HEROKILLER

Praise for Paul Tassi and The Earthborn Trilogy

The Last Exodus

"In *The Last Exodus*, Tassi succeeds in weaving together the space and post-apocalypse sub-genres into an enthralling adventure story of survival, trust, and hope. . . . Bottom line: a quick read, very enjoyable, highly recommended." —*Geeks of Doom*

"What would happen if you threw *Independence Day*, *The Walking Dead*, and *Guardians of the Galaxy* into a blender? I can't say for sure, but it'd probably look something like *The Last Exodus*. Tassi's book is a clear, clever and action-packed romp that will undoubtedly appeal to sci-fi veterans and novices alike." —Blake Harris, author of *Console Wars*

"Readers of Paul Tassi's *The Last Exodus* should get strapped in for a thrilling ride—this guy can really tell a tale!" —Michael Cobley, author of the Humanity's Fire trilogy

"A well-grounded, grim tale of first contact . . . Debut novelist Tassi gifts his characters with solid motivations and understandable responses to the postapocalyptic setting." —*Publishers Weekly*

The Exiled Earthborn

"Again, Tassi delivers a fast-paced action novel that hums along . . . a solid read that is perfect for a quiet weekend."

—*San Francisco Book Review*

"The space war between the human Sorans and their former slaves, the alien Xalan, continues in this fast-paced second Earthborn tale of raids and rescues. . . . A cliff-hanger ending almost demands that readers return for the concluding volume."

—*Publishers Weekly*

The Sons of Sora

"Tassi melds a coming-of-age narrative with a philosophical nod toward dealing with pain and sorrow in the midst of the horrors of war. . . . The epic vibe doesn't detract from the quieter truths, and small victories of the heart carry as much weight as clashes of space dreadnoughts."

—*Publishers Weekly*

HEROKILLER

A NOVEL

PAUL TASSI

Talos Press
New York

Talos Press books may be purchased in bulk at special discounts for sales promotion, corporate gifts, fund-raising, or educational purposes. Special editions can also be created to specifications. For details, contact the Special Sales Department, Talos Press, 307 West 36th Street, 11th Floor, New York, NY 10018 or info@skyhorsepublishing.com.

Talos Press® is a registered trademark of Skyhorse Publishing, Inc.®, a Delaware corporation.

Visit our website at www.talospress.com.

10 9 8 7 6 5 4 3 2 1

Library of Congress Cataloging-in-Publication Data

Names: Tassi, Paul, author.
Title: Herokiller : a novel / Paul Tassi.
Description: New York : Talos Press, [2018]
Identifiers: LCCN 2017046298 (print) | LCCN 2017051275 (ebook) | ISBN
    9781945863240 (Ebook) | ISBN 9781945863233 (pbk. : alk. paper)
Subjects: LCSH: Undercover operations--Fiction. | Contests--Fiction. |
GSAFD:
    Suspense fiction.
Classification: LCC PS3620.A86 (ebook) | LCC PS3620.A86 H47 2018
(print) |
    DDC 813/.6--dc23
LC record available at https://lccn.loc.gov/2017046298

Cover design by Paul Tassi
Cover art by Protski

Printed in the United States of America

For Michelle

PART I

"Boredom is rage spread thin."
—Paul Tillich

1

MARK JOLTED AWAKE TO something pawing at his shoulder. Drool spiderwebbed between his mouth and the wood. His unfocused eyes blinked and he saw a forearm being strangled by an angry purple octopus. A tattoo. Rayne.

"Mark," she said. His head tilted up toward her face. Rayne was mostly piercings and ink, with intense green eyes accented by a mask of makeup. She screamed at most customers, but she was nice to him, and he loved her for that. Except right now.

"*Mark*," she said, louder this time, which caused him to wince. He rubbed his eyes and she finally came into focus. Well, two of her did. And both looked annoyed.

"You know me, I'll serve you all day 'cause you're quiet, but you can't sleep. Laird will toss you in an autocab and you'll wake up in your driveway instead of my lovely bar."

Mark turned to look at Laird, who looked like an albino silver-back gorilla crammed into a boys' large black T-shirt. His build suggested an ex-college football player, but his vocabulary said nothing higher than Division 4. Mark absently thought of six different bones he could break in the man's body before he even hit the ground. Laird glowered at him, unaware of the imaginary ass-kicking he was receiving in Mark's head.

"Alright, alright," Mark said, his voice husky. "But keeping me conscious is probably gonna take a Spark and vodka."

"Coming right up," Rayne said with a smile full of rings.

Rayne mixed his caffeine/alcohol cocktail with machinelike efficiency, and Mark's eyes wandered up to the screen over the bar. He was greeted by moist lumps of indeterminate flesh, the sight enough to make him wrinkle up his nose on instinct. The camera panned out to reveal the full scope of the televised orgy, which was mostly sweat and uncomfortable grunts.

"God, Rayne, can we switch this shit? I'm going to puke all over your bar."

Mark gestured toward the TV, trying to change the channel with a swipe of his hand, but to no avail.

Rayne laughed.

"It's tuned to my bio; it won't work for you. Can't let just anyone mess with my set."

She made a quick flipping gesture with her finger toward the TV, and the stream rolled over to another similar, nudity-filled program. And another. And another.

"Hey, I was watchin' that!" came a cry from the back of the bar. Rayne and Mark ignored it.

"What, you don't like *Sexcapade*?" Rayne asked Mark, masking a smile. "You're the only one. It's the number one show on air right now by a mile."

Mark shook his head.

"I'm not some family-values nutjob, but come on. In my day you watched this stuff in the privacy of your own home with the blinds shut and deep sense of self-loathing. Not in a bar when you're trying to enjoy a drink."

"Such an old man," Rayne said, sliding the crystal blue drink his way. "At what, thirty-eight?"

He took a sip, and immediately his pulse quickened a half beat per second. By the time he finished it, he'd be out three extra hours sleep, no doubt.

"Thirty-five, asshole," Mark said, checking his reflection in the bar mirror. He couldn't blame her for the mistake. He might have said forty if he was looking at himself as a total stranger. Hell, he almost felt like he was seeing a stranger as is. He was half Chinese, but looked full-blooded with his father's face right down to the arch of his eyebrows. He was a few inches taller than his Amazonian, corn-fed mother, who if asked was a twentieth-generation Nebraskan. And there was just a hint of her blue ringing his brown eyes. But right now the dominant color infecting them was red. His cheekbones and jawline were normally cut from stone, but his entire face was puffy at the moment and he had a temporary tattoo of the woodgrain of the bar stamped on his forehead.

"Just turn on the football stream, will you?" Mark asked. "The Bears game should still be on."

Rayne obliged, and the TV flipped over to the game. But the screen showed a mostly empty field populated by medics, referees, and a half-dozen downed players. The fans in the stands were thinning out quickly.

"What the hell? It's over?" Mark said. "It's the second damn quarter!"

"Oh, I heard about this," Rayne said. "There was a big brawl and they had to cart off half the offensive line. I heard Grayson actually took a cleat to the eye."

"Seriously?" Mark said. "Like three-quarters of the roster is out already. I've seen little league teams with more talent than these called-up washouts."

Rayne shrugged.

"The crowds wanted fights. They got fights. Now they got a hell of a lot of hurt players. At least it's better than the NBA. They're talking about canceling the whole season after what happened out in LA."

"Ratings are still down," Mark said. "It's not doing them any good easing up on the fouls and ejections and fines."

"Well lord knows they're still trying."

Rayne flipped the stream to a NASCAR race that was under a red flag. The screen just showed an inferno of electric cars that were now little more than scrap metal after a 400 mph collision.

"I give up," Mark said, throwing up his hands. "Just put on a damn movie stream, I don't give a shit."

Rayne jumped to a new channel, and the familiar sight of writhing naked bodies returned.

"I said a movie!"

"This *is* a movie. That chick won an Oscar last year!" Rayne said, pointing at the gyrating woman onscreen. She flipped to a news stream this time, where, mercifully, everyone was fully clothed.

"Turn *Sexcapade* back on!" came the voice again from behind him. Mark turned around. He couldn't pin the annoyance to a specific person in the booths, but he suspected an irritating-looking group of college guys wearing Northwestern lacrosse zip-ups that badly clashed with every other article of clothing they wore. Though admittedly it was hard to match purple.

Rayne continued paying them no mind. She quickly flicked her finger, and the video now had sound, with the picture so clear it might as well have been a window. Mark took a swig from his electric drink, and found that he finally felt halfway awake. On the screen, an attractive blonde in a low-cut top filed a report from outside a large stone building in DC. She spoke in typical reporter sing-song.

"In a landmark decision destined to be the biggest of 2035, the Supreme Court has just ruled that effective immediately, Cameron Crayton's hit television event, *Prison Wars*, must cease and desist filming and broadcasting, having been found in violation of the 'cruel and unusual' punishment statute of US criminal law. Crayton's lawyers spent weeks arguing that because the program required the consent of the death row inmates, no laws were being violated, and the health and safety waivers signed by participants made the risks clear to all, but the Court ruled in a 5-4 decision that since the express purpose of the event was the death of a combatant, that it was in effect overruling their current sentence, and was in itself a form of capital punishment. *Prison Wars* draws the seventh most subscribers of any show in the nation, with twenty-five million weekly viewers tuning into its stream. A shutdown will dramatically impact the bottom line of Crayton Media Incorporated, and CMI stock is already plummeting in after-hours trading. CEO Cameron Crayton had this to say in the wake of the decision."

A man in a trim, pitch-black suit with an open-collar, garish red shirt appeared in front of a podium. The hands that gripped the metal were sixty, but his tight, smooth face looked no older than forty. His skin was tanned like evenly baked bread, and his teeth looked like they'd been carved out of marble.

"It was a tough decision, but I am satisfied with the split that we nearly convinced the court of the athletic merit of our program," he said with the poise of a trial lawyer spliced with the off-putting charisma of a politician. "Unfortunately, I understand the complications with the criminal justice system, and though I thank our partner prisons for their tireless support, I admit it is a tricky area of the law. Hopefully new legislation will ensure that entertainment isn't censored in violation of the First Amendment."

He smiled at the camera in a way that made Mark's teeth hurt. His sapphire eyes glittered with malice even as his face was robotically configured into something approximating cheerfulness.

"And while *Prison Wars* is no more," he continued, "we at Crayton Media have been hard at work on a new venture, something I think our audiences will love. Expect an announcement shortly, but for now, I'd say I've earned a good long nap."

Mark knew men like Crayton. They didn't sleep. His eyes told him that. He was simultaneously enigmatic and creepy, charming and unsettling. His face had been plastered all over the feeds after *Prison Wars* turned the media upstart into a mogul in the last year alone. But Mark wondered how fast CMI would collapse with its flagship show dismantled.

"They're shutting down *Prison Wars*?" asked Rayne, her stenciled eyebrows arched in surprise. "Shit . . ."

"Good riddance," Mark said. "That was a horror show."

"A really goddamn popular horror show," Rayne said. "My brother is going to be pissed. He loved that shit. I swear he must spend $100 a month on *Prison Wars* swag, not to mention the subscription fee."

The news was now showing highlights of *Prison Wars'* year-long run: enormous men exploding with muscle beating each other to pulp with pipes and chains. One man covered in blood and Russian mob ink of crowns and keys stared at the camera like he was going to eat it. "Drago the Undying" was a household name, more famous for killing eleven combatants in the ring than for the two dozen civilians he'd killed before that, including informants and their entire families. Hopefully now he would fade into obscurity like all the rest and meet his fate by lethal injection like he was supposed to before the *Prison Wars* circus began.

"This is what I fought for?" Mark said, gesturing at the snarling madman on the screen.

"Fought?" Rayne said. "No offense, Marky, but sitting in an Okinawa base playing video games for a few years during Cold War II isn't exactly sacrificing life and limb. You tell me how bored you were there all the time."

Mark boiled with sudden rage, but quickly quelled the fire in his chest. He was *way* too drunk if he was even hinting at what had gone on in China. It was time to go. He inhaled the rest of his drink and slammed it down on the table too loudly. That caught Laird's eye, and he lumbered around on underdeveloped calves to face him as he stood up.

"Hey, bitch," came the voice again from the back. "Turn the show back on now that the cranker's leaving."

Mark's theories were confirmed as he could now see the voice came from the college kid with the most punchable face of the group.

Rayne just glared at him and turned up the volume of the news. Mark didn't know what "cranker" meant, but the way the guy said it was unpleasant enough to make his fists clench.

"What the hell, bitch?" the kid said impatiently, his word choice surprisingly limited given the supposed caliber of his university. He was now attracting Laird's attention too. The oaf had always had a blindingly obvious crush on Rayne, and he darkened as he approached the table.

"Time to leave," Laird growled, and grabbed the loud idiot by the collar.

"Alright," the kid said, smiling to reveal dimples, holding up his hands like the bouncer had the power to arrest him.

But Mark slowed his walk to the door, seeing what was about to happen. The sandy-haired goon across from dimples had slid his shin behind Laird's boots. Dimples dropped his right hand and wrapped it around the neck of a bottle. Laird's beady eyes barely had time to register the threat.

A split-second later, the kid's nose exploded in a shower of blood and goo, causing him to drop the beer mid-swing and fling his hands to his face. The ketchup bottle Mark hurled at him like a lawn dart had not shattered, and it landed on the table with a thud. The five other Wildcats scrambled back in shock, the one about to trip Laird pulling his foot back immediately. The bouncer kept his grip on the kid's collar, hauling him out of the booth as he wailed. His friends trailed behind him, suddenly meek and harmless ducklings, and Mark held the door open as Laird tossed the kid to curb. As Mark passed on his way out, Laird granted him a nod of appreciation, which was the nicest gesture he'd ever made toward Mark since he'd started looming in the doorway six months ago. Mark stumbled past the dazed college kids trying to look up how to fix a broken nose on their phones, 911 clearly not an option due to the trouble it would bring with it. Their eyes darted toward him, but none made any moves his way, and if anything, they shrunk back as he passed.

Mark lurched over to his car. It took six attempts to unlock it with a fumbling thumb. He couldn't even open his door, but he'd made that ketchup bottle shot from a dozen yards while seeing double.

The training never leaves you, he thought, though he couldn't remember the exact drill where he was taught how to kill enemy combatants with condiments.

The door slammed shut behind him and he curled into a ball in the driver's seat of his car. The engine automatically started when it sensed his bio-signature. He looked at the dashboard where, ten years ago, a steering wheel might have been.

"Where to, Mr. Wei?" a pleasant female voice said, chipper with a faint chaser of sultry.

"Just home," he mumbled, turning himself so he didn't accidentally drool on the leather. The autocar kicked itself into gear, its Italian engine roaring before settling into a low purr as it crawled down the street. What the hell was the point of having an electric car with the equivalent of a six-hundred-horsepower engine when it always drove the speed limit? Another one of his unwise purchases.

The radio was squawking about the end of *Prison Wars*, the commentators wondering out loud how Crayton would recover.

"I wouldn't count him out," said the shockjock. "Do you know anything about that guy? Crayton's not someone you want to fuck with."

"What, he'll smile you to death?" said a woman, laughing.

"Just trust me," the other host said. "Whatever he's got cooking next, I have a feeling we've never seen anything like it."

2

MARK WOKE UP AN unknown number of hours later under his coffee table. The afternoon sun had set, meaning it was time to flip a switch and becoming something slightly better than a total waste of life. He didn't remember his car dumping him at home, nor the elevator ride to get to his penthouse condo in the Loop, but somehow he'd made it. Christ, he hoped Brooke hadn't been his crutch inside. The poor girl had been making eyes at him for three years, despite the fact that he'd embarrassed himself in front of her more times than he could remember, and probably a few times he couldn't. Hopefully today wasn't one of those. She was a sweet girl, cute too, but that part of his life was over. And it was entirely possible he was hallucinating her stolen glances and she was really just a nice person.

Mark yelled at his coffee machine until it stopped pretending it couldn't hear him and began brewing, and he stumbled into the bathroom where he hacked at his face with a straight-edge until he could see his jawline again. He pulled on some loose mesh workout gear and stuffed his bag full of the necessarily protein globules and vitamin inhalers. By the time he was done, the coffee machine had proudly announced the completion of his macchiato. His TV automatically turned on, meant to sync with the coffee being done, but he waved away the screen before he could be assaulted by genitalia.

The thirtieth-floor penthouse would have been gorgeous if Mark had even remotely attempted to keep up with the housework. Dusting and vacuuming were ancient rituals he couldn't even comprehend anymore. Sometimes he picked up pizza boxes and organized them into a skyscraper in the kitchen, but that was the extent of his attempt to pick up the place. Mark had a high-end robo-cleaner that made a valiant attempt at sweeping the floors for crumbs and dust creatures, but it had been unceremoniously killed in the line of duty after inhaling a sweat-drenched sock. It now stood as a monument in the corner that was now ironically also collecting dust. A German woman named Olga was the nuclear option who used to come in to make the place spic and span once a week, but a recent string of personal budget cuts made her services no longer required. The condo and car he'd bought with cash, so those could stay, but the money pile was starting to dwindle and sacrifices had to be made. Last on the chopping block was his bar tab, obviously.

At the time, three million dollars had seemed like a fortune, and it was certainly an outrageously large severance compared to what most poor saps in the Army or Air Force could hope to get. But he also saw how fast it could blow into the wind after you bought a few toys, made a few bad investments, and had no desire to supplement it with a new job. The only skills Mark had were ones he never wanted to use again. He drank to forget them, yet each night he remembered, drawn back to an eternal fitness and training regimen that was as much a part of him as breathing. It was the only reason his mind hadn't completely turned to mush after about three thousand gallons of rum. Nor did he weigh the five hundred pounds you'd expect from someone who had a cardboard tower of empty pizza boxes threatening to collapse in their kitchen.

He drained the last of his coffee before exiting his condo, at least somewhat less inebriated than when he'd entered. In the stairwell he found Brooke, glistening from a recent run, desperate to avoid

HEROKILLER

becoming the 60 percent of the country that was morbidly obese. She was certainly winning that war.

"Hey Mark!" she said, loosening a ponytail of curly blonde hair.

"Hey Brooke," he said, continuing to descend, but he suddenly ground to a halt.

"Did I . . . see you earlier?" he asked, failing to properly phrase the question in a way that didn't sound strange.

"Where?" she said, clearly confused. "Were you at the grocery store?"

"Nope, nevermind, must have been someone else," he said quickly. So she hadn't hauled him upstairs. That was good. She smiled all the same. Mark wasn't sure he'd seen her do anything *but* smile the past few years. But hers was genuine and reassuring, not forced and horrifying like the one he'd seen plastered on Crayton earlier. Her eyes were a blue pretty enough that Mark wasn't sure why someone would divorce her. But perhaps it had been the other way around, he guessed. He could snoop on the Deepnet for all the information about her he could hope for, but he just didn't care. Or he could have a single conversation with her somewhere other than a hallway or staircase. But again, why bother? He hadn't felt much need for human attachment before it all happened. But after? Never again.

He didn't even realize he'd stopped talking to her until he found himself downstairs. *I'm such a dick,* he thought to himself. But then he remembered the clown car of frat boys from the bar and felt a little bit better about himself by comparison.

As he leaned back in the driver's seat, his head spinning, Chicago was alive with cars going exactly the prescribed speed limit. No one honked. Not anymore. A few years ago self-driving was made explicitly illegal and auto fatalities took a nosedive. Granted, deaths from heart disease and stroke were at all-time highs, and joining a professional sports team in this day and age was no way to extend your lifespan, but hey, at least driving was safe now.

It was nearing midnight, right on schedule for Mark's bizarre not-quite-nocturnal life schedule. He spent about six hours abusing himself down at Rayne's bar, The Blind Watchman, and then passed out for a few hours before waking up for what was usually the better part of an all-night workout session in the only gym in the area that would accommodate such a thing.

After his car self-parked and opened its gullwing doors, Mark got out into the mostly empty lot nearly all the way sober. Inside the gym was the usual ghost town, with it being technically morning on a Wednesday, but that's how Mark liked it. He was so used to being alone in every other aspect of his life, he wasn't itching to work out somewhere with two hundred buzzing human gnats swarming the equipment. He'd accidentally wandered into the place during the daytime on a few occasions, and it had given him nightmares for a long while after.

First up was a nine-mile run, punctuated by bathroom breaks where he puked up the sins of the afternoon. Only two visits this time meant he was doing better than usual. He sweated through his clothes in about four minutes, the nearly silent treadmill content to absorb the deluge of droplets that could no longer be sucked into the fabric.

Then came two hours of weight training, both body resistance and with as many metal slabs as he could fit on the bar. Mark's solitude extended to not needing or wanting a spotter, not that there were many around at this hour who would have a prayer of helping him with the amount of weight he was pressing. Carlo could, but Carlo was always in the ring upstairs.

Mark was simply too bored to punch a bunch of misshapen bags over and over, so he adopted a sparring partner in the form of Carlo. The kid was only nineteen, but one of the top middleweight prospects in the region, with big dreams of UFC. Thankfully he'd avoided TV matches, which were engineered to produce injury and accidental death, but who knew how long that would last. Mark constantly tried to talk him out of pursuing a future in the league, and to date had done nothing but solidify the kid's resolve.

"What else am I going to do? Work at Boxmart?" Carlo said as he danced around the ring in front of Mark, clad in long black trunks. Tattoos curled out of his waistband like snakes, and he didn't just have a crucifix on his muscled chest, he had an entire goddamn stained glass window, complete with demons threatening to bite Christ's ankles as angels tried to lop their heads off with flaming swords. It was a little silly, but mostly terrifying, and the mural continued on his back as well.

"Boxmart won't get you killed," Mark said.

"Nah, fuck that," Carlo replied, waving a gloved hand. "I'm goin' straight to the top. My manager says he ain't never seen talent this young before."

"Well so long as you're humble about it," Mark said, lashing out with a strike that purposefully missed Carlo's jaw.

"Man, you hear about *Prison Wars*?" Carlo said, raising his eyebrows. Mark just rolled his eyes. "That's some serious censorship bullshit right there," Carlo continued.

"Do *not* get me started," Mark said, and let one of his kicks connect to Carlo's leg. Carlo winced, but pressed on.

"But for real though, those fools don't know how to fight, just beatin' on each other with pipes and shit. You think some child molester knows how to throw a proper punch? Bitch, please."

"Oh, and you'd show them?" Mark said, dodging a pair of uppercuts from Carlo, bouncing backward off the octagonal cage.

"Sure. They'd call me 'The Needle' for how many of those Death Row fools I'd smoke."

"Seriously Carlo, Boxmart isn't so bad."

"Fuck that," Carlo repeated, and Mark let him connect with a side kick to his ribs. He swore and rubbed the spot.

Carlo stopped dancing and grabbed a plastic waterbottle from the corner of the ring. He sprayed most of it on his face and a few drops made it into his mouth.

"I don't get you," he said, turning to Mark. "You come in here, drunk as shit half the time, and still manage to put up a fight. But it only feels like you're goin' ten percent at most. Are you a fuckin' Terminator or something?"

"Something like that," Mark said, actually cracking a rarely seen smile. He wiped it away as quickly as it had come.

In truth the cycle was just Mark's way of punishing himself. He drank himself half to death then spent all night pummeling his body until the toxins ran away screaming with tears in their eyes. He was a mess, but each night the gym pulled him back from complete collapse. His body itched for sparring sessions like these more than it did for alcohol. He drank out of boredom, not necessity. At least that was what he'd convinced himself.

And with that six-hour torture session, Mark dragged himself back into the car, ribs aching and stomach empty of everything but water and protein. This time he remembered the elevator ride upstairs, and he collapsed in his bed instead of a random piece of furniture or his rug.

He dreamed of them, as he always did.

WHEN CONSCIOUSNESS FOUND HIM again, the projected readout on his wall said 10:03. Four hours of sleep was enough, he supposed, and he'd survived on far less. His sheets were wrapped around his limbs like anacondas from his thrashing around. He untangled his arm enough to stretch out and reach for the thin clear bit of plastic folded up on his nightstand. He rested it on his chest. He unfurled the bendable screen and watched it flicker to life, the only light in the room as thick curtains suffocated whatever trace of the sun tried to come in.

This was the worst aspect of his surreal daily cycle of existence. The most addictive too. He could give a shit about having a drink all day if he really had to give it up, but not one morning passed without his glassy eyes staring at the translucent screen.

Mark remembered when he was young and his grandmother

showed him pictures of her when she was little. They were old photos, and the pieces of fading paper that chronicled her entire youth barely even filled a single shoebox.

Now? Contact lenses had cameras that would start recording when you uttered a codephrase. Practically every moment of your life could be documented if you had the drive space to save it all. When a hard blink took a photo, there were few moments you couldn't save forever.

His fingers flittered over the long list of files. Mark's living space was complete chaos, but the digital videos here were all meticulously organized, titled, and dated. He finally landed on one: "Spade Karaoke Bar, Okinawa - March 18, 2024."

This was before they were even together. Before the program. Less than a year after he got there.

The video quality wasn't great—just shot on a phone, not an S-lens, since it was over a decade ago. But it was good enough. The audio was serviceable, though his flexscreen had some trouble translating the ancient filetype.

At first it was only the backs of people's heads and the sharp chattering of regional Japanese, but soon the music kicked in. Mark didn't recognize the beat, but as soon as she started singing, it all came back to him. A ten-year-old classic pop-country song, sung in perfect English by a girl who had been born and raised in Japan. Though he wouldn't know that until later.

The camera panned around and there she was. She wore her hair down in long, wrist-thick braids that almost reached her waist, the style at the time. Her eyes were jade, barely visible through her bangs. In a high-neck sweater, she was more conservatively dressed than the vast majority of the other bar patrons, with the possible exception of a skirt and heels that made her legs look like a Scandinavian runway model's. She was gorgeous, which is why Mark had started recording as soon as she took the stage, but what had most impressed him was her voice.

The pretty girls who ended up singing onstage at bars like this were either failed pop stars who were lost without autotune, or were so shy their musical whispers could barely be heard over the beat as they stared meekly at the audience.

But not her. She sang with natural talent and raw confidence that somehow didn't approach arrogance. She was simply having fun, a smile on her face for the duration of the song, stomping her daggered heel in time with the music. He and everyone else were singing along with her, and Mark *never* sang. He remembered wondering if it was some sort of prank where a J-Pop star invaded a local podunk bar incognito, and then surprised everyone with a rousing performance.

BUT SHE WAS A regular girl with a magnetism Mark had never seen before, or since.

She was just Riko.

It was the first time he ever saw her.

AFTERWARD, THERE USED TO be another segment to the ritual. One where he'd reach under his bed and pull out the thing from its box. He'd stare at it, feel the cold weight of it in his hand. Wonder why he shouldn't do it. He took it out every day for the first two years, but the answer was always the same.

"She'd be so fucking mad," he'd whisper, and he'd put it away until the next morning. One day, he simply didn't take it out again, and hadn't for two years since. The answer was always going to be the same, he realized. No matter how much pain he endured, he couldn't dishonor her like that. Though the state of his everyday life wouldn't exactly thrill her either, he supposed. One thing at a time.

3

I T WAS AROUND NOON when Mark finally escaped from his condo and walked briskly for three blocks until he reached The Blind Watchman. Between the pancake house, the 7-Eleven, and the bar, he really never needed to leave a half mile radius outside his building during the day, and rarely did. As he approached the bar, he saw Rayne outside the door smoking.

"Hey, you want to go grab a coffee?" she asked, flicking away ash. "Before the uh, day's festivities begin?"

"A coffee?" Mark said, dumbfounded. "I, uh . . ."

"It's not a date, you loser. But you should get some caffeine in you. You look like a goddamn zombie. More than usual."

Mark eyed the door to the Watchman, then back to Rayne. Her red-streaked hair was twisted up into a bun today, and she looked dramatically more pale outside than in.

"Is Laird on the bar?" he asked.

"Yes," she said. "So hopefully no one will ask him to do anything more complicated than use the tap. If so, maybe the bar will survive my lunchbreak."

"Alright," Mark said, a yawn giving away that Rayne was right.

THE LINE WAS LONG due to an elderly patron poking at the automated dispenser like he was trying to break a Nazi code on a Turing machine. The JavaSpot had finally fired the last of its cashiers, and the entire place was now run by a vaguely self-aware dispensing device at which patrons picked their own ingredients and the monolithic silver barista brewed it for them on the spot. A lot of fast food joints and grocery stores had done the same recently, which coincided suspiciously with a rise in the homeless population all over the city. But machines made for poor conversationalists, so Rayne's job at the bar was safe for now.

Finally the old man surrendered and soon enough Mark and Rayne were sipping iced drinks at a nearby table. If this was a date, they would have been the most oddly matched couple in the world, with Mark now clean-shaven and in blank beige and black clothing. The only metal that had ever pierced his skin had been blades and bullets, while Rayne was riddled with the stuff. She wore a neon orange tank top that looked like it had been attacked by a wild dog. Unknown tattoos could be glimpsed through the holes exposing the skin of her abdomen. Her eye makeup was Egyptian, and today she wore faux-purple pupils that were glued to the looming screen above Mark's head.

"Oh wow, this is it then," she said, eyes widening. She took down her legs from their resting place on the table and sat up in her chair. Mark turned around to see what she was talking about, and was blinded by the wattage of Cameron Crayton's smile.

"Not this asshole again," he muttered.

"Shhh," Rayne said, "I want to hear this."

In fact, most of the patrons had gone dead silent and were staring at the screen. It seemed the torture chamber of *Prison Wars* really did have quite the audience.

Crayton wasn't on the steps of a courthouse anymore. Rather, he was clearly in some corporate office high up in Manhattan, as the glass behind him gave way to the entire sprawling cityscape. He stared straight at the lens like he was giving a presidential address, and spoke with the abrasive enthusiasm of a megachurch pastor.

"Hello, my friends! I know many of you were disappointed by the court's decision yesterday to take *Prison Wars* off the air. I certainly was as well; it's a project very near and dear to my heart. And yet, CMI marches on. Even before the decision, we have been planning for an expansion of the *Prison Wars* concept, one that we think will revolutionize entertainment in this country *forever*."

Mark looked at Rayne who raised a thin eyebrow.

"I give you the *Crucible*," Crayton said, making a sweeping motion to reveal a logo that had the words embossed in gold and wreathed with flame.

"No longer will we be confined within the walls of the prison system. The Crucible will bring our famed competition to the masses. A grand, nationwide tournament with only one victor. A duel to the death to crown the most formidable combatant in the country."

A few younger men in the coffee shop started applauding and cheering. Mark looked at them like they were psychotic.

"Is he saying what I think he's—" he began, but Rayne waved him off, eyes glued to the screen.

"The Crucible begins in sixteen cities around the nation. Preliminary matches will choose a champion from each region. These qualifiers won't require a mortal price, simply the will and ability to win, but once the final sixteen are chosen, the fights *will* be to the death."

More cheers from the JavaSpot.

"It is in tandem with this news that I announce the construction of Crayton Colosseum, a stadium that when completed will host the final tournament to a massive live audience, with millions more watching at home. We break ground in Nevada within the week."

Mark's head was spinning. How on earth was this really happening? How *could* it happen?

"Enrollment for the regional qualifiers begins at the conclusion of this message and can be completed online or in person. Registration will be open for two weeks, and so long as you're over eighteen years of age and a US citizen, you are free to enter. And while *Prison Wars* was an entirely male affair, the Crucible is open to both genders. I believe women are just as strong and capable as men, and I wouldn't dream of excluding them here."

Crayton peered into the lens with uncomfortable intensity.

"And now, perhaps, you're asking why. Why on earth would anyone volunteer for a tournament like this where the stakes couldn't be higher? You're not death row inmates after all. You have families and friends and your entire *lives* ahead of you."

That was the most reasonable thing Mark had heard him say yet.

"But it is for the future and for your families and friends I encourage you to fight. For those who qualify for the final tournament, I am guaranteeing a minimum payout of ten million dollars, even if the combatant falls in the first round. The amount will increase with each new stage, and ultimately culminate in a grand prize of one *billion* dollars, which the competitor will still be alive to spend."

The same cluster of jackasses was cheering. Even Rayne wore a crazed smile after hearing that figure.

"*A billion dollars?*" she mouthed at Mark, who simply looked stunned.

"I thank you all for your viewership, and I look forward to seeing you all tune in to the Crucible. Registration details follow this announcement, and I look forward to seeing sixteen of you in Nevada later this summer!"

Crayton dissolved and was replaced by a montage showing the various qualifier host cities. New York, LA, Atlanta, Dallas, Seattle, and then, of course, Chicago, before the list continued. The young men were still grinning like idiots, but the rest of the establishment appeared to be as dumbstruck as Mark. Once the video faded, the shop started buzzing with heated chatter about what had just been announced.

This is it then, Mark thought. *This is how it all ends.*

"WHAT I DON'T UNDERSTAND," Rayne said as they walked back to the

Watchman, "is how he's going to pull this off after the government just shut down *Prison Wars*. Like, how is this any less illegal?"

Mark shook his head and tossed his empty cup into an overflowing trashcan.

"I don't know, but he's got a plan. You don't organize something like this, promising a billion-dollar grand prize, plus invest what, another billion in this crazy new stadium, without having assurances it's going to work."

"Jesus," Rayne said, checking the readout on her phone. "I wish I bought his stock when it bottomed out yesterday. It's going through the roof right now. A 60 percent jump in the last ten minutes alone. His net worth probably just tripled."

"Well, he's got a colosseum to build," Mark smirked.

Soon they arrived at the Blind Watchman and Mark spent the next hour staring at a single beer before telling Rayne he was calling it a day, much to her surprise. He wandered outside and started walking until he was out of the Loop and deep downtown. The city seemed livelier than he remembered, and he overheard more than a few people talking about the announcement.

It bothered him more than it should have, but he couldn't shake it. He wouldn't watch it, of course, and no one was forcing him to. And in reality it was only what, fifteen people potentially dying? More would die from heart attacks by the time he rounded the next block than the tournament would actually kill. Still, he felt like a line had been crossed.

Now we're cheering as the desperate eat each other.

"CHRIST, THAT'S A LOT of blood," Mark said as he handed Carlo another towel. "Sorry about that, again."

Carlo waved him off and held the new towel to his lip. The white counter of the gym locker room had a worrying amount of diluted red on it. Luckily the only other people around were the old men who constantly occupied the sauna, though Mark wondered exactly what was going on in there this time of night.

"Think I never had a split lip before? I'm good, but even I take shots in the ring sometimes."

Carlo frowned at the mirror where his lip was starting to swell. Mark had connected with a too-sharp right hook and soon both of them were covered in Carlo's blood. Mark looked down at his shirt, realizing it was ruined. After stripping it off he tossed it into a nearby trash can.

"Well, there'll be plenty more where that come from when you sign up for the Crucible, eh?" Mark said, flexing out his sore hand.

"You're goddamn right!"

"What?" Mark asked in mock surprise. "Are we going to see the rise of Carlo 'The Needle' Rivera at last?"

"Ain't gonna be no child molesters in this thing. You enter that, you *gotta* know how to fight. Like me."

He patted his chest with gloves. Mark paused.

"Wait, are you serious? You're really entering?" he said, horrified. "Carlo, the thing ends with the *public execution* of fifteen people. Including you, if you make it that far."

"Nah," Carlo said, waving Mark off with his hand. "Not when I'm the 16th, sittin' on a throne of cash bricks worth a cool billion."

It was all Mark could hope for that if Carlo actually was entering, he would get knocked out of the running in qualifiers, which seemed likely. But what if he didn't?

"Carlo, the odds—"

"Man, please," Carlo said, starting to get visibly edgy. "The odds been against me my whole life. I'm fighting for rent money on the way to the top, yet no matter how hard I go at this thing, that noose just keeps gettin' tighter. They're about to take my mom's house away. My family only gets to eat because I put the food on their table. And I can only do that like half the time. You drive around in your fancy car and think people aren't killin' each other to survive already. I could be making three times what I earn now selling crank, coke, or stardust on my block, but I'm trying to do it right. Now this thing comes along and tells me I can take a run at a billion dollars doing what I do already? You're goddamn right I'm gonna do it. Set up my family for *generations*."

Mark shook his head. He knew Carlo's life was tough. His father was a Marine who had been killed in Afghanistan during the fourth surge of '23. His mother had raised him and his little brother ever since, but now he clearly wanted to step up to the plate. Bending over, Mark rummaged through his bag to get out a fresh shirt. Well, fresh was a relative term in a bag which smelled like a dying animal after months of laundry neglect.

"What happened to you, man?" Carlo's tone shifting now that Mark had dropped the issue. "You look like something carved you up pretty good a long while back."

Mark looked down at the thin, white scars criss-crossing his torso and knew Carlo saw the ones on his back. He quickly pulled on the new moldy shirt and turned around.

"When I was on base, a private got drunk and drove a supply truck into our barracks," Mark replied without blinking. "They patch-ed me up best they could, but I still look a little like abstract art."

"Intense," Carlo said, eying him somewhat suspiciously. Mark hoped he hadn't noticed how many of the cuts were perfectly straight and parallel. *That's Chinese precision for you*, he thought, shivering at the memory.

Carlo lifted up his arm to show a white jag near his armpit.

"Sixth grader tried to steal my bike when I was eight. He put a goddamn switchblade an inch from my lung."

"And he still only *tried* to steal your bike?" Mark asked, eyebrow raised.

"My puppy Hercules chomped his arm and I broke his eye socket with a rock," Carlo said, suddenly looking downcast. "Man, I miss that dog."

"Quite the puppy," Mark said, nodding. He heard a disturbingly pleasurable grunt coming from the sauna, and they both wiped off the counter and fled before whatever was happening in there escalated further.

ON THE WAY HOME, Mark drove past a long line of people standing in the darkness. He was confused at who would be out at 4 a.m. on a weekday, some with tents, others with folding chairs and beer coolers, but eventually he saw the banners reading CHICAGO CRUCIBLE REGIONALS REGISTRATION, and realized the line trailed all the way to a nearby office building.

Employees wearing Crayton Media badges were herding the lines into something resembling an angular snake to avoid spilling out into the road. The police were there as well, and blue and red flashing lights strobed in the darkness.

"Jesus," Mark said as he saw how many people were registering for a chance to die in front of millions. Did they understand what they were signing up for? Perhaps the qualifiers, a more standard fighting competition, attracted all types just trying to test their luck and brawn, maybe grabbing fifteen minutes of fame in the process. Out of all of them, only one would make it to event that actually forced you to kill other people. If this insanity even made it that far. Mark had to imagine the government was trying to decide how best to go after Crayton this time.

ONCE HE GOT BACK to the penthouse, Mark couldn't sleep. Despite six hours at the gym, he still had a seemingly endless amount of energy. As always, he reached for that thin, clear screen, and brought up the familiar file list.

"Som Chai Okinawa - April 3rd, 2024."

Another phone cam shot. The video showed him, cramming vegetables into his mouth with chopsticks.

"Why are you filming this?" Mark asked the camera. "This does not need to be filmed."

A giggle from behind the lens.

"I thought you should have a record of your first attempt at eating Thai," Riko said with an unseen smile.

"Attempt? I think I'm succeeding," Mark replied. "Give me that."

He took the phone from her and the view switched to Riko wearing a pale blue dress and sparkling black necklace that looked vaguely volcanic. Her long hair was wound up far above her head, and she was beautiful as ever. Their first date.

"Tell me," she asked, putting on a mock serious face. "How does a Chinese guy stationed in Japan hate all Asian food, Thai included?"

Mark chuckled through a mouthful of something unpronounceable.

"Because this Chinese guy is only half-Chinese, and he grew up with a very white mother who made very white food like macaroni and hamburgers all the time."

"And what's your excuse after you moved out?" Riko asked.

Mark looked from side to side.

"Umm, macaroni and hamburgers continued to taste better than . . . whatever this is," he said, poking at his meal with one chopstick.

"The fatherland would be so disappointed," Riko said, shaking her head.

"I think China may take more issue with me than just my food choices. But if we ever storm their beaches, I'll make sure they see me eating crispy honey shrimp or something, and maybe they'll take pity on me."

Riko laughed. Mark remembered how the entire room lit up whenever she smiled.

Mark heard something that sounded like a loud thud in the hallway. He bolted up immediately, the screen falling flat on the sheets. Scrambling under his bed, he came back up with his pistol and crept to the doorcam screen in complete silence. He took one look at what was on the monitor, and his heart nearly stopped.

"Oh shi—"

His front door splintered, then exploded.

4

POLICE KNOCKED. POLICE IDENTIFIED themselves. Police had POLICE written across their chests in big, bold letters. That's why, when the first man came in through the door in a blank helmet and flat, matte kevlar with no markings, Mark didn't hesitate when he pulled the trigger.

But the resulting click told him the firing pin was inoperable. The gun was a paperweight.

The armored man and the three others behind him had strobes mounted on the barrels of their submachine guns that lit up Mark's place like a dance club. Combined with a high-pitched sonic frequency designed to assault his ears, it was horribly disorienting. Dropping the useless pistol, Mark had to dive out of the way of silenced shots from the men in the doorframe. He heard glass shatter in the hallway. The men were shouting coded orders at one another, and Mark crawled to extract his M6 from its resting place taped under his living room couch. His hand felt around and found nothing. It was gone. His pistol. The rifle.

This was planned.

There were two other guns stashed in the house, but Mark already knew they would be broken or missing, and he couldn't waste valuable time chasing after them.

The men rounded the corner and Mark dove for the flashing barrel. The gun fired a hissing series of silent shots as it swung upward, and Mark wrenched it away from the man's grasp. He swung the stock into the helmeted face and the invader collapsed on the spot. Mark only had time to get off a pair of shots at the others, but even in the strobed darkness, saw rubber bullets bounce off their armor.

Capture, not kill.

That wasn't terribly comforting either.

They've come at last.

Mark caught a bullet that felt like a sledgehammer to his exposed shoulder. It spun him around, but he kept his balance and he dove into the kitchen.

As the next figure came around the corner, Mark reached up and grabbed a cylindrical grenade from his belt. He rolled it between the man's legs before spinning around to take cover behind the open door of his fridge.

The EMP blast exploded in the middle of the remaining three men. The strobe and high-pitched wailing stopped, and even the lights in the hallway blew out.

Mark used their newfound disorientation to charge into the group, slamming the first man's head through the drywall and firing a rubber bullet into the exposed throat of another figure, who went down to the ground choking. The third man recovered enough to raise his gun, but Mark kicked it sideways before shattering the man's helmeted face with the butt of his gun. The man stumbled backward into the hallway clutching his face, only to be absorbed into a black mass of armor. More men. At least another four.

A clear, indestructible riot shield slammed into Mark and the locomotive of men behind it propelled him down the entry hallway. Blue electricity crackled in the darkness, and Mark had to jump back as a taser lashed out through a slit in the shield toward his chest.

He yanked the shield toward him and spun around, catching the man holding it in the back of the head with a sharp elbow and he collapsed on the spot. A firm front kick bowled over the next two men, but the third hit him square in the chest with two rubber bullets, knocking him on his ass. The man fired another stream of bullets, but Mark rolled right. He grabbed the taser from the first downed man and slammed it into the side of one of the invaders struggling back to his feet. He convulsed violently and shrieked through his helmet. Mark dodged more shots and ran back to the living room as the remaining two men spread out to flank him.

He hurled a cordless lamp at one, and it shattered harmlessly across kevlar. He swung the riot rifle like a baseball bat, but the man ducked under it, and Mark felt an electric jolt hit his ribs as a knuckle taser sent an uncomfortable amount of voltage coursing through him. Doubled over in pain, he just managed to block an ascending knee from the man, and he shot up with an uppercut into his opponent's helmeted jaw. He heard a crack, and wasn't sure if it was the man's neck or his fingers, but he dropped all the same.

More shouting. More strobes. More dark figures storming through his door. Mark breathed heavily, clutching his side. Blobs of pain radiated all throughout his body where he'd been struck. His muscles were burning, his vision was mostly red blotches.

From the door, a thin red light cut through the darkness and landed on his chest. Mark thought it was just a laser sight, until his skin started heating up like he was starting to boil from the inside out. He stumbled forward toward the new figures, but dropped to his knees as his entire body felt like it was engulfed in invisible flames. Blue electricity leapt out from the shadows and made the unseen fire feel downright pleasant. The darkness consumed him fully, his body slipping into unconscious surrender.

MARK'S HEAD ROLLED FORWARD then snapped awake, and he instinctively jerked his hands and feet, only to find them chained to a table and chair respectively. He was seated in an empty stone room with polished aluminum furniture and a suspicious-looking wall to his right that was almost certainly transparent from the other side.

He'd been in many rooms like it before, but the question was whose room was it? Mark was just praying the first face he saw didn't look Chinese.

Gideon Gellar was not Chinese. Mark's eyes widened as his old handler walked through a seamless door on the opposite wall. The years had saddled him with another forty pounds or so, and his thick black beard was now streaked with gray. His skin was dark and his eyes smiled at Mark even if his face didn't. With him was a tall, silver-haired man with the stripes of a general on his blue uniform. He wore no nameplate.

"Are you fucking kidding me, Gideon?" Mark said, yanking at the chains. "What the hell was that about? Are you out of your goddamn mind?"

Gideon held has hands up as he and the other man approached the two chairs opposite Mark.

"Easy Mark, I'll explain—" he began, but Mark didn't relent.

"I haven't heard from you in three years and you throw a tac team through my front door to bring me in? You ever heard of a fucking phonecall?"

Gideon folded his arms.

"Can we just skip the next ten minutes where you yell at me, and I can tell you what you're doing here."

Mark's chest was rising and falling rapidly. He suddenly realized that he was now wearing a shirt and shoes. The other man's long face was expressionless. Gideon turned to him.

"He took out two teams unarmed. The third only got him with the laser."

"But they still got him."

"No one beats the damn laser, McAdams."

"Please address me as 'General' in the presence of the detainee."

Gideon waved him off.

"I ain't in your goddamn chain of command and I'm not paid enough to kiss your ass. You wanted him here. You wanted to see what he could do. Well there you go. Mark, this is *General* McAdams from Homeland."

"Will someone tell me what the hell is going on?" Mark said. He wriggled around and felt bandages under his shirt with some sort of med-goo slathered on his bruises and burns.

Gideon turned back to him.

"We need you back in the field."

Mark was already shaking his head by the time he finished the sentence.

"What the shit are you talking about, Gideon? I'm out, remember? I'm *way* the hell out."

"This is something special," Gideon said, the general beside him looking grim.

"Iran is cold, China is in flames. There are no more goddamn wars, secret or otherwise."

"Is he really that naïve?" the general said to Gideon like Mark couldn't hear him.

"Kid earned the right to be whatever he wants," Gideon shot back. "But I don't think he really *wants* to be drinking all day and being a gym rat all night. Tell me, Wei, what *are* you training for in that ring?"

"Nothing," Mark growled. Of course they were monitoring him. "And I don't owe you shit after what happened."

"You don't," Gideon said. "That's fair. If anything we owe you even more. And yet, we need you."

"*To do what?*" Mark finally bellowed.

Gideon and the general finally sat down as Mark's chest heaved with rage. His former mentor brought out a flexscreen and set it in front of him. A nauseatingly familiar face was on it.

"Cameron Crayton?"

Gideon nodded.

"If this is a hit, I might be tempted to oblige just because he's so goddamn irritating, but what's this all about?"

"Not a hit," Gideon said. "Crayton's got deep pockets. Too deep for running some moronic show for two years. We need to find out who's backing him, and why."

"Have you seen this?" the general asked, his voice stone. He waved away Crayton's face and a video began playing. A paunchy, white-haired man standing before a large hall was speaking. Congress. His nameplate read ALAN DRAPER, D-NY. He spoke with a Bronx accent, but it felt purposefully practiced to better connect with his constituency who didn't live in ten-million-dollar mansions.

"I'm bringing to the floor a job-creating bill that will provide gainful employment for hundreds of thousands of workers, and ensure the security of one of America's greatest exports, athletic entertainment," the senator said.

Mark looked at Gideon, confused. He nodded for him to keep watching.

"This bill will exempt athletic activity from criminal penalties regarding death or injury of voluntary participants. America is on the forefront of creating the most exciting athletic competitions in the world, and I fear that millions of potential jobs and billions of potential tax dollars could be lost if these new sports are entangled in red tape and court cases. Our economy is finally heading in the right direction, and a bill like this will only bolster America's recovery. I urge you to read it and lend your support to it. And I know our president will do what's right by the American people and sign the Athletic Protection Act into law."

Mark shrugged.

"So he bought himself a senator. I'm pretty sure I could buy one too if I invested in lobbyists instead of the market."

"He's bought himself more than one member of congress," Gideon said. "A large number, if the rumblings are any indication. And our White House sources tell us the president is even amenable to the idea."

"But the court—" Mark began.

"The Supreme Court shut down *Prison Wars* in a tight split, but only because it was interfering with the criminal justice system. And who knows when this would make it to them. The last show ran for over a damn year before the ruling."

"Alright," Mark said. "So raid his offices, get the data, and take him out for good measure while you're at it. What's the problem, and why do you need me?"

The general shook his head in obvious frustration.

"Crayton has access to more money than anyone in his position should. He's a billionaire, sure, but he's acting like he's the richest man on earth with how much influence he's buying to prep for this latest nightmare. We need to figure out where it's coming from. It looks like it could be the Chinese, but we need proof. Putting a bullet in his head isn't going to solve anything since he's just a puppet, and sending infiltration teams through his vents will only give us what he wants us to find. We need someone on the inside to get close to him. To gain his trust."

"So you want me to apply to be his secretary?" Mark said, half-smiling now from the absurdity of the situation.

The general looked at Gideon with a face that very plainly said "Is this guy serious?" before turning back to Mark. Gideon spoke next, his fists clenching into balls as he leaned over the table.

"Operative Wei, you are being recalled for assignment," he said. "Your orders are to enter the Crucible tournament regional qualifiers. And you are to win."

5

MARK TOLD THEM TO go fuck themselves, of course. The rest of the night had dissolved into a shouting match between Mark and General McAdams about his "responsibility" to his country, and all the various punishments he'd face if he refused. Mark brought up the ironclad contract he'd signed with the government granting his severance and cutting all ties with his former employer. McAdams laughed at the idea that a digital file with an electronic signature and seal allowed Mark anything of the sort. Mark, absent restraints, would have loved to crush the man's windpipe to stop the grating sounds escaping from it, but all he could do was glare. In the end, they said they'd give him time to think, and Mark was injected with something that made him faceplant on the metal desk within seconds.

When he woke up back in the condo, he found it had been put back together. Holes in the walls were patched and painted, a brand new door had been installed since the other one had been reduced to little more than a blast crater. Hell, even his pistol had its firing pin replaced, he discovered. The clean-up boys never missed a beat.

Mark himself was not so easily fixed. Though they'd treated his injuries, he limped around the apartment grasping at the various clusters of pain that emanated throughout his body.

He had known a day like this would come. Either it would be the government knocking at his door (or blowing through it, as it turned out), or the Chinese looking to finish what they started. Mark had given up looking over his shoulder, not particularly caring whether an assassin's bullet drilled through his skull at any given moment. He was almost annoyed it was Gideon who had found him first.

And for what? The most ridiculous assignment he'd ever heard of. He couldn't imagine why else they'd come to him unless their active agents were all occupied running ops that actually mattered. Entering a brutal TV gameshow didn't really seem like Homeland Security territory, and allowing the CIA to run an op on American soil instead of the NSA or FBI certainly wasn't kosher, even if it was a joint project. Yet last night wasn't a dream.

Christ, maybe it was, Mark thought as he rubbed his eyes and stumbled around his pristine apartment. The cleaners had literally cleaned, and his place was so spotless it would actually be a red flag for anyone other than Mark who'd been in his place in the last few years. Between the recently vacuumed floor and a body full of bruises, Mark knew it had all really happened.

He collapsed on his couch and draped his hand over his forehead, trying to process it all. He flung his palm at his TV, which turned on and bathed him in light and sound.

A male reporter with plastic white hair stalked the pavement, which was lined with hordes of grinning men and a sparse smattering of women. A camera followed him, and the banner across the bottom of the screen read THOUSANDS LINE UP FOR CHICAGO CRUCIBLE QUALIFIERS.

After watching a few unsettling interviews with potential participants fighting because they were either clearly unstable, in desperate need of cash, or both, Mark swept the channel away with his hand, He dove into his data drive, which had appeared on the screen in its place. He scrolled through the list of files and clenched his fist to open one labeled "Tenryu-ji Temple, Kyoto - August 26th, 2026." The playcount said this would be his 133rd time watching it.

Riko's dress was a thousand silk orchids sewn together to make one flowing fabric sculpture. The pearl white veil trailed behind her, floating in mid-air like a spirit. She approached the ancient stone altar wearing a smile meant only for him, with porcelain skin and bright green eyes that were heartstopping. The sight still took his breath away even now. As she reached his side, she bent over to him and whispered—

THERE WAS A KNOCK on the door. Mark waved the TV into blackness and bolted up, suspicious. Though if Gideon was back with another tac team, at least this time they bothered knocking. Or maybe it was the Chinese with that bullet after all. He craned his neck around to check the video feed on his wall. It was . . . Brooke? She stood patiently with her hands clasped behind her back. Mark limped over to the door and opened it. It still smelled like fresh paint. Much to his surprise, Brooke marched straight into the room without waiting for an invitation. As soon as she opened her mouth, he knew something was wrong.

"We need to talk, Mark."

Her ocean blue eyes blinked, and there was something in her gaze that unnerved him. He could count the number of times she'd stepped foot inside his place on one hand over the last few years, and it was almost always some grocery-related emergency about needing an extra egg or some sea salt. She'd invited him over for dinner a few times, which he'd always refused. He interpreted it as a potentially romantic gesture. But more than likely it was pity, he later realized.

Brooke was sweet and kind, but the stern-faced girl on the couch was neither, he could tell that from just the five words she'd spoken so far.

"I said, we need to talk."

This was not Brooke. Or rather, Brooke was not Brooke.

"Who are you?" Mark said, understanding.

"That's all it took to figure it out, huh?" she said, cracking a thin smile. "Just me dropping the act for a few seconds?"

"I said, who are you?" He flexed his fingers and his eyes darted to the various weapons resting in their hiding places.

"I'm the girl next door," she said, spreading her arms.

"You have five seconds, or I will kill you," he said through gritted teeth. Brooke rolled her eyes at the threat.

"God, Mark, calm down. If I was here to take you out, this would have been the world's slowest assassination."

Four years, by his count. It didn't make sense. Unless. *Of course.*

"You're my monitor."

"There we go," she said. "Can you sit down now? You're making me nervous."

Mark thought back to every encounter he'd ever had with her, and realized what a fantastic actress she'd been this whole time. Utterly flawless. It had honestly never even occurred to him.

"You're one of Gideon's. Why the hell did they put a monitor on me? What the hell have you been telling them all these years?"

"Mark, did you really think they were going to let one of their top operatives out and never keep tabs on them? You have to know better than that."

Mark's knuckles were white.

"Four years," he said. "Jesus."

"Hey," Brooke said. "Give me some credit. I don't spend all my time writing down every time you take a shit. I run plenty of local ops for Homeland that are far more important than being your shadow."

"What have you told them?" Mark repeated. "And why are you telling me all this now?"

"As for what I've told them, that's all locked away in a data center somewhere on servers a mile below the earth, I'm guessing, but you can imagine the highlights. You're generally a complete waste of space and a horrible mess after what happened. Understandable, but you're not a lost cause either."

Mark just shook his head, trying to comprehend it all.

"And as for why we're having this conversation, it's because I'm about to graduate from being your monitor to being your new handler, considering you're going back in the field."

"Oh God," Mark said. "Not this Crucible shit again."

"They asked me if you were ready for it. I said yes, but they wanted to test you anyway with that little tea party last night."

"That was a goddamn stupid thing to do," Mark said. "I could have killed any one of them."

"You didn't. But it wouldn't have mattered," she shrugged. "They were all Glasshammer mercs. I'm pretty sure you can get like a twelve-pack of those guys at Boxmart."

"I'm not entering the Crucible," Mark said. "It's absurd."

Brooke nodded.

"It certainly is, but Crayton is trouble. You know how big his file is?"

"How big?" Mark asked.

"It's non-existent."

Mark's eyebrows went up.

"What do you mean?"

"I mean in a data-gathering age when I can tell you what kind of cancer your dog died from when you were five, or your great-uncle's shoe size, we have nothing on Crayton. Not a thing. His public backstory is all air, completely forged. Behind it there's nothing. It's like he simply popped into existence, cash spilling out of his pockets. Now he's got half of Washington on his payroll and burning desire to get people on TV to kill each other. We need to figure out what the hell is going on, and we need you to help us."

"Us? You can't be more than five years out of the academy. You don't know what I—"

"I do know, Mark. I know it all. To take on this assignment, I got the full report. Even the blacked-out pages. Even the pages that weren't even pages."

She paused, her tone growing softer.

"I know what was done to you. I know what you had to do. I know what you lost. And I know what it means to be told you have to jump back in."

She leaned forward.

"I'm not here to threaten you. You know how this works and how uncomfortable the cell of an Icelandic blacksite is, and I know that doesn't scare you. But you know what else I know?"

He stared at her.

"I know that you want to do this. I know that you *need* to. I've watched you drift aimlessly through life these past four years in a fog. I expected this to be a short assignment given that you seemed like you were going to off yourself in the first month, but you didn't. Not the first year. Not all these years. You're waiting for something. For some purpose. Some reason to exist again. And I'm telling you, this is it. Crayton is powerful and very clearly a sociopath. That would be a dangerous enough combination on its own, but if the Chinese or anyone else have their hooks in him, that could spell disaster. This may be a joke op, hence them pairing you and meI together, but there could be something much larger going on here."

She waved her hand.

"But I'm not here to tell you to do this for king and country like Gideon or General McIdiot; I'm telling you to do it for you. Take this assignment and start living again. A person without a purpose is one of the most profoundly tragic things in existence, and I can't watch you wallow for one more day."

Mark gave a dry chuckle.

"But they put you up to this," he said. "It's the only reason you're talking to me now. Your orders are to get me to join. And let me guess you have a PhD in psych to boot?"

"Yes, they put me up to this; yes, those are my orders; and yes,

I am smarter than you. But what do you expect? Gideon used to know you well, but lord knows you've both changed, and now thanks to four years of intense stalking, I know you better than anyone. Probably even better than you know yourself. And I'm telling you to do it."

Mark could hardly believe what he was hearing, and who he was hearing it from.

"What's your real name, anyway?" he said, looking up at her.

"Take down Crayton with me, and I'll tell you," she said.

"No name is that interesting," he said.

"Then Brooke it is."

She stood up and walked toward the door.

"Forget China. Forget darkops. Forget Spearfish. Leave it all behind you. You've stared into that abyss for too long. Either jump, or come back from the brink. There's work to do."

BUT FORGETTING CHINA WAS impossible. Lord knows he'd tried, swimming in an ocean of alcohol for years. It was the sort of thing your mind should black out on its own out of shock and trauma, but they trained that out of you. You learn never to forget, given that some remote detail might stick in your mind through the horror of it all that would prove useful later.

When the CIA recruited him straight out of West Lincoln High, and offered to pay for four years of Caltech if he'd join them afterward, he'd gotten stars in his eyes. He'd be James Bond. Jack Bauer. Jason Bourne. All those heroes he'd grown up worshipping. A secret fucking agent. How cool was that?

He finished the four-year degree in three years, he was so eager to start and put his old life behind him. Almost immediately they shipped him out to Japan for training, and he discovered quickly that there were no sexy women to be rescued from maniacal villains.

No nuclear bombs to defuse in mid-air as they hurtled toward a major city.

There was only China.

The media dubbed it "Cold War II" and it stuck, a familiar identifier everyone hoped wouldn't morph into "World War III" instead someday. China's population had reached a tipping point. Increased pollution had turned cities from toxic to downright uninhabitable, and respiratory problems and birth defects were sweeping through the country like wildfire.

The US took it upon itself to poke and prod. The CIA would spark riots and whip up the fervor of the public to hopefully topple the communist regime. China responded with some not-so-veiled threats about ending the "tyrannical" global reign of the US for good, and both countries threw up nuke-zapping satellites into the sky that would hopefully prevent the end of the world. But no one knew if any of the tech would work. As such, the war was fought on the ground, in the shadows. Whatever shots were fired were heard and seen by no one. Almost no one.

Mark was recruited at the height of it all, and he learned quickly his ancestry was just as much a reason as his test scores and obstacle course times. He'd grown up speaking Chinese thanks to his father, who had left the country decades earlier, running away with an American tourist he met. He thought he knew everything about the culture there was to know, but the CIA crammed even more in his head in preparation for the part he was to play.

"They'll hate you, you know," Gideon told him. "Everyone in the Academy, all your friends, will think you turned. The government will disavow you completely. That's how dark this is going to get. But we'll bring you home in the end."

Mark's mission was more complex than simple spying. He'd defect to China and "accidentally" get caught after a few months undercover. He'd cut a deal to avoid immediate execution by Chinese death squad, and turn double agent, spying for them instead. But in the end, he'd still feed the US the truly deep, dark shit they wanted to know, and wait for final orders and eventual extraction. If he lived that long. They screened hundreds of candidates for Operation Spearfish, and Mark was only one of a few left standing as they hacked through the list. They told him Spearfish was the key to winning the entire war. Perhaps he was naïve to believe them, but it turned out they were actually right.

It was 2026. He was twenty-seven. He got married the day before he left.

A week later, the government sent him a video file. A beaming, crying Riko told him she was pregnant. She wanted to name their daughter Asami, after her grandmother.

Sixty-three days. That's all the time he had to be a flesh-and-blood husband and father once he came home and found a bright-eyed toddler with her mother's smile and his left dimple. Sixty-three days, and then it all shattered.

He was finally just too damn tired of doing nothing but sweeping the pieces around.

Hours after Brooke had left, Mark went and knocked on her door.

6

AFTER HE AGREED TO the mission, Brooke gave him everything they had on Crayton. The billionaire's public profile
was well known. The man gave interviews out to news outlets like
candy, and everything about the man was fully documented online,
from which tiny town in Norway his grandfather was born in to his
favorite A-list pornstar (Shyla Banxxx, it turned out). Gossip sites
had details on his diet, the locations of his half-dozen homes around
the world, the make and model of twenty different cars he'd been
spotted in during the last year alone.

And yet, when he looked at the NSA, FBI, and CIA files Brooke
had on Crayton, it was something else entirely. Everything that
actually mattered, his true family history, his childhood education,
all of it was smoke. Before he started showing up and bankrolling
start-ups with money pulled out of thin air, it was like the man didn't
exist. Even working intelligence for as long as Mark had, you rarely
saw anyone with a null file to this extent. It was common to see a
few years blank here and there when you pierced the cover stories of
assets and agents, but an entire lifetime?

But why? The question gnawed at Mark. Crayton was clearly
two shades away from insane, and his time with *Prison Wars* had
certainly accelerated the decline of American society to some small
degree, but a ghosted media magnate? It was bizarre. It had taken
the agencies five years of work to unravel all the threads, but Mark

couldn't find what had tipped them off to investigate him in the first place. Gideon had mentioned the Chinese, but that didn't make sense either. *That war is over,* he thought. *They lost.*

After Cold War II, when Spearfish came to a head during a schism the media would dub "The Red Death," China broke into five separate states, only one of them keeping the country's original name. They were all still feuding with each other to this day, and Mark couldn't imagine what on earth they'd be doing turning their attention back toward the US. None of them had the capacity to go toe to toe with America anymore, and no more than two of the five were ever allied with each other at one time given the volatile political landscape in the wake of the country's collapse. The Red Death hadn't killed them, but it had certainly rendered them impotent as a superpower.

But if this is MSS—if they have something to do with Crayton and all this madness . . .

The thought was unsettling. Mark owed the Ministry of State Security, the Chinese version of the CIA, a debt, and he had no doubt elements of the intelligence service were still operational, even if the war was over and China was more or less on fire.

He's still alive, said a dark voice in Mark's mind. The one that usually called him to drink. *You know he is.*

He shook the thought out of his head. *If he was alive, he would have come for you by now. They killed him. They showed you his corpse.*

A corpse, anyway.

Mark shoved the thought from his head. He'd jumped from the CIA to Crayton to China to the MSS to a man that still haunted his dreams. That was a quite a leap, even for him. And he was one paranoid motherfucker.

Zhou was dead. That was all there was to it. If this was actually a Chinese problem, it was a new one.

It won't bring back what you've lost, the voice said.

But now at least, he truly had nothing left to lose. And shit, that was what they were counting on.

BROOKE POKED A DUMPLING with chopsticks, distrusting the caliber of the take-out place they'd ordered from. They were in her apartment now, a sun-drenched loft with a lot of dying plants, and something that kept skittering around the wood floors. Mark only caught a glimpse of it every so often, and had yet to determine of it was a cat, dog, or some sort of domesticated rodent.

"So what do you think?" Brooke asked, finally deciding to pop the dumpling into her mouth. "Think you'll be able to embrace the new you?"

Mark stared at the flexscreen intently.

They took his car. They drained his accounts. They turned his cash-purchased penthouse into an underwater mortgage. Essentially all they left him with was his name.

Mark Wei was an alias he'd assumed a long time ago, and they let him keep it for this mission. But the parameters of the cover had changed dramatically. As Brooke explained, masking a smile the entire time, Mark was now an ex-Navy SEAL turned Glasshammer merc turned hopeless gambling addict. He'd made good money for a long while as a unit commander in the private military corporation game, but he'd lost millions over the past few years playing ultra high-stakes blackjack and no-limit poker at virtual and real-life casinos. Mark thumbed through a rundown of his fictional debt, and questioned how anyone on earth could seriously be eight million in the hole and still find places that would let them gamble. Brooke assured him it happened more than he thought. Even though it was a cover story, looking at the angry, glowing red numbers on the page made him wince a little bit. He felt downright bad for this desperate, fictional version of himself.

"He's also an alcoholic," Brooke said, "so that won't be too much of a stretch for you."

Mark ignored the dig, and kept sifting through the profile. No wife, no kids, minimal family. All true, and other than the gambling, Mark had to admit it *was* a little uncomfortable how much new the new life resembled his old one.

"I'm trying to wrap my head around this profile, but some of it seems really strange."

Brooke drowned the rest of her food with another packet of soy sauce. A ball of red-brown fur raced behind Mark so quickly he only saw the tip of its tail.

"Right now there are a lot of different types of loonies all trying to enter the Crucible," Brooke said. "You're going to see a ton who are just local meatheads trying to prove to the boys they're tough shit. Maybe they used to play football in college or were in an amateur boxing circuit. Maybe they won a few bar fights and think they can throw a proper punch. They'll enter, knock a few heads, but ultimately get their asses kicked by the real players, and go home with bruises and a tall tale."

"Who are the real players, then?" Mark asked.

"The ones who are signing up hoping they reach the stage where they can actually die. The insane, or the truly desperate. Those with a do-or-die reason to need the millions, or to prove themselves on a national stage. You'll get all types there as well, but most will have specific reasons for entering. The only ones that will make the cut will have to have some serious bite to go with their bark. Expect a lot of ex-military. Guys like you, and a few girls even if they're good enough. The Serious Shit Brigade."

"Saw a guy on the news," Mark said, remembering one of the interviews he'd seen the other day as hundreds waited on the street to sign up for the Crucible. "Some ex-cop who got fired after a shooting. Now he's broke and trying to pay his kid's medical bills, even if it kills him. Had death in his eyes."

"Exactly," Brooke said. "Guy like him will have the drive, but the skill? He better be a hell of a cop."

"So this is where the profile comes in," Mark said, understanding.

"You start going in there and dismantling folks in the ring, and no one's gonna believe you're a local stockbroker."

"Alright, I get the SEAL thing and the gambling debt now, but you had to marry me to Glasshammer?" Mark said.

"SEALs are not terribly well-paid, "Brooke said. "The big bucks come from the PMCs, as I'm sure you know. Plus it's easier to make their records cloudy if people go prodding. Almost everything they do is off-book, and we've got enough dirt on their entire board to make them do anything we want. Collaborating on cover stories is kids' stuff."

"Just so long as I don't have to go near them," Mark said.

Brooke shrugged.

"If anyone pokes around, you'll have two dozen guys you never met talk about how much of a badass you were during some op in the desert, though they'll hint you were the type of loose cannon that might blow a fat salary in Vegas if given the opportunity. Standard stuff."

"China anywhere in there?"

"Nothing in the story even remotely about China. Hell, they even thought about making you half-Japanese, but they didn't want to redo the surname. Your current ID has enough stuck to it to be useful in some aspects."

Half-Japanese. That stung a bit as Mark thought of Riko.

"You're already registered online, now you just have to show up to the actual 'audition,' as they're calling it, in a few days."

"Any idea what that entails?" Mark asked.

"Fighting, obviously, but details are murky past that. But you have to win."

Mark cocked his head.

"I have to take the entire *region*?"

"Crayton probably won't even look at you unless you're a city finalist. It's the only way you'll get access to him."

"Even for me, that's a tall order, considering the thousands I've seen lining up around the city. And lord knows how many signed up online."

"Mark, come on. I've memorized your file, remember? Your training is unparalleled. Your missions. The *Hóngsè Fēng* . . . "

Mark held up his hand.

"Alright, alright," he said. "I'll do what I can, but I'm not promising anything. They better have a back-up plan."

"They always do," Brooke said. "But, there's another problem."

"What now?" Mark asked. Brooke brought up a recorded news stream on her television.

"It seems like Crayton is bringing in ringers."

The first video was a report on how notorious serial killer Matthew Michael Easton had just been released from death row. Despite the fact that he'd killed twenty-three women with a hunting knife and being arrested in a fur coat made out of their scalps, the pair of detectives who had brought him in had been indicted on corruption charges, after it had been brought to light that they'd invented probable cause and planted evidence, including the coat, on Easton when they arrested him. The running theory was that the pair of them had actually killed the women, and their plan was to use the reclusive Easton as a scapegoat.

The elaborate liberation of Easton wasn't the only such story. Other news clips showed that a metro Detroit gang enforcer was set free after key evidence turned up missing. A white supremacist leader was exonerated after his judge was arrested for taking payoffs. And a Russian mobster was set free after two separate witnesses recanted their statements emphatically.

"They're all from *Prison Wars*," Mark said, finding the obvious thread. He was looking at Drago Rusakov, or Drago the Undying, as the show had anointed him. A fortress of a man shown beating a fellow prisoner to death in footage from the short-lived Crucible precursor.

"Yup," Brooke said. "Crayton's camp even had to issue a statement about it because it was so transparent."

She brought up a paragraph of text on her flexscreen.

"One of our many rewards to *Prison Wars* contestants was the use of legal aid to re-examine their arrests, trials, and sentences," the statement said. "Our lawyers have been shocked to discover what appears to be rampant corruption and incompetence in a few of the cases of our most well-known competitors. We have worked tirelessly to see that justice is served, and we are elated that these innocent men are going free as a result of our team's dedication."

"They are masters of bullshit, I'll give them that," Brooke said.

Mark could only shake his head. He turned back to his rice, but it was cold and hard on his plate.

"This all still seems like a joke. I've been out of the field for half a decade, and this is your first assignment as a handler. We're hardly cream of the crop."

Brooke nodded.

"Yeah, I get that, but you can be damn sure I'm not going to screw it up, if I ever want to have an actual career and work with actual operatives. No offense."

"None taken."

"Why'd you change your mind?" Brooke asked.

"Your pep talk."

"Really?"

"No. And don't ask again."

THE FIRST DAY OF auditions was weirdly mysterious. After receiving a message that was he was an "approved combatant," Mark scanned through the instructions to find only that they said to wear athletic apparel and report to a specific address. The building he was assigned to was a skyscraper downtown that turned out to be owned by a CMI subcorp, but other than the date, time, and vague dress code recommendations the invite said nothing else. Mark was sent hacked messages from other combatants by Brooke, but none said anything different. The only change was the address, and there were four or five buildings where auditions were being held. As it turned out, when Carlo got his message, he was assigned to the same one as Mark.

"I can't believe you signed up for this!" Carlo said as he glanced a punch off Mark's arm. They were walking to the entrance of 455 North Wells where the concrete tower loomed above them. "You were always talkin' so much shit about it, telling me not to do it."

He stopped.

"Wait, were you trying to get me out so you'd have an easier time cruising to the finals?"

Mark hadn't really considered that he could eventually fight Carlo. Given the odds, it seemed unlikely, but if they were paired up, Mark had been training with him long enough to destroy him. Well, destroy him gently. He'd feel bad if he embarrassed the kid.

"Nah, man. Just . . . I've got a few more money problems than I've let on."

"Money problems?" Carlo said, surprised. "But that car!"

"Bank took it," Mark said, the cover story starting to take over. Fortunately Carlo knew next to nothing about his personal life, despite their time sparring together. "They're about to take my place too."

Carlo held his hands up.

"Sorry, your business is your business. Just glad to have some company, even if I do have to kick your ass later!"

Mark grinned.

Inside the building, large, stainless steel letters were bolted into the wall over the reception area which read CHICAGO QUALIFIERS AREA C. Whatever company's masthead had normally been there was just a scuff on the wood. Mark squinted and saw that it used to say INFOTECH or INFRATECH or something like that. The name was different than whatever the Crayton subcorp on the lease was called.

A long desk had five receptionists sitting behind it, each a twenty-something girl with a plastered-on smile. Filing into lines were hordes of burly-looking men, some laughing and joking with each other, obviously groups of friends who'd signed up together for laughs, like Brooke said. Others were alone and silent, and seemed like the ones to watch out for. Out of the two hundred or so crammed into foyer, Mark could count the number of women on two hands. He was surprised there were even that many, despite Crayton's open invitation.

"Look at these chumps, man. This ain't even gonna be fair."

Carlo bounced around like he was in the ring already. Mark continued to scan the crowd. Steroid-blasted bodybuilders. Pudgy ex-linebackers. Those were the obvious ones. But others he couldn't get a read on.

It took about half an hour for him and Carlo to reach the desk. They split between the two closest receptionists, and Mark walked toward a diminutive brunette who looked slightly on edge from the rowdiness of the room. Mark tried to look reassuring with a forced smile. Her expression remained unchanged and he realized he probably just looked creepy.

"Hello!" she said. "Look here please."

She pointed a manicured nail down to the desk, and as Mark glanced toward the spot, a tiny light flashed briefly.

"Thank you, Mr. Wei," she said, his information now undoubtedly coming up on a screen he couldn't see. "You'll be in 1258 today. Elevators are back and to the left."

She pointed in the direction and Mark saw others filing into the open doors. He wondered how many fights would break out in the elevators themselves, judging by the energy of the crowd.

"Thanks," he said, and she slid him a clear digital ID badge with his name, picture, and a long number on it. The headshot was one that was submitted with his application, and had been one Brooke took on her phone in his apartment. He looked hungover.

He took the badge and turned to leave.

"Good luck!" the girl called after him, and it almost seemed like she meant it.

Carlo got out one floor below him, and told Mark he'd meet him afterward, whenever that was, at a diner down the street. The doors closed as he gave Mark a wink. A few more levels, and Mark stepped out onto the twelfth floor.

He wasn't sure what he expected, but from what he could tell the floor was deserted. Opaque glass doors didn't give anything away about what was behind them, and starting at 1200, he had to walk for quite a ways and around a few bends before he reached 1258. Once he did, his ID badge chirped and the door's lock clicked open. He walked inside, taking one last look around the eerily empty hallway.

Clearly, the space used to be an office. He could still see the tracks in the carpet that had once housed cubicle walls and the footprints of desk chairs. There was even a large, rectangular imprint and a black ink stain where a copier used to be. But it been stripped of everything and replaced with just one thing, a six-sided ring with clear polyglass walls, raised a few inches off the ground and almost touching the ceiling. Standing in front of it was a man and a woman in business attire, wearing bored looks and CMI badges. The man checked his flexscreen.

"Mr. Wei, is it? Welcome," he said in the most unwelcoming way possible. "Please familiarize yourself with the equipment provided."

He turned and gestured to a small table behind him. The woman said nothing and just stared ahead with lightless eyes.

Mark approached the table and saw two sets of lightly padded MMA-style gloves and two armored jock plates. He took the collection on the right.

"No weapons of any kind are allowed, nor any protective gear other than fabric clothing and what has been provided before you," the man said, clearly reading from a file on his screen.

"Scans indicate you have brought no contraband or restricted items with you, and Crayton Media Incorporated appreciates your respect for the spirit of the competition. Please make yourself ready for your bout, which will begin shortly."

Another click, and the door to the ring popped open. Mark wandered inside, and stripped off his sweatshirt and track pants. He wore a simple T-shirt with NAVY in bold, block letters across it, and a pair of loose-fitting white shorts. He kicked off his shoes and socks, and tossed all his extraneous clothes over the side wall of the ring. He velcroed up the gloves and shoved the jock down his shorts, praying Crayton had sprung for never-used gear.

The whole set-up seemed rather haphazard for a megacorp like CMI, but he stopped to think about how many times over this scene was probably being repeated around Chicago, and in all the rest of the qualifier cities. There were probably thousands of rooms just like this one, all set up in what, two weeks? He couldn't imagine the manpower that had gone into making that happen. He looked around for cameras and found tiny black half-orbs in the ceiling, and two more embedded in the corners of the ring. An audition indeed. And the two Crayton employees were what, referees? Judges? Was he in some sort of tournament? He needed Brooke to get more info on what the hell he was getting into during this qualifier stage. It seemed silly to feel uncomfortable given all he'd endured in the past, but the dim, torn-up office was strange, and the fact that he was auditioning to try and kill people on national television, and doing so for the US government, was so bizarre he felt like he was dreaming. He shook out the thought, and started swinging his arms and legs to warm them up. A minute later, the door to the office opened.

"This right?" came a voice from a large shape in the doorway. "I'm Mick Dillon. They said I should come here." The man flipped up the badge attached to his shirt.

"Yes, Mr. Dillon," the Crayton Media man said. "Please come in." The man approached the ring, and as he did so, the judge gave him the same spiel as Mark, which the man "Uh huh-ed" and nodded his way through.

"Let's do it!" the man said as he scooped up the gloves and jock at the conclusion of the reading. He glanced up at Mark for the first time, and the door popped open for him to enter the ring. He lumbered inside, threading stubby fingers through the gloves, and awkwardly trying to shift the jock in his pants as he walked.

Mark sized up Mick in about eight seconds. He was 6'4, 230, mostly muscle, but a fair bit of it flab. He was probably close to forty-five, and thankfully, Mark quickly deduced, one of the rowdy meatheads who had probably signed up as a boast. He had a thick black beard that stood out starkly against pale white skin, and beady brown eyes glinted under thick brows. His hair was tied back in a messy ponytail, and he wore a moderately clean tank top that revealed a small archipelago of isolated tattoos. He seemed to favor his right side, hinting at an old knee injury.

He eyed Mark, trying to size him up in a similar way, but no doubt doing so less effectively. He started with the obvious.

"Navy man, huh?" Mick said, pointing a gloved hand toward his shirt. "I was a Marine myself."

He tapped a stretched-out USMC tattoo on his shoulder.

"That right?" Mark said, not knowing what else he was supposed to respond with.

"So why does the Navy use powdered soap?" Mick called out.

Mark was confused. He knew the Navy in and out, but was this something he missed he was supposed to remember? If so, he was blowing his cover story already.

"Uhh," was all he could come up with.

"Because it takes longer to pick up in the shower!" Mick said, and roared with laughter. The two judges outside remained stonefaced.

Lovely.

He tried to give a courtesy laugh, but it was mostly just a smirk.

"And oh *shit*, they gave me an Asian! Don't tell me you know karate and taekwondo and all that shit!"

Some stereotypes were set in stone.

"You'll find out soon enough," Mark called back to him, and danced back and forth in place, continuing to warm up. Mick laughed. Mark realized he actually kind of liked the guy, despite the fact that he was a crude, vaguely racist moron.

"Gentlemen," the male judge called out from behind the glass. He and the silent woman were now sitting at a table facing the ring, flexscreens in hand. "Let's begin."

Mark waited for them to continue speaking. To explain what was to happen next. They said nothing, and just stared.

"So, ground rules?" he finally asked.

Nothing.

"Time limit?"

Nothing.

"Win conditions?"

Finally, the man spoke.

"Unconsciousness or submission. Now please, we have a great many people to see today. Begin."

From somewhere in the ceiling, a chime sounded. Mick and Mark stared at each other, practically dumbstruck.

"Alright, Navy," Mick said, curling his hands into fists. "Let's settle that old debate."

Mark was sure he was alluding to some Navy/Marines rivalry he couldn't care less about, but he had a mission. And Mick, bless his heart, was step one.

After making a single half circle of the ring, Mick threw out a heavy haymaker that had probably once made him the pride of his unit twenty years ago. But all it did today was sail right over Mark's head as he ducked under the swing and responded with a lightning-fast uppercut to both of Mick's chins.

Mark watched the man's eyes unfocus as he instantly crumpled to the ground. He did not move, and simply lay on the mat like a fleshy tumor growing out of the surface.

A few seconds later, another, deeper, chime sounded. The door to the ring popped open.

"Thank you, Mr. Wei," the man said, and motioned toward the ring door.

Mark looked back and forth between the prostrate Mick and the judge. Both he and the woman were now standing. She was scribbling something in her flexscreen with a stylus.

"Is that it?" Mark said, a bit confused.

"We'll be in touch," the man said, and reinforced his gesture toward the door.

Mark slowly approached it, turning back as he opened it.

"Shouldn't someone . . ."

"Mr. Dillon's vitals are stable and he will be attended to by medical personnel shortly. If you would please return to the lobby, you will receive further instructions."

This time he gestured toward the office door. Mark scooped up his pile of clothes next to the ring, and walked toward the exit, slowly shaking his head.

"MOTHERFUCKER BROUGHT A BAT!" Carlo exclaimed as he sat down at the table of the diner where they said they'd meet after the fight. Mark was already halfway through a grease-soaked burger when Carlo showed up.

"A bat?" Mark said, eyebrow raised.

"An aluminum one, too; not even wood," Carlo laughed.

"What happened?"

"They took it away. Said it was contraband or some shit. Guy said he thought they could use weapons like in *Prison Wars*."

"I suppose there's some sort of logic in that."

"Shit, they should have let him keep it. Wouldn't have mattered."

Carlo thumbed through the tablet menu, hungrily eyeing Mark's fries periodically.

"Who was he?" Mark asked.

Carlo shrugged.

"Some white dude. Decent boxer, but not used to getting kicked in the fuckin' head."

"So I take it you won?"

Carlo made a noise and a hand gesture that roughly translated to "bitch, please."

"Hey!" he called out to someone who wasn't their waitress. "Three more steakburgers and a diet soda!"

She nodded and smiled, and moved toward the kitchen.

"What about you? You don't even look like you broke a sweat."

Mark supposed that was true. He flexed out his hand, which ached a bit, but he had lingering bruises from the tac team invasion that still hurt more.

"Big, ex-Marine jackass. But he was harmless. Shit fighter. Lights out on the first straight upper."

"Of course, you train with *me*," Carlo said, swatting at Mark's arm. "Man, I'm glad to get out of there though, that place was creepy as shit. Freakin' robot referees writing things down. No crowd. No nothing."

So Carlos's experience was similar to his, then.

"What did they tell you downstairs after?" Mark asked.

"Come back Wednesday. You?"

"Thursday."

"Surprised none of this is on TV," Carlo said, motioning to the flat set over the bar currently showing yet another twenty-car pile-up in an auto race. "Kicked off all around the country today."

"And there *were* cameras," Mark mused.

"Really?" Carlo said, clearly not used to spotting surveillance like his life depended on it. "Shit, I didn't even see 'em."

"It's too early," Mark said, guessing at Crayton's strategy. "They have to narrow it down and figure out who's good and who's worthless. Broadcasting now would be like people tuning in thinking they'd be seeing the NFL, but getting Pee Wee football instead. No faster way to kill all this Crucible hype than that."

"When I'm done with this city, they'll have somethin' to watch, that's for sure," Carlo said, puffing his chest out, and snatching a handful of fries from Mark's plate.

"I'm sure," Mark said, and stared into the flames emanating from the racetrack on the screen.

7

MARK HAD FOUR MORE fights in the next two weeks, none lasting more than a minute. Upon returning to the same building each time, he saw the crowd get smaller and smaller, and the receptionists and Crayton Media wranglers all knew him on sight by now, though they still made him do the retinal scan every time, regardless.

His opponents began to get somewhat more competent, but he tore through them quickly all the same. A few days after Mick had gone down for the count he was paired up against a squat wrestler who kept diving for his legs until Mark finally just kneed him in the face so hard his nose broke. After that, the weekend brought him a veteran cage fighter who knew his way around the ring, but no amount of fearsome-looking tribal tattoos could save him from Mark's hard right cross that rendered him unconscious a millisecond before his head cracked into the polyglass wall.

Eventually, Mark's solemn judges were joined by two others, all four scribbling notes and checking the camera feeds on their flex-screens. They watched him dismantle a bodybuilder who thought two months of judo and ten years of bench press maxing was enough to know how to brawl. His muscles were like round globules of flesh glued haphazardly all over his body, which were good for absorbing Mark's blows, but once he went to work on the man's fragile joints, he was on the floor permanently within fifty seconds.

Mark was surprised by his last opponent, a woman. She was nearly as tall as him, and had stone-cut abs below a black sports bra that had flattened her to the point of androgyny. A buzzed head completed the effect. Her fighting style was erratic, but effective, a combination of a half-dozen different martial art styles, and for the first half-minute, Mark was actually on his back foot, fending off her lightning-quick high kicks. Finally, he simply grabbed her leg and swung her around into the cage wall, stunning her. She regained her balance, but Mark respected her enough not to pull his punches because of her gender. She blocked five, but the sixth ended the bout decisively. He offered her hand to help her up when she regained consciousness, but she simply glared at it, and got to her feet on her own, storming out of the ring and room shortly after.

"What's next?" Mark asked the now six CMI employees in the room.

"You'll receive further instructions downstairs," was the reply, the same as ever. Nothing had changed. Was he going to have to knock out every single person in the city? Brooke said the end was near, and he thought she was being purposefully vague about the details to keep him on his toes. "The show will begin soon," she said, and left him to wonder what that meant.

After Mark left, he got a ping from Gideon to meet him a few blocks from the building. He closed the door of the autocab he was about to get in, and headed east. He felt something wet on his cheek, and dabbed it with his finger. Blood. Probably from a rogue fingernail. He felt a little embarrassed that she had actually gotten through his defenses, even if it was just a scratch.

When he arrived three blocks later, Gideon was sitting on a bench, and Mark was half-surprised he wasn't feeding ducks bits of bread, judging by the age of his outfit and the gray in his beard. It had only been a few years, but his former handler looked like he'd aged a decade and a half. Mark supposed the same was probably true of him.

"There's our gladiator," Gideon said with a smile.

"Don't even start," Mark said, pointing his finger like a dagger.

"Have a seat." Gideon gestured.

Mark obliged, and watched a parade of joggers pass by. He touched his face again, but the blood had dried. He unshouldered his gym bag and laid it to rest on the pavement.

"Can I repeat how glad I am you're doing this? Not just for us, but for you. You look alive again."

"Until I'm executed on national television," Mark said, resting his elbows on his knees and clasping his hands. "Then maybe not so much."

"You know it won't get that far," Gideon said. "No way. Once you qualify, we think you'll be able to get what you need during training."

"Training?" Mark said, surprised. "What are you talking about?"

"In our digging, we've found bits and pieces of Crayton's Crucible plans. Other than building that monstrosity in Vegas for the finale, there's some sort of training period between qualifiers and the final tournament. Something up close and personal with you and the others who make the cut. And hopefully Crayton himself."

"Fantastic," Mark said, rolling his eyes.

"Get what you need there, and we can hopefully shut the entire thing down before it gets bloody."

"Alright," Mark said. "I have no idea how close I am to qualifying though. It's weirdly unstructured."

Gideon nodded.

"Brooke told me. Just stay on your toes, and don't get soft. You'll get there. But there is something you should know."

"Something besides the training period?"

"More pressing than that. A hill you may have to climb before you get there."

Gideon pulled out a flexscreen and brought up a mugshot of a man with tattoos creeping up his neck and spreading across his face like some kind of ink-scarred pox. Looking closer, Mark saw that there was a flaming swastika etched on top of his jugular.

"Who the hell is this?"

"Burton Drescher. One of the most powerful figures in the Aryan Brotherhood. Ran the entire federal pen in Terre Haute, Indiana. Rumored to have dropped more bodies inside than out, but only the latter were ever proven. Until recently."

Mark slowly started to recognize the man.

"He's one of Crayton's."

"Bingo," Gideon said, swiping the picture away and bringing up a video. It was footage from *Prison Wars*, and showed Drescher stomping a black inmate into pulp on the cement floor.

"Crayton had him transferred to one of his private shit show jails, and by the time they shut it down he'd racked up five bodies on camera."

"But he's out," Mark said, remembering vaguely the news report he'd seen earlier in the month.

"Crayton broadsided a judge with bogus corruption charges, and his lawyers tap danced their way into getting him released."

Gideon swiped again, and a gallery of surveillance photos of Drescher appeared, some satellite, some ground level. He was in Chicago. Mark was sharp enough to catch on.

"Wait, are you telling me that Drescher is enrolled in *Crucible qualifiers?*"

Gideon nodded.

"And not just him. Crayton got five out, including that nutjob serial killer and that big ugly Russian hitter. I knew the guys who took him down a decade ago, and as you can bet, they're mighty pissed."

"Don't tell me all of them are in qualifiers."

He already knew the answer.

"Five of the sixteen cities, yep. Including our precious little patch of land here. Drescher is your problem. I know you've been blowing through these other chumps like wildfire, but he might be an issue."

"I'll need a sheet on him," Mark said, rewinding the *Prison Wars* footage with a gesture.

"Already done. You can look it over, but the highlights include a stint with Special Forces before he heard Hitler's call and went KKK full-time. Got locked up downstate for burning a Pakistani family alive in their car. His lawyer's defense was that it was a malfunction with the gas tank, and he was at the scene because he was racing to help them. And most certainly was *not* pointing and laughing as they cooked."

The screen now showed the charred remains of an SUV and a few dark skeletal shapes inside of it. Gideon shook his head and closed the file.

"Just greenlight him," Mark said, thoroughly disgusted. "I'll do it myself."

"Can't," Gideon sighed, clearly wishing it wasn't the case. "He's high profile after his stint on TV, and him taking a bullet would set off an alarm. Even staging an accident would spook Crayton and make him look hard at whoever wins Chicago. That's why you've just got to kick his ass the old-fashioned way."

"Fine. Not a problem," Mark said, actually looking forward to the opportunity. "Why let them out? Why have them re-enlist?"

"I'm not a TV exec," Gideon said, "but audience appeal, name recognition, all that shit maybe. Or he just wants his own ringers so he can shape the finals however suits him. You know damn well every reality show in history has been halfway scripted, if not all the way."

"Well, at least I can throw one wrench in his plans," Mark said.

Gideon scoffed. "Soon enough you'll get to throw the whole damn toolbox. Just wait."

MARK STOPPED BY THE Blind Watchman for a quick beer or three, and spent an hour filling in an astonished Rayne that he'd actually signed up for the Crucible. She seemed more excited than concerned, which worried Mark a bit, but he would take all the support he could get, even if she had no idea why he was really doing it. He promised he'd buy her a less shitty bar to run if he won.

When he got home, he opened his door and his heart skipped a beat when he saw the back of Brooke's head peaking up over his couch. After years of coming home to no one, it was always jarring when she let herself in for one of her little pop-ins. He'd liked her better when she was just his doe-eyed neighbor.

"Good, you're back," she said, turning around. "A girl can only spend so long watching TV these days without wanting to blow her brains out."

"Long day," he said, tossing his bag into the hall. His place was slowly starting to fall back into its usual state of mess, despite Brooke attempting to tidy up whenever she stopped by. For her own sanity, she said.

"You hear the news? This thing is starting to heat up."

"What are you talking about?" Mark asked.

"Chase Cassidy just entered the LA Crucible qualifiers."

The actor? Mark was confused. "Well hell, this is going to be easier than I thought."

"I don't know, you see that scene he did in *Bloodrace*? He took out forty-five guys by himself!"

"That was all choreographed! No one actually got hurt," Mark said as he slumped down on the couch.

"True, but I heard he does all his own stunts," Brooke said. "I watched a special on him where it said he trains for eight hours a day when he isn't filming, and he has his own private dojo at his pad in Malibu. He's flown in trainers from all over the world to teach him every kind of martial arts there is. His fansites all say he can punch through brick walls."

Mark scoffed.

"That sounds like another one of his movies."

Brooke shrugged.

"His whole life is a movie. In any case, the Crucible just got its first celebrity endorsement. I have a feeling this is going to end up bigger than we can imagine."

8

T HE NEXT DAY, CARLO had invited Mark to his house for dinner, and Mark couldn't think of a plausible reason to say no.
Messages from Gideon and Brooke flashed in his alerts, but he
was starving and ignored them. He supposed he could go for some
Mexican food.

"I'm from Puerto Rico, you asshole," Carlo said after Mark said
that out loud. "Just smile and say you like Mom's cooking. That's all
it takes to be in with my family."

Despite being only a ten-minute jog from their shared gym,
Carlo's house was in a rough part of town. Lawns were left untended
and full of trash, and there wasn't a car on the street less than ten
years old.

Carlo's place was in better shape than most, and at least looked
like it had been painted within the past decade. But if what Carlo
said was true, they were on the verge of eviction. Inside, there were
already a lot of taped-up boxes, preparing for the coming storm.

Carlo was greeted by his mother and aunt. Mark was introduced
around.

"Nice to meet you, Mark, I'm Maria Rivera," Carlo's mother
said in heavily accented English. She was short with Carlo's brown
eyes and a warm smile. "This is my sister, Isidra, and her daughters Chella and Nicole." Two girls about ten and twelve giggled and
avoided eye contact while whispering in Spanish. Mark understood

"he's so handsome!" well enough, but was content to smile and nod, pretending not to know what they were saying.

"I'm Diego, Carlo's brother," said a young, lean boy of about thirteen. He gripped Mark's hand as firmly as he could.

"I've heard a lot about you all," said Mark with a smile. "Thanks for having me."

Mark was ushered into the family room and it was clear dinner was already in progress, as the table was lined with delicious-smelling food that practically resembled a Thanksgiving feast. But given how many people there were that had to share it, doing the math revealed that it still wasn't all that much per person. Mark was careful not to take more than a small share, even as Aunt Isidra kept piling more onto his plate. "You need your strength!" she maintained, as they knew he was competing alongside Carlo. His mother tsked disapprovingly, and it became clear that she was not a fan of Carlo's involvement with the Crucible.

"Why you in this craziness?" she asked Mark as they were all finally seated and eating.

"Need the money," Mark said, half-shrugging.

"Money, money, money, that's all I hear. More important things than money!"

"We need a roof over our heads!" Carlo said. "We need school clothes and food!"

"God will provide," Maria said, and crossed herself. Carlo just shook his head. "You two need nice girls, that's all. All this fighting for money. Just some nice girls, and you'll be settled right down."

"I've dated plenty of girls," Carlo said.

"I said *nice* girls," Maria shot back, waving a wooden spoon. "Not these girls with their short shorts and their attitudes. It's the damn TV. All the S-E-X," she spelled out in a hushed whisper so the children couldn't understand.

"Then we better move, 'cause that's all the girls we got around here," Carlo said, laughing. "When I win the Crucible, we'll go back to Miami. Get set up real nice."

Maria made a dismissive motion and went back to serving the younger children.

"You fight too?" Diego asked.

"I do," Mark said. "But not as good as your brother." He tapped his bruised cheekbone.

"No one's as good as Carlo," Diego said, tilting up his chin, and his cousins on either side of him nodded in assent. Carlo beamed from across the table.

"Maybe you someday, eh?" he said, and reached over to ruffle his hair, a gesture Diego tried to fight off. The table laughed.

Carlo's phone chirped and he casually fished it out of his pocket to check it. He broke into a wide smile seconds later.

"I'm in!" he shouted, turning the phone to show a congratulatory message from CMI that Mark couldn't quite read. As Carlo waved the phone around, he made out the word "semi-finals." The table erupted in cheers. Mark smiled and started clapping, before feeling a buzz in his own pocket.

He took his phone out, glanced at it, then tossed it across the table to Carlo. He read the message aloud.

"Congratulations on your admission to the CHICAGO Crucible Qualifier semi-finals. Only four competitors have been chosen for this honor, and your exceptional ability in the ring has earned you a place among them. An event is scheduled for 9:00 PM at 5587 Michigan Avenue. Black tie is optional, and a car will be sent."

"We did it, bro!" Carlo yelled, running around the table to hug Mark. "We did it!"

THE EVENT IN QUESTION was a lavish party thrown at a downtown club called La Machina. Carlo had insisted he and Mark share a limo to the event and CMI was happy to oblige. When they arrived they found a literal red carpet had been rolled out for them, leading up to a club that looked like a crashed spaceship from the outside.

A few minutes later, Mark was still seeing stars from the flashing cameras that had assaulted him on the way inside. He'd ignored all the questions shouted his way and made his way through the doors, escorted by refrigerator-shaped security guards who were smart enough to be wearing sunglasses to reflect the flashbulbs. Carlo, naturally, bathed in the attention, and Mark lost track of him as he stayed outside to pose for the cameras. He'd stayed long enough for the two of them to be photographed about ten thousand times with Carlo's arm hanging over his shoulder. It was supposedly something of a story that two friends and training partners had both made it to the qualifier finals together. They'd each face separate opponents in the semi-final, but if they both won, they could meet in the final itself.

Inside was the kind of high-end nightclub that made Mark instantly uncomfortable: thumping music so loud he couldn't hear himself think, a constant parade of free drinks that more often than not led to disaster, and now about two hundred girls in skin-tight, two-thousand-dollar dresses making eyes at him. He quickly realized it wasn't just because of his natural charm. At least one of the screens in the room was showing highlights of his fight with the bodybuilder. Another had Carlo's bout against the farmboy, and sure enough, soon Mark saw another screen showing Drescher hammering a muscled opponent into submission. He was the third then. There was still no sign of the fourth. He wished Carlo had followed him in; he shuffled around feeling lost.

That only lasted about ten seconds however, as a woman strode straight over to him and greeted him with a pretentious double cheek-kiss like they were old brunch pals.

"Mark, looking dapper as ever," she said, "I'm CMI vice president Vanessa Redgrave. I am *very* familiar with your work."

Mark felt like he'd seen her at his final fight, which had drawn more of an audience than the others.

"Pleasure," he said, nodding.

"You like?" she asked, gesturing outward toward the party, but in a way that also hinted that he was supposed to check her out as well. She wore a high-slit emerald dress with a tight corset top that showed off what was assuredly a $30,000 pair of breasts. Mark kept his eyes on the party.

"Very, uh, festive," he said.

"I would have thought this would be right up your alley," she said with a tinge of disappointment. "High roller that you are."

Mark had almost forgotten his degenerate gambler cover story. He really was rusty. He smiled and nodded.

"Absolutely."

"We have roulette and blackjack somewhere around here I think," she said. "All proceeds to charity of course," she said with a wink that could have meant any number of things. "Where's your partner in crime?"

"He's outside working the press," Mark said. "You know him."

"Absolutely," she said, "That's one of the things we love about him."

"And Burton Drescher?" Mark said, motioning at one of the screens where the man was now stomping on his downed opponent's chest. "What do you love about him?"

Vanessa's smile dimmed. "Mr. Drescher has proven himself a formidable competitor in *Prison Wars*, and we are grateful his wrongful sentence was overturned. It's fantastic he has decided to rejoin the Crayton family as a Crucible contestant."

That all sounded very rehearsed. Maybe Vanessa wasn't as soulless as she looked.

"Alright, enjoy yourself!" Vanessa said, clearly wanting to avoid any more uncomfortable questions. "Oh, David! Hello!" And she floated away, leaving Mark to endure more stares from a hundred different partygoers.

Brooke buzzed him, and he fished the translucent phone out of his jacket.

"Cameron Crayton is there."

FOR AN UNSETTLING HALF hour, Mark dealt with strangers swarming him, asking about his fights so far, his life, and so on. It was the first time his cover had been truly put to the test, but he knew about fifty pages of backstory by heart at this point, and once he got into it, it all came second nature. He told a few of his faux wild gambling stories and had those nearby roaring with laughter. Sometimes, he peppered in a few somber war tales, one of which actually brought a girl to tears. Most of the stories were real, and could be verified if anyone went poking around. Most just weren't originally his. He had a private laugh as he imagined *actually* telling them all the highlights of his life.

Eventually Mark escaped and managed to reunite with Carlo and his family. He took turns dancing with his mother and aunt, before being kidnapped by his cousins Nicole and Chella, who blushed constantly as Mark twirled them around. Carlo's brother Diego was around somewhere, no doubt in a teenage boy's paradise with so many stunning women around. Given the atmosphere, Mark really didn't think children should have been invited at all, but he saw a few other kids around, presumably more guests of guests.

And then, it was time. The lights all turned toward the large stage at the edge of the main dance floor. Rear curtains parted, and Cameron Crayton walked out into the light, arms extended, smile wide as ever. The crowd erupted in cheers, and Mark forced himself to clap. Crayton, clad in a silver tuxedo, moved with the grace of a shark, and his bright blue eyes were electric. After the applause died down, he spoke into an invisible mic embedded in his collar.

"Thank you, thank you," he said. "I can't make it to all sixteen cities, but I'm sure as hell glad I didn't miss Chicago!"

The hometown roared in assent for another minute.

"As you know, the Crucible is now nearly ready to air. The first broadcasts will be the semi-finals and finals of our city qualifiers featuring contestants who have been battle-tested for weeks now. The Windy City's four champions are here tonight!"

More cheers, and a few people he'd been talking to clapped him and Carlo on the back.

"To introduce them, I'll be announcing their pairing for their upcoming semi-final. First, we have Mark Wei, who will be taking on Josh Tanner! Come on down boys!"

More cheers and shoulder pats and Carlo yelling encouragement in his ear, and Mark slowly lumbered toward the stage, his heart hammering. He muttered curses under his breath. That meant Carlo was going to face Drescher in his semifinal. He wanted to get Drescher out of the way first, and have a friendly final with Carlo. But now? Carlo had to face the *Prison Wars* killer, and Mark was fighting . . . who exactly? Tanner. The name sounded familiar.

"Mark Wei is a former Navy SEAL who has served all over the globe before being recruited by prestige military contractor Glasshammer during peacetime. You've seen some of his highlights tonight, and he's one of the most brutally efficient and effective fighters I've seen around the country!"

Applause, as Mark reached the steps for the stage. On the wall was a giant picture of his face, and next to it, Tanner's profile shot. Mark suddenly remembered where he'd seen him before.

Crayton reached out his hand. Up close, Mark could see the tiny lines threatening to crack through his perfect skin. The smile was even more blinding up close, and the look in his eye was unreadable, and disquieting.

Mark shook his hand firmly, imagining how easy it would be to snap the man's neck in the next two seconds. It was tempting, but it wasn't the mission. *Though it would certainly send a goddamn message to the rest of the country watching this shitstorm.*

He released Crayton's hand, and the CEO motioned for him to stand stage left.

"And now here comes Sergeant Josh Tanner, formerly of the Chicago Police Department! He fights with an incredible amount of spirit and skill, and is entering the Crucible where he hopes to pay for his son's medical care. A true hero and role model for fathers everywhere!"

That was where Mark knew him from. He recognized Tanner from an interview on the news weeks ago during registration. He had a desperately sick kid and lost his insurance for some reason or another. Brooke was probably already sending him the guy's file. Mark's heart sank knowing that he'd be the one to send him home with nothing.

Tanner reached the stage and looked even more uncomfortable than Mark felt. He stiffly shook Crayton's hand and walked over to Mark.

"These two will face off in the ring a week from tonight. You will *not* want to miss it."

Behind them, more fight highlights played, some from Mark's older fights now, meaning mostly knockout punches and kicks. He got a brief glimpse of Tanner's style, which seemed to have a foundation in Muay Thai, which was unusual.

Mark turned back to Tanner and found something else unexpected. The man had stretched out his hand toward him.

Mark blinked for a minute, then reached out to shake it. They gave each other a quick nod, and locked eyes for a moment. Tanner's face was weather-worn, and didn't look like it belonged on top of a tuxedo. He had a hunted look about him, and Mark was further displeased he wasn't an asshole. Tanner gave a brief wave to his family in the crowd. A pretty redheaded wife with two kids in tow. The third was likely in no state to come.

"Such sportsmanship!" Crayton said to more applause. "And now, let's welcome Burton Drescher and Carlo Rivera!"

Finally, Mark saw Drescher wading through the crowd. His jacket was off and he had no tie. His shirt was unbuttoned to reveal a few of his chest and neck tattoos, and there was no hiding the ones on his face. He stalked through the crowd like a grizzly bear, and everyone hurriedly parted before him.

"You all know Burton from his time in *Prison Wars*, where he amassed an impressive 5-0 record. We were fortunate enough to help him overturn his wrongful conviction at the hands of a corrupt legal system, and Burton decided that his experience on our show would give him an edge in the Crucible, now that he's a free man. We're glad he's back with us!"

Yeah, okay, Mark thought. Drescher and four other ex-*Prison Wars* combatants just happened to all be sprung from death row, and then immediately turned around to enter another deadly tournament. Mark wondered how much Crayton had already paid each of them to sign up, or if simple threats had worked. Though threats didn't look like they'd have much sway on Drescher, no matter how much influence Cameron Crayton had.

After shaking Crayton's hand, he walked over to the other side of the stage, mercifully far away from Mark.

"And here we have young Carlo. One of the top featherweight MMA prospects in the country, and only nineteen! Carlo comes to us from just a few blocks south of here, a second-generation American by way of Puerto Rico, and is using his skills to secure a future for his entire family!"

Crayton was an expert in dancing around the fact that fifteen out of the sixteen entrants would be dead by the end of the year, and that was their way to "provide" for their families.

Still, Carlo bounded up the stage with a big grin and pumped Crayton's hand enthusiastically. He turned and waved to the crowd who couldn't help but cheer at the charming young man practically bouncing up and down on stage.

But Mark watched Carlo's face darken as he walked and stood next to Drescher, who was staring daggers at him.

"Gentlemen," Crayton said, but no handshake followed. Instead, Drescher leaned in and said something out of earshot to Carlo. The boy's face twisted with rage and he lunged at Drescher. Mark was milliseconds away from bolting over, but a half dozen dark-clad security staff emerged from the dark corners of the stage to pull the two apart. Eventually both calmed down, but still wore scowls.

"Wow," Crayton said. "Well if you can't tell, that's going to be one hell of a match!"

Mark was worried he was right.

"Now if you please," Crayton said. "When I said I was throwing a party, I meant a *party*. Drinks are free, and the dance floor is filled with some of the most beautiful women I've ever seen. Stay until tomorrow, if you can!"

Despite his professed love for the party he was throwing, as soon as the light was off him and the music started blaring again, he disappeared behind the curtain. Mark made a split-second decision and followed Crayton into the darkness. He needed to make first contact. Get on Crayton's radar.

"Excuse me, Mr. Crayton."

Crayton stopped and turned. Again, hulking security personnel stepped forward from the shadows, and one put a firm hand on his chest, preventing Mark from moving any closer. The man touching Mark towered over him. He had a granite jaw with buzzed silver hair and eyes discolored by double S-lenses displaying a dozen readouts on his retinas at once. An old scar was carved over his ear and wrapped around the base of his skull. Mark saw hints of tattoos poking out of the collar of suit, but couldn't make them out.

"It's alright, Wyatt," Crayton said with a smile. "Sorry. As my head of security, he's a little overprotective. You Glasshammer boys are always on edge, it seems. Might you have served together?"

Wyatt took his hand off Mark's suit and they stared at each other. Mark hoped he wasn't sweating, and his stomach felt like it has collapsed in on itself like a dying star.

"Blackfox Unit, Sudan, Kenya," the man said, his voice deep like an echo in a bottomless pit. He eyed Mark suspiciously.

"Redhawk Unit, Iran, Indonesia, and Azerbaijan. And a few more places I probably shouldn't talk about," Mark cracked a smile to break the tension. Wyatt didn't crack anything.

"Big company, isn't it? And getting bigger all the time," Crayton said.

Wyatt nodded, and retreated to the shadows. Mark caught a glint of his S-lenses in the darkness. *Glasshammer?* Shit. Mark didn't know that was where Crayton got his private security detail. Gideon and McAdams swore his cover was secure, but needless to say this was an additional complication he didn't need.

"But anyway, glad to actually meet you, Mark." He extended his hand again, and Mark shook it. "I'm off to Miami tonight, so unfortunately I don't have much time to chat."

"I know, and I apologize, sir," Mark said more submissively than he liked. "I just had to ask you something. If we get it to Vegas, and don't . . . make it to the end, how will our winnings be distributed? I don't have much family, never married, no kids."

Crayton nodded.

"I've seen," he said. "Bit of a lone wolf, are you? Well, we have that in common, as I'm sure you know."

Crayton had never married, and all paternity suits against him had been disproven over the years.

"You'll sign something to designate where you want the winnings to go in case you . . . are not the victor. Family, friends, charity . . . creditors," he said with a knowing wink. He really had been briefed on Mark then. But Mark doubted that this fictional version of himself would care much about paying his fictional loan sharks if he was dead. His story was that he was going big for the billion, or dying famous, at the very least.

"Thanks, sir. That's all I wanted to know. Have a safe flight to Florida."

"Thank you, Mark. It was a pleasure," Crayton said. "We've really got our eye on you." Another wink.

9

THINGS RAMPED UP QUICKLY. By the end of the next week, Los Angeles was about to crown its champion, the very first death-match contender. To celebrate, Carlo had invited himself and his brother over to Mark's condo to watch the final on his big screen, one of his few possessions that hadn't been repossessed or pawned to maintain his cover story.

"I can't believe he made it to the final," Mark said, shaking his head as he watched the highlights of Chase Cassidy's previous fights on the screen. "He's a goddamn actor!"

"And I told you that you underestimated him," Carlo said. "That dude is wicked good. Look at that form! He's got round-the-clock training whenever he wants it, and all they had to do was teach him to land punches instead of pull them."

"He's a total longshot, and he's still probably going to lose this final," Mark said, but he had to admit elements of Chase's fighting style were impressive. Even a few minutes into the fight, he'd managed to land some solid, stylish hits.

The camera swept through the audience of the Staples Center where the fight was being held, and from the signs people were holding, it was clear Cassidy was the crowd favorite. *Two billion dollars' worth of movies at the box office will do that*, Mark thought. His opponent was Alontis Sidner, a world champion kickboxer who was the pride of his scene, but had less mass market appeal. Cassidy was tall, but Alontis towered over him, and his reach was insane.

"Max Rage! Max Rage!" Diego chanted as Cassidy danced around the ring, dodging blows from Sidner five minutes into the fight. The Rage trilogy was one of Cassidy's highest grossing franchises, and the fictional disavowed CIA agent Chase played in them was a pop culture icon. But even cursory research revealed Cassidy hadn't had a hit in a while, and Mark wondered if the man would actually donate his Crucible winnings to charity like he'd claimed in interviews.

Cassidy darted in with a pair of hard jabs that caught Sidner off guard and split his lip. Carlo and his brothers cheered as blood dotted the mat. There was a knock at the door, and Mark checked the monitor to make sure the Riveras weren't about to be the victims of another unplanned home invasion. It was Brooke, so he popped the locks.

"Ah shoot, I missed the start," she said as she walked into the room holding a long glass plate.

"Well hello there," Carlo said, smoothing back his already close-cropped hair. "Mark, *who* is *this*?"

"My neighbor," Mark said as she moved around the couch. "Brooke. She comes by to bother me every so often."

Brooke gave him a mock glare.

"You can come bother me *any* time," Carlo said with a wide smile. Brooke grinned and set down the plate on the table.

"Thought you guys might want a snack, so I whipped up some chocolate chunk brownies. First batch didn't go so well, which is why I'm late."

"Awesome!" Diego exclaimed and dove into the pan practically face first.

"You just made a friend for life," Carlo said as he reached over and took one for himself. "Mark, we need to talk about where you've been hiding her," he said.

"She's a friend, Carlo," Mark said, rolling his eyes. "But she probably won't be if you keep talking. Watch the fight. Your boy is about to go down."

Cassidy was on the retreat, half keeled over from a number of kicks to his midsection. Mark turned and noticed Brooke's T-shirt, which had a DEATHSTRIKE logo on it.

"Aw, you too? Come on!"

"Oh, I'm sorry, are you too much of a snob to appreciate a good blockbuster?"

"If it's actually good," Mark said. "*Deathstrike* is total shit."

Deathstrike had Cassidy playing a globe-trotting mercenary with the most terrible Irish accent ever put to film. Even his fans regarded it as one of his worst outings, so Mark guessed Brooke was attempting to be ironic.

The man could fight though, Mark was starting to have to admit. Most other fighters would have been on the mat by now, but Cassidy was showing surprising resilience, and seemed to draw his energy from the crowd who hadn't stopped chanting his name since the bell rang. "*Cass-i-dy! Cass-i-dy!*"

Normally Chase Cassidy was an extremely good-looking statue of a man, with steel-gray eyes, perfectly tousled hair, a winning smile, and a physique that had landed him loads of shirtless commercial spots over the years. But now his eye was swelling and puffy and his chest was raked with trickles of his own blood, which poured from his nose and mouth. He still had that famous smile, but it was a sickly red.

The camera panned away from the ruin of Cassidy's face and showed Cameron Crayton himself applauding in a VIP box at the arena. Mark had asked about Axton, Crayton's head of security, and was sent a very thin file about one Commander Wyatt Axton, who had cleared out some rebel encampments during a few of the African civil wars. Deeper digging into redacted pages revealed that many of the "rebels" may have been women and children, but the

CIA hadn't looked too closely at the oversight. Now a collection of America-friendly dictators resided in their various thrones across the Atlantic, and Glasshammer secured some prime new contracts with the federal government for their efforts. But most pressingly, given how autonomous the divisions were within Glasshammer, Mark was promised that his cover story would stick, despite the uncomfortable connection. Crayton had hired his own wing for his security detail that were miles removed from the company Mark was supposed to have served with. Still, Axton had looked at him like he smelled a rat almost instantly.

Mark turned his attention back to the screen where the screaming crowd was practically drowning out the commentators of the match. Cassidy blocked kick after kick from Sidner and finally drove a stiff punch into the side of the taller man's knee. From the way he hobbled backward, Mark knew Sidner was hurt. He could barely even put weight on the leg. Most fights would be stopped after that kind of injury, but this wasn't most fights. As if to prove a point, Sidner lunged forward with a groin punch that Cassidy was barely able to deflect. The actor countered with a quick elbow that stunned Sidner and made him wobble toward the wall before his injured knee finally gave out. He struggled to his feet. Still no bell rang. Only unconsciousness or surrender would end this fight, and neither man had gotten this far to give up.

Sidner lurched upright and flung a few desperate punches toward Cassidy. The man danced back with a broad smile, his fatigue all but erased as the tide had turned his way. He planted a foot into Sidner's chest and the man bounced off the polyglass and stumbled forward. And then, as if straight out of one of his films, Cassidy launched himself into an airborne tailspin kick, his foot connecting with the edge of Sidner's jaw as he whipped around. By the time he landed, the kickboxer was sprawled out on the ground unconscious, a few of his teeth littering the mat. The crowd was deafening as Cassidy raised his arms in triumph. A tone finally sounded signifying Sidner was not getting up again, and Chase Cassidy became the first official combatant in the deathmatch tournament of the Crucible. Carlo, his brother, and Brooke were all hooting as loud as the crowd.

"Why are you so happy?" Mark asked Carlo. "He's your competition."

"Maybe," Carlo said, smiling, "But that was fuckin' *awesome!*"

The continued roar of the crowd said most of America was likely to agree.

ONE BY ONE, OTHER cities held their own semi-finals and finals within a few days of each other. Soon enough three others had joined Chase Cassidy as finalists and Mark's potential rivals, though he sincerely hoped Crayton was taken down before he'd ever step foot in the ring with any of them.

Mark watched the Dallas finals at the Blind Watchman, where Rayne had it playing on every screen and the place was more packed than he'd ever seen it. By the end of the night, it was a burly ex-NFL player named Naman "The Wall" Wilkinson who pummeled his opponent into submission. He was a hometown hero to football-crazed Texas, and it seemed he'd bring a sizable chunk of that viewership with him. His most devoted fans seemed quite forgiving that he'd retired before steroid abuse allegations against him could be proven. As if they needed proof. The man was a hulking semi-truck positively exploding with muscle. Mark guessed he needed the cash to pay his team of lawyers who had kept the NFL from coming after his Super Bowl rings.

Next up was Nashville, and Mark joined Carlo at his place for the event. They watched the festivities on an ancient flatscreen as his mother and aunt showered them with food. Mark was surprised to find a woman crowned champion of the region, a former Olympic gymnast named Soren Vanderhaven who had taken home four golds for the US at the 2028 games in Nairobi. Since then, she'd retired and spent years training to become an incredibly formidable fighter. Mark had assumed Crayton opened up the tournament to both genders for good PR, but he genuinely didn't believe he'd see any women as finalists. Only something like 8 percent of entrants were female, and putting a woman up against someone like Naman Wilkinson was asking for annihilation. But in the final, Vanderhaven absolutely demolished an ex-Army corporal twice her size with blinding speed and technical sophistication. And she certainly knew how to win the crowd over as well. Vanderhaven was shockingly gorgeous, with cerulean eyes and long, curled blonde hair she hadn't even bothered to pin up for the fight. She fought in flashy, revealing outfit that was just a few strips of fabric above lingerie, and quite a few below traditional ring attire. For most of the fight, the outfit and the sculpted body it was barely containing were all the commentators could focus on, until they realized that she was dishing out a hell of a beating. Rayne was absolutely in love with her, and informed Mark at the bar the next day that she was sorry, but she was her pick to win the whole thing. "I hope she doesn't kill you, though," she added, helpfully.

Mark watched the third and final fight before the circus came to Chicago in the penthouse level of the Crayton building where he'd fought previously. CMI had extended him an invite for every match, but he only accepted it once Brooke told him it could help him get in better with the staff, which could be useful. Vice president Vanessa was there, and wouldn't stop chattering away through the entire fight. Denver crowned a young, determined soldier named Ethan Callaghan as its champion, an ex-Green Beret who was fighting to pay for his wife's medical treatment. She had a late-stage brain tumor that could only be treated through completely experimental, wildly expensive drugs. The camera showed Callaghan's three children in the audience, all blond with green eyes like him. Given the profile this event would give him, someone like Callaghan could probably just start a fundraiser himself to try and pay his bills, but upon closer examination, the contract they had all signed forbade them from soliciting any kind of donations once they entered the Crucible. Smart from Crayton's point of view, given that such a thing would negate many contender's motivation for entering in the first place, but impossibly cruel as well. Someone like Callaghan's wife could literally die because of that clause. Even Mark breathed a sigh of relief when the young man won, before remembering that he was trying to shut down the entire tournament and Callaghan wouldn't get anything.

"Do you know he saved his entire unit from an ambush in Tehran?" Vanessa told Mark after he won the fight. "Carried five soldiers to safety while nursing three gunshot wounds of his own."

"They should pay him better," was all Mark could say in reply. Sometimes he felt sick at the severance package he'd gotten from the CIA while so many other soldiers were so badly mistreated and forgotten about as veterans. This kid deserved better than being forced to enter a spectacle like this to be potentially butchered in front of millions.

"He's a hero," Vanessa continued. "One of our best."

Was she talking about America or the Crucible? It was hard to tell with these people.

"I NEED TO KNOW what all this is for," Mark asked Gideon during a park bench meeting the day before the semi-final. "Tell me you turned up something on Crayton, and he's dirty and not just some sociopathic billionaire with an unhealthy love for ancient Rome."

Gideon gazed out into the park, looking as old as Mark had ever seen him. He seemed like a shell of his former self, back when he'd pulled Mark out of the fire. Well, the fire he'd thrown him into in the first place.

"Within the next few minutes," Gideon said, "a story is going to break. Supreme Court Justice Constance Wright has passed away."

"What?" Mark said, incredulous. "Is that true?"

Gideon nodded.

"She was eighty-four. She had a stroke. These things happen."

He paused.

"Except when they don't."

"What are you saying?" Mark said. "You mean . . ."

"Wright was the swing vote that killed *Prison Wars* for Crayton. His new 'Athletic Protection Act' his surrogates are peddling in Congress is about to pass the House and make its way to the Senate. It will squeeze past the left and land in the lap of our good friend President Ashford, who, according to our reports, received millions in re-election funding through various Crayton shell companies and subsidiaries over the course of the past few years. He will sign it."

"And the Supreme Court is the only roadblock left," Mark continued the thought.

"Crayton doesn't want a shadow cast over his little game with another prolonged court case. Ashford will appoint a new justice that will swing the *right* way, and this 'Crucible' becomes unquestionably legal."

"You don't think . . ."

"The president knows?" Gideon said with eyebrows raised. "No, I don't. I'm guessing he probably doesn't even know just how much Crayton has invested into him either. But he'll make the consideration all the same, given that he's got jelly where a backbone should be."

"Do you have proof? That Crayton had Wright killed?"

Gideon shook his head.

"If I did, you would be obsolete and we wouldn't be sitting here. I'm sure the autopsy will show us exactly jack shit, but this is not a coincidence. I'm telling you this to get you to recognize the *stakes* here. It's not just some nebulous threat or vague associations with foreign powers. If one of the new China Republics used Crayton or his company to kill a Supreme Court justice, that's an act of war. It should not surprise you to learn that Wright was also key in upholding the severity of the trade sanctions against China during Cold War II, and before she was appointed, she consulted on the legal aspects of Spearfish years before it was implemented as well. She's an old enemy to them."

Spearfish. Even the word made Mark nearly hyperventilate.

"Could it have been MSS directly?"

Gideon shook his head.

"Unlikely," he said. "The Ministry is still lurking in the shadows, but they don't have the resources to pull something like that off anymore. Not unless they used a hefty asset with reach and connections that was already here."

"Like Crayton," Mark said. "Or rather his guard dog, Axton."

"Exactly. So we need that connection. You may not find a handwritten confession from Crayton that he spiked her pill bottle, but all you need is a thread, and we can tug on it until he unravels completely. But time is of the essence, as you can tell. We don't know how this is going to escalate. What's he's planning. What MSS is planning for him. This tournament has to be a smokescreen for something larger."

Mark's head was spinning. His phone buzzed and he checked the alert. He caught a glimpse of Constance Wright's name in a breaking news headline.

He was worried he'd stumbled into another war.

10

THE LAST WAR WAS dark. The last war was cold. The last war was lonely. And it hurt.

It was mostly, sharp, stabbing pain. But later, he would realize, there was a deep, pervasive, sickly pain that would thread through his entire body and soul and never truly leave him. Pain that started with one man.

"My name is Zhou," said the smoking figure hidden in shadow. "And I would like to know yours."

Mark couldn't feel his arms because they'd been bound so tightly to the metal chair for hours. When they grabbed him, he tried to keep himself oriented, but all he could deduce was that they were leagues underground, and certainly no one was coming to save him. That wasn't the mission, after all.

"Please, I told you," he said in flawless Mandarin, "I'm Li Quang Wu, I work in—"

"I know where you work," Zhou interrupted. "And I know that position has allowed you access to sensitive information. Information that you have been broadcasting back to the United States."

"What? No!" Mark cried, exactly on script. He forced tears out of his eyes. "There must be some mistake, I'm being set up. You must have a mole in the office."

"We do," Zhou said coolly. "And it is you."

Mark braced himself. He'd already been slapped around by the guards who had wrestled him down there, but the blow from Zhou's fist was the first serious strike he'd endured since he'd entered the country over a year ago. The first of many to come, he knew.

Pain exploded through his eye socket as his head whipped back from the punch. The chair remained bolted to the ground, and his neck bore the brunt of the recoil.

Now, Zhou stepped into the light. He was tall, as tall as Mark, meaning he stood out among the shorter populace of the country. His brows were thick and his features implied he was pureblood Chinese, through and through. The right half of his thin face was flecked with tiny white scars that looked like ancient cuts from shrapnel. He was young enough to have fought in Tibet, Mark guessed, but he would have been little older than a boy. Dark eyes pierced him, searching for the truth.

Mark had thought he was ready for the second phase of his part in Spearfish. But now, locked in a dark, freezing room a mile underground, staring at this man with death in his eyes, he wasn't so sure. This was the plan. Work as an MSS underling to solidify his cover, and transmit periodic reports to the US. The goal was to be stealthy enough to look like a pro, but just repetitive enough over time for the monitors to recognize a pattern and discover his malfeasance. Few spies were given a mission to get caught, yet here he was. Now he had to last long enough for them to believe he was a hardened US asset, but eventually break so they knew he could be turned. Many spies had died with their mouths shut, claiming ignorance until the end. Though part of Mark thought he could do that if he had to, he thought of Riko and the unborn Asami, and was glad his mission was to survive.

If he could, that is.

The second, third, and fourth blows all landed just as hard, and eventually Mark stopped counting and simply tried to maintain consciousness. He was told during training, during all the abuse he'd endured, that the CIA had studied Chinese interrogation techniques. That nothing they'd do to him would be worse than what they were putting him through. He had to believe them, as it was the only thing that had made the torment bearable. Knowing it was for the greater good, and that it was as bad as it would get. The beatings, the waterboarding, the humiliation and degradation. He'd done it all in mission prep, he could do it again if it meant completing the task at hand and getting back home to his family.

"Bring out the kit," Zhou called out to someone unseen in the darkness. A graying man stepped forward with a small suitcase. Zhou opened it, and Mark's eyes widened as the knives glinted in the gloom. Some were straight as arrows and razor sharp, others were jagged and grotesque and looked purposefully dull.

Zhou smiled a hateful smile.

"Choose."

Too many nights he still woke up with fire radiating from old scars. The wounds were long healed, of course, but for a few seconds every day he felt like he was back in that chair again. Most days he was glad there was no one sharing his bed to see him flush with that kind of panic. Most days.

Today he woke up alone as usual, the violent images slowly drifting from his consciousness. Remembering that horrible hole made him almost grateful for his current assignment, which was practically a vacation by comparison. Crayton was insane, that much was clear to Mark, but evil? He didn't think so. But if he was in fact in league with China somehow, that would change the equation. An operative with the hearts and minds of the American public was dangerous, no matter how he got their attention.

And he had gotten their attention.

THE NEWS WAS FLOODED with reports and speculation about the next city finals, Chicago. In a few hours, he'd step into the ring with Josh Tanner in front of tens of thousands live and millions on TV. The last set of matches had crept up to twenty-five million live viewers. Not *Prison Wars* numbers, and there were still about a dozen porn programs ahead of it, but the Crucible qualifiers had seen their ratings rise every week. Brooke told him that they could expect thirty million for his match at the very least, and more once he got to the finals.

Even though Mark knew he would beat Tanner, the rest of the country was apparently not so sure. He flipped on the TV as he got dressed and a roundtable of panelists on CMI's sports stream were debating his merits.

"I've seen the footage, and I'm not impressed," said a former heavyweight boxing champion turned commentator. "Wei's style is all over the place, and relies too much on a single knock-out blow. That may have worked well and good for the chumps in the lower brackets, but now he's facing some serious competition from here on out. Tanner is no joke."

Footage played behind them of Tanner pummeling a downed opponent with furious strikes.

"And how can you not be in Tanner's corner?" a blonde female anchor asked. "He's fighting to pay for treatment for his sick son while Mark Wei is what, fighting to pay off some gambling debts?"

"To be fair, Melanie," interjected an older man with a curled mustache. "Wei is something of a war hero. During the Iran incursion, he received a purple heart for injuries sustained in the field."

That was how they explained away his scars. He was supposed to have been caught in a blast from an IED. It was flimsy, but most knew it wasn't polite to question how a SEAL got a purple heart and the scars to match. In this case, the government's word was law.

"I know about his service," Melanie said, "But after that he signed up with Glasshammer? That's a red flag to me. You've read about what they did across Africa in '32. Was Wei there for that? What kind of orders did he follow?"

"I think we're getting a bit off-point here," a fourth man said, bald, with a wide smile and a loud tie. "This is fundamentally about their abilities as a fighter, not the content of their character. Do we even want to start talking about the kinds of things Burton Drescher has been accused of?"

That was answered with complete silence and awkward stares all around.

"I didn't think so, but the man gained fans and fame all the same for his ability to *fight*. *Prison Wars*, and now the Crucible, never claimed to be creating role models. They want to find the best fighters in the country. And sometimes those are the kinds of people who have done bad things."

"Fine," Melanie said, waving her hand. "But I'm rooting for Chase Cassidy and the guy with the sick kid."

"To each their own," the man said with a smile before turning to the camera. "We'll be right back with more on Chicago Cruci—"

Mark waved the screen off and rubbed his eyes. There had just been a roundtable discussion about him on TV. *This is getting more and more surreal by the day*, he thought. It was hard to believe after spending so long in complete isolation and darkness, that he was now being thrust into the light. It's not as if the CIA hadn't recruited public figures as assets before, but to turn one of their ghosts into a fully fledged celebrity was absolutely unheard of. Mark assumed the agency had bypassed the president completely on this because of his ties to Crayton. Whatever the case, Mark couldn't help but feel that somehow, this was going to end up being even more of a mindfuck than Spearfish by the time it was all said and done. And at least now, he had nothing to lose.

THE LIMO WAS EMPTY. Carlo had gone ahead to take his place in the VIP booth with his family, where Mark would be watching his fight against Drescher the following night. Mark rode in silence as the car made the short drive to Wrigley. Crayton had actually managed to pay off the MLB to move a Cubs game to a different night in order to rent the stadium for the semi-finals. The finals were reportedly going to be in the even more massive Soldier Field a few days from now.

As they approached the stadium, the streets were lined with fans who hooted and hollered as he passed. There were thousands lined up, many of whom probably wouldn't even get inside. But as the car slowed, Mark saw a different kind of bystander pressing up against the metal gates, with police officers holding them back. They were angry, very angry.

Mark squinted to read their signs, expecting some kind of anti-Asian sentiment. Cold War II had made some elements of the American public (and government) distrustful of anyone who looked even remotely Chinese, and even after the collapse, that hadn't gone away completely. But Mark saw no slurs as the light illuminated their placards.

THE END IS NIGHT one sign read. Reading the sign-holder's lips, it sounded like she was mouthing something similar.

ROME BURNED FOR ITS SINS, said another.

There were dozens, hundreds of protesters, many with vaguely religious elements written on their signs about the moral decay of the country and how the Crucible was essentially a sign of the end times. Mark couldn't disagree, and stared at one of the simpler signs that seemed to sum it all up.

WHAT HAVE WE BECOME?

The protestors were screaming at him, and a few broke through and began banging on the windows of the car. They didn't know it was actually him in there, but any other VIP executive or attending celebrity was still someone they wanted to yell at. Mark regarded them calmly, recognizing bulletproof glass when he saw it, but he wanted to roll the window down and say that he agreed with them.

Wrigley loomed large behind them, clouds obscuring the moon above it. Light shone out of the field and into the sky like some kind of promised land, and it was that sight, not the protestors, that gave Mark chills.

INSIDE, THE ADRENALINE WAS starting to get to him. It coursed through his veins like lightning, and he found himself tapping his leg uncontrollably as one of his trainers wrapped his wrists. There was a whole flock of them, old men with thinning hair and noses broken a dozen times each. All were chattering in his ear about tactics and strategy. He couldn't even remember any of their names. The only person he wanted in the locker room was Carlo, or even Gideon. These men didn't know him. They were cashing a check from Crayton and pretending to care if he got beaten to a pulp in the ring. Maybe they got a bonus if he won, which explained their fervor. Mark just nodded, but he was mentally muting all of them. Even Crayton's camp didn't seem to understand this wasn't a normal fight, like boxing or MMA. This was something else. Something primal. You couldn't coach that. These were men and women with death wishes. Some dreamed of glory, sure, but not Mark. Not Josh Tanner either, he imagined.

He could hear the crowd outside. A low roar like a swarm of disturbed hornets. Mark's energy spilled out past his bouncing leg and he stood up, hopping back and forth. His trainers slapped him on the back and smiled, seeming to think he was fired up, dollar signs in his eyes. Honestly, the only thing Mark was dreaming about at the present moment was squeezing Crayton's neck until his retinas detached.

A trainer held up his phone for him; a single message was on the translucent screen.

GET HIM BRO!

Carlo. Mark couldn't help but smile. He turned and jogged toward the door, the trainer army at his back.

The hallway was dark, lit only by the glow of the field outside.

He could see the floor seating, and the circular arena sitting somewhere around where second base used to be.

This is insane, he thought, one more time. After so many years in the shadows, it made his skin crawl to step out into the light.

Cameron Crayton had pulled out all the stops. Like the other fights Mark had seen before, now that he was the final four in the city, production of the Crucible had gone into full effect. This was no rank, torn-apart office with a pair of judges solemnly observing his fight. This was sixty thousand people, each determined to scream louder than the one standing next to them. Mark realized he was walking into a theme song, a blaring new-wave rap track he'd never heard before in his life, and the entire crowd seemed to pulse with the beat. Even he couldn't help but bob to the rhythm as he walked through the screams toward the ring. A video played on the giant screen over center field, some cut-together production that relayed his entirely fictional life story like it was a documentary. It focused mostly on his military career, his heroics as a sailor, then as a SEAL, then even at Glasshammer, where they'd concocted some tale about him rescuing a band of aid workers in Jakarta or something. He could barely even hear the narration over the deafening crowd. He finally reached the stage and stripped off his shirt, revealing at last his full collection of scars he'd sustained at the many edges of Zhou's knives. To everyone else, they were war wounds, and the crowd collectively gasped as they saw the intersecting lines covering his upper half.

Tanner was already there. Mark had missed his intro, which was assuredly five minutes of footage of his poor dying son. Mark sure as hell didn't want to see that for the eightieth time; he felt bad enough. Tanner was also shirtless, and had a smattering of disjointed tattoos. A cross. A clover. The names of his children etched on his ribs in what appeared to be their own handwriting. He eyed Mark with the hunger of a starving animal. Suddenly, Mark realized that while he had nothing to lose, Tanner had *everything* to lose, which in this case was probably much more dangerous.

An announcer wearing a sparkling suit with pearl white hair and teeth strode into the middle of the ring. The wireless mic clipped under his throat boomed throughout the entire field, and swaying masses slowly grew silent as he introduced the two fighters.

Mark was met with a smattering of boos mixed with the cheers. Either there was an anti-Chinese bent to the crowd, or they just didn't like his gambling and mercenary work. Tanner, on the other hand, had everyone cheering at the top of their lungs and stomping on the bleachers like madmen. Mark supposed if he was in the crowd, he'd be rooting for the man across from him, too.

The announcer reiterated the rules, because there was no referee. In effect, there were no rules. No rounds. No off-limit blows. They were to fight until one of them was physically unable to continue, though Crayton's judges were known to use a loose definition of that phrase. More or less, you were either unconscious, or you were begging for mercy. Mark knew from the look in Tanner's eye that the latter wasn't even an option for him.

The announcer's voice, the din of the crowd, all of it became like white noise to Mark. He scanned the seats for Brooke, looked to the boxes for Carlo and Crayton. In the third row, he caught a brief flash of a narrow, hard face, flecked with scars. He looked again, and the dead man was gone.

Mark shook his head, and rubbed his eyes. He saw himself on the giant screen, fifty times larger than life, looking bewildered. Underneath the feed were numbers. Four. Three. Two. One. A familiar chime.

He should have been paying closer attention.

Tanner's fist connected with his temple, and everything went white.

11

MARK HIT THE FLOOR as the crowd leapt to its feet. His vision slowly flickered back, just in time to see a shin about to crash into his face. He rolled back and Tanner's kick went wide. Mark spun up to his feet, and shook his head. He had a momentary flashback to tenth grade when Johnny Kalowski sucker punched him after football practice because his girlfriend had passed Mark a note in class. After he'd gotten that one shot in, the next few minutes resulted in Johnny Kalowski's jaw being wired shut for the following month.

Tanner's hit wasn't cheap, though; Mark was just off his game. Had he really thought he saw *Zhou* in the crowd? Was he actually going insane? Mark took a breath and collected himself, able to dodge a fresh flurry of elbow strikes from Tanner, who was now shifting into full Muay Thai mode. Where the palest white man Mark had ever seen had learned to be an expert Muay Thai fighter, he had no idea. Honestly, he'd rather buy Tanner a beer and talk about it than beat him half to death in front of all these people, but that didn't seem terribly possible in the present moment.

Tanner threw out a few more kicks, showcasing a flexibility that was more reserved for yoga instructors than ex-cops. He was exceptionally fast, and Mark had to break a sweat deflecting the incoming blows. His highlight reel really didn't do him justice. In person, Tanner was a lot more formidable than Mark had imagined.

He's fighting to save his son's life, said a voice in his mind, but Mark shoved it away. He had to. He threw a punch.

It missed.

Tanner ducked under and countered with a stiff uppercut that rattled every single one of Mark's teeth. He backed away and shook it off, allowing himself a snarl of anger. Tanner the desperate father was melting away, and the man before him was becoming simply an opponent to be destroyed.

Mark flew off his back foot and hit Tanner hard across the face with an aerial right hook. Before he could even recover, Mark planted his foot in his chest and sent him crashing against the polyglass. The stunned Tanner threw up his arms to block, but Mark went low and sunk a trio of jabs into the man's ribs. He could have gone a few inches lower and probably ended the fight right there, but he was still holding onto a little bit of restraint and decency, at least.

Tanner gasped on the last hit, and threw out a counter punch of his own that glanced off Mark's shoulder. He lunged forward and wrapped Mark up, but Mark countered with a quick judo throw that planted Tanner flat on his back. Mark leapt a few feet in the air and came crashing down with a knee that probably would have caved in the man's chest, but Tanner was still quick enough to roll out of the way. Much to Mark's surprise, Tanner spun around and countered with a winding kick to the back of his head, which sent him stumbling forward.

Even though the ring kept some of the sound out, the crowd was in frenzy. Mark wasn't on the outside looking in, but even he knew that *they* knew this was more than a normal fight. The audience could feel his anger. Tanner's desperation. There were *stakes* here. Not just a prizefight with two rich guys looking to get richer. In that moment, Mark thought that maybe Crayton wasn't crazy after all, and he really had tapped into something here.

But it was only a moment, as his head was snapped back into the ring by a square punch to his eye that drew blood. He staggered back and grabbed Tanner's wrist when he swung again. Tanner whipped around, not missing a beat, and slammed his elbow into Mark's ear, which caused him to lose his grip. Immediately, Tanner jammed a knee into the meat of Mark's thigh, which almost caused him to collapse on the spot. He'd rather be fighting a boxer that only knew how to use his hands, or a bodybuilder that didn't know how to use anything at all. Tanner was potentially lethal, and it was clear he deserved to be there.

Mark blocked the next knee strike, and countered with a downward elbow of his own planted in Tanner's sternum. Tanner lunged with another strike, but Mark grabbed him and flung him sideways through the air and into the wall. Even if the crowd was on Tanner's side, they couldn't help but cheer at that.

Mark kicked Tanner as he tried to rise, once, twice, three times. Tanner finally blocked and slowly got to his feet. He was favoring his left side, and Mark struck hard at his right leg, which he'd landed on wrong. It gave out as expected, and Tanner crashed to the mat again.

"*Stay down!*" Mark growled at him, out of earshot of the cameras, he hoped. "*This is over.*"

Tanner either didn't hear him, or didn't listen. He scrambled to his feet and dove at Mark, but got a forearm across the bridge of his nose as penance. Mark shifted his feet and drove a hook into his jaw, and Tanner went to his knees. When he looked up, his eyes were unfocused, but still open. That exact blow had knocked out dozens of other, much tougher looking men throughout Mark's life.

Mark could feel the blood trickling down his face from a cut near his eye, but Tanner looked even worse. Mark saw a white fleck on the ground that might have been a tooth. Tanner raised his fists.

"*Just stop!*" Mark hissed again. He didn't want to humiliate the man, even if he had to beat him.

Tanner swung wildly again, and Mark dodged like the punches were in slow motion, which they practically were. Tanner's strength, his speed, were draining quickly. Finally, Mark caught his arm, spun him around and wrapped him up in a chokehold.

"*It's over,*" Mark whispered in his ear. "*I'm sorry.*"

"*It . . . can't . . . be . . .*" Tanner choked out as Mark's grip tightened around his femoral artery. He struggled violently, like a man facing death, but as the seconds passed, the thrashing slowly subsided. Mark wrenched upward, pulling even tighter. He saw a crazed, bloodied face on the giant screen overhead. His own. Tanner's eyes were rolling back in his head, and tears were spilling out of the corners.

Mark kept pressing the artery, and left the windpipe intact, not wanting to do any lasting damage. Finally, Tanner blacked out completely, and Mark lowered him gently to the mat. The crowd was quiet. It wasn't the victor they wanted, and it also definitely wasn't the explosive conclusion they expected. Mark heard pattering of a few cheers, a few boos and more than a few outright sobs. The chime sounded. He was a city finalist.

The announcer returned.

"Your winner, Mark Wei!"

He held Mark's battered hand aloft as Tanner slowly started to come to. The look on his face when he realized he'd lost would haunt Mark forever.

12

MARK SLEPT FITFULLY FOR the next twelve hours or so, his body exhausted and bruised, but his mind firing on all cylinders whenever he closed his eyes. He worried about Carlo and his fight. He thought about Josh Tanner's son. He thought about Spearfish. And Zhou. And Riko. And Asami. He thought about killing. He thought about dying.

Until finally, he had to think about the mission. Crayton's people were sending an autolimo as they always did, and Brooke had outfitted him with the necessary gear for his first meaningful exchange with Crayton. It wasn't much, but it would prove useful all the same, provided everything went as planned.

Mark called Carlo from the limo, which was the best he could do since the combatants were forbidden from associating with each other before the fights, even if they were friends. Ultimately Mark decided he'd rather face Carlo in the final than Drescher. Not that he was scared of Drescher, but he didn't want Carlo mangled by the man. Better Carlo win and the two of them could have a friendly final based on the actual spirit of competition, not blind rage or desperation. Mark was already planning which knock-out blows would be effective but undamaging to Carlo in their theoretical final. But first, Carlo had to get there.

"Use your speed," Mark said. "The man's a tank, but he won't be able to keep up. His reach and power won't matter if you can get inside."

"Mark, come on, you do know I do this for a living, right?" Carlo said on the other end of the line.

"Yes," Mark said, "But MMA still has weight classes, rules. We didn't have either when I served, so I might have some useful sage advice for you yet."

"Yeah, yeah," Carlo said with an unseen smile. "Well, I rewatched his old *Prison Wars* tapes and he suffered a bad break in his left arm about a year and a half ago. Steel pipe cracked that shit right in half during his match with what's that guy's name? Some mafioso."

"Enzo Cavatti," Mark said, more familiar with *Prison Wars* than he'd have liked to be, now that he'd watched both seasons multiple times as background research for the Crucible mission. "Though as I recall, the pipe ended up in Cavatti's windpipe by the end of that fight."

"Right, but point is, that's exploitable. I've got a half dozen different ways I can tweak that arm alone."

Smart kid. Smart fighter.

"Just don't forget to focus on defense. Trying to block will probably get you killed, so dodge whenever you can instead. With the haymakers he throws, he'll get off balance soon enough if he's hitting nothing but air."

"Yeah, yeah," Carlo said. "That's always been the plan. Don't worry, old man. You'll get your grudge match with me in the final."

Someone said something out of earshot.

"Oh shit, I gotta go. I've got like six interviews before warm-ups. Time to get this beautiful face on TV."

Mark chuckled.

"Good luck, I'll see you after."

"No luck needed."

As a finalist, Mark was invited to watch the fight from Crayton's private box at Wrigley, which would allow him to get close to the man far ahead of schedule. Anything that could possibly speed up the mission and abort the Crucible earlier was a welcome development. The wood-paneled box had seated presidents and princes alike at one point or another, but now it housed Crayton and his assortment of VIPs, with Mark among them. As he entered, he was greeted with a scent of a thousand ancient cigars that had wormed its way into the wood and upholstery over the years. A few men were actively smoking new ones, and everyone turned to stare as he entered. By now, everyone in the room instantly knew who he was, and the bruises still spreading across his face would make it clear to anyone who was confused. He was the Talent, and it was clear he was in a room with the Money, which was exactly where he needed to be.

Crayton himself was the first person brave enough to actually talk to him, and he acted like they were old friends, greeting Mark with a firm handshake and a palm on his shoulder. Wyatt Axton loomed behind him, and Mark saw the lump of a large caliber pistol in his coat as his hands remained crossed in front of him.

"Hell of a fight, Mark," Crayton said through his shark smile. "I've watched the replay four times already. Your technique is flawless!"

He stared a little closer at the biggest bruise near Mark's eye and winced.

"Well, almost flawless," he laughed. "Come on, we've still got some time before the fight and there are a bunch of folks who have paid a hell of a lot of money to get to sit in the same room with you tonight."

"I'm sure you're the one they'd rather be talking to," Mark said with a smirk. Crayton leaned in and lowered his voice.

"That may be, but that's why I need to throw you at them instead," he said, his smile still fixed. Mark wondered if he ever stopped smiling. Behind him, Axton was his polar opposite; he had probably never smiled in his life. His eyes never left Mark for a second.

As Crayton introduced him to everyone from CFOs to talk show hosts, Mark constantly scanned the room. Suited security lined the walls, with Axton forever attached at the hip to Crayton himself. But from what Mark could tell, Crayton hadn't gone so far as to outfit the box with any anti-surveillance tech. Mark periodically pretended to check his phone for messages, but really he was getting data about the unseen frequencies rebounding around the room. There was nothing that would detect a bug, nor what he was going to attempt later that evening.

Mark was now rubbing elbows with the types of men and women who spent more on fuel for their private jets in a year than Tanner would need to help his son. Mark swallowed the thought and contracted the right muscles to make his smile reappear as he was introduced to the actual owner of the Cubs, the team that was supposed to be playing on the field below until they were preempted by a gladiator match.

After too much socializing for Mark's taste, the festivities were about to begin, and everyone took their seats. The plush recliners were so comfortable, Mark wouldn't have been surprised if patrons normally spent more time sleeping in them than watching baseball. But if the Crucible qualifier pre-show was meant to do one thing, it was to wake the audience up.

A line of two dozen women were in the ring where the clear walls had not yet been put up. Even from a distance, it was clear they were unnaturally beautiful, and soon enough the monitors in the box zoomed in enough to confirm that. They wore short, sheer, flowing robes that left little to the imagination. They were clearly meant to be cheerleaders of some sort, but instead of pom-poms they wielded sword hilts with flowing ribbons streaming out of them. Music started blasting, and the girls launched into an elaborately choreographed routine that was equal parts athletic and erotic. Mark squinted at the monitors above, and swore he recognized a few women from TV programs where they wore even less.

"What do you think of the, uh, what are we calling them, Vanessa?" Crayton asked. Mark had a prime seat next to the man himself.

"The Muses," his vice president answered from behind him. Mark could never seem to escape her. She glanced at him with a quick flash of something unknown in her green eyes.

"Ah yes," Crayton said. "The Muses. I like the name, but the execution I'm not so sure about. Mark?"

"Oh, uh, they're very . . . talented," Mark said, unsure of what else to say.

"Oh, come on, Mark. I didn't pay these girls an ungodly amount of money to take a night off from fucking on TV for *talented*," Vanessa said. They *were* porn stars then. Mark wasn't imagining it. He'd missed this entire spectacle yesterday when he was behind closed doors before his fight.

"They're ridiculously hot," Mark said with a frat-boy smile, knowing that was the desired response.

"Thank you!" Vanessa said, throwing her hands in the air. "I told you, sir. That will engage the prime demo even more. Best of both worlds. Tits and ass-kicking."

Crayton waved her off.

"I don't know," he said. "It's all a bit crass for my taste."

Mark had to stop himself from spitting out a sip of bourbon at the irony there. Instead he choked down the drink.

The dance continued, punctuated by whistles in the crowd. An assistant buzzed by Crayton's ear, holding a phone.

"Sir, another call. It's urgent."

"Block the number. All those numbers," Crayton said, suddenly sounding annoyed. "No more calls. Tell him our business is concluded, as I've made explicitly clear already."

"Of course," said the man. Mark heard the faint sound of the hinges of a door closing before catching a few barely audible words from the man. In Mandarin.

"Wŏ hĕn bàoqiàn . . ."

My apologies . . .

China. A thread. But who was it? And why was there tension with Crayton?

"Everything okay?" Mark lightly pressed. Crayton waved his hand.

"Of course, of course. Just an irritating advertising partner who can't take a hint."

That was all Mark could hope to get for the moment, and further inquiries would draw suspicion. Though it was significant in that doing business with any of the Chinese Republics was presently illegal.

Mark turned to Crayton.

"Mr. Crayton, can I ask you something?" he said.

"Cameron, please. I have enough people calling me Mr. Crayton all day."

"Sure," Mark said, but didn't rephrase. Instead he just asked, "What made you want to get into this?"

"Into what?" Crayton said. "Sports entertainment?"

"Uh, yes, but this new kind you've invented. With . . . high stakes," Mark clarified.

"You don't have to dance around it, Mark," Crayton said. "You're one of the few risking your neck out there after all."

"Fine," Mark said, with Crayton giving him some leeway to be direct. "The deathmatches. Why not just buy a sports team? Or get into porn like everyone else?" He gestured toward the writhing women on stage.

He knew he wouldn't get the real story, but he wanted to see how Crayton reacted when probed, and what his rehearsed answer would be.

Crayton smiled, but it was different. It almost seemed genuine.

"You're a smart man, Mark, so I'll be straight with you. I suppose I'm supposed to say the money. That's part of it, to be sure, but it's more than that. To me, it's hope. It's healing. It's honor. To you as well, I believe. Or else why would you be here?"

That was a trap Mark almost fell in.

"More competitive than sports, more entertaining than porn, then?"

Crayton tilted his head back and forth.

"To some. Traditional sporting events are dying, even if they all don't realize it yet. I'm sure you've seen it yourself, with every league in disarray, trying to draw fresh eyes with brawls and rule-bending. Pornography is the current mainstream trend, yes, but what real *challenge* is there to producing that?"

"I suppose it's pretty straightforward," Mark said, nodding.

"But this?" Crayton continued. "Convincing brave men and women they want to die for glory or money, and convincing the public they want to cheer for it? That's taken some doing."

Like bribing two branches of government and killing off members of the third, Mark thought. Crayton continued.

"But do you know what I realized the secret is?" he asked. Mark was suddenly intrigued.

"I don't."

"It's pre-packaged war. The most entertaining spectacle of all."

Mark was confused.

"How do you mean?"

Crayton sat back in his chair and folded his arms across his lap.

"What were the two most significant conflicts of the last fifteen years?"

"The Iran Incursion and Cold War II," Mark answered automatically.

"And how many American lives were lost in each?"

"Eight hundred in Iran. Thirty-three in China," Mark said, repeating the official tally. Naturally he knew both statistics were bullshit.

"Those numbers are low, thankfully, the lowest they've been

for any major 'war' in ages. We're mostly fighting with robots and drones and computer viruses now."

"And that's a bad thing?" Mark said, eyebrow raised.

"Of course not," Crayton said. "But it's left the public hungry. Hungry for heroes. For glory. For blood."

"Both wars had heroes," Mark said, starting to get a bit hot.

"Of course," Crayton said. "But what was their reward when they got home? What was yours? A paltry check from the government and being forced into working for a mercenary outfit?"

Mark paused to consider it, and imagined how he should react given his cover.

"And I'm one of the lucky ones," Mark said, slowly getting where Crayton was going with this.

"I'm glad you're smart enough to realize that," Crayton said. "Others work for minimum wage or live on the streets. Our *veterans*! I've seen men pawn their medals for food."

For liquor or drugs, more like, Mark thought.

"And as brave as you all were, there was no glory in those wars. Iran was a rap on the knuckles for threatening Israel. We poked China until it ate itself to ensure our continued economic dominance. Before that, Afghanistan, Iraq, Korea, Vietnam. All those lives, for what? All those heroes that came back damaged, broken, forgotten."

Crayton grew silent, but the bass still pumped throughout the stadium. The Muses continued to rhythmically swordfight with fluttering ribbons.

"So how do we create new heroes? How do we inspire a nation fatigued by pointless violence meant to make the rich richer, and little else?"

"The Crucible?" Mark offered, following Crayton's twisted logic.

"In here, we will *contain* war. We will fight not with nations, but with individuals. Here we offer the chance to live forever. To grant the brave and their loved ones the rewards they deserve."

"But it's entertainment," Mark said, gesturing toward the dancing Muses.

"All war is," Crayton said, "whether the public will admit it or not. How high were ratings of the livestreams when we first marched into Iran? How many people waved flags like America was a sports team to cheer on? But it was all futile. A pointless conflict with more pointless deaths. We want to feel proud again, and no war has achieved that since we toppled Hitler."

"Millions died to make that happen," Mark said.

"And now millions don't have to!" Crayton countered. "Don't you see? Only a few, and it will energize the nation in a way that we haven't seen in nearly a century."

Mark was silent, he wasn't sure what to say. He didn't want to be a grinning sycophant, but didn't want to be overly aggressive either.

"For too long we've rewarded bravery with empty gestures," Crayton continued. "Flags and fireworks. The Crucible will shower the country's bravest warriors with millions, and their names will live forever."

And you'll make money hand over fist, Mark thought. *The rich get richer.*

"That's why I'm here, I guess," Mark said, deciding it was best to placate him. "I feel like I'm owed more than I got."

"You are, my friend," Crayton said, placing a firm hand on his shoulder. "You are."

As the dancers left the stage, Crayton turned to chat with the round-faced guest seated at his right, the mayor of Chicago.

Crayton was good, Mark realized. That entire speech was tailored directly to him. If Mark was the man he was pretending to be, he no doubt would have been moved by the whole "heroes that get what they deserve" speech, crafted for a wounded vet who had lost everything. Hell, part of it actually spoke to Mark, the true Mark, who had lost even more than this false version of himself had. *Wasn't he owed more?*

But it was all bullshit, of course. Sure, there were veterans and soldiers alike in the Crucible, but what about the athletes? The actors? The martial artists? The *Prison Wars* murderers? Crayton's logic fell apart there, and Mark was sure if anyone else had been sitting beside him, he'd have an entirely different tale planned for them.

Still, Crayton wasn't wrong about war, nor the public's perception of it. China's collapse after The Red Death was one of the most profound American victories in the country's history, but where were the parades? Where were the medals for soldiers like him who fought only in the dark? There were none. Nothing short of a full-scale invasion and a few atom bombs would have satisfied the public's need to see heroes kill and villains die. China's demise was too clean on its surface, and Iran was little more than a quick sucker punch. No wonder they were so rabid when the Crucible came along. Crayton had indeed picked his moment well, Mark had to admit. But that didn't make him anything more than a snake offering the hungry a poisoned apple.

Mark's train of thought was interrupted by a ping from his phone. He slid it out of his pocket and read Brooke's message.

"I think Drescher has 47 lbs on Carlo. I wished him luck!"

It was code. It meant there were forty-seven cell signatures in the room. She was supposed to let him know when that number was at its probable max. The mention of "luck" meant go. Mark looked around and saw that everyone had in fact taken their seats ahead of the imminent start of the fight, and no one else was coming or going. He flicked to the correct symbol in his homescreen, a decoy photo editing program, and opened it. He watched for six seconds as his phone leeched all the data from all mobile devices in the room. Thousands of terabytes were uploaded to Brooke in almost an instant.

Another message appeared. "Great view I'm sure," it said. More code. The transfer was a success, and she'd begin decrypting immediately. A message about food would have been a signal to retry. If somehow anyone was monitoring his phone, the conversation would have looked innocuous.

Mark briefly scrolled through the list of transferred data. A phone registered to Crayton himself was there, as were a dozen and a half other Crayton Media-issued devices including flexscreens and S-lenses like the ones Axton wore. A potential goldmine, depending on what they revealed when cracked. Mark slid his phone back into the pocket of his suit and the lights dimmed. A bombastic dance track starting blaring, and a spotlight shone on Carlo entering the crowd from the dugout area, smiling as wide as Mark had ever seen.

13

MARK SPRINTED THROUGH THE corridors of the stadium past fans in the refreshment lines gawking at the monitors. His heart was racing as he tried to remember the blueprints, which he'd only glanced at during mission prep, and figure out a way to get down to the main field. He spotted an "employees only" door and slid through it as a dazed vendor walked out rubbing his mouth.

"Jesus," the man was muttering aloud.

Drescher didn't have forty-seven pounds on Carlo. It was more like a hundred. It was the reason that normal fighting events had weight classes, rounds, and referees. So disasters like this couldn't happen.

Mark took a hard right and blew past a dusty row of broken seats that had been extracted during a recent renovation. He ignored Brooke's messages, which he only saw part of as he glanced at his phone during his full sprint.

"MARK DON'T—" was all he could see, but he knew the rest. He didn't care.

Carlo's technical sophistication and speed had eventually counted for nothing the moment Drescher finally landed his first punch, six minutes in. It sent the kid rocketing back into the glass, and he was too dazed to block the follow-up hook. Mark saw his eyes roll back in his head before he hit the mat.

But that wasn't the end. By Drescher's third punch, to an already downed, unconscious Carlo, the chime sounded. Then the kicks began. One. Two. Three. Thunderous football punts directly into the crucifix on Carlo's back like Drescher was trying to kick Christ off the cross. The in-ring mics picked up the sound of bone cracking. By that point Mark had already leapt from his seat next to Crayton and was out the door by the time the ring's gate opened and security began wrestling Drescher away.

"That'll teach you to eyeball me you fuckin' spic!" was the last thing Mark heard Drescher bellow. Fuck the mission. Fuck everything. He would kill him.

Mark had finally made it to the ground floor, and followed the signs to a dark hallway where the dancing Muse girls were standing around looking frightened, not knowing if their finale was canceled due to the EMTs flooding the area.

Blowing past them all, Mark ran into a wall of security guarding the mouth of the tunnel.

"Sir, this area is—" one began before Mark stiff-armed him in the chest. He spun wildly down to the ground and the other three guards drew their tasers. Mark dodged their electric swings and disappeared into the floor crowd before they could stop him.

Stumbling through the seating outside the ring, Mark ripped away bodies as he made his way to the glass enclosure near where the pitcher's mound would normally be. When he reached the edge, he saw Carlo's mother sobbing. The cousins were emulating her wails. His aunt was trying to shield his brother from looking into the ring. Diego caught his eye as Mark pushed past more security and climbed the steps to the ring.

Carlo was wearing a plastic neck brace and wasn't moving. His eyes were swollen shut, and Mark prayed he was only unconscious. Mark saw one of the EMTs with a mobile heart rate monitor on his wrist, and watched the lines rise and fall far apart from one another. Too far apart.

Mark whipped around and looked for Drescher, but the only trace of him were bloodied size fourteen footprints leading out of the ring. They'd taken him away long before Mark had reached the floor. He was probably already in an autolimo by now and Mark was furious he'd missed him.

Mark knelt beside Carlo and watched his chest rise and fall ever so slightly. EMTs were screaming at him to clear the area, but he couldn't hear them or the rest of the crowd.

Until suddenly, he stopped and listened. They were cheering. They were fucking cheering.

The ride to the hospital was a blur. Even in its so-called emergency mode the autocab would only go five over the limit. Mark had been practically thrown from the ambulance, but he made sure that Carlo's mother Maria rode inside with Diego. His aunt and cousins followed with Mark in a painfully slow autocab.

The hospital was bright and deathly quiet at the late hour, even in the emergency wing. All hands were on deck to receive Carlo, who, according to a shaken Maria, had reportedly died for a minute in the ambulance before he was shocked back to life.

The doctors were trying to firm up their diagnoses, but all agreed on a few points. Carlo had sustained severe damage to his neck and spine and had broken at least four ribs and one of his legs. But it was hard to get a full gauge of his potential pain or mobility status because he simply would not wake up. He was being taken to a brain scan when Mark finally answered his phone.

"What?"

"Mark," Brooke said. "You need to come in."

"I'm with the Riveras."

"I'm worried about you."

"You're worried about the mission."

"That too."

Mark stalked down the hallway, his body wired despite the late hour.

"I don't give a damn about the mission. That wasn't a fight. That was a hate crime."

"Mark, you knew this is what this was. And this won't even be as bad as it gets. We have the phones now and—"

"I don't care about the goddamn phones!"

Mark remembered now why for years he'd tried not to get attached to anyone. Now, someone who had barely been an acquaintance not that long ago was nearly dead and causing him to lose his mind. It was like it was happening all over again.

"I need the night off, for Christ's sake." He calmed his voice down a bit, knowing that would reassure her. "I have a fight in a day and a half. I'm still on track. Crack the phones. Let me know what's in them and we'll go from there."

"Alright," Brooke said, sounding a bit more hopeful. "But come in tomorrow morning. Gideon wants to meet."

"Fine," Mark said. "This better be worth it."

"You want to make Crayton pay? Stay with the mission and bring him down. The right way."

Mark hung up.

Carlo's scans would take hours, and most of the exhausted Riveras were asleep in his room. He was way too jittery to sleep.

I need a goddamn drink.

A few hours later, Mark had no idea where he was. He remembered a blinking neon sign with a brand of beer he liked. Opening bleary eyes, he saw a bottle of that beer in front of him. Beyond it sat a dozen and a half overturned shotglasses. He tried to swear, but his brain lost the word halfway through.

Some yelling, a punch. Concrete scraping his palms. When he came too again, he was wandering the aisles of a liquor store, a bottle of something brown in his right hand, and something clear in his left.

There was no clerk. Just another faceless robotic monolith demanding payment. This one actually required a breath test to sell alcohol, but Mark waved his phone in front of it and a military-grade hacking tool fried the circuits of the whole unit. He stumbled out the door and into a waiting autocab.

He couldn't feel his face. Or his hands or feet. He felt nauseous and couldn't remember how many times he'd thrown up already. The stain patterns on his shirt said at least twice. He wobbled toward the line of a thumping club, and pair of bald, burly bouncers dragged him by the neck away from a gaggle of laughing girls in short dresses. To free himself, Mark tried an elaborate judo throw, which only managed to rip one of the bouncer's shirts, and it was Mark that got tossed into a wall instead.

It was getting darker, if that was even possible. The moments felt like years. He was staring at water, though he couldn't tell if it was a river or a lake or a drainage ditch. He threw away the remaining empty bottle in his hand, which sank silently. He went to throw something else away but stopped when he realized it was his phone. And then he did it anyway, the slim, glowing piece of plastic disappearing into the black water after sailing twenty feet through the air.

Where are you, Riko?

Why did you have to go?

He realized he was speaking out loud, yelling at the night itself. "Because I deserved it," he said. "And now I'm in hell."

HE HAD DAMNED HIMSELF in China, of course. After Zhou had surgically removed his soul through weeks of torture, there was nothing left but a shell. The training hadn't prepared him for that. Nothing could have. No one would have gone knowing that was in store, and they had to have known that. But if he didn't finish the mission, there was no point to it all, and he'd never see Riko again, or meet Asami. It was the only thing that kept him sane.

But the horror had only begun.

"My superiors believe your desire to turn is genuine," Zhou said.

Thankfully there was no knife in his hand, which was a rarity. "The information you've provided has been very helpful to them, they say."

Hope. There was hope. After "breaking" and admitting he was a spy, Mark had been offering up information to the Chinese the CIA had told him to give away as enticement. Submarine positions. Japanese codebreaking cyphers. Drone surveillance schedules. Useful, but ultimately not damaging enough to pose a serious threat to US interests. Enough to get his foot in the door.

"I just . . . want to help," Mark choked out through chapped lips. He was lucky to get water even once a day. Food came every three or four and even the rats in his cell wouldn't touch it.

"I still think you are a lying snake," Zhou said in Mandarin. "But it is not up to me. And I am due for a promotion for my role in helping you see the light of our glorious republic."

After all this time, Mark didn't think Zhou was really a true believer. Just an ambitious man trying to climb the ladder of chaos. And he was another rung.

"They ask something of you," Zhou said. "It will mean you leaving this cell. Rice and meat every day. Your own quarters."

Mark's heart leapt in his chest involuntarily. This was it. What he'd been waiting for. The chance to become a full double agent, and finally, maybe, be treated like a human being again. Unless this was another one of Zhou's cruel jokes.

"Think I am fucking with you?" he said, reading Mark's mind. He arched an eyebrow that had a tiny scar running through it. "I wish I was. I would bury you alive in here for eternity for your disgrace. But instead . . ."

He produced a keycard. As he ran his finger over the center of it, Mark's electronic cuffs beeped, and then opened. Mark rubbed his raw wrists and pulled himself to his feet.

"Thank you," he managed to spit out. Zhou merely frowned.

"Come, they are waiting."

Mark limped after Zhou out of the cell, half considering clawing his eyes out with his overgrown fingernails as revenge for the abuse he'd endured. But again, all it would do was widow Mark's wife and orphan his child. The CIA often chose operatives based on their *lack* of family ties, but Mark couldn't imagine how this mission could be done by someone without them.

They didn't have to go very far before arriving at another cell only six over from Mark. The rooms were soundproof, so it was impossible to tell how many were occupied. Mark was sure the blacksite, which he guessed was several miles under Beijing, was full with new political dissenters China was rounding up daily. Or at least they had been the last time he'd seen daylight.

The door opened. Inside were three figures at a table, faces hidden by shadow. Two wore suits, one had the stripes of an admiral. Mark's pulse quickened. All were smoking. Everyone smoked here.

Maybe they'll all just die of lung cancer.

They said nothing. Suddenly Zhou stripped the rags from Mark's shoulders. What was left of his prison jumpsuit was torn away, and he was naked before them. Mark was used to such embarrassment by now, but was not expecting what came next. A hose and a mist of soap. Attendants emerged from the walls and violently scrubbed him from head to toe. They shaved off his mangled beard and buzzed his matted hair so he was almost bald.

Zhou threw a uniform at him. A soldier's uniform with no rank on it. He gingerly put it on, enjoying the sensation of actual clothing brushing past clean skin. His sudden lack of hair made him cold, but he didn't mind. He laced up his shoes and donned his hat. Everything fit to perfection.

He turned to Zhou, who was holding up a mirror.

"The traitor reborn."

Mark did a double take. He almost didn't recognize himself. His face had lost what little fat it had, and his skin was gray as ash. He could only imagine what he'd looked like *before* being cleaned up. But now he realized perhaps there was a reason Zhou had never cut up his face, nor removed any fingers. He was at least, to some extent, valuable.

"I'm ready to serve," he barked, turning to the table and clicking his heels together in salute. The gesture was minimal, but painful all the same. Everything hurt. Always. Maybe that was over now. Maybe.

The figures regarded him in silence still. One of the suits lit a new cigarette.

"And serve you shall," one finally growled from the darkness. He waved his hand toward Zhou.

Zhou nodded and took a chair from the corner. It was metal, and Zhou fixed it to the ground with bolted clamps. It was the same chair Mark had sat in many times before.

No, no, no, no, Mark's mind raced. Not more. Not again. That's all this was. Just a big headfuck. He should have known.

But Zhou didn't restrain him. Instead, the door opened and two more guards shoved a hooded figure inside, dressed in a relatively fresh-looking jumpsuit.

The guards slammed him down in the chair and secured the restraints. They pulled the hood off the prisoner. It was a young white man with an overgrown Army buzzcut and a face full of bruises. He glared at the room in silence.

"This is Lieutenant Oh-Connor. Special Forces. We caught him trying to sabotage a nuclear plant in Lianyungang last week, trying to make it look like an accidental meltdown. The People's Defense Force killed most of his team, but a few members escaped. We have been asking him where they might have gone. Now, we would like you to ask him."

Mark turned to regard the battered American soldier. His gut was churning.

"Lieutenant, what are the evac procedures for your unit? Where are they being extracted?"

The man looked surprised at Mark's perfect English, but the answer he gave was the one Mark expected.

"Lieutenant Marcus O'Connor. United States Army. Service Number 8355521. D.O.B. 6/22/2002."

Jesus, he was three years younger than Mark. He blinked.

"Lieutenant, we must know where—"

Zhou interrupted him.

"We have asked him like this. And like that," he said, pointing to the recent bruises on O'Connor's face. "Now, you ask him like *I* ask."

An aide handed Zhou a suitcase.

The kit.

Mark's heart was in his throat. Zhou opened it, and presented the array of knives. Some of them were still crusted with blood. Possibly *his* blood.

Could he just take them and kill everyone in the room? Everyone in the blacksite? No, of course not. He was weak from starvation and he'd be shot inside of two seconds. His breathing became shallow and he was dizzy. His hands wouldn't stop shaking. Embers burned from cigarettes in the shadows. This was it. This was the last test.

Mark turned to Lieutenant O'Connor, the young man's eyes now involuntarily wide with fear.

"Choose."

14

MARK'S BRAIN SLOWLY TRANSITIONED into consciousness, the lights coming on one room at a time in his head, though some places remained permanently dark. His vision was blurred, his throat felt like he'd swallowed sand. He vaguely was aware of having control over his arm and flung it toward a nearby glass of water. His middle finger caught the rim, and flipped it. What soaked into the carpet smelled like jet fuel, and he didn't imagine it would have been very hydrating. His stomach wrenched at the smell, and slowly even more pungent scents trickled in. Urine. Bile. What had to be some kind of dead animal. Or maybe it was just him.

He blinked, and the room became a little more clear. The tragic wall art and comforter with ancient stains indicated a motel room. His hand fumbled around so he could try and pick himself off the floor, but it slipped on a slick brochure that had probably once been on the nightstand.

MADISON: A PLACE FOR FAMILY FUN, it read, and the picture showed a smiling family canoeing down a river.

Madison? As in, Wisconsin?

Mark had no idea how he'd gotten there. The clock blinked 12:00 but the light behind the curtains said it was probably around mid-afternoon. He reached into his pocket for his phone, but found nothing but uncomfortable dampness.

His head was reeling and he took a single step and fell straight back onto the bed, which had been stripped half-bare by a thrashing madman, most likely him. He rolled his head around and looked for clothes other than his own, thankfully finding nothing but the sock and shirt he was missing. His shoes were nowhere in sight.

It hasn't been this bad in a while, he thought, his brain forming each word with a sharp prick of pain. *Not since it happened.*

Suddenly, the door was flung open and Mark was baked in searing, torturous light that made his mind catch fire. The cloudless Wisconsin sky felt like the ozone layer had vanished and the sun was burning all life on the planet away, starting with him.

In the doorway, an angel of death loomed. Mark reached for a gun he did not have, and tried to vault away to the other side of the bed but just rolled over and bumped his head on a lamp, which crashed to the ground. It felt like his veins contained more alcohol than plasma.

The figure approached and mouthed something he couldn't hear, though he recognized his own name. He felt a sharp prick in his shoulder and saw the plunger of an injector release something lime-colored into his veins.

It was China. It was Crayton. He tried to fight but his arms felt like he was swimming in tar.

Slowly, his head began to clear. Just a little, but enough for his eyes to finally focus on the face in front of him.

Brooke.

His ears started to work too.

"Jesus, Mark."

She sat on the bed as he remained crammed into the corner between the mattress and the wall. Another figure was behind her, one he could now easily recognize. Gideon. And he did not look pleased.

"I knew you were a mess when I put you on this op, but I thought you were past something this stupid!" Gideon yelled. The volume made Mark's head throb.

"What did you give me?" Mark said, his speech one long slur.

"Think of it like eleven cups of coffee," Brooke said, putting the empty vial back into a little plastic case. "Military grade hangover cure."

Mark almost corrected her to say he was still drunk, not hungover, but thought better of it.

"Carlo?" he asked, squinting. The light still burned.

"Critical, unconscious. The Riveras wondered where you went off to," Brooke said.

Gideon folded his arms.

"We don't have time for this," he said. "We're going to have to airlift you back to the city. Goddamn Wisconsin? And you ditched all your trackers and made us go full bloodhound on you? The brass is pissed about this. They want to pull you."

"Too late for that," Mark said, shaking his head.

"I know that," Gideon snapped. "But you might be out of the running anyway if we don't get you back in time for the fight. "

"That's Friday," Mark said, flinging his arm out dismissively. "I'll be fine by then."

"Mark," Brooke said, holding up her phone. The news portal she had open displayed a headline that made his eyes widen, letting in even more burning light.

WEI VS. DRESCHER: BIGGEST CRUCIBLE MATCH YET?
FIND OUT TONIGHT

Tonight?

Below that, there was a running countdown clock.

2:45:32

2:45:31

2:45:30

"Oh shit."

MARK COULDN'T THINK OF two things that went together more

poorly than air travel and alcohol-induced vertigo. He spent the entire trip back to Chicago dry-heaving, because there was nothing left in his stomach to evacuate. Brooke injected him with a few more colorful liquids that were meant to treat various symptoms normally exhibited by rescued POWs.

Gideon was trying to walk him through a debrief, and because of how quiet the new hexocopters were, he didn't even have to yell. Still, anything above a whisper was torture to Mark, meaning he was only really hearing half of whatever Gideon was saying.

"We had to send the mobile data you ripped to Langley. The CMI-issued tech is beyond anything we can crack in the field. Might take a little while. That level of security is a red flag in and of itself. Elsewhere, the rest of the crowd had more middle-aged naked selfies than I'd care to see. If we dig enough we'll find some kickbacks and favor trade among their little incestuous club, but that's par for the course and not what we're after. Crayton and his people are way more on their game. Nothing in the preliminary decrypt even hints at China."

Mark was nodding, but was really only thinking of Carlo, battered and broken in his hospital bed.

"I want to see him," Mark said, and Gideon looked annoyed that he clearly wasn't paying attention.

Brooke knew who he was talking about, and shook her head.

"No time. At this rate we'll have to have you parachute onto the field to even be a half hour late."

THEY DIDN'T DO THAT, of course. They had to drop him outside the city and plant him in an autocab to take him home where a limo with an impatient escort staff was waiting. Five of them jumped on their phones when he rolled up, all letting their various bosses know that he had actually been located. All looked like they had just escaped the gas chamber.

"Don't worry, boys," Mark said, forcing a smile. "Party ran a little late is all." His mannerisms, speech, and breath certainly all said that was true. But he left out the part about the "party" being a blackout rage bender that landed him in a city he'd never travel to of his own free will 150 miles away.

When he finally pulled up to Soldier Field, the sun had set. He was still mostly drunk. And fully angry. Brooke's cocktail allowed him to walk and talk, but beyond that was anyone's guess. Still, he knew he had enough fuel in the tank to beat a thug like Drescher. Not just beat him. Tear him apart.

Crayton's team had ridden in the autolimo with him the whole way, ensuring he didn't go MIA again. They refrained from asking him prying questions, but once the doors opened, Mark realized they were going to let him be picked apart by vultures.

Mark had avoided the press pretty well so far since the Crucible propelled him to at least local notoriety. If he qualified for the main event, half the country would know his name. And it all started now, with dozens upon dozens of cameras pointed his way. The camera flashes reignited his dormant migraine and he stumbled out of the car with two buttons open on his hastily assembled pre-fight dress outfit.

Mark charted a course straight through to the stadium, trying to mute out the rabid press corps as much as possible and squinted to mitigate the flash photography. Some questions were screamed so loud he couldn't ignore them.

"Will you avenge Carlo tonight?" a psychotic-looking beauty queen asked him, shoving a wand mic in his chin.

"Avenge?" Mark growled.

"Reports are that he's in a coma, and has serious injuries. Burton Drescher has gone on record saying that he wished, and I quote, that he'd 'killed the little wetback.'"

Mark stopped and swerved around to face the throngs. They all stepped back a couple feet.

"Burton Drescher is a disease," Mark said, eyes bleary and bloodshot as he looked into the lens. "To this tournament. To this country. To the entire human race. I will *eradicate* him."

The press stopped shouting long enough to cheer.

SIXTY-THOUSAND FANS CLAPPED LIKE a waterfall as the Muses finished their latest dance routine. Mark hadn't bothered to look at the monitor in the locker room, and had forced all his faux trainers to leave. The Soldier Field crowd was sold out and then some, with extra seating crammed in to accommodate the last few thousand who wanted to see what was being pitched as the biggest fight of the Crucible so far. There was a story now. *Revenge.*

Mark's knee bounced up and down uncontrollably as he buried his face in his hands. His head had been spinning for hours, and despite Brooke's magic cocktail, it didn't seem like it would stop any time soon. But even on his worst day, he should be able to beat a brute like Drescher, right?

An intro video started playing. His. It was a new one this time, no more heroic tales from days gone by. Rather, a voiceover and security cam footage from his local gym.

"Best friends and training partners, Carlo Rivera and Mark Wei entered the Crucible together to prove their worth as fighters."

The screen showed shots of them sparring late at night at the gym.

"Though from different backgrounds, they were inseparable, with the same big dreams of a better life, and each were convinced they'd see the other in the finals."

A dramatic pause.

"And then, tragedy struck. In his semi-final match with Burton Dres—"

Mark let out a primal scream, grabbed a discarded practice football helmet from a nearby locker and hurled it into the TV, the thin screen spiderwebbing and shorting out as the helmet bounced on the tile floor. The bullshit was suffocating. His anguish and anger was being pre-packaged and sold as a *goddamn product*.

He didn't want to fight. He wanted to burn the entire stadium down.

Again, Mark was last to enter the ring. The clouds above the field threatened rain, but if there was thunder, it was drowned out by the roar of the crowd. As he walked out from the player's entrance toward the lit-up ring, he heard something he never expected, and half thought it was an auditory hallucination, the booze playing tricks on him again.

"*Wei! Wei! Wei! Wei!*" the crowd chanted, stomping their feet with each repetition. It was a far cry from his tepid reception at Wrigley. It seemed they loved Carlo and wanted to see justice for him. The narrative was working. How could it not?

In that moment, Mark forgot about the mission. Crayton's corruption. His own anger. Hell, he almost forgot he was drunk. In that moment, he absorbed the cheers of the crowd and felt more alive than he had in years. It was downright euphoric. He smiled. He waved. He became what they wanted him to be. The white knight, there to slay the dragon. He was poised to be the hero, a title he'd never been able to wear publicly.

But the dragon looked murderous. Drescher was in the ring, punching air, but he turned to face Mark as he made his way into the ring amid the fanfare of the crowd. His sneer was encased in a pencil-thin goatee, which rested under a crooked nose and the blue eyes of the Master Race. His dyed black hair was already wet with sweat.

Drescher was almost as wide as he was tall, and stood a few inches shorter than Mark. He lacked the chiseled muscles of a cage fighter or bodybuilder, but he was solid as concrete from head to toe. He was the kind of guy you'd see pulling tractor trailers or flipping monster truck tires in strongman competitions.

His full litany of tattoos was on display: flaming swastikas, SS emblems, iron crosses and a host of pagan-looking symbols and nonsensical numbers that Mark assumed were part of the neo-Nazi movement, which somehow never seemed to dissolve, even close to a century after Hitler's death. Mark also was close enough to make out a German phrase inked across his chest in medieval-looking letters, ARBEIT MACHT FREI.

The man's not just a disease, Mark thought. *He's a fucking plague.*

Anyone else would have been terrified. The man before him was the closest thing to evil incarnate that walked the earth. But Mark had stared into darkness so long it had lost all power over him. He divorced Drescher from the legend. From the Aryan Nation terrorist. From the *Prison Wars* gladiator. He was just a man. A man who had hurt his friend.

"Tell me," Drescher growled at him, circling like a predatory beast. "Were you fuckin' him? The little spic?"

Mark's blood boiled, but he remained silent.

"I've been hearin' all about your late-night training sessions, and neither one of you showed up to Crayton's party with a bitch on your arm. Makes sense." He snorted.

Mark was mildly concerned he was seeing two Dreschers talking shit, but shook his head to refocus. He hoped he wasn't going to vomit up whiskey or something worse into the middle of the ring.

"The chink and the spic. An epic love story for our time."

The announcer was presenting each of them to the crowd, but Drescher just kept going.

"Well, he should be fuckin' dead, but from what I hear he's a vegetable. Guess that means you'll need some lube next time you wanna—"

Mark was done. With Drescher. With holding back. With all of it. The announcer dove out of the way midway through his presentation as Mark speared Drescher through the midsection, pulverizing the air from his lungs. They crashed into the polyglass wall, Drescher miraculously remaining upright with his solid, low center of gravity. He hammered two shots directly into Mark's ribs, which made him release his grip. Mark thought he'd puke right then and there, but his organs merely bounced around inside him. Drescher took advantage of Mark's discomfort and hit him with a hard right cross that dropped him straight to the mat. The man had the force of a Panzer tank behind his punches, and his kicks too, Mark learned as Drescher's foot met his abdomen and spun him around in a full loop. A few more of those and he'd be in the hospital bed next to Carlo.

Mark regained his footing, aware that he wasn't quite the ruthless fighting machine he imagined after two and a half days of nonstop drinking. Drawing energy from the frenzied crowd, he blocked Drescher's next two strikes, but found out he had been right in his advice to Carlo. The punches threatened to break his forearms if he kept them in place, so he was forced to try to duck and weave out of the way instead, his arms already turning beet-red from the blows.

Again, he just wasn't fast enough and one left hook caught him alongside the ear and sent him tumbling to the ground. It hit him with so much force he couldn't even hear whether or not the crowd was cheering or booing when he got up, and it took everything in him to dodge a second swing that would have taken his head clean off.

There was no style here to understand. Drescher was a street fighter, always improvising. Just when Mark thought he was getting a handle on the punches, Drescher dove into his waist, picking him up and slamming him into the wall. This time it was Mark who lost his breath, and as he gasped to get it back, Drescher stuck three stubby fingers in his mouth and yanked him down to the mat by his jaw. Mark was so caught off guard, he couldn't dodge the foot that slammed into his face immediately after. An inch to the right and it would have shattered his nose, but it drew blood all the same. Liquid was also leaking out of his ear, he realized, and he was more disoriented than ever.

Mark rolled away and righted himself once more, this time more slowly. He realized he was going to have to try to go on the offensive if he wanted a prayer of surviving a fight he thought was supposed to be a sure thing. Then again, he was supposed to be sober.

Mark lashed out with a few strikes, but the ones that landed didn't even make Drescher flinch. Mark jabbed at a skull tattoo near his kidneys, but it took five full blows before Drescher even cringed. And his counter overhand dropped Mark to one knee. The crowd gasped.

Spinning up with a kick, he caught Drescher under the jaw, which caused him to stagger back. It was an opening. He raced forward, almost losing his balance, and launched himself into the air. This time, he landed two rotating kicks before he hit the ground, and Drescher clutched his chest. Mark ducked under a clothesline and countered with backward elbow, a move he borrowed from Josh Tanner. Now Drescher was the one bleeding, and Mark felt new life pouring into him as Soldier Field erupted in another chant of his name. He took a running start and propelled himself off the wall, bringing his fist down for a knockout blow to Drescher's tattooed face.

He caught him.

Drescher had one hand wrapped around his arm and the other under his thigh. They hung there for a moment, suspended in a grotesque ballet, before Drescher whirled around and flung him up into the polyglass. Mark fell a solid seven feet after contact, too dazed to avoid smashing face-first into the mat. And just in case that wasn't enough, as he rolled over, Drescher's next kick was aimed straight at his crotch. Mark felt pain like he hadn't experienced since the chair in China, and his vision was blinding white. Drescher grabbed him by the hair and slammed him down over and over. If they were on concrete, his brains would have been spilled all over the ground already. Mark struggled, but Drescher sensed escape and collapsed completely on him. He wrapped his meaty arm around Mark's neck and pressed his elbow into his vertebrae. The force increased with each passing second until there was only one conclusion.

He's going to kill me, Mark realized. And then he understood.

He had to stop treating this like a fight. A boxing match. An MMA brawl. Like something with rules. With boundaries. This was survival. This was the deck of the *Hóngsè Fēng*. This was the library of West Lincoln High.

Mark bit into the flesh of Drescher's arm until he understood what human meat tasted like. The man howled and wrenched back, losing his kill-grip on Mark's neck. He stepped back and looked at the deep chunk missing from his forearm, which was now a bloody glob on the ground. He roared and swung at Mark with a hard left. The arm that had been broken by a pipe in *Prison Wars*.

Mark broke it again.

The move was effortless. Bend the right way with the right force and it doesn't matter how much muscle surrounds the bone. Drescher's left arm was crooked to the point of uselessness, but practically immune to the pain, he still charged.

Stomping down hard into his kneecap, Mark heard that crack too. Drescher lurched forward, slamming into the mat. Mark followed him down to the ground, landing on him with a knee specifically designed to detach one of his kidneys. Even if he missed, he'd take two ribs with it. More cracks. The ring mics picked up every sound and the crowd was delirious with excitement.

Drescher pulled himself up with his remaining good arm. He turned to face Mark, blood pouring from his nose, coloring his torso's tattoos a vivid crimson. He was trying to mouth something but Mark suspected he'd split his tongue open. From the way he was breathing, it seemed like Mark's last strike had punctured one of his lungs.

He could have thrown a punch to end it all. Drescher would be out cold and he'd be sailing into the finals as the triumphant avenger.

But he thought of Carlo, who might not ever wake up. He

thought of Crayton, who was responsible for this shitshow. He thought of the Pakistani family that had burned alive at Drescher's hand and instead of justice their killer was turned into a superstar.

He didn't throw that punch. Instead, he lashed out with the flat of his hand.

It caught Drescher in the throat, and a wet crack told Mark that he'd collapsed his windpipe. Drescher went down to his knees, clawing at his neck, unable to suck air into skewered, liquid-filled lungs. At last, his sky-blue eyes released their rage, and were wholly consumed by fear.

Mark watched Burton Drescher drown in his own blood live in front of thirty-five million people.

PART II

"You may live to see man-made horrors beyond your comprehension."
—Nikola Tesla

15

"WELCOME TO SPORTSWIRE, I'M Jayce Harrington, and there's only one thing anyone's talking about this morning. Am I right, Melanie?"

"Absolutely, Jayce. In case you've been struck blind or deaf, Cameron Crayton's Crucible tournament claimed its first victim last night, veteran *Prison Wars* participant Burton Drescher, killed in the ring by newcomer Mark Wei. Johanna Viseberg and Turk Smith are joining our discussion."

"Thanks for having us."

"Now, there have been a few deaths in the Crucible so far, correct?"

"That's right. During the various, non-televised qualifying stages, there have been reports of a few accidental deaths from injury in the ring or, on a few occasions, heart trouble. But the debate today is whether or not Mark Wei *purposefully* killed Burton Drescher for critically injuring his friend and training partner Carlo Rivera in a fight earlier in the week."

"If you watch the fight, near the end, you can see something changes in Wei. His moves become more precise. His last four blows each broke a bone, according to our analysis."

"This is what you get when you bring in soldiers, not fighters, Jayce."

"Expand on that, Johanna."

"These men are trained to subdue with lethal force. So lethal force is what you're going to get. And could you blame Wei after what Drescher did to Rivera? That fight was also above and beyond what was necessary."

"I have to chime in here, I think we're missing an important point."

"Yes, Turk?"

"Have we forgotten that the entire *purpose* of the Crucible qualifiers is to enter a tournament that Cameron Crayton specifically said is a fight to the death? And we've already seen this with *Prison Wars*! Why should Mark Wei killing Drescher, even intentionally, be such an issue if we've already accepted all that?"

"Well Turk, as you know, the Supreme Court ruled against *Prison Wars*, specifically the 'purposeful death' component of the competition. While Cameron Crayton's 'Athletic Protection' bill aims to correct that, it's only passed one house of Congress. He's hoping to have it signed by the time the Crucible itself starts later this summer, but for now, that kind of competition is technically still illegal."

"It's a gray area, Melanie. I don't think you can prove that Wei even *had* intent to kill Drescher. Four boxers died in the ring last year alone on the pro circuit. Six cage fighters, after the rules changes. I don't think this is different."

"Johanna, you're a veteran fighter; was that final blow by Mark Wei meant to kill?"

"If I just watched the footage by itself? Hard to say. It's a valid strike that with less force could merely disorient your opponent. But in the larger context of the situation, it seems likely it was meant to be lethal."

"I believe they call that speculation."

"And I don't mean to be improper here, but is anyone really going to be mourning Burton Drescher? The guy was a scumbag, he killed a family from—"

"I'll remind you that he was cleared of those charges."

"Maybe, but I think Wei was doing the world a favor."

"Word has it that the Aryan Nation has issued a host of death threats to Mark Wei, the Rivera family, and even Cameron Crayton in the wake of Drescher's death. Like him or not, he was a pillar of his own community, and by surviving *Prison Wars* he grew himself quite a public fanbase as well."

"Here's the question, though: what does Crayton *do* about Mark Wei? Does he kick him out of the tournament?"

"Why bother? The next stage will have combatants killing each other anyway. What's the point?"

"It sets a bad precedent for the rest of the qualifiers, for one."

"I'm sorry, but that's bullshit. You sign up for a tournament that has you killing people, you shouldn't be surprised when people start dying."

"We're going to take a quick break, but when we come back—"

TWO WEEKS LATER, THE Crucible rolled on, and Carlo's condition hadn't changed. The mission itself had stalled, with almost nothing valuable trickling in from all the phones Mark had collected. What little info was gleaned went straight to command and bypassed him entirely. All that was relayed to him was that it was "essential" that he remain embedded in the tournament.

Mark and Brooke were leaning on a rail near the end of Navy Pier, surrounded by crowds who had showed up to nearby bars to watch the Seattle qualifier finals. Mark wore a baseball hat and wide, pitch-black sunglasses to prevent anyone recognizing him. His skin crawled every time he was out in public now with his profile so high. Everyone was still talking about Drescher's death in the ring. Crayton had issued a public statement clearing Mark of any intentional wrongdoing, and law enforcement wasn't bringing any charges against him either. Mark's face still had traces of the bruise from that night, and his cheek flared with pain whenever he had to chew anything harder than bread.

"We also wormed our way into his mail server, so we're still getting incoming messages, too," Brooke continued. She was also wearing sunglasses, but for more traditional reasons. Her curly blonde hair kept flying in front of her face, propelled by the wind. In frustration she finally threaded it back into a ponytail.

When she was done she showed Mark her phone where a message was illuminated.

SENDER: vredgrave@craytonmedia
RECIPIENT: crayton@craytonmedia
SUBJECT: Wei

"This is our chance, sir. With Wei killing Drescher, we can DQ him and replace him with Josh Tanner. His kid's still alive. He's still the best story. Please consider it. For the record, creative agrees with me."

-Vanessa

SENDER: crayton@craytonmedia
RECIPIENT: vredgrave@craytonmedia
SUBJECT: Re: Wei

"Wei stays. This is the last I'll hear about it."

-CC

Mark tossed the phone back in her lap.

"What's this have to do with the mission?"

"Well, it shows Crayton's got a soft spot for you at the very least. Plus he opened up a bit to you the night of Carlo's fight."

"That was all smoke. And it's going to take a hell of a lot more than being teacher's pet to extract anything useful out of him."

Mark winced as he saw a couple look in his direction as they passed by. They kept going and didn't say anything. Somewhere out there were at least two plainclothes agents making sure the Aryan Nation didn't try to murder him. So far, no one had made any attempts. Mark looked at Brooke, who had visibly hardened since being the bumbling girl next door he'd known for years. Her shy smiles were replaced by a wrinkled brow and pursed lips most of the time. Over time, Mark grew increasingly sad that she was a part of this at all. She probably was recruited straight out of Stanford and thought she'd win Cold War II through sheer determination and a positive attitude. Now what was she? A babysitter turned animal tamer, cracking the whip around the lion to make sure he didn't eat anyone else.

There was a loud cheer from the closest bar, and Brooke turned her head.

"Sure you don't want to watch the end of the fight?" she said.

Mark shook his head.

"And see some poor old man get his ass beat? No thanks. Not really in the mood."

Mark couldn't remember the names of the Seattle finalists, but one stood out, a wrinkled, bald Asian man in at least his mid-sixties. The Crucible didn't broadcast much about him other than he was supposed to originally be from somewhere around the Nepal/Tibet region and had been involved with the border war there in some capacity. He eventually was naturalized after living in the US for a few years once immigration became streamlined at the beginning of the Ashford administration. What was his name again? It was on the tip of Mark's tongue.

A louder cheer from the bar interrupted his thought process.

"Holy shit," Brooke exclaimed. "The old man won."

She showed him a livestream on her phone she'd flipped on in secret. The short, bald man simply stood and bowed to his opponent, who was unmoving on the floor.

67-year-old Shin Tagami Crowned Seattle Champion, the banner read.

Tagami? Japanese then. Mark wondered how he got wrapped up in the border war on the other side of China. In any case, at least Mark wasn't the only Asian finalist anymore, for whatever that was worth. And sixty-seven? That seemed insane. Mark now regretted not watching the match to see his fighting style, but they were already showing replays. It was mostly Chinese kung-fu, including a thunderous knockout palm strike on his much larger, much younger opponent that was so fast Mark and the cameras barely caught it. He was intrigued.

For a split second he looked up, expecting to see Riko so they could speculate about the man's migration from Japan to China. But it was Brooke, of course, and his question caught in his throat. Mark realized that the last time he'd been to the pier was with Riko. And Asami. They rode the giant Ferris wheel and little Asami threw up on both of them. They might have even sat on this bench after the ride, cleaning up, he remembered. Mark laughed at the thought, which drew a strange look from Brooke.

"What?" she said.

"Déjà vu. Let's go."

Mark spent the next few days trying to avoid Crucible hype as much as possible. The press was beating down his door for interviews, still morbidly fascinated by Drescher's death, but he dodged them all, a move command actually agreed with. Crayton him-self was hopping all around the country for events. Unlike Mark, Crayton never turned down the opportunity to do an interview or three, and Mark was sick to death of him and his damn tournament. That could not be said about the general public however, as the Crucible's ratings continued to climb, leapfrogging several top porn programs and recently ticking by the numbers put up by *Prison Wars*. The Crucible was a fully-fledged phenomenon, and Mark could only imagine the viewership if the Vegas deathmatch tournament actually made it to air, though it was still up to him to ensure that didn't happen. Problem was, after all this time and even fairly exten-sive personal contact with Crayton, he still felt miles away from that goal. No matter how hard he looked, Mark still couldn't see the Chinese angle in the tournament.

Eventually Mark decided to start watching the finals again. He'd have to sooner or later via replay, so he figured he might as well catch them live. Instead of attending one of CMI's lavish viewing parties or eating popcorn with Brooke on the couch, he went to the hospital and watched the remaining bouts with Carlo. Well, next to Carlo anyway, who was pumped full of tubes and had his eyelids taped shut.

Mark talked to Carlo like he could hear him, and for all he knew, maybe he could. He did play-by-play of the action along-side the announcers, and critiqued the styles of the combatants. Together, they watched all the remaining finalists earn their spots. There was a veteran MMA fighter, a young boxer, a female SEAL, and as Mark suspected, three *Prison Wars* survivors. While Mark had put down Drescher, four others were still competing. One was a Triad lieutenant who had been knocked out by a burly lumberjack of a man in Salt Lake City during that region's finals. But the other three had made it through: Ja'Von Jordan, a gangland assassin from Detroit, Matthew Michael Easton, the crazed woman-scalping serial killer, and then of course the *Prison Wars* legend, the massive

Drago "The Undying" Rusakov. The monstrous Russian had nearly killed his final opponent, a young martial artist, but had managed to only break both of his arms and most of his ribs. A few days later, when he was downgraded from critical condition, it became clear Mark was still the only finalist who had killed someone in the ring.

The last city was Charlotte, and Mark was surprised to see another woman in the finals, making it only the fourth time it had happened. Two had made it through: the scowling SEAL from Atlanta and Soren Vanderhaven, the vivacious former gymnast who had been plastered all over the airwaves for weeks now in the wake of her Nashville win. This time, Mark was surprised when the woman's bio came up on the screen.

"A . . . ballerina?" he said, turning to an unconscious Carlo. The fight commentators clarified.

"Aria Grace Rosetti was the principal dancer in New York's second largest ballet company until she unexpectedly quit five years ago and moved to Raleigh. She's been dancing since she could walk, and has also trained in many schools of martial arts, which she believes works synergistically with dancing. Reports say her family is not supportive of her decision to enter the Crucible."

The feed cut to an interview with a teary-eyed older couple.

"She doesn't need to do this," the mother said, her voice cracking. The woman's gray-haired husband stood stoically beside her. "I don't understand what's gotten into her these past few years. Our daughter needs to be back on the stage! Not in this terrib—"

The clip quickly ended, and the feed switched to Rosetti in the ring.

"She's going it alone," the announcer said. "But she's certainly got some fans in the house tonight."

"Wow," Mark whispered to the silent room as he saw her.

The woman onscreen was gorgeous. If Soren Vanderhaven was a real life Barbie doll, Aria Rosetti was like a fine marble statue, carved by hand, every line and surface detailed to perfection. She was tall and lean, as a dancer would be, and two decades of training for the stage and the ring had toned her muscles from head to toe. There was a power to her that wasn't reflected in her size, but simply her presence. Her deep brown eyes flickered with life, and her long, chestnut hair was drawn up into a high ponytail. Her cheekbones were sharp and her nose was small and pointed, but there was nothing severe about her face. It looked oddly gentle, especially given the task at hand.

Mark turned to Carlo and knew he'd be making some wildly inappropriate comment if he was awake. Instead, the announcers were doing it for him.

"That body! My god!" the color commentator said. Naturally, they never said anything like that about the men who were almost always rippling with muscle during their own fights. Unlike Vanderhaven, Rosetti wasn't spilling out of her outfit in the least. She wore black cropped athletic pants and matching sports bra, perfectly normal ring attire, yet the commentators were acting like she was in a string bikini.

No such remarks were directed at her opponent, a hulking, white dump truck of a man covered in tattoos that made him look almost gray from the neck down on camera. Mark thought he might be another *Prison Wars* veteran. Instead he learned that "Rex," as he was simply called, was a prominent member of an upstate "motorcycle club," a.k.a. biker gang, which also explained his foot-long, gnarled beard. He'd broken the jaw of a champion prizefighter in the previous round to secure his spot in the final. The announcers were already making "Beauty and the Beast" jokes.

Mark didn't want to watch. It was moments like this that made his stomach churn. Either he'd see this woman get beaten to a pulp by a troll, or she'd somehow manage to beat a man twice her weight and advance to a tournament where she would almost certainly die in front of millions.

It was the latter, to his surprise.

The fight, it turned out, was a thing of beauty. Rex charged at her like an enraged elephant, swiping at her with arms as thick as her waist, but she deftly dodged him until he started to visibly run out of steam. Her movements were fluid. Not a literal dance, but the influence was obvious. Everything she did was so smooth it seemed like she'd choreographed the entire fight beforehand, and her mangy dance partner had never rehearsed. He stumbled badly, struck by needle sharp kicks and quick jabs whenever she found an opportunity. There was a precision to her a moves that other few fighters had. She targeted nerve clusters, vulnerable muscles, weak joints. She was never going to knock him out with a haymaker, but she wove a tapestry of pain that had him crawling on his hands and knees by the end of the fight. Mark's heart leapt into his throat when Rex finally grabbed ahold of her leg as she went to kick him and landed a few hard blows to her midsection that disrupted her rhythm, but she was strong enough to take it, and wrenched herself free before he could get any further advantage. Mark saw a flash of fear in her eyes, as she knew that if she was caught like that again, he could maul her in seconds. She circled him slowly, and inexplicably went in for the same kick that got her grabbed the first time. Mark yelled at the screen, but realized mid-expletive that it was a feint. As her opponent lunged again, she spun and leapt over him, whipping her back heel around and planting it in the base of his skull. Between that impact, and the front of his head slamming into the mat thereafter, Aria Rosetti finally had her knockout. She smiled and bowed and the crowd adored her.

The sixteen were chosen.

16

MARK CUT THE S-LENS out of his thigh for the fifty-third time. It didn't hurt anymore, and like the other fifty-two times, the tiny casing slid out covered in goo. He dabbed at the cut, which stopped bleeding almost immediately, and rolled his pants back down.

Even as a flipped agent, China would never give him unrestricted terminal access, so it was his only way to communicate with command now that he wasn't permanently bound to a chair. He was deep, very deep, into Phase II of Spearfish, and Phase III was fast approaching.

The micro S-lens, which he popped out of the casing and slid into his eye, was his true wire to Washington. He had a separate decoy lens he told China he was using to report back to the US, but they monitored every letter and punctuation mark he sent them, AI subroutines scanning for codes in each transmission. So far, they'd been satisfied he was pulling his weight, and instead of beatings and blades he'd been getting hot meals and an actual bed like the one he was lying in now. The mattress felt like it was stuffed with tree bark, but it was better than the floor. Or the chair.

The S-lens flickered worryingly, but finally blinked on. The overlay showed only one incoming message from command, prefaced by the usual SENSITIVE tag like all the rest. Like he'd ever be sifting the through lens messages in public. If he wandered into the wrong part of the base with the right kind of electro-surveillance, he'd be caught and in front of a firing squad by morning. And that wasn't a figure of speech. In his short time working for the Chinese he'd seen political dissenters rounded up and executed routinely. Zhou made him watch. He was just thankful he wasn't forced to participate.

Mark was still haunted by the sky-blue eyes of Lieutenant Marcus O'Connor, which brimmed with tears as the knives tore his flesh. They could have never prepared Mark for that. It was the turning point. He was all in after that, or else all the horror would be for nothing.

On any given day, he thought he was going insane. Juggling messages between China and the US, sending false info back and forth while scraping together real intel whenever he could. It was almost impossible to keep track of the lies and the truth, but if he slipped, even once, he would be back in Zhou's chair, or more likely buried in one of the mass graves that did not officially exist a few miles outside the seaside base.

Mark blinked through the S-lens's settings, trying to bring the imagery back into focus.

Mark jolted upright as the door blew open. He immediately blinked the S-lens to clear and bolted up to stand at attention. Zhou was in the doorframe . . . smiling? That worried Mark more than a scowl. He was further unnerved when Zhou stepped forward and clasped his shoulder. Old scars contorted in strange ways across his face, which wasn't used to expressing happiness.

"Sir?" Mark said, hating the word. He prayed Zhou couldn't see the faint trace of the lens in his eye, but there was no way to lose it now.

"That frequency you gave us," Zhou said. "We used it."

"And the drones?" Mark asked. "Destroyed?"

"Not destroyed, we actually *landed* them. We took them straight out of orbit and right into our palms, so to speak. The machinery alone is worth billions, and the sub-orbital propulsion technology we can now engineer from the American designs is priceless."

If your country survives that long, Mark thought. He forced a smile as well.

"I am glad to be of service," he said. Langley said they could part with that tech, but they were paying a steep price to keep him relevant in the eyes of the Ministry of State Security.

"Due to my part in securing this material as your operator, you are now addressing *Major* Zhou of the MSS."

Mark stiffened his stance and saluted once more.

"Sir."

"The formalities can wait. I have come to congratulate you personally on a job well done."

Mark nodded stiffly.

Zhou looked back out into the hall briefly, then pulled something out of the back of his trousers. Mark flinched instinctively, but relaxed when he saw it was a bottle. A quarter of it was empty already, implying Zhou had already started celebrating.

"This was my father's," Zhou said. It was perhaps the first personal thing he'd ever revealed to Mark. He seemed to be high off his achievement, and buzzed from the liquor. Mark barely recognized him as the same stern-faced monster from the cold cell miles underground.

"He said we would share it when I enlisted," Zhou continued, looking over the golden label of the brown bottle. "But he did not live to see the day. I would ask that you share it with me now. We have earned it, I would think."

Mark nodded, and Zhou sat, uncorking the bottle and pouring it into two plastic glasses on the table. It smelled ancient, delicious.

"To the glorious Republic," Zhou said as he raised his glass.

"To Major Zhou," Mark said.

"WE'RE LIVING AT HIS *house?*" Mark said, incredulous. "I don't understand." He was staring at the digital plane ticket that had showed up in his mail along with a congratulatory note from Crayton himself for making it to the finals.

"It's not a house," Gideon said, pacing near Mark's window, peering outside through the shutters. "It's a compound. The man literally grew a sixty-acre oasis in the desert and built a thirty-foot wall around it."

"There's the main mansion, three guest houses, two gymnasiums, six pools," Brooke said, reading about Crayton's palatial Las Vegas estate.

"And you think there will be something incriminating there?" Mark asked.

Gideon nodded.

"It's been weeks and crypto has taken precious little out of the phones and mail servers. I know they don't tell you much, but honestly, there isn't much to say. China is nowhere to be found."

"So you think he'll keep physical evidence if he wipes digital clean? Doesn't seem likely."

"He needs weight on China just like they need weight on him. Especially if they're butting heads now. If you can't find any goddamn secrets in that fortress then you're the worst agent I've ever heard of. Something is there, you can count on it. He spends more time there than at any of his dozen odd homes around the world. And we've searched most of those already."

"When do I leave anyway?" Mark asked Brooke. She flipped through her screen.

"You're heading out in time for the curtain pull-back on the Colosseum. Crayton only lives a few miles from the site, which is another few miles outside the Strip itself."

Mark re-read the message again. *Your journey begins in earnest now. The Crucible will evolve in ways you never imagined.* What the hell did that mean?

"I still don't even understand what's happening now. He's moving us all into his compound? All sixteen of us who are supposed to kill each other by the end of the summer? And what are these changes to the tournament he's talking about?"

"I'm sure he'll explain it when you get there," Brooke said.

"You're supposed to be explaining this stuff *before* that happens," Mark said, annoyed. "I don't like going in blind, and I feel like I know next to nothing about what this asshole has planned at any given moment. How am I supposed to prove his ties to China when we can't even get the Crucible's itinerary down?"

"I assure you we are working on it," Gideon said. "Suffice to say I don't think you'll be in much danger sipping piña coladas at Crayton's pool, so calm the hell down. It'll be a miracle if he finishes that monstrosity in the desert by the end of August anyway. I doubt he's going to risk your health before then."

"How reassuring," Mark said, growing angrier. "*Nothing* about this has felt right from the start. China. CMI. Even Langley. And on top of it, we don't even have a roadmap. A compass. A goddamn north star to tell us where this mission is going. This is not Spearfish. At least we had a plan there, however fucked up it got."

Mark noticed Brooke cringe almost imperceptibly.

"This *should* be cake compared to Spearfish, but yes, that's the problem. We don't *know* the stakes," Gideon said. "It's your job to figure them out."

"And your job to help me, in case you forgot."

"I don't need this shit, Mark. I have enough to deal with. McAdams is breathing down my neck every day about your lack of discipline, which *might* be worth it if you yielded any significant intel."

"I'm sorry, was cloning the phones of every top Crayton Media executive shitty intelligence gathering? Man, you guys have really raised that bar."

"Stop," Brooke said. "Both of you. Mark, Gideon put this whole thing together and knows what he's doing. Gideon, with all due respect to your ability to fire me or drop me in a hole in Cuba, Mark has earned the right to be a little pissed. We took a secret agent and made him one of the most famous people in the country. That's way outside the lines. Everyone he's ever met is in danger, and one's already halfway to dead."

Mark and Gideon were silent and sullen. Gideon rubbed his beard but kept his mouth shut. Brooke was a third of his age and his subordinate, but clearly knew him well enough to press his "off" switch in an emergency shutdown procedure. Mark's too, for that matter. She was right, infighting was getting them nowhere.

"You will have anything you need on the inside," Gideon said. "We'll get it through whatever security he has. Rest assured knowing that at least. By the end of your stay, there should be no stone left unturned in that gaudy place."

Mark looked at the pictures of the compound on Brooke's screen. "Jesus, it really is ugly, isn't it?"

The tension broke, and everyone laughed. Gideon's was deep from his belly, and Brooke snorted through her nose, looking embarrassed. He could have a worse team, he supposed.

MARK WASN'T GETTING OUT of Chicago that easy. Somehow, Rayne had managed to rope him into a going-away party thrown at the bar. Laird made sure no press or uninvited guests got inside, and so it was just Mark and a hundred of his closest friends. Or rather, a hundred of Rayne's closest friends, the ones she deemed suitably cool enough to be there. The only person Mark knew there besides the staff was Brooke, who had snuck in a back entrance to avoid the photographers outside.

Thankfully, Brooke had come, meaning he had someone to talk to other than overly exuberant fanboys. It occurred to him she probably never really socialized working this city gig for the Agency. Lord knows he didn't. It was interesting to see her in fashionable bar clothes talking and smiling like a normal human. Years ago, she'd be exactly the type of girl he and his buddies on base would be hounding to come home with them. And she'd be the type to politely decline, he guessed.

"Buy me a drink?" she said with a sarcastic smile as he approached

"Mine are free," Mark said. The crowd parted and dispersed as they went to the bar.

"What'll it be, lovely?" Rayne said, not even breaking a sweat despite the insanity at the counter.

"Whatever . . . that is," Brooke said, pointing at the remnants of Mark's drink.

"Coming right up," Rayne said. "Mark, we're going to need to have a chat about this one later," she said, jerking her head toward Brooke. "You've been a sad sack this whole time with this girl living across the hall from you? Sorry, but you'll get no more sympathy from me from here on out."

Mark grinned and Brooke laughed, carefully avoiding a snort. She'd had a few as well, it seemed. Gideon would be so disappointed in the pair of them.

"You could at least look like you're enjoying yourself," she said as Rayne handed her the drink and waved away her money. She skipped across the bar to take a new order.

"I actually am!" Mark said. "I promise. Thanks for coming. At least I know one person who doesn't work here."

"Well, everyone here wants to know you, that's for sure," Brooke said, motioning toward a gaggle of girls in impossibly short shorts glancing his way in the corner of the room.

"Christ, are they even eighteen? Does Rayne babysit them?"

Brooke laughed.

"You're handling this all pretty well, I have to say."

"You mean other than going on a bender and drunkenly fighting a Nazi and cracking his windpipe in front of thirty million people?"

"Yeah, other than that."

They finished their drinks.

AT THE END OF the night, Mark did in fact bring Brooke home. But given that they practically lived next door to one another, it was hardly some sort of great conquest. They were in Brooke's apartment for a change, and she lay on her couch with her arm draped across her face. Mark had taken up residence on the floor, the ceiling starting to spin above him. Looking left and right he saw mounds of animal fur that had evolved into tumbleweed-like shapes under the furniture.

"God, I am not in college anymore," Brooke moaned. "I don't know how you drink so much."

"It's not a skill I would recommend acquiring," Mark slurred.

Brook lunged across the table to fumble for her flexscreen.

"Should we go over mission brief—"

She tried to bring the screen to the couch, but her grip slipped and it ended up smacking Mark in the face as he lay on the floor.

"Ow! What the hell?"

"I'm sorry!" Brooke choked out, but she was laughing uncontrollably. Mark rubbed his forehead and smiled. Brooke covered her mouth with her hand, but couldn't stop giggling.

"And no, no goddamn mission briefings. We can take one night off, can't we?"

"I'm not sure how effective a strategy session would be right now anyway," Brooke said, finally controlling her laugher.

Mark was silent for a while, folding his hands on his chest. His flight left in what, five hours? At least it was a private jet, so he could show up five minutes beforehand if he wanted. At this rate, he'd be lucky if he woke up for it at all.

"I still can't process how insane this assignment is," he said.

Brooke peered over the side of the couch, resting her head on her hands.

"You know whatever's going on, he has to be stopped."

"I know," Mark said. "But at this point, I'm starting to think he needs a bullet in the head more than a trial. Money can buy justice. Or rather, injustice, if the need arises."

"The parameters could change. It could be on the table. But I'd like to avoid spending my thirties in a cell somewhere," Brooke said. She looked at him and cringed, clearly remembering his Chinese imprisonment. "Oooh, sorry," she said.

Mark waved her off.

"You get a pass for being my guardian angel the last few years."

With the light above her streaming through her long, blonde curls, she did look rather angelic. Mark felt a powerful urge to kiss her. And not for the first time, he realized. He felt a sharp twinge of guilt.

She disappeared back over the couch, and Mark soon heard long, deep breathing. She was out, and he closed his eyes and let himself drift away as well.

17

OME DAYS, MARK COULDN'T quite understand the trajectory of his own life. Five years ago he'd been sucking the bone marrow out of rats to keep himself alive in a freezing underground cell. Today, he was sitting in a plush recliner on a private jet being served champagne by what appeared to be a runway model wearing a flight attendant's uniform.

Now that the finalists were chosen, Crayton was escalating things further, apparently giving each the royal treatment before their nearly inevitable death. For Mark that involved a private flight to Las Vegas in one of Crayton's many personal aircraft, a brand new vertical-takeoff N-jet that was practically silent. The thing was more spaceship than passenger transport, and it was like being in a floating dining room in the sky, complete with ornate furniture bolted all around the cabin and, somehow, a motion-stabilized chandelier hanging from the ceiling. It was exactly as absurd as he expected from Cameron Crayton. Even more so when he realized there were probably fifteen other identical jets in the air, each ferrying their winning combatant to Vegas. As the half dozen flawless flight attendants smiled in his direction from the rear of the plane, he wagered they would probably take more than just his drink order if he asked them.

Instead, he thumbed through article after article about Crayton on his flexscreen, learning how the man had supposedly made his billions through almost prescient investments in every kind of company under the sun. Before he formed CMI, Wall Street had christened him the "Believer," a man who had faith in tiny companies that almost always blew up after being graced by the golden touch of his investment. A nano-tech firm specializing in robotic surgery that today led the field. An autocar manufacturer, which rose to put old giants out of business. Hell, Mark learned that he'd even been an early investor in JavaSpot, the coffee place that put millions of baristas out of work with its automatic dispensers. The man had fingers in every pie by the time he was thirty, and used the fortune to start CMI, drawn to mass media by what he deemed "a natural inclination toward showmanship," which was the understatement of the century. His investments grew alongside his business, and he was currently the eighteenth richest man in the world. Mark suspected he was probably higher on that list if anyone could actually manage a full audit of his assets. Most men in his position inflated their net worth when they could, but Crayton tried to downplay his at every turn. Mark made a mental note that Brooke should investigate other early investors in the companies Crayton had "believed in" decades earlier. He was either King Midas himself, or had the biggest streak of luck Mark had ever seen in picking winners. Alternatively, it seemed possible someone was crafting his luck for him, perhaps.

The flight was short, and two drinks later, Mark had touched down at a private tarmac outside the Vegas Strip. Even from a distance, he could see the looming, shrouded shape of Crayton's Colosseum in the desert. From Brooke's intel reports, the outer shell had been finished in record time, with more than a few worker deaths hushed up by CMI after they forced the crews to work at a breakneck pace. The interior and outer grounds were still under construction and would be through the rest of summer ahead of the main event. But Crayton wanted to broadcast that the stadium was coming along swimmingly, hence the forthcoming reveal of the façade, which had been constructed under the secrecy of massive

tarps and screens, only bits and pieces poking through to the sun-
light. Spy footage from the press only showed an arch here, a bank
of windows there. But now it had apparently come together enough
to make a big press event out of it, which was where Mark was currently heading.

After that, it was straight to Crayton's compound for . . . well,
Mark still had no clue, much to his dismay. "Training," was the
only buzzword that kept coming up in hacked internal messages.
Reportedly Crayton was flying in people from all over the world
to Vegas, not just the combatants themselves. Support staff? It was
never made explicitly clear in any of his messages to his underlings.
There were also a lot of references made to something called "The
Crucible: Heroes and Legends," which was pitched as "Stage II" of
the grand tournament, with qualifiers being the first. It also sounded
suspiciously like the name of potential TV show, so Mark guessed
that whatever was coming, it would be broadcast nationwide.

It was a bizarre feeling to have grown sick of seeing his own
face on TV, but there he was, sitting in an autolimo on the way to
the Colosseum, staring at a screen where a panel of forty-something
women on an entertainment show were debating the ranking order
of the "hotness" of the Crucible's male combatants. Chase Cassidy
led the pack, naturally, and Mark found himself in sixth place out of
thirteen, sandwiched between Miami boxer Asher Mendez and Salt
Lake victor Moses Morton, a burly, bald white man with a prominent mustache who had knocked out a *Prison Wars* fighter in his
final.

"Mark Wei over Morton?" one woman said. "But those *shoulders*
Moses has, my god! I just can't get enough."

"I'm not sure he'd flip sides for you, honey," another woman said.
"He and his husband have been married twenty years this June."

"Isn't that always how it goes, ladies?" the first woman said, and
the group dissolved into laughter.

Mark found he was ahead of all three *Prison Wars* killers on the list, and in dead last was the Vegas winner himself, a homeless veteran known only as "Manny," who fought like a rabid, cornered animal and had pretty severe burns covering half his face and neck. The women grimaced when his unsettling picture came up, and they quickly shooed it away so they could go back to talking about Cassidy's chiseled jawline. Mark just shook his head and tried to wave away the channel, but it wouldn't go anywhere. The set wasn't tuned to respond to his bio, much to his dismay. Fortunately, it was only a few more miles to the stadium, which loomed large on the horizon.

Mark now had to hear the women swoon over Rakesh Blackwood, second place on the list, and one of the more eyebrow-raising contenders. He was actually a billionaire himself, the lone son of a deceased oil baron, but showed little interest in the family business, leaving everything in the hands of his board of directors. Rather, he was recognized as one of the world's foremost thrillseekers, having been the first in line when space tourism reopened after the Hermes VI disaster in 2029. His quest for adrenaline had taken him from cliffdiving to autoracing to big game hunting, and now to the Crucible itself. The show played a clip of Blackwood, barely thirty, with piercing brown eyes and the smile of a Bollywood superstar, talking about how the Crucible was "the final frontier in pushing humanity to its limit," implying he'd tried everything else under the sun that had the potential to kill him, and had grown bored. For the past few years Blackwood had been learning martial arts with the best instructors money could buy, which led to a decisive victory in San Francisco. It was hard to know who was the bigger media darling, Blackwood, Cassidy, or Soren Vanderhaven. Each seemed to be doing their damndest to win the crown, flooding the airwaves with interviews since their respective wins. In contrast, Mark had done zero. But he suspected he wouldn't be able to get away with that for much longer.

When the limo stopped, Mark was ushered out past the

swarming press camping at the base of the towering Colosseum. Mark saw a lofted empty stage in the distance and thought he caught a glimpse of football god and Dallas victor Naman "The Wall" Wilkinson towering above the crowd a few hundred feet away, smiling and flexing for the cameras. Mark was only out in the open for a moment before he was quickly ushered into a nearby tent and set upon by stylists who cut and tamed his hair and stuffed him into a slim-fitting suit that had somehow been perfectly tailored to his exact measurements. An approving gaggle of men and women nodded their heads when they were finished, and Mark had to admit he looked more stylish than he had in years. Or ever, really. A few dabs of camera-friendly makeup and he looked twenty-five again.

"God, I feel like a monkey," Mark heard someone say as he was finally released from his stylist captors. He looked up and saw a recognizable face, Ethan Callaghan. On screen he was always surrounded by his adoring family, including his sick wife, but here where no guests or entourages were allowed, he was alone, just like Mark. Callaghan wore a similar suit, only light gray and with an even trendier tie. He looked as uncomfortable as Mark felt, if not more.

"Yeah, I know the feeling," Mark said, pulling at his collar. It wasn't actually tight, with everything measured perfectly to the millimeter, but he did it for dramatic effect all the same.

"Ethan," Ethan said, extending his hand, not presuming Mark knew who he was.

"Mark Wei," Mark replied, shaking the hand. Another vet with a sick family member. It reminded him painfully of Josh Tanner, but Ethan looked more alert and alive, like he had some kind of hope, rather than being lost in a pit of despair. By making it this far, he had at least assured his family $10 million in winnings, which had to be enough to cover whatever outrageously expensive treatment his wife required. Though he might have to hurry up and die for her to get it.

"I'm sorry about your wife," Mark said. "How is she?"

"Worried," Ethan said, bypassing her health. "Begged me not to do this, but you know, desperate times . . ."

"I know," Mark said, nodding. "I definitely know. I'm here, right?"

Ethan gave a short laugh. "I suppose so."

His face darkened a bit.

"And I was sorry to hear about your friend. Carlos, was it?"

"Carlo," Mark said. "He's stable, but still hasn't woken up. Hopefully that will change soon."

"Absolutely," Ethan said. He was a good-looking kid. Only twenty-eight, Mark had read, but he'd still get carded at any bar. He had sand-blond hair, bright blue eyes, and a muscled frame without being bulky. He was just a little taller than Mark, but maybe weighed a few pounds less. Time spent as a Green Beret had made him a hell of a fighter, Mark had seen in his clips. Not to mention he had a hell of a reason to fight. Speaking of, Mark heard the vibrations of a phone and Ethan fished his out of his pocket. The screen lit up with a picture of a beautiful, smiling woman.

"Oh shoot, gotta take this," Ethan said, looking apologetic. Mark nodded as he answered.

"Hey, honey. Yeah just got here. We're about to go on stage in a little bit."

Mark started to wander away to give the impression of privacy.

"Guess who I just met?" he heard Ethan say when he thought he was out of earshot, but Mark was trained to listen when others weren't.

"Mark Wei! Yeah, that one. Seems like a cool guy."

Their conversation turned to toddler nap schedules and medical bill due dates, and Mark tuned them out. Someone wearing a CMI badge and head-mic tapped him on the shoulder, and motioned for him to follow.

It was sweltering on the stage. Despite enormous fans blasting mist in their direction, the Vegas sun was unrelenting, and Mark had sweated through his suit several times over. He imagined the same was true for everyone lined up next to him.

He stood shoulder to shoulder with Callaghan, flanked on the other side by a towering figure he recognized as Moses Morton, who, to his good fortune, was wearing a white linen suit. Next to him was someone Mark could place only vaguely. The MMA fighter maybe? Hagelund? Then, Soren Vanderhaven, wearing the only outfit that would be considered climate appropriate, judging by the amount of skin it let breathe. And she was also kept cool in the shadow of Drago Rusakov, whose massive frame could have probably shaded the entire crowd if they'd raised him up a bit.

They were all there, all sixteen, lined up on stage like some sort of bizarre beauty pageant, or farm animals waiting calmly to be ushered into a slaughterhouse.

In the center was Cameron Crayton himself, addressing a crowd at least fifty thousand strong who had trucked out to the desert for the unveiling of the Colosseum. The first few dozen rows were made up of press alone, judging by the sea of camera equipment. Screens were vaulted up at various points in the crowd for those who couldn't get close enough. The cameras panned across their faces as they stood baking in the heat. Whenever the frame focused on Chase Cassidy, who was standing six bodies down from Mark, the crowd let up a little cheer despite the fact that Cameron was still speaking.

"... Crayton Colosseum will truly be a new wonder of the world. A worthy home for the sixteen bravest people I've ever met standing behind me today. Behold, a new era in sports entertainment!"

He flung his arm behind him dramatically, and a bunch of tiny hisses indicated that anchors were being released. Slowly, the massive tarps covering the walls of the arena floated down to its base, revealing the building underneath.

It certainly looked finished, at least from the outside. The influence of Rome's original Colosseum was obvious from first glance. It had the same tiered archways that wrapped all the way around its oval shape, but while the original had maybe four levels, if Mark recalled correctly, this one had seven, and the entire structure as a whole was far bigger than the original ever was. Instead of stone, it was mirrored glass and blue-gray steel. It was simultaneously modern and ancient. Mark had to admit it was rather breathtaking, if only for its scale. Even if the insides were still hollow, it was remarkable to think a structure of this magnitude had gone up so quickly, no matter how many workers had been mixed into the mortar in the haste.

"With a capacity of 250,000, it will be the largest stadium in the world, bar none. The viewing screens on either side of the arena will be big as football fields themselves. Inside there will be five-star restaurants and bars with the finest drinks imported from all over the globe. There will be lower-cost seats for the common man, and luxury boxes for those that can afford them, so accommodating and welcoming they double as hotel rooms. The Colosseum will provide the best athletic viewing experience in the life of anyone who steps through its doors. Period."

Mark and the rest of the combatants on stage craned their necks to see the building behind them. The sun was now reflecting off its arched windows, making it even hotter than before. Forget a billion dollars, this thing had to cost at least three. Insanity.

"Naturally, construction continues, as you can see, but all this and more will be included by completion for the final tournament three months from now. Not to mention we still have a bit of landscaping work to do where you're all standing."

The drew a chuckle from the audience, currently standing in the desert outside the Strip that would have been the kind of place the mafia buried bodies before Crayton came and built a stadium on top of it.

Crayton began introducing the various competitors on stage, who gave a wave when he reached them. Mark noticed the faint glimmer of something shining a few feet in front of Crayton as he

PAUL TASSI

spoke. He quickly deduced it was an exceptionally thin shield of bulletproof glass. Crayton was a public figure, sure, but far from the president or someone with similar security needs. Yet he had a bulletproof screen in front of him and was constantly surrounded by a squad of mercs? Mark wondered if Crayton was fearing a very specific threat.

"And next is Mark Wei, Chicago winner, and our first competitor to get his hands dirty!"

The crowd cheered as Mark gave a slow wave and stiff smile. That was a cute way of saying that he'd killed his last opponent. Though, across the stage, the *Prison Wars* veterans probably had at least a hundred bodies between them if the charges against them were true. And that wasn't even counting the ones they killed in Crayton's televised freakshow the past two years. The scrawny kid, Easton, shot Mark a burning look that set his teeth on edge. Meanwhile, Rusakov regarded him with the impassiveness of a city-sized meteor slowly falling to earth. Given how much of a problem Burton Drescher had become, Mark was not eager to see what havoc these new psychopaths would wreak if given the chance. And truth be told, he didn't know nearly enough about everyone else on stage either. If they'd signed up for this thing and gotten this far, it seemed likely they were not entirely sane, and were almost certainly dangerous.

After Crayton's conference ended, the scene was something of a madhouse. The combatants were pulled every which way by sweaty employees wearing CMI badges, and Mark had no idea where he was going now. Was he supposed to give the suit back? It certainly needed a good dry cleaning at this point.

Eventually he was herded toward a dust-covered SUV autolimo that had pulled up on a not-yet paved road behind the stage. The gaggle of CMI employees assigned to him said that it would take him to Crayton's compound a few miles away where there was a private reception for the "guests," as he and the others were called.

Mark opened the door and was about to step inside when he saw someone was already in it. It was Moses Morton, the enormous, mustachioed man in the white linen suit.

"Oh, sorry," Mark said. "I can get another one."

"Plenty of room," Moses said with a wide smile, spreading his arms. "This is pretty damn big, even for me."

Mark hesitated.

"And it's got cold beer," Moses continued, holding up a drink.

Mark was convinced. He crawled inside and sat opposite Morton. The man tossed him an ice-cold bottle that mirrored his own.

"You're Moses, right? I'm Mark," he said, and they shook hands. Morton's bald head was bright red from the sun and the burn creeped down onto his thick, muscled neck. His shirt had a few buttons loose and showed a forest of chest hair. He took a sip of his beer with rolled up sleeves showcasing forearms as wide as Mark's head.

"Pleasure," Moses said. "Feels good to be in the AC, doesn't it?"

Mark nodded. The limo had started to move.

"You took down that *Prison Wars* guy, right?" Mark asked. "The Triad?"

Moses nodded slowly.

"Very fast. Very talented. He certainly didn't make qualifying easy."

Mark was surprised at the man's humility.

"Kind of unsettling to fight a trained killer, I have to admit," Moses said, taking another swig of beer. "Erm, no offense."

Mark just chuckled.

"Where I've worked, most would probably take that as a compliment," he said. "And yeah, you're right."

"Your man. Drescher, was it? He was a real piece of work."

No judgment, no praise. Interesting. Mark didn't know what to make of this guy. He looked about forty-five and like a real-life manifestation of Paul Bunyan. Mark just nodded at his statement.

"What did you think of the Colosseum?" Mark said, changing the subject. Moses's eyes lit up.

"Fascinating design. Really captures the beauty of the original while modernizing it quite well. And the size! Rome's could only seat about eighty thousand, and this is what, triple that?"

"I think so," Mark said.

"The original was called *Amphitheatrum Flavium*. It was built by emperors in the Flavian Dynasty, shortly after Nero. The name 'Colosseum' is supposedly derived from the 'colossal' statue of Nero that was once planted nearby." Moses spoke quickly, full of excitement.

"Interesting," Mark said, eyebrow raised. "History buff?"

Moses laughed.

"Sorry, I tend to go off like that. History professor actually. Brigham Young."

"History professor?" Mark said, curious. "How did you end up here?"

The desert streaked by them as Moses pulled another beer from the cooler in the seat, and dabbed it on either side of his head. Despite the AC, he was still sweating.

"Always had an interest in two things, history and sports. I have five brothers and two sisters exactly my size, so needless to say it was a physical household growing up. Football, hockey, and such. I got into wrestling, and won a few state titles back in the day. Soon after that, I learned with a body like this, if you stop being active, it will turn to jelly just like that." He snapped his fingers.

"So I've been training ever since. I spend some time coaching kids downtown when I'm free. Hard to pry those video games off their faces, though," he chuckled.

"And history?" Mark said. So far, the combatants weren't at all what Mark had expected. And had been weirdly friendly to boot.

"That was always my true passion," Moses continued. "Had a brother in the NFL for a spell. My sister was a professional bodybuilder. All the others mostly moved heavy objects full time. But me? I always loved history. I used wrestling to land a scholarship and double majored in history and classic literature. A doctorate later, and I was a professor at my alma mater."

"Quite the journey," Mark said. He reached toward the cooler for a new beer, but Moses beat him to it and tossed him another bottle.

"It's certainly off the beaten path," Moses said, nodding.

"And the Crucible?" Mark pressed.

Moses shifted uncomfortably.

"I'm not really one of those people with a 'good' story," he said with air quotes. "A 'proper' reason for being here. Like that kid who's trying to save his wife. Or that actor who's giving all the money to charity. I'm just here because I was born in the wrong century."

Moses laughed at what was undoubtedly a quizzical look on Mark's face.

"It's something my husband has always said. I've always loved the great battles and warriors of history. Growing up, I always wanted to be a knight, a viking, a centurion. But the modern world and its futile wars never held any appeal to me. My husband thinks I'm forever stuck in the past, wishing I'd been born living under Caesar Augustus or King Arthur, cracking heads with maces and enjoying a lack of indoor plumbing."

Moses turned to glance out the window and took another sip of beer.

"I read. I play VR games. I do historical reenactments. I'm one of those nerds you see running around the forest wearing chainmail and swinging replica broadswords, pretending he's a Knight of the Round Table. Met a lot of fun folks there. But again, in the end it just isn't what I'm looking for."

"But the Crucible . . ." Mark said, following the path.

Moses nodded.

"A true-life gladiator bout for our time? I could hardly believe it. I had to try. I didn't think I'd get anywhere near the final tournament, but somehow, here I am."

"What does your husband think of all this?" Mark asked.

"Nolan is . . . supportive," Moses said hesitantly. "He's seen me go through a lot. Aimlessness, depression. He said it was the first time in a long while he'd see me really come alive when I was talking about entering. He said he wouldn't deny me that feeling, no matter the risks. Calls it my mid-life crisis." Moses laughed.

Mark thought about the millions that would potentially go to Moses's husband if (most likely, when) he died, but kept his mouth shut, not wanting to assume anything or be an asshole.

"Anyway, sorry to talk your ear off. I know we just met, but that's sort of just what I do. Always have. Nolan would be scolding me right about now, as I haven't even asked a thing about you."

"You gave me beer, that's good enough," Mark said. "And trust me, you're *way* more interesting than me."

"Nolan said I shouldn't try and make friends here. That it was stupid considering what we've all signed up for. But I don't know, that's just who I am," he smiled broadly. "Hard for me to hush-up like a churchmouse, particularly around such fascinating folks like yourself. Where did you serve again?" Moses asked, about to put Mark's memorized cover story to the test for the thousandth time.

But the limo slowed to a halt. Both of them turned and looked out and saw an enormous iron gate joining together two towering stone walls. Two huge, gold-scripted Cs were embossed on each side of the gate.

"I guess we're here," Mark said. The gate slowly parted and the limo crawled inside. It was hard to believe the sight that lay before them.

18

CRAYTON'S COMPOUND WAS EVEN more outrageous than the pictures made it appear. It was a literal oasis in the desert, with lush gardens and rolling hills, and Mark thought he even saw a lake in the distance as the limo drove through the grounds.

Perched on various mounds of artificial earth were the mansions themselves, three "smaller" ones that were multi-million-dollar guest units, and then the larger manor, which looked like an odd fusion of Buckingham Palace and the Vatican, with hints of modernism thrown in there just to screw with the aesthetic even further. A sign of Crayton's inclination toward the Greeks and Romans, there were a few towering columns. But his style was a blend of an incredibly diverse array of time periods.

Surrounding the entire estate was a wall thirty feet high and meant to keep out everything from the prying eyes of the press to the harsh winds that would aim to sandblast the expensive architecture. As the limo rolled toward the main house through the private drive, Mark saw a fine mist covering the grass and sculpted bushes as they passed. Some sort of advanced irrigation system that ensured the desert island paradise didn't dry up under the Nevada sun. Mark wondered why he picked this precise spot in the country to set up his fortress, but supposed he understood the appeal of building his own little mini-city in the middle of nowhere. Even cursory research showed that the parties Crayton threw here were supposed to be legendary, and he was known to host political fundraisers on the grounds as well, where more than a few backroom deals were likely to have taken place, among other hidden sins. Mark was on the hunt for all the secrets the gaudy monstrosity held.

The driveway straightened out and they were now flanked on either side by enormous figures carved from stone, wielding swords and spears, angled to hoist their weapons over the road. There were close to a dozen by the time they reached the end, and each was probably three stories tall, planted on a rectangular stone base.

"Incredible," Moses said, a look of childlike wonder on his face. "I think that one is Alexander the Great," he said, pointing toward a curly-haired figure. "And that has to be Pyrrhus of Epirus," he said of a statue with a crested helm. "And that one's either Sun Tzu or Genghis Khan, I'm not sure," he continued, pointing again.

The limo stopped and the doors opened automatically. Mark stepped outside and found himself at the base of one of the final statues in the line. A figure towered above him holding two swords. He was face to face with a bronze placard.

SPARTACUS, it read, along with a brief history of the gladiator-turned-revolutionary's uprising in ancient Rome. On the other side of the car, Moses was gazing up at a spear-wielding warrior. Mark raised his eyebrow in a question, and Moses answered.

"Achilles," he said, with wide smile. Crayton was a man after Moses's own heart, it seemed, decorating his grounds with the greatest warriors and military minds mankind had known. All the statues looked brand new, untouched by dust or even bird droppings.

A line of limos had formed near the base of the main manor, and Mark started recognizing other Crucible combatants as they trudged up the stairs. Naman Wilkinson, Asher Mendez, the one they just called "Manny," looking frazzled and lost in a crumpled suit. Mark saw the *Prison Wars* trio of Ja'Von Jordan, Matthew Michael Easton, and Drago Rusakov moving as a unit as they exited the same limo. *A gang leader, a serial killer, and a hitman walk into a mansion,* Mark thought, the beginning of some twisted joke. The three were strange bedfellows to be sure, but it appeared their time at *Prison Wars* had created at least some sort of bond between them. That probably wasn't a good thing.

Mark left Moses to stare at the row of statues as he made his way up the stairs. He reached the giant oak doors at the same time as another man, who paused to let him pass. He looked up to nod in appreciation and found himself staring into Chase Cassidy's steel-gray eyes.

"After you," Cassidy said with a paparazzi-friendly smile. Mercifully, there was no press allowed inside the compound. The pair of them walked in and Cassidy extended his hand.

"Pleasure to meet you, Mark," Cassidy said, shaking firmly. "I'm a big fan of your work."

It was clever quip, referencing Drescher's death while also being a line he was probably fed all the time as an actor. In truth, Mark kind of hated most of Cassidy's movies, but the global box office disagreed.

"Good to meet you," Mark said. There was an understanding that passed between them that Cassidy himself needed no introduction.

"Crayton's really added on to this place," Cassidy said as they walked through the foyer, which was laden with gold and marble. "I was here in '32 for the *Prison Wars* launch party. He only had the one guest house then. And those statues outside have to be *brand* new."

"He certainly has . . . interesting taste," Mark said, uncomfortable in this kind of conversation. He realized Carlo, Diego, and Brooke would all be freaking out to know he was speaking to *Max Rage himself* at this very moment. While most of the other contestants looked out of place in their new fancy clothes, Cassidy was right at home in red carpet-style attire, assuredly an outfit he already owned rather than one provided to him by Crayton's stylists. The man ran his hand through his hair, wiping away a trickle of sweat, but the gesture looked like he was posing for a *GQ* cover shoot. He was about as physically flawless as a human being could get between perfectly symmetrical and proportioned features and a body that could have been a model for one of the statues outside. Way too pretty to be wrapped up in something like this.

"Is that Rakesh?" Cassidy exclaimed, as the lean Indian man walked toward them. He had a similarly tailored suit that probably cost more than the limo that had driven them here.

"Chase, sorry I missed you at the ceremony," Rakesh Blackwood said. "Dreadful setting. I mean the desert, for two hours? Good *lord*."

Blackwood was on eye level with Mark, but was acting like he wasn't even there.

"I never thought I'd be dragged back to *this* place again," he said, rolling his eyes. "It's an assault on the senses. If father hadn't insisted I'd never have stepped foot through the door for that dreadful gala a few years back. And now we have to *live* here? My god, I thought the torture was reserved for the arena."

"Oh come on, Rakesh," Cassidy said, shifting his smile to reveal a hidden dimple. "It isn't that bad."

"I'm sure it's heaven for all these . . . *others*," he said, tilting his head toward Moses, who had just walked in the door and was still gawking at everything he saw. "But I'd rather be in my Bellagio penthouse and commute."

Clearly not a part of the conversation, Mark started to leave, but Blackwood finally turned and addressed him.

"Which room will I be in?" he said to Mark. "I assume Crayton wouldn't dare put me in one of the *guest* houses."

"Uh," Mark said, confused. "I have no idea. Why would I—"

Cassidy interrupted.

"This is Mark Wei," he said. "From Chicago. Killed that Nazi in the ring. He's not one of Crayton's gophers."

"Oh!" Blackwood exclaimed. "I do apologize," he said in a tone that in no way suggested an apology. "I thought you were a butler. But I see he has us *all* standing around then."

Blackwood extended his hand, and Mark was tempted to break every finger on it. But he resisted the urge and only shook it.

"I'm going to find another drink," Blackwood said. "And none of that swill they were serving in the cars. Excuse me, gentlemen."

Blackwood strode away and Cassidy turned back to Mark.

"Billionaires," he muttered. "I kind of hope he dies first."

Mark had to laugh at that. He imagined Cassidy would be a bit irritating, but compared to Rakesh Blackwood, he was a delight. Mark saw Ethan Callaghan walk through the doors, and gave him a friendly nod, which was returned. He started to walk over to him, but an older, bearded man who *did* actually look like a butler cleared his throat.

"Excuse me, ladies and gentlemen. The house staff will begin directing you to your rooms, where you will be allowed to freshen up after the day's events. Dinner will be served in the main manor in two hours, and you will be joined by Mr. Crayton himself, who relays he has very exciting things to share about your stay here. He has asked to convey his deepest gratitude that you've joined him here in his home, and he looks forward to seeing you all tonight."

After that, the group split, and Mark was surprised to find he was assigned to the main manor while others were being carted out to the guest houses. He saw Cassidy and Blackwood were staying there as well, and possibly a couple others, but they disappeared down winding hallways before he could be sure. The place was a maze of ornate wood, precious metal, and expensive stone, and Mark's room ended up being even more lavish than he imagined. It was as big as his entire condo, with an emperor-sized bed (was that even a size?) and a full entertainment suite that took up one of the towering walls. Even the bathroom seemed to stretch on for miles and had a shower with about two dozen heads along with a tub that could comfortably fit ten. Mark suspected that it had likely been filled to capacity at some point, given the stories he'd heard about Crayton's gatherings.

He blinked through the messages on his S-lens, but found

nothing. Though phones and lenses weren't banned on the grounds, he was waiting to hear from Brooke, who was supposed to hack Crayton's network when Mark entered, and set up a secure feed they knew couldn't be monitored. It must have been taking her longer than they expected, so for now he was on his own.

Mark used his phone to sweep the room for cameras and audio bugs. He couldn't find any, but knew he'd have to search more thoroughly later. He checked every wardrobe door and drawer, and found nothing but an endless amount of clothing tailored to exactly his size. There was everything from gym attire to a full tuxedo. Mark laughed out loud when he saw a screen on the inside of the closet that had a picture of "recommended dinner attire," pointing him to a specific sport coat and shirt combination hanging nearby. Mark guessed that Blackwood and Cassidy didn't have these kinds of suggestions, and it was just for the rubes like him who had never dined with a billionaire before. Mark wondered how the women might react to Crayton's fashion algorithm picking out their dresses and heels for them.

Mark showered, blasted from all sides by the jets of hot water in the sauna-sized enclosure, and put on the recommended outfit because he really didn't give a shit if Crayton wanted to play dress-up with him. He glanced at a loaded bar cart at the foot of his bed, but thought better of mixing a drink. After a few beers and hundred-degree heat, all he wanted was water, and naturally there was a fridge full of it nearby.

Mark was still inspecting the room when he realized time had flown and dinner was calling. Dinner was quite *literally* calling, as his TV turned on and the microthin screen displayed a message read by a soothing female voice telling him that he should make his way to the "second dining hall." It also showed an overhead map of where exactly that was, and Mark made a mental note of the blueprint of the manor, which would undoubtedly be useful later.

He walked through the halls, passing a host of maids and

manservants, all of whom stopped what they were doing and greeted him with a polite smile and nod as he went by, which he did his best to return.

On the way to the dining room, he caught a glimpse of Kells Bradford, the Atlanta winner and second female combatant to qualify. She was one of only a handful of female SEALs who had ever completed the program, and Mark was not eager to talk to her. His cover story had also made him an ex-SEAL, and he didn't want to be pressed on the finer points of the program by the genuine article. But when they saw each other, she simply met his eyes momentarily and kept walking. She was wearing a long violet dress that displayed impressively muscled arms, but she looked more than a little uncomfortable in it, and was clearly unsteady in her heels. It seemed talking to Mark was the last thing on her mind, and he was content to let her wobble on ahead of him in silence.

Finally, they reached the dining room, which had vaulted ceilings and expensive-looking paintings lining the walls. The table was enormous and was probably carved from a redwood. Eight seats were on either side, with one at the head. Other combatants had already filtered in and were either chatting or taking their seats. Many, like Bradford, appeared perfectly content sitting in silence. Others were deep in conversation, and Mark saw Ethan and Moses chatting in the corner. Moses waved at him as he entered.

Mark hated dinner parties enough as it was, but this was something else entirely. They were in some billionaire's twisted dollhouse fantasy, and not to mention everyone in the room was either a murderer, or had signed up to become one. Mark really wished Brooke was in his ear right about now.

He circled the seats and found his nametag on the middle on the left side of the table. The place settings were exquisite, naturally, with more utensils than he had any idea what to do with. Above the plate was something rather odd. It was a beautiful marble sculpture of a wolf, about a foot and a half tall, howling toward the vaulted roof of the dining hall. An interesting decoration, though one he wouldn't have thought to find at a dinner like this. A quick cursory glance revealed other stone animals around the table. A tiger. An elephant. Mark was a bit confused, but a chime sounded and he took his seat. On his left, Drago Rusakov sat down and threatened to snap the legs of his chair. Mark met his eyes briefly and felt a cold chill creep through his spine. The man said nothing, simply glared, stroked his thick beard, and turned away.

On his right was a far more pleasant sight. The dancer from Charlotte, Aria Rosetti, slid into her chair and ran her fingers over the statue in front of her, a horse reared up on its hind legs.

"Hi," Mark said with a half-smile. Rosetti turned toward him and her lips parted in a polite smile.

"Hello," she said, and pulled a lock of curled chestnut hair over her ear. She was wearing a sparkling blue dress that clashed with every other color in the room, but still managed to look great. He opened his mouth to say something else, but was interrupted by another chime. Cameron Crayton entered the room.

"You found it!" Crayton said, raising his arms and flashing his trademark smile. "I know it can be quite the labyrinth in here. Don't worry, we only hire the best minotaurs for security!" He nodded toward Wyatt Axton, his silver shadow, lurking near one of the exits.

The joke drew few chuckles, though Moses Morton guffawed loudly. He was seated on the end next to Soren Vanderhaven and looked like he was having the time of his life. Vanderhaven, her blonde hair done up in elaborate, winding braids, looked bored, and kept glancing across the table at Chase Cassidy.

"I wanted to thank you all for joining me here," Crayton said. "Apologies for having to use the second dining hall, but the first is still being renovated."

Mark looked around the opulence and could only imagine what the *first* dining hall might look like by comparison.

"I'm sure you're all starving, but I just wanted to go through a few things before we begin this journey to the Colosseum. You've all been instrumental in making this show a hit, and I know you will continue to do so!"

Mark sipped his wine and stole a glance behind him at Rosetti, who was resting her chin on her hand, regarding Crayton with curiosity.

"You may be wondering why you're staying here for the next three months until construction is complete on the Colosseum. This is for a few reasons, but first and foremost because Phase II of the Crucible is about to begin. We're calling it 'Heroes and Legends.'"

That matched what limited intel Brooke had managed to extract from CMI.

"Over the course of the summer, your life here will be streamed live across the world. Crucible fans will watch you train, and see how the most fearsome fighters in the country interact with one another, for better or worse."

"A reality show?" Cassidy called out from his spot six down from Crayton.

"Of sorts," Crayton said with a knowing smile. "One that will introduce the world to our formidable roster of champions."

"What about those who need no introduction?" Rakesh Blackwood said, smirking.

"Then they will perhaps see a side of you they don't know," Crayton said, his tone cutting.

"Can we opt out?" Kells Bradford said, rubbing the back of her shaved head with her hand.

Crayton shook his head.

"The paperwork you've already signed gives us license to broadcast your time here for *Heroes and Legends*. If you protest, I'm afraid you'll be replaced by your runner-up, and forfeit the money you've already earned to them."

That made Bradford's eyes widen. She kept silent, indicating that perhaps the live show wouldn't bother her *that* much.

"There are no recording devices in your rooms, which allows you privacy there. Elsewhere, we have cameras and microphones embedded all over the property, as well as a few drones you may see buzzing around from time to time. No pesky camera crews will be crawling all over you, don't worry."

On cue, two miniature gyrodrones flew in from the outer doors of the room and slowly drifted in a line down each side of the table.

"Say hello to America," Crayton said. "We're live right now."

As the drone passed Moses, he waved at it eagerly, mouthing "Hi, Nolan" into the lens. Chase Cassidy gave a mock salute. Soren Vanderhaven's expression changed from melancholy to upbeat in an instant as she beamed at the camera drone. Mark simply nodded at the one that passed by him, while Aria Rosetti gave it a little wave.

"You won't be able to watch the broadcast yourself, but just know that unless you're in your room or using the lavatory, chances are you're on television in front of an audience of millions. Do with that information what you will," Crayton said.

The drones vaulted upward and took up orbiting positions around the crystal chandelier.

"There will be few rules while you live here, but there *are* rules. First, unless you're training, there are to be no physical altercations amongst you. We wouldn't want to spoil things for the tournament itself. Second, you must remain on the premises until the Crucible begins in earnest, and are only allowed visitors during a predetermined period in the future. Other than that, your time is more or less your own as you prepare for what lies before you."

Mark scanned the table, and was surprised to see someone he hadn't noticed at all yet. Hunched between Naman Wilkinson and Ja'Von Jordan was a small, older Asian man. Shin Tagami, Mark remembered. He'd probably been around all this time, on stage at the conference and here now, but it was genuinely the first time Mark had consciously seen him. It probably didn't help that he was at least a head shorter than everyone else at the table, the women included. He looked dramatically out of place, but was sitting contently across from a graceful stone statue of a crane.

"What's with the animals, Crayton?" Rakesh Blackwood said, addressing Crayton informally as only a fellow billionaire could. But he voiced something they were all wondering.

"Ah," Crayton said, his eyes lighting up. "A creation of our marketing department. These statues were made for me by the sculpting genius who also created the towering wonders outside. Each represents a symbol that will be now be associated with each of you going forward in this tournament."

Mark stared at his wolf. Next to it was Rusakov's hulking, horned bull.

"The idea is that now that all of you have risen to fame, it's good to have something to associate with your 'brand,' as it were. Sports teams have icons and symbols as we all know, and merchandise flies off the shelves as a result. We thought a similar approach would work in the Crucible. So grow familiar with your symbol, as it will be with you until the end."

Everyone was now paying special attention to the statues, which suddenly held much greater significance.

"Should I be insulted?" Aria Rosetti said, turning to Mark as she gestured to the horse in front of her.

"It's very pretty," he offered, which drew a smirk.

Chase Cassidy eyed his roaring stone lion with pride. Ethan looked similarly pleased with his bald eagle, wings spread. Others were less satisfied.

"Is this a . . . jackal?" Blackwood said, gesturing at the beast in front of him. "A bit of a low blow, don't you think, Crayton?"

"I did not choose the symbols," Crayton said with a twinkle in his eye which indicated to Mark that probably wasn't true.

"Uh, gross, what is this?" Soren Vanderhaven said, eyeing something that looked insect-shaped in front of her. "A bee?"

"It's a hornet, dear," Crayton said.

"Can I trade?" she asked, looking stricken.

"No trading."

"So, are you a pack wolf or a lone wolf then?" Aria said, examining his statue.

"The latter," Mark said. "At least that's how they view me, I imagine. Your stallion really is quite nice, you know."

"Oh, don't placate me," she said with a grin. Mark smiled involuntarily.

"I don't want to get off track here," Crayton said as the table started muttering among itself about their assigned creatures. "As the most important announcement is yet to come."

Everyone hushed up at that.

Mark's mind immediately raced to the "changes" referenced in the hacked emails. This all was already insane enough, as is. He couldn't possibly imagine anything else that could make the Crucible any more surreal. The camera drones hovered expectantly above them.

"As many of you may have guessed, I have something of an attachment to ancient Rome. It's a fascinating period in history that, I'd argue, has never seen its equal."

Crayton reached down and delicately grabbed something that Mark couldn't see, as it was obstructed by a floral centerpiece.

"I've collected many treasures throughout my career, but this remains my favorite."

He raised the item, and Mark could see it clearly. Balanced atop Crayton's open palms was an ancient-looking shortsword.

"This gladius belonged to Marcus Attilius, a gladiator who fought for the emperor Nero in 64 AD. It's nearly two thousand years old. No doubt many archaeologists watching are screaming at their sets that I have this out of its case."

Mark's eyes narrowed. Where was this going?

"With it, he killed two undefeated gladiators, and managed to absolve himself of all his debts, which is why he'd stepped into the arena in the first place. Not a slave, a volunteer. It's a priceless weapon, and a true artifact of history, having thrilled untold crowds in millennia past."

He paused.

"I want the Crucible to have artifacts of its own. I want our crowds to cheer and worship you like those gladiator-gods of old. That can only be accomplished one way. A way to give the people what they really want to see, but are too timid to admit."

His eyes glinted.

"Today, I'm announcing that when each of you stands on the sands of the Colosseum, you will not fight with your fists. You will be armed and armored."

Mark felt every heart in the room stop.

19

Dear Mom,

Today was the first day of gladiator camp. I made a few friends. One is named Ethan who's from Colorado and the other is Moses from Utah. They're really nice. There's a girl here who I think is kinda cute. Also, they said we're going to slaughter each other with weapons when camp ends, so that's fun. Gotta go, training starts early tomorrow.

Love,

Mark

MARK LAY IN HIS bed, staring at the ceiling. His stomach was dissolving bits of lobster and steak, but he'd left most of it on his plate, unsettled after Crayton's announcement.

In truth, it wasn't the ceiling he was looking at, it was Brooke, who had taken up residence in the corner of his S-lens. She'd managed to excavate an encrypted pipeline into the compound, and they were now able to speak freely without risk of interception or eavesdropping.

"Seriously? Weapons?" Brooke said. "Given his hard-on for

Rome, I guess we should have seen this coming. And *Prison Wars* had weapons, I guess."

"Those were lead pipes and glass shivs," Mark said. "These are fucking swords and axes and I don't even know what else. Medieval shit. That's half the reason we're here for this long. They're flying in instructors to train use to use goddamn melee weapons and fight in full plate armor."

"Do people still know how to do that?" Brooke said.

"You'd be surprised," Mark said, thinking of how Moses positively lit up when the news was announced. Someone like him who had at least *held* these kinds of weapons before would have a big advantage. The rest of them knew how to fight with their fists and feet, but weapons? That was something else entirely. Mark had done some extensive knife training, obviously, and learned how to make use of improvised objects in hand-to-hand combat. But the concept was almost entirely foreign. No one had ever put a battle axe or broadsword in his hand at the CIA, that was for sure.

"We need to shut this down, fast," Mark said. "This tournament cannot happen. Some of these people, they're not what I thought they'd be. They shouldn't be here. No one should."

"I know," Brooke said. "I looked into what you told me. I started pulling investment records for all Crayton's early seeds, looking for a Chinese connection."

"And?"

"Zero. Not even a whiff."

"Goddamnit."

"*But,*" Brooke said, the word filling Mark with hope for a brief moment. "I thought I'd look into these companies' early *competition.*"

"What? Why?" Mark said. "What would that show?"

"Not a lot so far, but I'm still looking. In at least one case, though, the Crayton-backed robotic surgery company PrecisionPoint was neck and neck for mass adoption with another company, Exoware."

"What happened?"

"Exoware was printing parts in China, and suddenly the government stepped in and shut down one of their largest factories for pollution violations, which crippled production. What do you think happened then?"

"PrecisionPoint landed the contracts," Mark said slowly.

"Exactly," Brooke said. "Crayton's investment went from hundreds of thousands to tens of millions in just a few years. And that was just one company."

"That's good," Mark said. "That's really good."

"I'm going to keep hunting for stuff like this, but I'm going to send what I've got to Gideon. See if they draw the same conclusions at Langley."

Mark nodded his head, feeling a bit renewed from the breakthrough. But something told him that Crayton was a freight train that was going to be hard to stop before the tournament started. They'd need more, way more.

"They have me in the main manor. I'll figure out a way to start searching the place on my end. They've got cameras everywhere for this damn show though, I'll need some help disabling them."

"On it," Brooke said. "Well, almost on it. These camera feeds are all hooked in through the CMI network, which will be a different beast to break through. Will have that capacity soon enough though, don't worry."

"Thanks," Mark said. "I appreciate it. You're doing great, seriously. I know I gave you and Gideon a lot of shit, but I'd be nowhere without you two. Thanks for watching my ass."

Brooke smiled through the camera briefly, then regained a straight face.

"Just be careful. Glasshammer's crawling around everywhere in that compound, and even if you've met a few nice guys, there are stone cold killers in there with you."

"I know."

Brooke paused.

"Pretty messed up, having you all live together and get to know everyone before you're supposed to kill each other on camera."

"Crayton said something about it 'raising the emotional stakes' for both us and the audience. And yes, this is all fucked up in every conceivable way."

The next morning, tiny, self-driving electric carts lined up outside. It seemed to be the most efficient way to shuttle everyone around the sprawling property. Mark sat inside the first one in line. He didn't see anyone else coming out of the doors, so he told it to go, and off it went, already programmed to zip over to the second guest house, which Mark could see a ways off.

He still couldn't get over how strange the surroundings were. It was like being in an incredibly well-maintained microcosm of a cross between Central Park and the surreal rose garden of the Queen of Hearts in *Alice in Wonderland*. The greenery was punctuated only by the mansions and the outer wall, which was almost invisible in the distance because of how large the property was. There were beautiful gardens, cubed hedges, enormous fountains, and yes, Mark realized as they drove along its edge, definitely a lake in the middle. Huge trees that didn't look like they should be indigenous to the Vegas desert were clustered together to make little groves of shade, and Mark could only imagine what the water bill for the place must be. Somehow, the air felt at least twenty degrees cooler inside the compound than out. Mark hadn't figured out how Crayton had managed that little climate control trick. Mark squinted to see if they were actually inside some kind of giant clear dome, but it appeared Crayton had stopped short of planting a moon base in Nevada.

Soon enough, they arrived at the second guest house, and Mark saw other combatants filing inside. He caught up with Ethan, who shook his hand.

"Get much sleep?" he asked.

"Not really," Mark said. "You?"

"Nah," Ethan said, though he did look more well-rested than

everyone else shuffling through the halls. "Was not expecting that little twist," he said.

"I don't think anyone was," Mark said. He thought about what it would be like to shove a sword through this kid's chest. The notion was laughable, like some sort of bad dream, but that was exactly what he was supposed to do a few months from now.

The two turned a corner and walked into what could be best described as museum. With one very particular type of item on display.

There were weapons. Dozens of them. No, hundreds, Mark saw, as he entered the wide-open space. Each had its own stand or case, but as he drew closer, Mark saw that none of them were actually behind glass. There was every type of melee weapon Mark had ever seen in a history book or a movie. Swords, spears, shields, axes, maces, daggers, flails and . . . that was about all he could name. There were countless other types, different kinds of blades protruding at odd angles, or blunt-force weapons that looked like they could crush your bones if you just looked at them the wrong way. As they moved to the center of the room, they saw Moses looking around at the racks on the outer walls like he was in heaven. Light beaming in from the skylights above completed the effect. So far only Moses and the *Prison Wars* crew seemed pleased with the weapon announcement.

"This collection is just *stunning*," Moses said as they drew closer. "Some of these aren't even replicas! They're the real thing! I saw a halberd that had to be at least six hundred years old, and you can just reach out and touch it! Incredible."

"Everyone's gotta have a hobby," Mark said. Ethan chuckled.

"Hey guys," said a small voice from the center of the room. Standing between fighters a solid foot and a half taller than him was a young kid wearing a CMI LABS polo with double S-lenses sparkling in his eyes. He couldn't have been older than twenty.

"Guys, if you could gather around," he said. Everyone ignored him.

"Guys . . ." he said, his voice pleading.

"Hey!" Chase Cassidy barked, assuming the leadership role. "This young man needs our attention."

That made the chatter cease and everyone turned to face center. Drago Rusakov glared at Cassidy, who had cut short his conversation with Ja'Von Jordan, but he folded his tattooed arms and turned to the young man in the middle.

"Thank you, Mr. Cassidy," the kid said with an awkward bow in the actor's direction. "My name is Arthur Stemkowski. I work at Crayton Labs in Burbank, and Mr. Crayton has kindly flown me and my team out here to help you with this next phase of the Crucible. I have a dual doctorate in chemical and mechanical engineering, and I promise, I am older than I look." He paused for laughter, and none followed. The best he got was a stiff chuckle from Moses.

"So you're here to what, prep us for the SATs?" Matthew Michael Easton said with a sneer. He flipped his stringy bangs out of his face, and his ghostlike blue eyes flashed from side to side. Even his voice was creepy, like a string of sour notes in a song you already hated. The thought of planting a nearby mace in his skull was not unappealing, Mark realized.

"Hah, uh, no, rather, I'm here to help you craft custom weapons and armor to help suit your combat needs for the Crucible."

That drew a few appreciative nods from the crowd, which seemed to suddenly acknowledge the potential usefulness of the young man in front of them.

"Normally, I design military-grade hardware, but this is a special treat. We are going 'old school,' as it were. No guns, no projectiles, no electronically assisted anything. Just metal, leather, carbon, and whatever else we can cook up," Arthur said, rubbing his hands together.

"Very soon, I'll be working with you to design a weapon and armor set to meet your exact specifications. I won't train you how to use them. That's, uh, obviously not my department," he said with a nervous laugh. "But my team and I will build whatever your heart desires. Within, um, the stated rules of course."

He spread his twiglike arms and pivoted around.

"The point of bringing you here today to Mr. Crayton's private collection is to give you a taste of the types of weapons you can use in the Crucible. Anything you see here can be replicated, and most likely improved with modern day technology, for use in the Crucible. Armor design and fitting will be another day, but for now, your instructions are to just get a feel for what *type* of weapon you think you'd be comfortable using. And remember, weight matters. If you think something is heavy now, it will be even heavier when you're wearing armor. You'll have no power assist in your suit to help share the load. If you have any questions, I'm right here, but for now, feel free to explore. And yes, the edges *are* sharp, so please don't accidentally dismember each other and get me fired, heh."

The group made their various ways to the edges of the room. Opera music started to play over hidden speakers, and Mark looked up and saw camera spheres embedded in the ceiling, and at least one drone drifting lazily around twenty feet up. He kept forgetting they were on TV.

"Jesus Christ," he said, as he ran his hand over the handle of a long axe. "We're really through the looking glass now."

"I don't even know where to start," Ethan said. He picked up a spiked ball attached to a stick with a chain. It dangled dangerously by his shins, and he began to wind it up as Mark took a step back.

"Ah, ah, ah," Moses chided as he stepped in and gently put his hand on the handle before the ball gained momentum. "I would avoid that," he said. "The flail takes a *lot* of training, and you're still probably going to end up smacking yourself in the face. Trust me,

I've seen it happen. At this one Renaissance fair in '28, a guy lost an eye trying to show off with one of these."

"Alright," Ethan said, putting the weapon back, "what would you recommend?"

Moses took a step back and sized him up.

"Offense or defense?" he asked.

"Can't have both?" Ethan replied.

"Of course," Moses said. "If that's your game, I'd probably recommend a sword and shield combo. Here, try these."

Moses lifted a tower shield from its resting place and grabbed an old-looking sword to pair with it. Ethan took both and buckled a bit under the weight of the shield.

"Wow," he said. "Even heavier than it looks."

Moses laughed, "That's what training is for. Try a few swings."

Ethan stepped back and parried and thrust a few times. His form looked surprisingly good, from what Mark could tell.

"Impressive!" Moses said, apparently agreeing. "You're a natural. Never done this before?"

Ethan smiled. "Nah, not much call for this kind of thing in Iran, right Mark?"

Mark raised his eyebrows. "Right."

A loud clatter startled them all, and they turned to see Aria Rosetti looking sheepish with the bladed end of a giant double-headed axe sticking out of the wooden floor.

"Uh, it was heavier than it looked," she said, echoing Ethan's line. She tried to pull it out of the ground, unsuccessfully. Behind her, the pro-fighter pair of Dan Hagelund and Asher Mendez were snickering.

Mark stepped in to help her, but Moses was closer and reached her first.

"No worries, miss," he said. He ripped the axe out of the floor with one motion and slung it over his enormous shoulders like it weighed nothing. "We all have to work within our weight class!"

He put the axe back on its stand and fingered through some nearby blades.

"For you I think . . . these, maybe."

He pulled out two matching short swords, each about as long as her arm. She took them in hand, and though they dropped in her grip momentarily, she was able to hoist them up into something resembling a fighting stance.

"That's more like it," she said. "What are you, some kind of blacksmith?"

Moses laughed that contagious, deep laugh of his.

"If only," he said. "Just an enthusiast. Moses."

He offered his hand, and she took it. The size disparity was comical.

"Aria."

"And this here's Ethan and Mark."

"Hello," Ethan said, smiling warmly and shaking her hand. Mark offered his as well.

"The Wolf," she said, nodding.

"The Horse," he replied. She frowned in mock outrage.

"I'm going to stick with *Stallion*," she said. "Sounds prettier."

"Well at least you avoided being the Wasp," Mark said, jerking his head toward Soren Vanderhaven across the room. She was twirling a long spear around with worrying skill. Next to her, Chase Cassidy was fighting phantom enemies with a katana.

"What about you guys?" she asked.

"Eagle," Ethan said.

"Grizzly," Moses said. Mark hadn't seen his statue. It certainly fit, and naturally, Moses seemed to love it.

"I was never one of those girls who wanted a pony growing up, but whatever, I'll deal with it," Aria said.

She swished the swords around, which cut the air between them.

Moses picked up a large maul that looked like it may have once been a tree trunk.

"If you've got the size, you're supposed to use it," he said. "That's how battles used to be won with weapons like these. Don't think I'd be much use with a little sword-needle in my hand."

Mark had no idea what to grab, so he simply picked up the nearest sword.

"Bastard sword," Moses said. "The favorite of many a knight. Can use it with one hand or two because of the extended grip. But it would be tough to pair with a shield."

"I like to be mobile," Mark said, giving it a few practice swings. It was uncomfortably heavy, and he could feel the muscles burning in his forearm already. Ethan playfully swatted at his blade with his own, and sparks flew between the steel as they met.

"Want me to test that shield out?" Mark menaced.

"Uhhh, I'm good for now," Ethan said, laughing nervously.

"Excuse me, Arthur," Moses called out. "How many weapons are we allowed to use in our fights?"

"Whatever you can carry," Arthur said, excited someone was actually talking to him. "But I would advise against overloading."

"He's right," Moses said, turning back to them. "You can strap four swords to your back, but if they make you twice as slow, you'll be dead in a hurry."

"Maybe just a little extra then," Mark said, and picked up a long knife from a nearby table. He noticed there wasn't a blade under a foot long in the bunch. Nothing too small and sharp that could be thrown as a projectile. Or at least nothing that was *supposed* to be thrown.

All four of them were now holding some sort of weapon. For a moment they paused, and the smiles drained from their faces. In that instant, they seemed to realize that this wasn't a game. They could all potentially be tasked with murdering each other by summer's end.

And yet, somehow it didn't matter. They could ignore it a little longer.

"Breakfast?" Aria said. "I hear you can just yell 'pancakes' in an empty room here and someone will bring them to you in less than a minute."

"Sounds like a plan," Ethan said, "I'm starving."

As they put their weapons back, Mark watched Shin Tagami, slowly shuffling around the room, hands behind his back. He hadn't touched a thing, and quietly let himself out a back entrance.

After indulging in a breakfast that left each of them, even Moses, completely stuffed, they walked toward the exit of the guest house with the intention of exploring the grounds before they headed back to continue playing with weapons. Training didn't begin in earnest until the following day, allowing at least a short period of adjustment to their new surroundings, and Mark realized that he'd probably just eaten his last chocolate chip pancake for the summer. Aria said she'd spoken to the staff and Crayton's team had drafted "recommended" meals for them in order to keep them in fighting shape, which was meant to join roughly six hours of fitness training each day, on top of specific instruction relating to armor and weapons. Mark was exhausted just thinking about it. He was going to completely give up his nocturnal schedule and possibly quit drinking altogether.

Of course you can, he thought, *it's not even an issue.* Though just the thought of it actually made him want a glass of whiskey. Of course competitors were *allowed* to eat or drink or train as much or as little as they wanted, but to be taken seriously, he'd have to put in the work like he was actually attempting to compete and win. It would look more than a little suspicious if he spent his days lying in bed having pizza and beer delivered to him by the help while everyone else was out working their asses off. It seemed Crayton was counting on self-discipline being a determining factor to victory rather than skill alone. Their current accommodations were akin to a luxury vacation, but they'd have to treat their training like a day job.

The four of them were about to try and walk over to the lake, but when they exited the guest mansion, they saw something happening outside.

Crayton's security detail, a few wearing suits, but some wearing Glasshammer-issued riot armor, were surrounding a man with wild hair and a crookedly buttoned shirt paired with what appeared to be a swimsuit. Mark circled around and saw that it was Manny, the homeless veteran no one seemed to know anything about. Medical personnel were attending to one of the suited guards nearby whose white shirt was streaked with red. Manny raised his hand, and Mark saw that he was clutching an axe with crimson on the blade. The head was misshapen and jagged, like something a caveman might have crafted. Moses would know. Manny was yelling something unintelligible, and Mark saw that there were already at least three pairs of taser hooks in his skin, which appeared to have done nothing. The other guards were taking aim with weapons that Mark at least *hoped* were loaded with non-lethal rounds.

"Sir, again, put the axe *down*. You cannot take weapons from the display area without permission," a guard said.

That was generous, considering one of their own was lying on the ground with a chest wound. Mark imagined the guards were supposed to handle the "talent" with kid gloves, no matter what happened. But this guy clearly need to be in a room with padded walls.

"Stay back!" Manny yelled, finally saying words Mark could understand. "You're all fascists! You're Chinese spies! This is a prison camp for those who *know*."

Aria looked nervously at Mark. Ethan and Moses conferred among themselves. Manny turned and saw them. The burns on his face made Mark cringe involuntarily.

"Rise up, friends!" he called out, waving the axe. "Free yourself from the bonds of tyranny! We cannot live in the chains of false gods!"

"Hey, man," Ethan said, extending his hand. "Just calm down and—"

Ethan was interrupted by the whine of an electric engine. A dark SUV slid on the gravel and dug a trench through the nearby grass as it skidded to a stop. The door flew open, and a figure sprang out of the back seat like a released caged animal.

Wyatt Axton stomped toward the circle of guards with fury in his eyes.

"What the *fuck* is going on here?" he asked. Though the scene was pretty clear. "No one has a goddamn tranq on them? Jesus Christ."

"We put two in him already," one guard offered. "But—"

"Shut the fuck up, Martinez!"

Axton pushed past two guards who couldn't get out of his way fast enough. He wore a tac vest with no shirt underneath, which showed off arms like bundled steel cables. There was a submachine gun slung across his back and a Desert Eagle on his hip, but he made no motion to equip either.

Manny pointed the bloodied weapon at Axton.

"Behold, the servant of the beast! The white dragon emerges from the lake of fire!"

Axton didn't slow his gait at all. He marched straight up to Manny who immediately swung the axe toward his temple. Mark flinched out of instinct, but all four of them were rooted to the ground.

Axton ducked under the swing and slammed his fist into Manny's stomach. Seemingly immune to pain, Manny swung again and again, Axton weaving out of the way much more quickly than a man of his heft normally could. He struck back with targeted punches that should have floored Manny, but now Mark understood why the man had probably won his qualifier. Nothing fazed him.

But even more impressive was Axton himself, who moved with robotic speed and precision. Finally he grabbed the axe itself and ripped it out of Manny's hand. He spiked it into the dirt, blade first, and turned back to the wildman in front of him. Manny leapt at him, but Axton caught him by the shirt collar, and wrenched him down so his face crashed into Axton's knee. Even if he seemingly couldn't feel pain, biology simply shut his brain off, and he crumpled to the ground unconscious.

"Get some more sedatives in him immediately!" Axton roared. "And someone double check his meds. Whoever was in charge of administration is getting thrown in the fucking desert. And *you*, bunch of idiots standing around with your dicks in your hands. Ten of you couldn't take him? You had to interrupt my morning coffee? Everyone here is losing a week's pay."

None of the guards said a word.

Axton stalked past them as the guards converged on Manny. He glared at Mark and his group as he passed, and then disappeared behind the black glass of the SUV, which sped away back toward the main mansion.

"Remind me never to mess with *that* guy," Ethan said, rubbing the back of his neck.

Mark realized he couldn't keep ignoring the fact that Wyatt Axton was going to be a problem.

20

WE HAVE HOOKS INTO Glasshammer," Mark said later that night, chatting to Brooke on the S-lens. "We can't get him transferred, reassigned?"

"No way," Brooke said. She had the hood up on her Yale sweatshirt and looked like a parody of a hacker. Bits of curly blonde hair poked out the sides of it. "Do you know how many flags that would raise? You do not want to stir the pot and try to pry this guy off Crayton's personally assembled detail."

Maybe not, Mark realized. He rubbed the backs of his arms. The rest of the day had been spent playing with more weapons in Wing C, and by the end, everyone had pretty much made their pick. Despite being in relatively good shape, he could already tell his body would be screaming tomorrow.

"I see what you're saying," Mark said. "But if there's anyone that's going to find me out, or catch me looking somewhere I shouldn't, it's him. And something tells me I wouldn't just be tossed out of here. I'd wake up with my throat slit. You read what he did in Africa."

"Allegedly," Brooke offered.

"Bullshit, allegedly. I know we have those records."

"If you're thinking we blackmail him, that's going to go poorly for everyone."

"Ah, forget it," Mark said, closing his eyes and making his lens HUD disappear. "I guess I'm stuck with him. I just need to stay off his radar. Fortunately I wasn't the one who went crazy today and almost killed a guard. Who *is* that guy anyway?"

"Did some digging," Brooke said. "His real name is Manuel Varkas. Served *five* tours in Afghanistan, was on the ground for the Iran Incursion too. Did some hush-hush shit. Supposedly found a stash of chem weapons in a bunker somewhere and something went wrong in disarmament. Nerve damage and healthy dose of PTSD messed him up real good. He burned through his vet benefits and has been living on the streets for years. Entered the Crucible with quite literally nothing to lose, and he's managed to hang on to at least pieces of his spec ops training, it seems."

Nerve damage. Explained why it looked like the man couldn't feel pain. And his face, of course.

"Poor guy," Mark said. "Deserves better than this."

"That may be," Brooke said. "But be careful. He may not be an evil prick like those *Prison Wars* assholes, but he's clearly a hazard."

Mark couldn't disagree.

"Oh, I've got something you'll like," Brooke said, fiddling with her flexscreen out of his line of sight. An image popped up in a new window opposite her video feed.

"What is this?" Mark said. He squinted to zoom in.

"It's the full blueprints for Crayton's compound. Every inch, updated through the last six months. I hacked his contractor's servers and pulled all the files."

All four mansions, all the grounds. The detail was exquisite.

"This is perfect," Mark said. "Great job."

"And it gets better," Brooke said. "Ta-da"

On cue, hundreds of little blue dots populated the blueprints like stars. Inside, outside, on the walls, everywhere.

"Cameras," Mark said. "You did it. You got into the network."

"I'll credit Gideon's Langley team for doing a lot of that heavy lifting, but yeah, we're in. I can show you where every camera for *Heroes and Legends* is. I can show you the cameras Crayton doesn't want you to see. And I can turn them off and loop them if need be. You can pretty much have the run of the place now, if you can avoid live human beings."

Mark quickly jerked his head left and right.

"There aren't any in here, right?" he said.

Brooke shook her heard.

"That much he was being honest about. Thank god. If not, you'd probably have Wyatt Axton breaking down your door as we speak.

"Don't joke about that," Mark said, slightly chilled.

"Anyway," Brooke continued. "Your first target should be Crayton's office. It's right in the main manor on the third floor. I'm sure it's locked up tight, but if you scope it out, we can get through it." Brooke's eyes narrowed and she put her finger on her lip. Mark practically saw a tiny lightbulb ignite over her head. "I'll try to get into Glasshammer's comm link network and maybe do a trace on the guards that way. More little dots for your map that you can avoid."

"Thanks Brooke," Mark said. "You're really kicking ass out there."

Brooke came dangerously close to blushing.

"I did some of it, but Gideon helped too. I hear even McAdams is pitching in bodies to help with the back-end work. I think that Exoware info perked their ears up a bit."

"Whatever works," Mark said. Crayton was starting to feel a bit less untouchable.

"How's Carlo?" Mark asked, upset with himself he'd forgotten to ask until now.

"The same," Brooke said, her eyes lowering. "But they're hopeful. Don't worry, he's in good hands."

It was too easy to get sucked into Crayton's fantasyland. Mark had to stay focused, and remember why he was doing this in the first place. Drescher wasn't the only person responsible for Carlo's coma, after all.

Mark couldn't sleep, so he decided to creep up to the third floor and scope out at least the exterior of Crayton's office. In the dark, the place was a maze, but rather than have Brooke turning on and off cameras and trying to eye guards for him, Mark simply acted like he was going to one of the manor's libraries that was a few doors down from Crayton's office.

It was indeed hard to avoid running into maids and valets and security personnel whenever he turned a corner. Actually breaking in was going to be something else altogether, and would require a lot of help from the outside.

Finally, Mark reached the third story and slowly passed by two double doors joined by a pretty heavy-duty-looking e-lock. He casually glanced at his phone as he passed and pulled the data from the lock itself with the press of a button. Brooke could analyze it later and hopefully build him a key.

He kept walking and decided he should actually stop by the library on his way back to keep up appearances. Maybe even read a paper book for nostalgia's sake. He pulled the large door open and jerked to a stop.

A robe-clad Chase Cassidy was sitting on a long, leather couch behind a table filled with piles of books. Opposite him, sitting exceptionally close with her legs draped over his, was Soren Vanderhaven, wearing a pair of sweats and a T-shirt that looked oddly chaste. When she saw Mark in the doorway, her head jerked toward him like a babysitter who had just been caught having her boyfriend come by. Surprise transformed into a strangely intense rage in her eyes, but then that too melted away, and she forced a beauty queen smile, and put her hand over her mouth, the picture of supposed embarrassment. Cassidy merely grinned.

"Sorry," Mark said, feeling he'd almost certainly ruined a very specific kind of moment. As he backed out of the entryway, Cassidy gave him a quick wink, while Soren was now glaring through her tight-lipped smile. Mark closed the door slowly. As he did so, he saw a camera drone hovering above the pair of them.

Mark sent the lock data to Brooke, and while he should have

been planning his infiltration, he couldn't stop thinking about the Crucible itself. Despite his best efforts, he was actually *strategizing*, trying to figure out who might fare the best given the new addition of weapons to the equation. He spent a good deal of time doing research on his flexscreen, and figured that at least a few combatants could probably handle weapons well.

Moses was the obvious choice, as he was more of an expert than the actual experts Crayton had brought in to instruct them. Ethan showed surprising skill with the sword and shield, despite having no previous training Mark could find in his bio. That wasn't something taught in the Special Forces, he knew that much.

What worried him a bit was that he dug up an old Chase Cassidy movie called *Shogun Rising* where he played a white samurai in Japan. The film had trained him *extensively* in the use of the katana, the same kind Mark had seen him wielding earlier. Granted, prop fighting was different than real-life combat, but Mark had underestimated him before, and here Cassidy was, having proved himself after getting legitimately bloody in the ring.

In college, Soren Vanderhaven had been a baton twirler (of course she was) in addition to her gymnastic pursuits, and was probably the most coordinated person in the compound, so her ability to quickly pick up this style of fighting was assuredly second nature.

Mark was more confident that fighters like MMA-expert Dan Hagelund and boxer Asher Mendez would struggle un-learning everything they knew in order to wield weapons. Though he had seen Mendez practicing with some kind of spiked fist weapon the previous day, which meant he could possibly figure out a way to adapt.

Out of the *Prison Wars* group, all Ja'Von Jordan's murder charges were firearm related, and Drago Rusakov mostly crushed people to dust with his bare hands. But Easton, the serial killer, had shown incredible skill with shivs in *Prison Wars*, which had racked him up six kills on the show in addition to the dozens of women he'd scalped. And lord only knew there were a million different kinds of knives to choose from in Crayton's collection. Mark itched his scars. He hated knives. He already hated Easton. He secretly hoped this mission went on long enough to see him dead.

He checked the time.

Shit.

He was late.

"HELLO MR. WEI!" ARTHUR Stemkowski said as Mark crept into a room that looked unlike any other in the mansions. There were no elaborate murals or finely carved furniture in there. It was a lab, through and through. It looked like a cross between an auto body shop and someplace where scientists were trying to cure cancer. There were giant machines with purposes Mark couldn't fathom, but also microscopes and fridges full of test tubes. Arthur's small frame was dwarfed by the machinery that surrounded him. His floor-mounted computer terminal was quite a bit taller than he was.

"Hi," Mark said. "Sorry I'm late."

"No worries," Arthur said. "The next appointment isn't for a while yet. Did you enjoy yourself yesterday?"

"With the weapons? Sure. It was definitely interesting."

"And am I right in having pulled this weapon as the type you're interested in using for the Crucible?"

Arthur gestured to the bastard sword Mark had spent the better half of the previous day swinging around. Moses had told him it was the genuine article, at least five hundred years old. Thankfully, he'd managed not to break it, despite Ethan's best efforts when they were sparring. But he'd notched up the blade pretty badly, he realized.

"Yeah, that's it," Mark said. "And a knife too, if that's possible."

"Of course," Arthur said, nodding eagerly. "I like the selection. It's a very flexible weapon, and a good size for your build. I'm thinking carbon steel. Nothing more durable, and it'll be razor sharp."

"You're the expert," Mark said. He noticed a few camera bulbs in the ceiling.

"But today is really all about armor," Arthur said. "Have you given it any thought?"

"A bit," Mark said. He wasn't lying. He was spending far too much time thinking about this kind of stuff, he realized. "I want to be mobile and ventilated above all else, but still protected. Can you do that with a full suit?"

Arthur nodded excitedly.

"Absolutely," he said. "So no 'land tank' loadout for you then?"

"Are people doing that?" Mark asked, eyebrows raised.

"A few," Arthur said. "Some of the . . . larger gentlemen. But with the bulk of that much protection, they're sacrificing speed. However, the opposite is true as well. Miss Vanderhaven has requested a very . . . unique armor set that will certainly be, uh, mobile and ventilated, shall we say. But rest assured yours won't be styled the same way."

Mark could only imagine what that was going to look like, given her previous fighting ensembles.

"And one individual," Arthur continued, "has actually refused armor altogether."

Mark was incredulous.

"Seriously? Who?"

"Ah," Arthur said. "I am remembering now that I was told not to gossip. His eyes flitted toward the camera. Let's just focus on your own suit, shall we?"

Arthur flung up his hands and conjured a three-dimensional display on an enormous monitor in front of him. Different pieces of armor plating appeared, and, as he waved his hands around like he was conducting an orchestra, the various pieces flew across the screen and connected with one another.

"Pauldrons . . . here, reshape a bit. Breastplate . . . heat reflective."

Mark could only make out part of what he was muttering. Every so often he was asked for his input about which piece he liked or didn't. Or how much weight he was willing to sacrifice for flexibility. It was enough to make his head spin.

"Oh," Arthur said, his eyes widening. Mark could see at least a dozen different readouts on the S-lenses covering his irises. "I almost forgot. How would you like your symbol integrated?"

"My . . . symbol integrated?" Mark repeated.

"You are . . ." Arthur checked a readout in his lens. "The wolf, correct?"

"Yeah," Mark said. "But what do you mean?"

"In the spirt of proper, uh, *branding*, Mr. Crayton has requested that your symbol be integrated into your armor in some way. It can be a pattern, a logo, Actually, I can forge you an entire wolf's head helmet if you like. That would look terrifying!"

"Uh, no thanks," Mark said. "I have to?"

"Those are my instructions," Arthur said, growing a bit nervous that Mark was resisting.

Mark really couldn't care less about making a fashion statement or helping Crayton sell T-shirts. He threw up his hands in surrender.

"You know what, I'll leave it up to you, man," he said. "Just no wolf helmet. And don't give me like, a tail or anything."

Mark could see the wheels turning in Arthur's head.

"Alright," he said. "I may have an idea. You won't get your armor and new weapon until the tournament is about to start, but I'll assign you training gear that should mimic its weight and feel well enough. The delay is regrettable, but I have to build sixteen of these, after all! Well, fifteen, thanks to, uh . . ." he trailed off before he said the name. Mark could not imagine who would turn down armor in a competition like this.

They spent another solid hour mixing and matching plating before Arthur saved the build file.

"I believe it is time for my appointment with your compatriot, Mr. Callaghan."

"My compatriot?" Mark asked.

"Oh I forgot, you do not watch the show. Yes, well, *Heroes and Legends* seems to indicate that you and Mr. Callaghan have something of a friendship, do you not?"

Arthur sounded a bit forlorn, like he was unfamiliar with the concept.

"Uh, yeah," Mark said. "Couple of the folks here are good people. He's one of them, I guess."

"Yes, yes, I agree," Arthur said, smiling.

"What else has the show *indicated*?" Mark asked, curious.

"Hmm, well, let's see. Mr. uh, Manny had an incident with the guards yesterday, and he's currently being remedicated. Oh! The highlight hour spotlighted the fact that Mr. Cassidy and Miss Vanderhaven seem to be growing . . . close, but, oh, um, I seem to be gossiping again," he glanced nervously at the cameras overhead once again. "Thanks so much for coming in!"

"OF COURSE I'M GETTING armor! Are you crazy?"

Moses Morton was wheezing in between breaths. They'd been running for six miles now, and Moses started looking like death around four. He was certainly strong, as Mark had watched him deadlift roughly the equivalent of a semi-truck in the gym earlier, but his endurance needed work.

"I figured," Mark said, having barely broken a sweat.

"I think I drove that kid nuts. I was in there for four hours, fussing over every detail of the armor. And you should see the maul I'm having him make. It's exquisite! I based it off a seventh-century . . ."

Mark had a tendency to tune out when Moses started going off on one of his history lesson tangents. He turned his gaze outward to the path they were running on, which snaked all around the compound. Electric carts were zipping back and forth with maids shuffling towels and laundry around. Glasshammer security patrolled the grounds periodically wearing suits that looked stifling.

". . . and the armplates have a bit of Germanic influence. It's really going to be quite the ensemble. Do you know how long I've dreamed about designing my own set of armor? I'm going back for another session with Arthur to put the finishing touches on the design."

That much talking caused Moses to slow his pace, holding up his hand for Mark to fall back.

"Just . . . need a second," he panted, his jog now little faster than a brisk walk. "Nolan's always telling me I need to run more. If he's watching the stream, I'm never going to hear the end of it."

Moses pointed upward to a hovering drone high up in the sky that was much larger than the tiny dragonfly-like ones that were normally zipping around the mansions. The bulbs in its core made it look like cameras were sprouting on it like cancerous tumors.

"Nolan been calling a lot?" Mark asked.

Moses nodded, holding his side as he ran.

"Absolutely," Moses said. "He's been busy setting up the scholarship fund now that the paperwork's been signed."

"What scholarship fund?"

"Oh, that's where the money's going!" Moses said. "However many million I end up with when this is all said and done, I decided I'm creating a scholarship for students interested in history. Depending on how much I win, the fund could send thousands of kids to college for free. Tens of thousands even!"

Mark was taken aback.

"Whoa, really?" he said. "You're keeping none of it? Or . . . not giving any to Nolan?"

Moses laughed.

"Nolan's a partner at the top law firm in Salt Lake. Has been for ages. For our fifth anniversary, when I was still teaching at community college, he bought us a house in cash. Trust me, he couldn't care less about the money."

"Still, it's tens of millions, maybe more."

Moses shrugged as he jogged.

"We just like giving back."

"That's great," Mark said. It seemed as if he'd been wrong guessing at Moses's husband's motives.

"I can't wait until he gets to come here and see this place for visitors' weekend," Moses said. "He'll be blown away. I mean, he'll think it's tacky, but it's hard not be a *little* impressed."

Mark looked around the beautiful garden they were passing through, filled with arcing trees and a rainbow assortment of exotic flowers, and had to agree.

"When is visitation anyway?" Mark asked.

"Didn't you hear? It's practically right before the tournament starts at the end of August," Moses said. "You know, so we can . . . say good-bye if things don't go our way. Who do you have coming?"

Mark hadn't even thought about that. Brooke obviously couldn't. Rayne? He doubted she could leave the bar for that long. Maybe Carlo's little brothers and his mother? But they should probably stay by his side. Mark drew a blank past that.

"Um," he said.

Moses looked embarrassed.

"Sorry, I didn't mean to . . ."

"It's okay," Mark said with a half-smile. "Lone wolf, remember?"

"Hah!" Moses laughed. "Of course. Oh, did I tell you about the bear fur I'm embedding into my armor? Faux of course, I'm not a monster. Who would possibly turn down armor? Do you think it was one of the girls?"

"Why them?" Mark asked.

"Well, I don't know, maybe it's too heavy? Err, is that sexist? I'm not trying to be sexist," Moses was flushed.

Mark laughed.

"I don't think so, but maybe, who knows."

"I still feel a little bad about potentially fighting women," Moses said. "Do you?"

Mark shook his head.

"I've seen what some of the ones here can do. Trust me, you don't need to feel bad."

"I know, it's just . . . I was always brought up very strictly in terms of how to treat a woman. Opening doors, pulling out chairs. I mean, I grew up and married a man, but still. Fighting women is just a little strange."

"You didn't fight any women in qualifiers?" Mark asked.

Moses shook his head.

"Well, that's all very chivalrous, but I would put that out of your mind. Trust me, anyone here deserves to be here. And can probably hold their own."

As if to prove a point, Kells Bradford suddenly sprinted past them on the path, her skin glistening with sweat, tiny buds embedded in her ears audibly blaring music. She hadn't heard them, then. She was moving fast, as least twice their pace. Her muscled legs took her around the next corner, leaving them behind.

"Man," Moses said. "Maybe I really am too old for this. Can't keep up with you kids."

They rounded the corner and saw Shin Tagami sitting cross-legged on the grass in front of a tree. As they rounded the bend, Mark saw his eyes were shut.

"If he's here, you certainly can be," Mark said.

"Oh god, I'm done," Moses said as they passed Tagami, who didn't acknowledge their presence. "I can't win this tournament if I die of a heart attack."

"More tomorrow," Mark said, clapping a hand on the big man's shoulder.

"Only if you bench twenty more than you did today," Moses said. Mark groaned. The man had already forced him to his absolute max earlier.

"Deal."

They slowed to a light jog and turned again to try and find a quicker way out of the garden. Instead the hedges grew taller, and it became harder to see where they were going. The trees were thicker as well, which let them hide from the sun. The jog turned into a walk, and the soreness in Mark's muscles returned from the previous day's weapon experimentation. He was ready for bed, and it was barely mid-afternoon.

Something odd pricked his ears. A muffled yelp. An animal? Mark peered into the brush.

"What?" Moses said.

"Did you hear . . ." Mark said, holding his finger up, stopping to listen.

Another sound. Then a word. "*Please.*" The tone was strained, pleading.

Mark tore through the bushes with his bare hands, and ripped through the other side. There he saw a young girl in a black maid's uniform being pressed up against a tree, her hair being grabbed and pulled upward and tears spilled down her cheeks. Another hand was around her throat.

Easton.

The lanky creep wore a tank top that showed surprisingly muscular arms. Mark could see the bullet wound scar in his shoulder that he'd suffered during his arrest. He let go of her throat and turned toward them.

"Oh hi," he said, as if nothing was wrong. "Nice day out, isn't it?"

"Let her go, Easton," Mark growled. He tensed. Ready to strike. Moses crouched as well.

"What?" he said, "Me and Mimi here were just getting to know each other. Isn't that right?"

He looked at her, but her terror-filled eyes were locked with Mark's.

"You want to get kicked out?" Mark said, trying logic. "They see you and . . ."

"No cameras here, friends. No little flying snitches either. Just us and the beauty of artificially crafted nature. Now please, run along so I can finish my conversation."

"I don't think—" Mark said, but heard the brush rustle. Drago Rusakov lumbered out from behind a tree.

"What is happening?" he said, his Russian accent thick.

"These gentlemen were interrupting me."

"Go away," Rusakov glowered, turning toward them. He was even taller than Moses, and was blocking out the sun better than the trees.

"She's coming with us," Mark said.

"She is his," Rusakov said. "Do you not know? Everything here is ours. Food. Drinks. Women. Ours for being brave. For facing death. Riches for the damned."

"That's not how it works, my friend," Moses said, his voice stern.

Mark took a step forward toward the crying girl. Easton wrenched her hair tighter and suddenly whipped out a large knife from the belt of his dark paints, the blade aimed at Mark. Rusakov flexed and puffed out his chest. The man was probably the most terrifying human Mark had ever seen. Beady black eyes narrowed and the wind whipped his long beard. He curled his fist and Mark tried to read the Cyrillic letters scrawled on his knuckles.

Suddenly, as if appearing from nowhere, Shin Tagami was suddenly standing at the edge of the brush, having arrived in complete silence.

He walked slowly over to the five of them, the girl now turning her tearful gaze to the small old man. He was walking with a wooden staff that was taller than he was. He was completely bald, and didn't even have stubble on his face. He was wrapped in a long kimono, and held his fingers to his lips in a "shhh" motion as he approached. But he made no sound.

He walked up to the girl, Mimi, and made a beckoning motion toward her. She tried to take a step toward him, but Easton wrenched back on her hair, and she let out a little shriek. He pivoted around and pointed the knife toward Tagami.

"What, old ma—"

Almost too fast to see, the top of Tagami's staff lashed out and smacked Easton's hand that was holding the girl's hair. He released his grip on the maid, who stumbled forward toward Mark. Easton cried out and made a move with the knife, but the staff flashed again and hit his wrist so he dropped it blade-first into the earth. One final swing cracked across his face, and his skull rebounded off the tree behind him. He crumpled to the ground.

They were left staring at Drago Rusakov, who hadn't blinked since Tagami lashed out. There were now three of them, but Mark had a sinking feeling the colossal, legendary *Prison Wars* champion might be able to still beat them all to death on a whim, if he wanted to.

"Go," was all Rusakov said. That was enough for Tagami, who turned around walked slowly toward one of the mansions in the distance.

"Come on," Mark said to the maid. "Let's get you back."

He took Easton's knife and tucked it in his pocket, resisting the desire to plant it in his neck. Rusakov had wandered back into the trees like a forest troll.

"Thank you," Mimi called out breathlessly to Shin Tagami. The old man paused but didn't turn around. He gave a slight nod, and continued walking through the garden.

21

TIME WAS HURTLING FORWARD, pulling them all to their inescapable fate as the Crucible's final tournament loomed. Mark had snooped through the mansions, dodging guards and servants alike through Brooke's tracking systems, but found nothing of use. After all this time, they were still trying to crack the security of Crayton's main office, which was taking a worrying amount of time for a supposed team of experts at Langley.

Training was no longer an abstract concept and had been integrated into their lives fully. After they had spent a week playing with wooden practice weapons, they'd been upgraded to blunt steel, which weighed a hell of a lot more and had the potential to cause serious damage, despite the lack of a razor edge. They also wore armor meant to mimic the form and weight of the set Arthur was crafting for them. Crayton's team offered one-on-one training with all of the weapons experts he'd brought in, but Mark, Moses, Aria, and Ethan drew comfort from their little clique, and mostly sparred with one another. As time progressed, other groups had formed as well, the *Prison Wars* trio, obviously, but Asher Mendez, Naman Wilkinson, and Dan Hagelund had formed some kind of "professional athlete" club that sparred together and didn't talk to many others. Chase Cassidy and Soren Vanderhaven were rarely spotted more than ten feet from each other, and Rakesh Blackwood tagged along like a third wheel whenever possible, though his hungry looks at Soren were more than a little transparent. The rest were mostly loners. Mark almost never saw Tagami, Manny, or Bradford, who he assumed were training in isolation. Mark saw the strategic benefit in that, but it was hard to pry himself away from his group, who made ten hellish hours of training every day bearable.

"Moses!" Aria shouted. "I've told you a hundred times to stop pulling your punches. I'm a big girl, I can take it."

Moses swung his maul at her, but probably at no more than half speed.

"I'm sorry, dear, I'd just feel terrible if I broke something."

Aria lunged at him with a flurry of strikes from her dual swords, which Moses was forced to deflect. The dull clang of metal bounced around the gymnasium. Moses's bulky practice armor was known to crater the floor, and construction crews had been in and out all summer fixing the damage. Mark's was much lighter, but it was still enormously heavy compared to a spec ops darksuit. He hoped Arthur's final variant would prove to be a bit lighter and more mobile, as he'd requested.

"Very good!" Moses said to Aria as she kept striking. "But remember: when lunging with one sword, keep the other up to protect yourself."

Moses had turned into their de facto trainer, as he was more of an expert on wielding their weapons than the men Crayton had flown in. He'd shown Mark how to switch grips on his sword from single to double-handed, and back again. He was still fumbling with the transition, but was catching on quicker than most. Ethan, surprisingly, seemed to need the least instruction of all.

Mark hopped back as Ethan lunged forward with his shield, which he'd downgraded from the enormous "tower" to more manageable "kite." His practice sword was pretty close to a gladius, the type of short sword used in ancient Rome. Mark had range on him with his longer blade, but Ethan was incredibly adept at blocking his strikes at every turn. It would still be a while until their weapons and armor were built by Arthur and ready for use, so for now they were mowing through Crayton's training gear, averaging a snapped blade or split shield every other day or so.

In the midst of fighting, Mark glanced over at Aria, windmilling toward Moses with her swords. She still had trouble keeping the blades aloft over an extended period of time, but she never lost her grace, and Mark found himself—

"Ah shit!" he yelled as hot pain spread through his shoulder.

"Oh, sorry, did I get you?" Ethan said, a look of embarrassment on his face.

"That's kind of the point I guess," Mark said, wincing through a smile. The blades were dull, but the tip of Ethan's gladius was sharp enough to break skin if he found a crack in his armor. A trickle of blood streamed down the metal of Mark's shoulder. He set his sword down, pulled the pauldron off and clamped a towel over it, but after a minute realized he'd probably need it sewn up. The pain was so intense it was blurring his vision.

"I think you hit a nerve," Mark choked out.

"You been to the doc yet?" Ethan asked. Mark shook his head. "It's a few floors up, I'll take you."

Aria and Moses looked at him and the now-red towel with concern, but Mark assured them he was fine and took off with Ethan. A camera drone drifted silently behind them as they walked.

The "doc" turned out to be an Army medic turned vascular surgeon named Dr. Hasan who had a perfectly sculpted white beard and eyes so dark they were almost black. The medical bay was as elaborate as Mark expected, given that Crayton had clearly spared no expense on anything in the compound. Hasan had a full support staff of nurses and techs and enough equipment to run nearly any test that needed running. Mark saw there was even an onsite surgical wing, though that didn't seem to be necessary at the present moment.

"Sliced clean through a nerve cluster," Hasan said, confirming Mark's theory. "Must hurt quite a bit."

"I've had worse," Mark said. Hasan glanced over the litany of scars on his chest.

"I can see that," he said. "How did you say you got those again?"

"Shrapnel," Mark said. Hasan's eyes narrowed suspiciously.

"Mhm, well, this one just needs some sealant, and I'll give you something for the pain."

Before he'd even finished the sentence, he'd jabbed Mark with a small injector that shot something dark blue into his shoulder just below the wound.

"Uh, I really don't want morphine screwing up the rest of my training day."

"It won't," Hasan said. "And it isn't morphine. We call this *drexophine*, and you won't find it outside the military. Brand new. Passed all its trials with flying colors, but it's so expensive to manufacture, only the government can afford it. And not much of it, at that."

"Drexophine?" Mark said, rubbing his shoulder.

"Don't ask what's in it, bunch of stuff that will sound Greek to you. But it's complete pain management without foggy-headed side-effects. Non-addictive too, if you can believe that."

Mark couldn't, but half a minute later and his shoulder felt like it had been dipped in a cool spring. And his head felt totally fine. It worked so well it was disconcerting. Dr. Hasan filled his wound with sealing gel and wiped away the last of the blood before wrapping it up in a bandage.

"All set, son," Hasan said, clapping Mark on the shoulder. Mark winced, but realized it didn't actually hurt. Hasan winked at him. Mark wandered through the exit, where he found Ethan on his phone in the hallway looking pale. He looked up at Mark, then kept talking.

"Thanks for the call, I appreciate it," he said. "Just please let me know if anything changes. I love you so much. I can't wait to see you in a few weeks. Tell the girls I miss them when they get home from school."

Ethan slid his phone back into his pocket and blinked away tears as quickly as he could manage.

"Shoulder good?" he said, turning to Mark. "Not a fatal scratch?"

"Yeah, it's fine," Mark said, touching the bandage. "They gave me something for it, crazy stuff."

"Oh right, drexo-something. They gave me some when Moses cracked my rib a few days ago. That stuff is magic."

There was a long pause as they walked down the hallway.

"Everything good?" Mark finally said.

Ethan tilted his head back and forth.

"My wife's prognosis changed," he said. "They just downgraded her from a year to live to no more than six months. I thought . . . I thought she was doing better. To look at her, you wouldn't even know . . ."

Mark put his hand on Ethan's shoulder as they walked.

"Sorry to hear that, man."

"It's frustrating, you know? I earned ten million by being here, but I can't give it to her yet for the operation, and I can't even spend these next three months with her. I'd jump off the roof right now if I thought it would save her."

Mark noticed the camera drone still following behind them. He shot it an angry glare.

"If she's got six months, that's still enough time," Mark said, trying to be reassuring. "And visitation weekend is just a few weeks away. It's already August."

"Yeah, I know," Ethan said. "But Christ I really don't want to lose her. What if they downgrade again? What if after all this, the treatment doesn't even work? It'll destroy my girls. It'll destroy me."

Mark felt a knife in his gut. Ethan had so much riding on this tournament, and it was his job to dismantle it. It was Josh Tanner all over again, but he actually knew Ethan. Or at least felt like he did by now. It made him nauseous.

Behind them, the camera drone continued to watch impassively, broadcasting Ethan's misery for all the world to see.

"HOW'S THE SHOULDER?" BROOKE asked in his S-lens as Mark retired to his room for the night.

"You saw that?" Mark said. His shoulder was fine. Better than fine. A single dose of drexophine had erased all traces of the pain he'd felt earlier. He wondered how long that would last.

"I don't think you understand just how much you're being filmed," Brooke said. "They upgraded the show last week to have a dedicated live feed of each one of you going so that people can 'subscribe' to their favorite fighter. And then they're cutting the highlights together into a two-hour show every night. Ratings aren't what the fights were, but they're not bad either."

"I keep forgetting about all the cameras," Mark said. "Hopefully I haven't made that big of an ass of myself while training."

"You could do worse," Brooke said. "Plus, everyone's mostly watching Cassidy and Vanderhaven get cozy. And your friend broke a few hearts today with the news about his wife."

"Ethan?" Mark said.

"Yep," Brooke replied. "Poor kid."

Poor kid indeed.

"But yeah, tonight's the night," Brooke continued. "We have bigger things to worry about. I have Crayton's office key."

"Really?" Mark said. "Jesus, took long enough."

"You wouldn't believe the encryption," Brooke said. "But we're going to have a good window tonight. Crayton's at some gala in the city and shouldn't be back for hours. Axton is with him."

"Just tell me what I need to do," Mark said.

Mark and Brooke worked out a relatively simple pattern to get him around the compound unseen. She'd scout ahead with the cameras to see where Crayton's Glasshammer guards were, then cut and loop the cameras so Mark could move invisibly. Mark couldn't just be non-lethal, he had to be a ghost. He didn't even want to *look* at a guard, much less have to choke one out. As such, he was almost entirely reliant on Brooke to see him through.

The manor was eerie at night. The lighting was dim and it was so late even the maids had all gone to bed. Mark could hear the creak of patrolling security on the wood floors, but Brooke made sure they never crossed his path. Even with the stop and go of Brooke's camera tricks, it didn't take more than five minutes to ascend to the top floor where Crayton's office was. The library was dark, meaning Mark didn't have to worry about interrupting another rendezvous between Cassidy and Vanderhaven.

Mark tapped his phone and loaded up the cracked keycard config. He waved it across the lock, and the doors to the office popped open a little too loudly for Mark's taste. He stole inside and closed the door behind him. The lights came on immediately.

"No cameras in here," Brooke said. "No mics either."

"You could have told me that beforehand," Mark said. "Anyone could have been in here!"

"Yeah, absolutely not," Brooke said. "I told you, it took a whole team a week to crack that card data. I have a live feed of Crayton sipping champagne downtown, so you have nothing to worry about. Trust me, Mark."

Mark had to trust her, and realized he didn't have any time to waste. He scanned the room, which was every bit as lavish as he'd imagined, filled with enormous paintings that looked plucked straight from museum walls and twisted metal sculptures that were assuredly supposed to be modern art. The desk alone looked like it weighed a thousand pounds, and knowing Crayton, it was probably carved from the hull of some ancient war galley or something. Mark noticed something odd immediately.

"There's no computer," he said. "No flexscreens either. Nothing electronic at all."

"He must take it all with him," Brooke said.

Mark shuffled through the papers on the desk. Most appeared to be earnings reports for various Crayton-owned subsidiaries, and none seemed to be particularly eye-catching. Still, Mark blinked through each page, taking photos and instantly uploading everything to Brooke.

He circled around the desk and opened the drawers. He found a few books, more papers, and some scrolls that unfurled into blueprints for early drafts of the Colosseum. Below that, there was one final drawer with a maglock on it. Mark tried the room key crack on his phone, and it sprang open.

The entire drawer was a form-fitted case for a .45 magnum with a DNA ID-FIRE chip slapped on the side. Mark scanned it on the off chance Crayton had perhaps committed a multiple homicide with it and maybe they could get him that way.

"Wouldn't that just be a dream?" Brooke smirked when he sent the data. "Yeah, it's clean," she confirmed. "I doubt it's ever even been fired."

Mark looked over the weapon, which appeared brand new, and had to agree with that assessment.

"Shit!" Brooke exclaimed, and the office went pitch black. Mark instinctively ducked behind the desk. He eyed the magnum as he heard two guards pass outside the hallway. He could vaguely make out what they were saying.

"Did you see Soren tanning on the roof this morning?"

"Nah, but Walker told me about it. I have to catch the re-stream."

"Yeah, there were like five camera drones circling her the whole time. God damn what I'd give to . . ."

The voices trailed off as they reached the end of the hall.

"Shit, sorry," Brooke said as she remotely snapped a few of the lights back on. "I have like five monitors up at once. I looped the cameras but didn't even consider light coming through the cracks of the door."

"I'm not sure any light can make it through," Mark said. "But just keep it dim, I'll make do."

Mark looked at the drawer, which seemed just a bit too deep for a gun case alone, and he started feeling around the edges. After a minute, he was ready to give up, but he felt a little notch near the back. With the tip of his fingernail, he slid a small mechanism over, and the entire bottom of the gun case delatched.

"Think I've got something here," Mark said.

Inside did not appear to be a signed confession letter implicating Crayton in the death of Justice Wright, nor a full printout of the funding he'd received from China. Rather, there was just a small, flat box. Mark slowly picked it up and heard something rattle inside. He stood up and put it on the desk where it was fully illuminated by the light. Mark's eyes widened as he saw sloppily etched Chinese characters on the lid.

"Whoa."

"What does it say?" Brooke asked. She could read Mandarin, but the letters were jagged and it was probably tough to see through the S-lens.

"Unless I'm missing something here," Mark said, running his fingers along the carved letters, "it says 'White Devil.'"

"What the hell?" Brooke said. Mark fingered the latch and the box swung open. The wood smelled ancient. In the low light, it was hard to make out what was in the box. Mark poked gently with his finger and moved it closer to the desk lamp.

"Uhhh," he said, zooming in with the S-lens and taking some pictures. "Are these what I think they are?"

"Are those . . . teeth?" Brooke asked, wrinkling up her nose.

Mark peered at the tiny white nubs in the box, and picked one up. It did look like a tooth. A child's tooth, but one exceptionally yellow, and with what appeared to be a small hole stabbed through it. He looked at the others, and they were all the same.

"I don't understand," Brooke said. "Crayton doesn't have any kids."

"That we know about," Mark said. "But I don't think this is that. There are way too many teeth here for just one kid, and I'm guessing no illegitimate child of a billionaire would have to go without dental work. Most of these are warped and rotted and badly stained. That doesn't just happen after you take them out. And I think there are a few adult ones mixed in here too. But these holes . . ."

Mark shone a light through the tooth.

"I could take one to scan the DNA," he said.

"There won't be any left in those if they're as old as they look," Brooke said. "And we have to leave everything. Who knows if he has some late night teeth-counting ritual or something and will freak out if one's missing."

Mark put the tooth back and peered at the lid of the box. It was white, offset against the wood's rich brown. He clawed the top and peeled back what was stuck to the wood. A photo.

It was old, faded, and singed. In it, there were two smiling faces, a man and a woman, both blond.

"Is that Crayton?" Brooke asked.

Mark peered closer. He could see the resemblance. And yet . . .

"No, I don't think so. But a relative, maybe? This guy looks like he could be his brother, but this picture is pretty old. They stopped making Polaroids decades ago, and this looks older still."

"Crayton doesn't have a brother," Brooke said. "And here are his parents."

Through his S-lens she showed him a photo of a good-looking couple, also blond, taken about thirty years ago.

"Hunter and Helena Crayton," Mark said, reading the caption.

"They were nobodies. They owned a little hardware store in Idaho," Brooke said. "Both died in a plane crash when he was young. One of those tiny Cessnas. Hunter was a hobbyist pilot."

"This is from his file?" Mark said, looking back and forth between the two couples.

"Yep."

"I thought you said his file was bullshit."

Brooke paused to consider that.

"I don't know what to think anymore."

Mark snapped several photos of the Polaroid.

"Run them through facial scan. See if anything pops up."

Brooke tapped a few keys.

"Nothing on a quick pass, but I'll have to dig into it deeper with a more robust database later."

The resemblance to Crayton was eerie. Crayton was practically a perfect balance of the pair of them, his blue eyes and her wide smile. "Hunter and Helena" were also blond and handsome, but the similarities pretty much stopped there.

"What, so Crayton lied about his parents?"

"Or someone lied for him."

"What does that mean? They don't look Chinese to me."

"Yeah I noticed, thanks. Just find out who they are."

Mark snapped some pictures of the teeth, and closed the lid.

White Devil.

What on fucking earth.

22

THE MESS HALL WAS freezing, as it always was. Everything was steel, the floor, the ceiling, the benches, and there were no windows, only vents pouring in cold air to keep the staff "alert." Those were Chinese workplace standards for you.

Mark sat alone, poking at his hardened rice with chopsticks. His presence in the mess was an upgrade from being served meals while locked in a room. He'd proven himself an asset and earned a few privileges as a result. And yet, no one in the base wanted to sit with the *pàntú*. The traitor.

Mark didn't care, and at present, it was especially unimportant. Though it was easy to lose track of time on base, he knew what today was. Or was supposed to be. The start of the final phase of Spearfish, meaning by the end of the week he would be a hero or dead.

Something *was* happening. He could hear a buzz in the air. News was being passed around like a virus. Had it worked? Had it begun?

His thoughts were interrupted by Zhou slamming his hand down on the table, jostling his bowl. Zhou's eyes were wide with a mix of excitement and fear.

"Did you hear?" he asked Mark.

Mark shook his head.

"What's going on? What's everyone talking about?"

"General Lin is dead."

Mark's heart leapt. He feigned shock.

"What? How?"

"An explosion in the mountain base. No survivors yet. They are excavating the wreckage, but Lin himself has been confirmed dead."

"Who . . ."

"A flag was planted on a peak overlooking the base. It flew the colors of the Gold Tigers, Commander Wu's rogue unit in the north. They have more power and reach than we thought."

The misdirection for the magic trick meant to kill a country. It was supposed to be the CIA's masterpiece. And Mark was one of the brushes.

"And yet Lin was our political enemy, no?" Mark asked. "Is Admiral Huang pleased?"

Zhou's eyes flashed angrily at him.

"We do not cheer the death of our countrymen!" he snapped. But then he softened and lowered his voice. "Though Lin was a danger to China itself, and we are glad to be rid of him. But Wu is clearly an even greater threat."

"What of Commander Wu's whereabouts?" Mark asked. There were three top military figures and two politicians all vying for influence in China, and their clashes had been the cause of rising tensions for years now. One was Admiral Huang, who had close ties to the MSS and was the man Mark and Zhou worked for. Mark had long suspected he was one of the shrouded men in the room when he'd taken the knives to the poor captured US soldier. Mark rarely slept a full night without seeing the pain in that man's eyes before the light went out of them completely. *It was for the greater good* was all he could say to comfort himself, and it didn't help at all.

"Wu denied the attack, but he is a lying dog so that means nothing. Admiral Huang consults with Prime Minister Jiang for a course of action, though naturally I am sure Chairman Xianyu will oppose whatever they suggest, obstinate fool that he is. Admiral Huang has himself moved to a secure location as intelligence indicates he may be a target as well, given his influence."

"Moved?" Mark said. "Where?"

Zhou glared at him.

"That is not information you need to know," he said, and Mark didn't press the issue. But it didn't matter. If Zhou knew, that was enough, as Mark had secretly squirreled away his security credentials for weeks now. He had two days to figure it out, in any case.

Tomorrow, the rogue Wu would die if the Spear did his job. Then Mark would hunt down Huang. Then the Prime Minister and the Chairman would be dead by the end of the week. If all went to plan, China would burn by Saturday as chaos reigned and leaderless armies turned on each other after years of instability. A civil war to splinter China to bits. The mountain Spear team had ensured a successful beginning. He wanted to shake their hands for that.

This was it. One man to kill, and he could go home.

CRAYTON WOULD OFTEN DINE privately with the Crucible combatants. As the weeks progressed, he requested meals with Mark more than most to talk training, politics, and war stories. Mark almost never left a meal with Crayton feeling anything less than creeped out. Not because the man exuded the aura of a treasonous insane person, but because more often than not, he *didn't*. He was charming, eloquent, and had a disturbing ability to make you feel special, like somehow the two of you were old friends despite the fact he was throwing a tournament to celebrate your impending death. Mark casually asked Ethan and Moses how their interactions with Crayton were, and both said they just plain liked the guy. Only Aria expressed hesitation.

"He's very nice and flattering, but there's something just . . . off there," she said as she and Mark walked toward the man-made lake in the middle of the compound one night. There was one specific bluff that overlooked the water, where Mark had seen Shin Tagami meditating, and he was curious to see the view for himself. But after dinner with Crayton, it had gotten dark quickly, and it was getting a bit hard to navigate by the light of the moon alone.

"What do you mean, 'off?'" Mark said, even though he knew exactly what she meant.

"I don't know," Aria said, trudging up the hill a bit ahead of Mark. "Half the time I wonder if he's an android. It's like he's simulating human emotion instead of actually feeling it. Every time I talk to him it feels like a performance. And hell, maybe it is, with these damn cameras always around."

She pointed upward to one of the larger, bulbous drones in the sky.

They'd almost reached the top of the small hill, where a solitary tree branched upward toward the stars. Given the incline and the height of the tree, it even towered over Crayton's monstrous warrior statues back by the mansion. Below them was the lake, sparkling with moonlight. It was almost impossible to believe this was all man-made.

"I can see what the old man likes about this spot," Mark said as he sat down by the base of the tree. Lights flickered in the windows of the four mansions, and little beams indicated patrolling guards around the compound. In the distance, over the wall, was the dim glow of Vegas, poisoning the night sky with its neon. But even still, looking straight up, Mark could see the stream of the Milky Way through the branches of the hulking tree.

Aria sat down next to him, crossing her arms over her knees. She stared out into the dark water.

"This feels like some synthetic version of purgatory," she said. "Waiting for either heaven or hell on the other side."

"But most of us are damned," Mark said.

"No, we all are," she said. "Why else would we be here? We are the lost."

"The lost?"

"Lost in anger. Or grief. Or greed. Or vanity. Or all of it."

Mark looked at Aria, her profile flawless in the moonlight. Her wavy brown hair was black in the darkness and fluttered behind her as a hot breeze blew over the wall. She was heartbreakingly beautiful, and Mark hated that he could literally think of nothing else besides that when she was around. And yet, he'd become almost addicted to her presence. She was a ray of light in the darkness of this insane and increasingly terrifying mission. Ethan and Moses were as well, he supposed. But Aria, she was something else entirely.

"Can I ask you something?" Mark finally said. Aria turned toward him and brushed the hair from her face. "Why the hell are you here?"

Aria turned back to the lake.

"I mean," Mark continued, "everyone's got their reasons, but most are public knowledge, and if not, at least people are telling the right kind of lies. But not you. Never anything. Not even an inkling."

Aria remained silent.

"From what it sounds like, you had it all. One of the best dancers in the world. A supportive family. A great life."

"Jesus, Mark," Aria finally snapped. She flashed him a look of anger he'd never seen her wear before. "You think you know me because you watched the CMI recut of my life they turned into fight promos?"

"No!" Mark protested. "Shit, sorry. I just meant, you don't seem like one of the damned. I *want* to know the real story."

More silence.

"But I understand if that's something you want to hold close," Mark continued. "Believe me, I understand."

Mark felt like an idiot, pushing so hard. But Aria was a mystery he actually wanted to solve, unlike Crayton and his box of teeth and the rest of this mess of shit.

After another uncomfortable silence, Aria pivoted around to face Mark, sitting back on her knees. She bent in close, her hair brushing past his cheek. When she spoke, her lips were almost grazing his ear.

"This isn't a story for the cameras," she said. "This isn't a story for anyone, really. But you hurt the way I hurt. I can tell. I can see it in your eyes, every day. So I'll tell you. Only you."

"How do I hurt the way you hurt?" Mark whispered back. "What do you mean?"

"Listen, and you'll know," Aria said.

Mark fell silent.

"My sister, Olivia, and I have always been competitive. She's two years younger than me, so always a little slower, a little weaker. Not by much, but enough.

"My parents thought we could make each other strong, so they pitted us against each other our entire lives. Dance, sports, martial arts, anything they could think of where we could push each other to be the best.

"It worked. I constantly beat Olivia in nearly everything, first because I was older, meaning stronger and faster, but later because of the confidence I had believing I was the best. That let me beat her and other girls even when age became a hindrance instead of an advantage.

"It worked for her, too. Because she was always chasing after me, it made her strong. She dominated the competition in her age group, because *I* was always the standard. She never reached me, but never stopped trying.

"But when we were adults, it took a dark turn. Our parents kept pushing us. We'd audition for the same the same companies, the same roles even. I'm pushing thirty, and I felt like I was thirteen again. Our parents demanded that I show no mercy on her. *It's for her own good*, they always said.

"Eventually it started to seep into Olivia's skin and bones like a disease. The years of successes that felt like failures because she wasn't *quite* as good as me. She practiced harder, longer than ever before. She was determined to beat me. To *win*.

"We were both up for principal dancer in the Metropolitan

Ballet Company, one of the best in the world. I trained for months, and so did she, but she wouldn't even speak to me by then, after so many years of competition that had mutated into life or death struggles for the love of our parents and our own sanity.

"I snuck into one of her solo rehearsals anyway, and I was stunned. She was brilliant, beautiful, and absolute perfection. She performed a routine so complex, so physically eloquent, it was hard to fathom. It was career-making.

"I went to my audition shaken, but did well. Better than well. I made the other girls look like first year Juilliard students. But I was afraid of what was coming from her after what I'd seen.

"But she never showed up. She skipped her audition entirely, and a day later I was awarded the spot.

"I celebrated, I partied with my friends, I thought the world was mine.

"A week later, I got a phone call. I could barely recognize my mother's voice, her throat was so raw from sobbing. Olivia had broken her leg in one of her final rehearsals the day before the audition. She was admitted to the hospital, her leg was set, and she'd be starting therapy once it healed. While her doctors were confident she could eventually walk normally again, the break was so bad they told her she wouldn't be able to dance professionally going forward. For fun, sure, but not at the level she'd been training for.

"When she finally was released from the hospital, Olivia went home to her apartment in the city, took a hot shower, and dragged a razor blade through an artery in her injured leg. Her roommate found her body the next morning.

"I tried to dance after that in my new role as principal for MBC, but it was hollow. The joy was gone. My drive, my inspiration, had evaporated. It was her. It had always been her. Even when I thought I hated her as we grew older, I was lost without her. I quit, and my parents lost their minds. It was only then I realized what they'd done to my poor sister all these years. What I'd done. Who we'd turned her into."

Aria pulled back from Mark, her whispered story finished.

"See? I am one of the damned after all."

Mark couldn't hide the tears in his eyes.

"So you punish yourself here, like this?" he asked. "Why?"

"It's the ultimate irony, isn't it? It's only punishment if I die. If I'm *not* the best for once. But then I can see her again. Perhaps if I make it through, I can lift the darkness from my life, but it's so hard to see the other side. You know that feeling, I think."

Mark's eyes narrowed.

"Why do you say that?" he asked. "I'm here because of—"

"Gambling debts?" Aria said, eyebrow raised with skepticism. "Maybe that's true, but you've lost someone too, haven't you?"

Mark said nothing, but his poker face was slipping. Aria's story had knocked the air out of him.

"That kind of loss attaches itself to you," she said. "It's invisible to most, but can easily be seen by someone else who has it too."

"What does my loss look like?" Mark said, his whispered voice breaking.

"The loss of love, I think," Aria said softly. "The loss of more love than anyone should have to lose."

Fuck.

"And something tells me it's a story you'll never tell."

Aria and Mark were jolted out of the moment by the dull, piercing wail of an alarm sounding in the compound, echoing off the walls. It was a rising sound like an air raid siren. One by one, floodlights came on everywhere, illuminating the grounds in faux daylight. The purgatory paradise was suddenly a military base on full alert.

"What's going on?" Aria said, standing up and surveying the surrounding area. From the hilltop, they could effectively see the entire camp.

Mark squinted and saw figures sprinting from a side entrance of the main manor. There were three of them, clad in black, and they fled inhumanly fast toward the outer wall. Behind them, guards emerged, led by Wyatt Axton. He let loose with a stream of silenced SMG rounds, and his fellow guards followed suit.

"Holy shit," Aria said, craning her neck to get a better look, but Mark pulled her down. A stray bullet could go anywhere.

The three figures reached the wall and began to scale it like spiders, with no ropes Mark could see. They had some sort of grappling gear attached to their hands. Two made it up the wall in record time, but Axton took aim at the third as he neared the top. Mark couldn't see where the figure was hit, but he fell backward from the wall twenty feet to the ground. Axton and the others swarmed him, and Mark heard the roar of engines being revved outside the base. Axton flung his hand out to a unit of approaching guards, apparently directing them outside.

Axton plowed his fist into the injured invader, who went limp. He grabbed him by the neck and dragged him back to the mansion, where they disappeared through the same side door they'd emerged from. The alarm continued to sound. Mark wanted nothing more than to slide in his S-lens and ask Brooke what the hell was going on.

"Did they just *shoot* someone?" Aria asked, eyes wide with panic. "Who were they?"

"I don't know," Mark said as calmly as he could manage, "but we need to get inside."

CAMERON CRAYTON HIMSELF APPEARED on Mark's TV when he reached his room later that night after escorting Aria back to hers. His smile was faded, reduced to a mere grin, and the alarms had long stopped blaring, and the lights had returned to normal.

"Apologies for the late hour," Crayton said, the message playing on every screen in the compound Mark was sure, and probably on

TV as well. "But there was an incident at 10:30 p.m. this evening, and I wanted to ensure everyone who may have glimpsed it during the stream that there is no cause for panic."

Only Crayton would be a dressed in a suit this late with his hair perfectly combed. Mark was eager to hear his official explanation.

"A small group of overly zealous Crucible fans managed to gain entry into my estate and slip past security. It seems their intent was to pay one of our combatants, the enigmatic Mr. Cassidy, a visit. Chase has long been the target of such . . . enthusiasm from fans, so this isn't out of the ordinary. Fortunately, we don't believe the parties involved had any ill-intent toward him. They have been apprehended and turned over to local authorities. We wish them no harm, but I must state emphatically that this kind of behavior is unacceptable. We all love our brave fighters, but we must respect the law and the bounds of good taste."

Mark rolled his eyes at that.

"Thank you for your attention, and I know the rest of you will respect the sanctity of our training area in the future."

Mark stared hard at Crayton's eyes. He could see something in them, a tiny hint of fear.

"Well, what did you make of that?" Mark asked Brooke in the S-lens after the broadcast went dark.

"You saw more than me," Brooke said. "Not only did the intruders not pass by any of the cameras on the way in, all the footage from when the alarms sounded was cut from the livestream. Past that, even though I'm in their network, they wiped *everything* almost as soon as it happened. Maybe if I'd checked ten minutes earlier I could have grabbed something, but I was eating a late dinner. Sorry."

"Well I can tell you what I saw," Mark said. "And it wasn't any 'crazed fans' who moved like that. I'm pretty sure they were wearing lizard suits to get over that wall."

"Lizard suits" was slang for the LZ-600 series, a tactical espionage loadout where flat surfaces could easily be climbed with thousands of microscopic hooks on the hands and knees.

"And that wasn't rubber Crayton's security was shooting at them," Mark continued. "I bet there's someone scrubbing blood off the wall right now. I'm guessing the other two got away and they have the third on lockdown, if he isn't dead."

"What are you saying?"

"I think you know."

"A hit team?"

"Well they sure as hell weren't here to molest Chase Cassidy. These guys were pros."

"If this is China . . ."

"I didn't think they'd take it this far. I know Crayton's security has been tight, even for a billionaire, but this? A potential hit? Christ. This is big."

Mark rubbed his eyes, which temporarily blacked Brooke out of his vision.

"So what happens now? Isn't the enemy of my enemy my friend?" Mark asked.

"Langley won't see it that way. They need to know whatever the hell's going on between Crayton and China, if that's actually what this is. They're starting to really crack open that investment data I showed you. More Chinese connections defunding the competition of his start-ups, or otherwise screwing them over via proxies. A pattern is forming."

"And Gideon still thinks he's on the hook for Justice Wright, doesn't he?"

Brooke nodded.

He couldn't stop thinking about the lethal effectiveness of Wyatt Axton. If anyone could do his wetwork . . .

"Alright," Brooke said, yawning. "I can't stare at these damn video feeds any longer. I'm going to bed."

"Before you do, try to see if they stashed that guy they shot somewhere in the compound," Mark said. "If they're keeping him onsite, I could question him and might be able to break this thing open."

Brooke was still finishing her yawn, but nodded.

"Alright, alright. I'll pore through data all night and you can just relax on that giant-ass pillow you call a bed."

"Thanks," Mark said with a smile. Brooke blew out an annoyed sigh and killed the feed.

If it really was an assassination attempt on Crayton, Mark was a little sad it had failed.

23

VISITATION DAY ARRIVED. FOR many, it meant a joyous reunion with friends and family after a summer apart. But what it really meant was that the following week they'd all start hacking each other to pieces in Crayton's arena. It was amazing how fast time had flown, and despite a thickening intel file on Crayton, one final order from Gideon told him that they still needed more for any of it to be actionable. That meant Mark, and all the rest of them, would have to fight. And he would have to keep hunting, however he could.

As for the weekend itself, he'd actually invited Rayne, but she was busy opening up a second bar in the city now that the Blind Watchman's popularity had exploded. Brooke flying out for a neighborly visit was still not advisable given that they didn't want Crayton or his security digging into her.

Still, Mark was curious to see who arrived for the other guests, and it was always fun to watch new arrivals to the compound stare at Crayton's towering statues like the estate was a new wonder of the world. Mark supposed the Colosseum itself actually was.

Starting Friday morning, limos began rolling up through Crayton's gates and unloading friends and family members of Crucible combatants. The first to arrive was Soren Vanderhaven's enormous clan, with two younger sisters, eight cousins, and a mother, all as gorgeous and blonde as Soren. All nearly fainted at the sight of

Chase Cassidy. He and Soren had been something of an unofficial item for a good long while now, which the *Heroes and Legends* audience ate up with a spoon.

Let's hope she doesn't have to jam that spear down his throat in the first round, Mark thought. He wasn't entirely convinced their romance was genuine, as both seemed to know exactly how to play to the cameras, and he suspected Soren especially was just trying to get inside Cassidy's head. Under all that sweetness and light and makeup, he could sense something dark and ugly. She reminded him a bit of Crayton in that way, forever putting on a performance to hide what lurked under the surface.

Mark planned to leave and simply train by himself all weekend, trying to get a competitive edge over those who had visitors. Out on the grounds, he could already see Shin Tagami practicing his different stances, and Kells Bradford sprinting around the path as she always did. They weren't expecting visitors either, then. Manny had disappeared entirely, and rumor had it that Crayton's security had him confined somewhere, though Brooke hadn't managed to track him down.

As Mark turned to head to the gym, Moses stopped him.

"Wait, wait, wait," he said. "He's here!"

A limo door opened and a tall man with wavy, dark-blond hair swept back over his ears stepped out. He broke into a wide smile as soon as he saw Moses, and the two jogged to a quick embrace and a kiss. They separated, and they walked toward Mark, Ethan, and Aria.

"Guys, this is Nolan," Moses said, beaming. "Nolan, this is . . ."

"Of course I know!" Nolan said. He had a slight Australian accent. "I watch the show, don't I?"

He extended his hand to Mark.

"Mark, pleasure. Moses won't stop talking about you," he smiled, his tan face crinkling. He was exceptionally handsome and built like a rugby player. He and Moses looked less like a couple and more like a professional wrestling tag team.

"Ethan, I'm so sorry about your wife," Nolan said, dropping the smile. "Is she coming this weekend?"

Ethan nodded.

"She is, bringing the kids, too. The doctors gave her the green light. She's very mobile, considering."

Nolan gave an empathetic nod. "I can't wait to meet them." He turned to Aria, who was eyeing a limo rounding the driveway. "And Miss Rosetti," Nolan said, bending his knees slightly and kissing her hand. "I watched a re-stream of your MBC performance of Swan Lake last week. I was in tears. Absolutely stunning."

Aria smiled.

"Thank you, Nolan. You're as charming as your husband."

"He wishes," Moses said with a belly laugh, and put his arm around Nolan. "Alright, I have to show him the statues."

Nolan rolled his eyes.

"And the history lessons begin," he said as they veered away. "Nice to meet you all, see you later."

They waved good-bye and Aria turned back to a parked limo. The doors opened, and a familiar-looking man and woman got out. Mark recognized them from the news. Her parents.

"No, no, no," she stammered. "I told them not to come. I *specifically* told them not to come!"

Mrs. Rosetti gave a weak-wristed wave. Aria glared at her, tears forming in her eyes. She turned around and stormed straight back to the manor. Mark made a move to follow her, but Ethan put a hand on his shoulder.

"She's gonna have to figure all that out herself," Ethan said. "Trust me."

Mr. and Mrs. Rosetti looked sad and bewildered as their luggage was unloaded from the trunk. Mark would have felt sorry for them if Aria hadn't told him what she had that night at the lake.

Another elderly woman got out of a limo, and Mark was

surprised to see that none other than Matthew Michael Easton walked down to meet her and immediately took her two huge suitcases into his arms. As they walked up the path toward the manor, Mark saw her eyes widen and point at him. Easton looked confused, but she shuffled toward him and he was forced to follow.

"Is that Mark? Mark Wei?" she said, squinting through an ancient pair of glasses. Mark guessed she was at least eighty-five, possibly older. "I'm Miriam Easton, Matthew's grandmother."

She extended a wrinkled hand adorned with costume jewelry, which Mark shook gently.

"Nice to meet you, ma'am," he said. Easton stared daggers at him from behind her.

"I just wanted to say, what were you thinking the other night?"

"Excuse me, ma'am?"

"You and Aria at the lake. That was the most *romantic* thing I've seen on TV in a long time! Why didn't you kiss her, you big dope?" She swung her purse so it bumped Mark lightly on the arm.

"Uhhh," Mark said, at a loss for words. Ethan was snickering.

"You're young! You only live once. You're not married are you?"

Mark paused for a beat too long.

"I'm not."

"Or a *gay* like that Moses?"

"Nope."

"Then don't let that slip away again," Miriam said, shaking her crooked finger in his face. "A girl like that only comes along once. Oh, and maybe you can help my poor Matthew here. He's never been able to find the right girl either! I think that black girl could take a shine to him. Kelly, I think is her name. Don't you think?"

Mark was trying not to burst out laughing picturing Easton and Kells together.

"Sure, ma'am, most definitely."

It seemed pretty clear the poor woman either knew nothing

about Easton's crimes, or had decided to erase them from her mind entirely.

"Anyway, nice to see you in person. Outside of Matthew, you're my favorite stream to watch!"

She hobbled away with Easton in tow, who shot Mark a glare. When she was far enough away, both he and Ethan erupted in laughter.

"Oh wow," Ethan said, finally composing himself. "That might be my favorite moment of the summer."

He was still catching his breath, he'd been laughing so hard.

"So yeah, Mark, why *didn't* you kiss her?"

"Please don't make me kick your ass before your family gets here."

The energy in the compound was dramatically changed, with the guests lightening the mood of combatants and staff alike, despite the deadly tournament beginning in just a few days. Crayton himself was popular, shaking hands and literally kissing babies in some instances, and he invited everyone to the re-opened main dining hall for a massive brunch that featured metric tons of gourmet food lining the walls and long tables that sat everyone and their visitors comfortably. Mark had been unable to pry himself away to go train, and sat with Moses, Nolan, Ethan, and his family. Aria and her parents were nowhere to be seen.

Across the way at another table, Ja'Von Jordan's family roared with laughter about something, and they made an odd mix with Rusakov's menacing Russian clan, who didn't laugh at anything and seemed pretty drunk even at 11 a.m.. Easton eyed Soren Vanderhaven's cousins hungrily as his grandmother chatted away with Rakesh Blackwood's mother, a pretty woman wrapped in an expensive-looking sari.

Ethan's wife's name was Lily, and the three children she had in tow sat more still during their meal than Mark would have imagined. Caden was seven, Sadie was five, and Kellan was three and a half. All were picture-perfect adorable, and Sadie especially made Mark's heart ache.

Asami would be a few years older than her now, he thought, as he tried not to stare and freak the girl out. The Callaghans were a friendly but rather quiet bunch, seemingly intimidated by the situation at hand. It was hard to blame them.

Lily was exceptionally pretty, like a former Miss Whatever State She Was From, though she looked skinnier than was healthy, and was quite pale as well. But still, she looked far better than Mark anticipated, supposedly having six months to live. He still didn't quite grasp the disease corroding her brain, but it was obviously not appropriate brunch conversation.

"I feel like I know you two already," Lily said, "I watch the stream so often. The kids loving seeing their dad every night before bed, even if he *is* getting his ribs wrapped up by a doctor."

"Ah," Moses said. "I believe I am to blame for that."

"I believe if my husband was using his shield correctly, he might have avoided that, so I'll blame him," she said, and the whole table laughed.

"Isn't Daddy brave on the TV?" Lily asked Caden who nodded emphatically.

"Yes," the little boy said. "He looks like a knight."

"Fights like one too," Mark said, rubbing his shoulder. "I can attest to that."

More laugher. Mark noticed a camera drone hovering around their end of the table specifically.

"I'm going to grab some more pancakes before Moses eats them all," Mark said.

"Please do," Nolan said, "with my thanks."

Mark walked over to one of the side tables where servers were standing around at attention, waiting for any tray to get even a little bit low so it could be immediately replaced. The food was incredible, like a buffet thrown for royalty. Mark scooped up his pancakes and turned around. Standing at his knee was little Kellan.

"Hey bud," Mark said, crouching down. "Looking for some more bacon?"

There were tears in Kellan's eyes.

"I don't like it here," he said. "It's so loud."

"Yeah, it is," Mark said. "We'll go outside soon, and that will be better. There are a lot of fun parks here."

Kellan looked back toward the table.

"I want my daddy!"

"Okay, sure," Mark said, extending his hand down to the little boy. "Let's go back and see him."

"No!" Kellan yelled, stomping his foot. "I *want* my *daddy!*"

"We can go to him, he's right there!"

The table was a little far; perhaps Kellan couldn't see him. Mark made the executive decision to pick him up, and Kellan promptly burst into tears.

Lily sprang up as he approached the table.

"Sorry," Mark said sheepishly. "He said he wanted his dad."

"I'm right here, Kellan, don't worry!" Ethan said, but Kellan was inconsolable.

"Looks like someone needs a nap," Lily said. "Do you have kids, Mark?"

She cringed right after she asked the question. If he did, their absence during visitation was obvious.

"Not yet," Mark said, forcing a grin. "And it's looking unlikely."

That was the closest anyone came to mentioning the looming deathmatch all meal. This weekend was supposed to be an island of happiness in a sea of dread. All the blood and death on the horizon wasn't real yet, but Mark knew it would be very soon.

After the meal, the groups separated and began taking in the grounds at their own pace. The joy of seeing their loved ones was starting to give way to a sense that they might not see them again after this. By the end of the following week, the sixteen-person tournament would be down to eight. A culling by half. It was hard to believe, and the shock of it was starting to sink in, it seemed, judging by the tears Mark saw around the estate.

All he felt was frustration. Crayton was too careful, too slippery. Despite mounting evidence, there wasn't enough to move on him. Mark knew the CIA didn't actually care about whether the tournament happened or didn't. They weren't going to try a half-assed takedown just to possibly save the lives of eight people who had more or less volunteered to die. Their endgame was Crayton and Crayton alone.

Mark watched Moses and Nolan wander into the park and saw Ethan and his family retreat to his mansion. He thought maybe he should try to track down Aria, but Ethan was right, he probably shouldn't overstep. Elsewhere, he'd be a third or fifth wheel anywhere he went at this point, so he headed to the gymnasium to grab his sword and train. He could smell death in the air, and it frightened him. After what had happened in China, it was easy to feel invincible, but he'd never faced anything like this. This was a twisted nightmare of a mission in ways he was still only beginning to comprehend.

As Mark turned to head to the gym, he saw another autolimo pull up on the pavement. A late arrival? Maybe Tagami or Manny did have a visitor after all.

The limo parked and the outer door opened before an attendant could grab it.

Out stepped Brooke, her curled blonde hair worn down and dancing on her shoulders. She wore a red sundress and a smile, probably caused by the look on Mark's face.

"Uh," Mark said as he approached the limo. She wrapped him up in a hug and whispered in his ear.

"They beefed up my girl-next-door cover. Just a friendly neighbor paying a pal a visit."

"Alright, then," Mark said, unable to stop smiling. "Wow. I just—"

"But I'm not your surprise," Brooke said, stepping back and grinning wildly.

The door on the other side of the limo opened.

Before Mark even knew what was happening, Carlo was sprinting around the back of the car. As he cleared the bumper, Mark saw his legs were fully wrapped in a pair of mech-braces, their electric motors whirring, rebalancing from the rapid movement.

"Who's a fuckin' Terminator now?" Carlo said, beaming.

Mark embraced him like a brother, and tried his best to hide his tears from the camera drones.

24

WHAT THE HELL, GUYS?" Mark said as they walked around the grounds, Carlo keeping pace easily with his braces. From the back, Mark saw they were actually laced up under his shirt and into his spine.

"Sorry, sorry," Carlo said, still smiling. "I told Brooke not to say anything. I wanted to surprise you and didn't want to be video chatting your ass when I was still stuck in bed like a waste of space."

"I can't believe it," Mark said, shaking his head.

"His recovery has been phenomenal," Brooke said. "They're putting him in the top 5 percent of all cases that sustained his type of injury. I've never seen someone bust his ass so hard at rehab therapy."

"Yeah, well next year apparently I gotta get good at swords and nunchucks and shit if I'm gonna make it to the final tourney," Carlo said.

"Carlo, you can't seriously . . ." Mark began.

"Oh, don't even start," Carlo said. "I ain't trying to get my mobility back so I can retire and play golf! I'm gonna be back and better than I ever was."

"The doctors agree," Brooke said, heading off a possible argument. "With enough time to heal, they expect a full recovery. The braces really help with muscle regeneration and stimulation, but he shouldn't even need them in another month or two."

"Expensive as all hell, though," Carlo said. "Yet another reason to sign up next year. I'm gonna be paying these off the rest of my fuckin' life."

He tapped the metal.

"Anyway, now that I'm here I should probably thank you for murdering that Nazi dickhead for me. I was gonna do it myself until they told me you beat me to it. I bet that caused quite a shitstorm."

"Not as much as you might think, actually," Mark said.

"More to follow, right?"

"No doubt," Mark said, meeting Carlo's fist bump. He could tell Brooke knew the boast was hollow.

"This place is a trip, huh?" Carlo said, looking at the fake forest around them. "Give white dudes too much money and they just go crazy. Statues and jungles and stadiums and shit. But hell, I'd trade anything to be in your shoes right now."

"You might not think so after this week," Mark said.

"You better not die on me, Wei," Carlo said. "I bet my last $100 that you're going to win this thing. Even my brother is rooting for you over Max Rage now. Don't disappoint him!"

Through the trees, Carlo spotted the Vanderhaven clan on a stroll, a gaggle of platinum blondes with deep tans, whose giggling could be heard from afar.

"Christ almighty," Carlo said. "You have *got* to start making some introductions."

Mark and Brooke laughed. It felt incredible to have him back, and Mark felt lighter than he had all summer. At least one thing had gone right.

After a lengthy tour of the estate, Mark let Carlo get settled into a room in the main mansion. Carlo deemed it "fuckin' awesome" and spent ten minutes playing with the shower alone. Mark and Brooke retreated to his room, which earned a wink from Carlo, but in reality it was the only safe place they could talk away from the prying eyes and ears of the Crucible cameras. Mark couldn't care less about the implication to the viewers at home.

"I'm guessing you're here on business," Mark said. "Not just as Carlo's escort."

Brooke reclined in one of the plush chairs that littered Mark's room while he leaned against the wall opposite the TV. Out the windows, he could see the snipers on top of the walls that had been posted there since the "crazed Cassidy fan" break-in. Crayton was clearly rattled. Brooke noticed him eying the guards. The sun was starting to set behind them.

"Yeah, that's exactly why I'm here," she said. "I thought getting up close and personal with Crayton's security systems would let me locate where they're holding whoever they captured."

"Sounds good," Mark said. "When do we start?"

There was a dark look on Brooke's face, and he knew whatever she was going to say next wasn't going to be good.

"I actually found them a few hours before my flight left," she said, pulling out a flexscreen. "This was recorded thirty-six hours ago, about six floors under where we're standing in some deep, dark sub-basement. I couldn't even route you there if I tried. The feed is video only. No mics anywhere near there."

She played the video, which was grainy and warped. An old camera, probably not meant to even be recording.

Mark squinted and could make out a figure hung by their hands from the ceiling, a bandaged bullet wound near their ribs. As he looked closer, for a brief second he saw Zhou's scarred face in the fuzzed image. But he blinked again, and the visage was gone. Another illusion. The figure was actually a woman, Asian, with close-cropped hair and a lean, muscled frame. Her lizard suit had been stripped off and was shredded in a heap by her feet, her toes barely grazing the ground. She wore the bloody ruins of a fiber undermesh, which was riddled with burn marks and knife slits.

"They tortured her," Mark said.

"I've already been going through the older footage from this," Brooke said. "She never said a word. Didn't even scream."

"Has to be MSS," Mark said. "She looks as Chinese as they come, and if they're not supposed to talk, they don't. Not ever."

"She never did," Brooke said ominously.

Another figure stepped into frame, and Mark recognized the scar on the back of his head immediately. Wyatt Axton. He barked something at her the camera didn't pick up, but she remained stone-faced. Something in his hand flashed too fast for the footage to capture properly, but the end result was clear.

The woman hung dead, the hilt of a knife sticking from her neck as fresh blood poured down her chest.

"They take the body out and do God knows what with it," Brooke said. "Probably burned. I really don't think she gave them anything. I tried to ID her, but facial capture is useless."

"They're all ghosts," Mark said, still staring at the screen after the footage cut out. He was slightly shocked by her execution, which was uncharacteristic for him.

"Can we use this?" he asked. "Crayton's head of security killing in cold blood?"

"It's in the file," Brooke said. "But again, it's not a smoking gun for Crayton himself. A lip-read complete confession would have worked wonders, but she never even opened her mouth."

Christ, Mark thought. He certainly couldn't say the same was true of him when Zhou ripped through him with his knives years ago.

THEY KEPT TALKING UNTIL the sun dipped down behind the wall, and the Glasshammer snipers were black dots against the pink sky out of the window. Mark heard a ripple of laughter from a floor down. Brooke put away the flexscreen and turned to leave.

"Better get out of here before the *Heroes and Legends* audience starts buzzing about us," Brooke said with a half-smile.

"Ah, whatever," Mark said. "It's nice seeing you outside of an S-lens, you know."

Brooke turned back toward Mark, and leaned against the door.

"You could stay, you know," he said.

Something unspoken passed between them. They both knew what it was.

"I think someone might not like that," Brooke teased, defusing the tension. "Miss Rosetti?"

"What?" Mark asked.

"I caught the episode from the night of the invasion. They put a nice little spotlight on your moment by the lake before they cut out all the other footage. I'm sure she was whispering something quite nice in your ear."

Brooke was smiling, but her eyes were a bit sad.

"No," Mark said. "It wasn't like that. It isn't like that."

"Mark," Brooke said, her tone changing into something sharper. "Why do you think that matters to me?"

"You know why," Mark said. And there it was. He didn't even have to be drunk to say it.

"It's not . . ." Brooke said. "It can't be . . ."

She looked frustrated at not being able to find the words. Mark had moved closer to her, but the look on her face made him stop. It was pain, pure and simple.

"You heard about the mountain team, right? For Spearfish?"

"I, uh, of course. I know they succeeded," Mark said, caught off-guard by the topic change. "They never told us anything about the other Spears. Deniability. Why?"

"It was a team of three," Brooke said. "They were supposed to set charges after infiltrating the base to blow the whole thing up with General Lin inside. The first piece of the puzzle."

"And they did," Mark said. "But what does—"

"Once they got out," Brooke continued. "They realized there

was too much shielding in the walls for their remote detonation signal to go through. They only had one choice."

Mark stared at her.

"One volunteered to sneak back in. Actually, they all did, as the story goes. But in the end, they drew straws, as they only needed one to bring the remote back inside the base."

"I don't understand," Mark said. "How do you know all this? You weren't even in the Agency back then, and they don't share that shit with *anyone*."

Brooke blew out a sigh.

"It was my brother, Ryan, who detonated the charges himself. He was a field op like you, hand-picked for the mission. They never recovered his body, as it was either blown up by the blasts or crushed by the collapse of the mountain itself. He's still there."

Mark blinked, stunned.

"My family buried an empty box. My parents were told he died in a training accident, and they begged me to drop out of the military altogether. They didn't know I was also training for the Agency. They already lost one child; they couldn't lose two."

"I stayed. I resisted field work for their sake, but then Gideon put an assignment on my desk. One of the Spears needed a monitor. One of the few who made it back. Deep, deep cover. Had seen and done some of the most serious shit of the entire op. He'd returned to the US, but then lost his wife and child to Chinese retaliation when his cover was breached. He was an asset too valuable to cut away completely, and they needed an eye on him. His new name was Mark Wei."

Brooke paused. Mark didn't even know what to say.

"I know you're not Ryan. I don't view you like that. But that's why I signed up, and what you've meant to me. Needless to say this whole thing is pretty . . . complicated." She lightly touched his arm. "We can't make it any more complicated."

Mark's heart broke a little bit. Partially for Brooke, what she'd lost, and what she'd done to try and help him. Partially for himself, as he knew she was right.

"I'm sorry," was all he could say, though it spoke to all manner of things.

She nodded and left.

CAMERON CRAYTON CALLED IT the "Heroes and Legends Ball." Everyone else in the compound was calling it the "End of the World Party." *Eat, drink and be merry, for tomorrow we die.*

Sunday night came too soon for those who had shown up to say good-bye to their gladiators. But the party was the final hurrah, one last bash before Monday brought with it the anticipated (or dreaded) lottery, which would determine the tournament bracket and official match-ups.

It was a black tie affair, of course, since it was Cameron Crayton they were talking about. He was also celebrating the fact that the president had finally signed his Athletic Protection Act, meaning the Crucible could proceed without legal ramifications. Mark dressed in his tux, and found Carlo looking similarly stylish. Brooke was jaw-dropping in a short gold dress with professionally applied hair and makeup, but Mark realized he needed to stop looking at her like that.

The party was everywhere. It started in one of the main manor's great ballrooms, but spilled out into every other room soon enough. Rarely a second went by where a waiter didn't pass by with a tray of top shelf drinks, and Mark allowed himself to indulge for a night after a summer of cleansing purity. After just a few bourbons, he was already feeling pretty great, and he realized that his tolerance had dipped dramatically.

All the children and elderly visitors had gone to bed, the party not even kicking off in full until eleven. The camera drones were everywhere, documenting the events of the evening for the grand finale of *Heroes and Legends*. Soon enough, Brooke split off from the main party area to "do some snooping" as she put it, determined to use her in-person access to Crayton's security and data stores for good purpose. Lord knew Mark hadn't been able to pry anything that useful from the compound, and maybe she'd have better luck.

Crayton had allowed a few of his VIP friends to join the festivities. Mark saw a few well-known CEOs and celebrities, and at least one sitting senator among the crowd. But more eye-catching was the full roster of Crayton's Muses, the porn-stars-turned-performers that were to have a revived role in promoting the final Crucible tournament. They were unmissable in their sheer togas, each one physically flawless. He saw them flock toward the Crucible combatants in particular, and soon enough he watched Rakesh Blackwood steal away with two of them tucked under his arms. Mark didn't need to imagine what Rakesh had in mind for them.

"Hi!" someone shouted from behind him. He could barely hear over the blaring music. He turned and saw a stunning redhead with black streaks in her hair wearing one of the Muses' signature white togas. The translucent fabric left little to the imagination, and he caught Ethan's wife, Lily, eying her incredulously from a little ways off.

"Hey there," Mark said. "I'm Mark."

"And I'm Carlo," Carlo interjected, sliding in his hand before Mark's even reached her.

"Nice to meet you both!" she said with a flawless smile. She couldn't be older than twenty, Mark figured. "I'm Shyla. Cameron *insisted* that I meet you, Mark."

She rolled her head toward Crayton, who was standing a ways behind her talking to the senator. He recognized the gesture and raised his glass toward them with a wink. Mark had been out of the game a while, but he understood the implication.

"I was wondering if you could show me where you practice?"

Shyla said, all innocence. "I haven't been to the gym yet. And I hear they have a pool!"

Mark's head danced with images that he quickly waved away. Standing next to him, Carlo's eyes were wide, and he was barely masking a smile.

"Actually, Shyla," Mark said. "It would mean the *world* to me if you would let my friend Carlo here take you on that tour. I have a few things to take care of here. Is that okay?"

Mark was almost offended that Shyla looked a bit relieved. She lit up when she turned to Carlo, who was grinning from ear to ear.

"Of course!" she said, and Carlo offered his arm to her. "But will you, um, be sure to tell Cameron this is what you wanted?"

There was a hint of fear in her eyes. Mark nodded, trying to be reassuring.

"Absolutely," he said.

"It's a pleasure," Carlo said, his charm dial broken off at 11. "This way. And let me just say how much I love your work . . ."

The two walked toward the ballroom exit, and Carlo turned back toward Mark, mouthing "thank you" with a look of heartfelt gratitude on his face. He was so skilled in his mech braces, he wasn't even limping.

"Mark!"

He felt a hearty slap on his back that would have made him spill his drink if it wasn't already empty.

"Drink this whiskey."

Moses handed him a rocks glass of brown liquid. Mark downed it without hesitation.

"Now drink this whiskey."

This one was from Nolan. Mark complied.

"Settle a bet. Which is better?"

"I don't know," Mark said. "I might need some more samples."

Both of them roared with laughter. In their tuxes standing a full head taller than him, they looked like a pair of action heroes presenting at the Academy Awards.

"These Muses keep attaching themselves to me like barnacles," Moses said. "I don't think they got the memo." He jerked his head toward Nolan.

"I saw their queen bee talking to you," Nolan said to Mark. "No interest there?"

Mark shook his head.

"In another life maybe. For now, I'm content to play wingman."

"Speaking of," Moses said. "Where's Aria?"

Mark hadn't seen her. He wondered what had become of her and her parents. He'd glimpsed them briefly over the course of the weekend, but only from afar.

"Don't know," Mark shrugged.

"And that pretty blonde one," Nolan said. "Where's she?"

"Around," Mark said, with a smile. "But to answer your next question, she's just an old friend. Nothing more."

Moses eyed him suspiciously.

There was a loud roar and Mark turned to see that Drago Rusakov and Ja'Von Jordan were grappling in the corner, their respective entourages trying to pry them apart. Rusakov had Jordan by the throat and shoved halfway up the wall by the time security swarmed them.

"Trouble in paradise?" Moses asked. It was unclear what had sparked the conflict between the *Prison Wars* vets.

"I suppose it's too late for them to get thrown out of the tournament," Mark said.

"Tonight, I'm guessing anything goes," Moses said.

25

MOSES WASN'T WRONG. As the night progressed, the event devolved from an initially stuffy black tie affair into something much more primal. Mark stumbled around the mansion. He'd lost track of how many drinks he'd had, but if he was conscious, he deemed that it wasn't enough. Many of the Muses weren't even wearing their togas anymore and writhed unencumbered on top of antique furniture to pulsing bass. Mark saw Naman Wilkinson and Kells Bradford making out forcefully against the parlor wall, the SEAL finally having come out of her shell on the eve of despair.

Mark wandered the halls aimlessly. He stumbled toward a doorway only to have a shirtless Dan Hagelund get up in his face before he could enter.

"Private party, Wei."

Mark saw fuzzy shapes behind him that snapped into focus. Soren Vanderhaven was stripped to the waist and wrapped around Asher Mendez. Fire burned in her eyes as she caught Mark's gaze. Hagelund slammed the door in his face.

So much for that fairy tale romance, Mark thought, thinking of her summer-long courtship with Chase Cassidy. Though lord knew what he was doing. Last he'd seen him downstairs, there'd been a half-dozen Muses swarming him like gnats.

Mark swung by his room, desperate to change his shirt, which was covered in brown liquid he hoped was liquor. He stumbled inside and tore his shirt off like a crazy person shedding a strait-jacket. He jolted upright when he heard a splash. Creeping around the corner, he peered into the cavernous bathroom. The tub was full, overflowing actually, and bubbles danced like clouds on the surface.

"Finally," a feminine voice said from the bubbly mist. "I thought you'd never show up."

A woman stood up, stark naked, suds and water sliding off her pale skin. She was Asian, Japanese, Mark guessed. As she walked closer, Mark saw that she looked like . . . she looked a lot like . . . *No, no way. Not Riko. Don't even think it.*

"I'm Kay," she said, "I'm a friend of Shyla's. And Mr. Crayton's. They said I should come see you."

She was slurring, badly. She slipped on the wet tile, and almost lost her balance entirely, her sexy strut turned instantly chaotic. Mark jumped in to steady her. She took that as an invitation to fall into his arms, and pressed herself to his bare chest.

"You should come in the tub," she giggled. Up close, she still looked a little like her. It was eerie, almost. It made him sick.

Her eyes were unfocused. She was definitely on something. Heroin, maybe. Ecstasy. That new party cocktail that had been on the news lately. Paradise? Paralyze? Mark couldn't remember. For all his vices, he wasn't up on his designer drugs.

"You should sleep," he said. More giggling. He scooped her up in his arms and carried her toward the bed.

"What? Okayyyy, this is good too," she said. "I'm gonna make you . . . I'm gonna make you feel . . ."

But she was already passed out by the time he lay her down and covered her with the comforter.

Mark brought up the TV display and called for a medical alert.

He buttoned up a new shirt and slipped out of the room as a pair of staff EMTs arrived. They could deal with her.

THE ORDEAL WAS SO bizarre, it was almost enough to sober him up, so he slammed a few more drinks before he made his way out of the mansion entirely. After that, things started to get patchy. He was in the dark forest. By the lake. Then at a guest mansion. He knew where he was going.

The party's tendrils hadn't reached this place, and the manor was quiet, dark. Mark stumbled up the stairs and found the door he was looking for. He knocked. Too hard.

On the third attempt, she answered. Aria was wearing a fringed black dress with lace heels that made her nearly as tall as him. Her hair was long and one side was tucked behind her ear. A thin silver chain was around her neck.

"Hey," Mark said.

"Hi," she replied.

"You didn't go to the party," he said.

"I did," she said, "But it was getting weird, to say the least. And Moses said you'd already left."

She was looking for him?

"You were looking for me?"

"Maybe," she said. "My parents finally left. We spent half the weekend fighting. It was exhausting. I needed a break. Come in."

Mark entered, mentally sobering himself up as much as he could manage. He was walking straight, at least.

Aria's room was as spacious as his own, but she had a balcony overlooking the row of statues back by the main mansion. They were lit up from underneath at night, and looked like giants trying to stab at the stars.

"Drink?" she asked, motioning to her expansive bar cart. Mark noticed a bottle of wine already open and half empty.

"Actually, just water. Or coffee if there's any."

Aria smiled. She reached into the fridge and pulled out two bottles, one clear, one full of chilled cappuccino. Mark took sips from both. They hit the spot in the desert heat. He was suddenly embarrassed to be this drunk, a kind of guilt that rarely plagued him.

"She's not your girlfriend, is she?" Aria said. "Brooke."

Mark laughed.

"You're the only one to guess that right so far," he said.

"And she's definitely not the one you lost."

Mark darkened.

"No."

"I know why you're here," she said.

Mark was silent.

"And you probably know why I was trying to find you."

Still silent.

"It isn't real, you know. What we're feeling. It's just this place. It's what we're doing. It's what we're about to do."

"I know," Mark said.

"It won't fix you."

"It won't fix you, either," he said.

"I know."

"Then why are we here?" Mark said. "What are we doing?"

"Because this is all we have," Aria said, wet green eyes shimmering in the dim light of the room. "These little moments, where maybe we can pretend someone still loves us."

Mark swallowed a hard lump in his throat.

"I should leave," he said, getting up.

"You should," she said, rising with him. Before he could say anything else, she took two steps forward, and her lips were on his.

"Make me believe," she whispered, pulling away. "Make me believe it's okay if the world ends."

She reached behind her back and with a twist of her wrist, her dress fell to the floor.

"I will," Mark said, breathless at the sight.

For tomorrow we die.

IT WOULD ACTUALLY BE Tuesday before anyone died. Monday was the lottery, and the tournament itself began the next day. Mark woke tangled in Aria's sheets. She was already gone, as he might have guessed. He hitched an autocart ride back to the main mansion, where Crayton's staff were hard at work cleaning up the disaster that had befallen the place last night. Mark stepped over a passed out Russian mobster and made his way to his room. Thankfully, there was no one in it this time. Even his tub had been emptied and scrubbed, his wet sheets replaced. He showered and shaved and took a half dozen aspirin to quell his pounding headache. He wished he had some of the doc's drexophine, that was how bad his skull and eyes ached. It had been a long while since he'd had to deal with the misery of a hangover. He certainly didn't miss it.

Once he was cleaned up, he heard a knock. He opened the door, and Brooke walked in.

"Christ, you look like shit," she said. "Bad time to fall off the wagon, you know."

"Just for a night," he said, rubbing his eyes. "Can you blame me? Where did you go yesterday?"

"Everywhere I could find without Crayton's security shooing me away, but I don't think I raised any flags."

Mark's brain couldn't even form another sentence. He needed coffee. Or he needed whatever Brooke had injected him with before his fight with Drescher, but that was probably too much to ask.

"Anyway, I managed to poke into a few dataports," she continued. "Didn't find any dead Chinese assassins. Oh, but I scrounged up some of Wyatt Axton's travel logs. He was recalled to DC for a Glasshammer summit when Justice Wright was killed. So that's not nothing."

"Gideon see it that way?" Mark asked, eyebrow raised.

"'Something something *circumstantial evidence* something something.' You know him. But it's worth prying into."

"I don't want to go anywhere near that guy," Mark said. "But that's really good. I feel like you did more in a night than I did all summer."

"Maybe they sent the wrong infiltrator," Brooke said with a smile. "Time to take Carlo back. Walk us out?"

"Of course," Mark said. He wished more than anything they could stay.

But no one could stay. The morning departures were tear-filled, and Mark could barely watch Ethan say good-bye to his wife and children, possibly for the last time. The same for Moses and Nolan. And he was almost a little sad when Miriam Easton didn't cry at all, seeming to believe she'd see Matthew in just a few more days once he was done with "summer camp," as she called it.

Carlo looked more sad to say good-bye to Shyla than Mark. The Muse was now wearing a tank top and shorts instead of a toga, and she and Carlo lingered, fingers laced, before he left to talk to Mark.

"I owe you so much, man. Forget Drescher. This is the best thing you've ever done for me. Gonna see her again when I'm out here for your fight."

"Awesome," Mark said. Carlo shifted one of his braces.

"And I'm gonna see you too after that," he said. "Remember, the little bro is counting on you. So is my money."

That was about as sentimental as Carlo would get, but Mark saw the faint twinkle of tears in the corners of his eyes. He gave him and Brooke a pair of hugs as they piled into the limo.

"This isn't over," Brooke whispered into his ear. "You know that. Just win, and we'll keep going. We'll get him. The net is closing, I can feel it."

Mark nodded.

"And about the other night," she said. "I'm sorry."

Mark waved her off.

"You were right," he said, his voice low. "And thank you. For volunteering. For everything you've done for me. If I make it through this, I'll try to live a less fucked up life, the way your brother should have been able to. It's a gift. One I didn't deserve."

"You did," Brooke said, touching his arm. "You still do. Don't forget that. And I will *always* have your back."

And then they were gone, and everything plunged one level deeper into madness.

THE LOTTERY WAS TENSE. No one talked. Not even those who had gotten friendly over the past few months. Mark couldn't even look at Moses or Ethan. Aria was on the opposite side of the room. He had a significant chance of being told within the next half hour that he was supposed to murder one of them at the whim of a billionaire and tens of millions of his fans. The drawing was broadcast everywhere, and Mark heard CMI employees whisper about the records the stream was breaking.

"Sixty million," one said. "The servers are starting to buckle."

It had worked then, this summer of "getting to know" the combatants with the *Heroes and Legends* reality show primer. Mark had only seen secondhand reports, but supposedly everyone in the country had been tracking his every move for months. Well, *almost* his every move, thanks to Brooke. Mark didn't even want to know what the program had shown of his evening last night. At least there was no camera in his room or Aria's.

Mark looked over and was surprised to see Chase Cassidy and Soren Vanderhaven holding hands like nothing scandalous had happened. Either Chase didn't know what Soren had been up to the previous night, or he didn't care. It seemed likely they were just good actors, playing a part. Mark suspected that was likely the case. Their plastic smiles all but confirmed it for him, and Soren had given him more venomous looks than he could count at this point. There was no way she was the petite southern belle she pretended to be. Crayton's voice jolted him out of his fixed stare. He had a fresh haircut and a light blue suit with an open collar underneath. Mark swore he looked younger every time he saw him.

"Ladies and gentlemen, we are gathered on this historic day to seed the bracket for the most significant athletic tournament in human history."

Cameron Crayton, madman, traitor, and always the king of understatement.

"These sixteen men and women represent the finest fighters in this great nation of ours. And in a little over a week's time, eight of them will be immortal, living forever in our hearts and minds as the bravest of the brave."

In other words, half of them were going to be wormfood, probably sent home to their loved ones in pieces.

"There will be one match a day from tomorrow until the following Wednesday. Eight in all. The bracket you see above," he motioned to a large, thin screen that hung above them all which displayed an empty bracket with sixteen slots like they were about to start a March Madness pool, "will be filled in presently. Our randomized algorithm will pair the fighters without any regard for weight, skill, gender, popularity. It will simply be that, random."

Mark wondered why they needed an unbiased algorithm that worked just as well as picking names out of a hat. Not enough drama there, he supposed.

"I've brought in outside experts to examine our systems to determine that the selection system is perfect. I don't want any Vegas bookies on my back," Crayton chuckled.

The room was silent except for a few courtesy laughs from CMI staffers. The audience at home was probably laughing their heads off, though, Mark thought. Crayton had that effect on idiots.

"The draws here will be in order. The first two called will fight tomorrow. The next two, Wednesday. And so on. This is what it's all been for. All the matches, the training, the heartache, the drama. All for the glory of the Crucible."

All for the glory of Cameron Crayton, Mark thought.

"And," he said, pressing a few keys on his flexscreen. "The first fighters will be . . ."

The only drumroll was the thundering of every heart in the room.

"Mark Wei."

Of course. Of course he was going first. *God fucking damn it.*

His heart stopped. His stomach twisted. His mind raced. Crayton's pause was the longest two seconds of his entire life.

"And Chase Cassidy!"

26

THE REST OF THE event was a blur. Mark remembered shaking Cassidy's hand, the man trying to look as strong and confident as he did in his films, but with a tiny hint of terror behind his eyes.

Mark heard the other names called, cheers, gasps, and so on. Moses was fighting Mendez. Ethan was fighting Jordan. Aria was fighting Easton. That last one made him a bit ill. The bracket quickly filled up, but he'd have to process it all later. He had to fight in less than twenty-four hours, and immediately after the lottery concluded, he was led away by CMI staff to meet with Arthur, who had finally finished crafting his armor and weapon.

"Sorry for the delay," Arthur said, "But there were some materials complications with all the suits. Your practice gear, however, should allow you to slide into the new suit with ease, and swordplay should be easier, if anything, given the blade I've designed."

Mark just nodded, still trying to process the pairing with Cassidy. He didn't particularly like the man, but he'd been watching his movies half his life. The first part of the Max Rage trilogy had been his third date with Riko at the makeshift theater on base. The man was an icon.

But most importantly, he was not a killer.

The Crucible roster was full of soldiers and criminals who had killed before. But the athletes and this *actor*? This was when they were at an innate disadvantage. Cassidy excelled at training, Mark had seen that much, but it was another thing entirely when you were being asked to plunge that very real blade into very real flesh. Could Cassidy do it? Could his time at the Crucible graduate from publicity stunt to a murderous rampage through the bracket? Mark doubted it, but he'd underestimated Cassidy before, and he knew he shouldn't again. Who knew what kind of man was really lurking behind that pretty face? The fact that it was the kind who'd sign up for something like this worried Mark.

"Just slip this on first," Arthur said, offering him a fiber under-suit. "It will help make it all more comfortable."

Mark snapped out of his daze and stripped, zipping himself into the base layer. After that, Arthur began pulling armor out of boxes. The black plates that looked nonsensical by themselves, but as Mark watched in the mirror opposite him, they began to take shape the more of them Arthur added. He was rattling off all sorts of stats about their chemical composition, but Mark couldn't process most of it.

"Will it stop a blade?" Mark asked plainly. "That's the main concern."

"That depends on the blade, and the angle," Arthur said, speaking in his usual rapidfire. "There's a difference between being poked with a shortsword and crushed with a greataxe. Protect your joints and the cracks, that's what your instructors tell you. You don't have a shield, but I would avoid using your arm for direct blocking, as appealing as that option may be in a pinch. A sharp blade could get through even the dense plating there. And my blades are *sharp*."

Mark swung his arms in and out, and walked around in a circle. The weight was the same as the practice gear, but this refined suit was much more comfortable. The plates didn't jostle for position on his body; they glided in and out of one another effortlessly. It was masterful engineering.

"You gave up some protection to be mobile," Arthur continued. "But you've still got plenty. Hell, these plates could actually deflect *bullets* from most angles."

Arthur was finishing up with the final few pieces. Armored to the neck, Mark looked like a cross between a combat droid and a superhero. It was much more modern than he was envisioning, given Crayton's obsession with the past. The matte black made him look rather terrifying. Arthur handed him a helmet that looked like it had been pulled off the body of an intergalactic bounty hunter. Mark had to admit, it was pretty cool. He tried it on and found the entire interior of the helm was translucent, giving him a full field of vision. That was without question military-grade tech, as Arthur had hinted at earlier.

"Well, it's not a wolf's head," Mark said, taking the helmet back off. "Where is the wolf anyway? I thought that was mandatory."

Arthur smiled.

"Don't you see it?"

Mark peered at himself in the mirror. Suddenly, like an optical illusion, the visage appeared to him. The overlapping plates on his chest, shoulders and abdomen were arranged in a way that gave the vague impression of a wolf's face, eyes, ears, snout. It was almost seamlessly integrated, both menacing and beautiful at the same time.

"That's fucking fantastic," Mark said, unable to hide his excitement about the ensemble. "Great job."

Arthur beamed.

"But now, the *pièce de résistance!*"

He opened a long, flat box that had been sitting near them the whole time.

Arthur lifted the sword out like it was a holy relic, and it certainly looked like one. It was long, maybe a centimeter or two longer than the practice bastard sword he'd been using. The hilt was black to match his armor, but the blade was such an intensely mirrored silver it was practically white in the brightness of the lab. The cross-guard and pommel were stylized to match his plating. The effect made it look like a futuristic movie prop rather than anything medieval, but Arthur assured him it could do some very real damage.

Mark took it into his hands, and found that it was exceptionally light. At least half a pound under the practice sword.

"I know, I know," Arthur said, seeing his reaction. "I was supposed to match the weight of what you've been training with, but when I found those extra ounces I could shave off, I couldn't resist."

"I mean, that's great," Mark said, turning the sword over in his hands. "If you didn't sacrifice durability. This thing's not going to snap on me, is it?"

"Never!" Arthur said. "No way. Or you get your money back."

"It's free, and I'll be dead," Mark said.

"Yeah, uh, bad joke," Arthur said, scratching the back of his neck.

Mark practiced a few quick stances, and Arthur hopped back to be as far from the edge as possible. He could be fast with this, Mark realized. Very, very fast. He was kind of in love, even from the first few swings.

"That blade might be my favorite of all of them," Arthur said. "I can't wait to see it in action. Err . . ."

Mark ignored the perceived offense.

"What can you tell me about what Cassidy's using?"

"Ah, yes, I'm meeting with him right after you."

Mark eyed another pile of crates nearby. Another long flat one sat on the floor.

"But I'm not allowed to discuss that," Arthur said, his eyes darting to the side.

"Not even a hint?" Mark said, snapping the sword into a magnetic holster on the back of his armor.

"Well . . . I'm not breaking the rules to remind you that he was in *Shogun Rising*."

"Riiight," Mark said, eyes narrowing.

"So you may have some . . . flashbacks to that film when you face him in the arena."

He'd settled on the katana then. Mark had seen him use a multitude of weapons, but he stuck with that one the most. And it probably meant lighter armor as well.

"That'll do," Mark said, and Arthur breathed a sigh of relief he wasn't going to be interrogated further. Mark began stripping the plates off and Arthur reassembled them on a nearby mannequin. As he reached for his leg plate, Arthur stopped.

"Oh, and before I forget," he said. He grabbed a long, thin piece of plating near the calf and something clicked. A foot-long, flat knife slid out of the shin.

"For emergencies."

A crazed Hollywood superstar was about to try and decapitate him with a katana as 250,000 people cheered live. Mark's entire existence was a nonstop state of emergency.

Mark had a few hours later that night to practice with the new armor and sword to get used to them more. He was amazed how comfortable both felt, and despite the added weight and a complete lack of electronic-motorized assistance, he felt he could still move pretty damn well. His days of doing backflips during fights were probably over, but Arthur had delivered on the promised mobility. The training gear had been adequate for the summer, as now all the forms, stances, attacks, and parries he'd been practicing came even easier. It was like training with weighted gloves, then finally being able to slip on the real thing, and punch twice as fast. Or at least, that's what it felt like.

He was tempted to practice all night, but knew that wasn't smart. He needed sleep, though that was going to be hard to come by. He thought a drink might help, but decided the wiser course was probably to just walk around the grounds for a bit to settle his nerves.

Though the cameras were gone with the bracket being the last episode of *Heroes and Legends*, security was heavier than ever, and Mark passed an entire battalion of patrolling Glasshammer guards as he made his way toward the lake. He thought of Axton and the woman in the basement, and how the man would probably do the same thing to him if he was discovered. CIA or MSS, Crayton seemed like a nation in and of himself as of late, and he would protect his interests accordingly.

Mark made his way to Shin Tagami's meditation bluff, but stopped midway up the hill when he heard music drifting down to him and saw a shadow moving up near the top.

As he drew closer, he realized it was Aria. The music was classical, a score to a ballet he'd never seen. Wearing a flowing crop top and fitted yoga shorts, she was performing to an audience of crickets and fireflies, the drones having long fled. Mark crept into the shadow of the tree, not wanting to disturb her as she pirouetted and . . . well, that was the only vaguely ballet-related term he knew.

But it didn't matter. The language she was using transcended actual words. It was mesmerizing as she moved against the low moon, her long limbs moving gracefully with the melody. It wasn't all ballet, he thought. She simply went where the music took her, which resulted in all manner of hypnotizing movements. It was tantalizing without being overtly erotic. It was raw talent without being showy. She was simply made to do this.

Mark forgot all about the impending doom of the next day. He had to refrain from bursting into applause when she finished, and shut the music off from her phone on the ground.

She didn't jump when she saw him. Just smiled.

"You should be sleeping," she said.

"This was better," Mark said. "I . . . needed that."

"To spy on me dancing?" Aria teased.

"To see something beautiful."

"Quite the line there, Mr. Wei," she said with a weak smile,

"No line," Mark said. Her expression changed and he could tell she believed him. The darkness crept in and the playfulness departed.

"That was my sister's routine," she said. "The audition she never performed. I memorized it just from watching it once. That's how stunning it was. It's seared in my mind and strangely, it's the only dance that brings me any kind of peace anymore."

"Brought me some as well," Mark said. He noticed she didn't seem shaken at all from her pairing with Easton on Sunday. She was one of the last fights, but lord knew he didn't want to bring any of that up now. He looked behind her toward the wall. The snipers were invisible in the darkness. The statues weren't lit tonight, making the whole estate nearly pitch-black outside of security flashlights and insomniacs in the mansions.

"First time I've danced all summer," she said. "I didn't want to with the cameras still around."

"Can't blame you for that," Mark said.

Neither of them wanted to mention the previous night. Not to rave about it. Not to decry it as a mistake. They were both just content to let it be what it was. He felt *something* for the girl in front of him. But it wasn't just one thing. Attraction, pity, friendship, sadness, love, and guilt. He hadn't been with anyone else since Riko. Not until last night. All of it was a tempest inside him. It was paralyzing.

"Can you tell me about her now?" Aria asked, reading his mind. "Now that the flying cameras have gone?"

She gestured above them to a night sky free of drones.

Mark hesitated. He knew what training said. It was a risk. To him. To the mission. Even to her. He couldn't.

But he did.

"The car just exploded," he said, his voice low. "Bomb wired straight to the battery. They didn't even pretend it was a malfunction. I was in a meeting. Another debrief. The endless fucking debriefs. I didn't believe it when I got the call. It was *US soil*. That was a fucking act of *war*. It was impossible. But then I saw the mangled pile of ash and bone. I saw the crater in my driveway."

Aria looked confused.

"Why?"

"It was supposed to be me. For something *I'd* done. I was going to take the car that day, but I was worried about fucking *parking* because I got a ticket last time since I'd lost my pass. Jesus, how stupid."

Aria stood silent.

"It wasn't just her," Mark said. "It was both of them. It was my entire life."

"A child."

"A daughter."

Silence.

"Did you find them? The ones that did it."

"It was one man. He was just angry. At me. For what I'd done. They killed him trying escape by boat. Nuked him with all the brimstone a Hellbird could offer. I saw his pile of ash and bone too. It didn't help. Nothing could."

"Nothing but this," Aria said. The Crucible, was the implication. His penance.

She didn't understand. Not fully. How could she? He'd already said way too much. But if she was a Crayton plant, he was dead already. And he was practically past the point of caring.

But there was no hidden mic. No security team emerged from the shadows to take him down and torture him until his mangled cover story broke. It was just her, with tears in her eyes, feeling that same mix of pity and love, perhaps.

"Do you think you'll see them again?" she said. "If you fall tomorrow?"

"I don't know," Mark said, feeling lightheaded. "I wish I could believe that."

"Was last night . . ." she began, finally daring to broach the subject.

"It was what I needed."

"And what do you need now?"

"I don't know. This is all starting to feel like some kind of fever dream."

"I know."

"I'm sorry if . . ."

She stopped him with a hand on his chest.

"No apologies. Right now just stay with me here. It's just us and the stars. No more eyes. No more ears."

Aria led him by the hand to the base of the colossal tree that overlooked the lake. She peeled off his shirt, and then her own. She was even more beautiful in starlight. Mark knew he was sober this time, but everything was drifting between fantasy and nightmare. Nothing felt real. Like he could just wake up at any moment.

"Forget the pain," Aria said. Brooke said. Riko said. Their faces blurred together as one.

"Remember the love. Remember what it was like to live."

Mark felt like he was falling. She whispered, "Oblivion can wait."

PART III

"What is my greatest ambition in life?
To become immortal . . . and then die."
—Jean-Luc Godard

27

THANKS FOR TUNING INTO SportsWire, your *only* stop for the best Crucible news and commentary. I'm Jayce Harrington, joined as always by my cohost, Melanie Mitchell. And of course, our panel wouldn't be complete without our favorite guests, Turk Smith and Johanna Viseberg."

"Glad to be here, Jayce. You excited?"

"Of course! How could anyone not be? You've seen the crowd that's inside Crayton's Colosseum right now. Simply unprecedented!"

"That's 252,144 in attendance. Security's tight, but I'm willing to bet a few more snuck in."

"Well it's certainly not something you want to miss, though I'm told many of our international viewers are going to have to do just that, isn't that right, Turk?"

"Correct. Countries all across the globe have banned public access to the Crucible stream, and our beautiful faces here in the commentary booth. What a crime!"

"Why is that, do you think?"

"They keep citing 'America's culture of violence' and other non-sense, but please, this is an *athletic competition* and deserves to be treated as such. This is the USA at its best, if you ask me. Great stories. Great competition. Freedom and honor."

"You can hear that in the roar of the crowd, and today's match hasn't even started yet."

"And who *is* your pick in today's first match, Jayce? We haven't even touched on it yet."

"Good point, Turk! It's easy to look out our back window into the faces of a quarter million fans and get lost. As a reminder to our viewers who have managed to avoid any sort of news outlet the past few days, our first match is between the Lion of Los Angeles, A-list action star Chase Cassidy, and the Windy City Wolf, ex-Navy SEAL Mark Wei."

"Ex-mercenary too, don't forget."

"Yes, Melanie, you're always quick to remind us of that. I take it Cassidy is your pick then?"

"He is, but not just because I dislike Wei. I think as an actor who is used to screaming fans and media overload, Cassidy is probably going to have a cooler head than Wei out on the sand today. Combined with obvious physical skill, I think he'll come out on top."

"Johanna, do you agree?"

"I can see that argument, and it's something that might benefit many of the athletes in the tournament as well, from Naman Wilkinson to Dan Hagelund to Soren Vanderhaven. But I wouldn't discount actual military training as a means of learning lethal force. And I'm sure none of us can forget that we've already seen Mark Wei kill in the ring before it was even mandatory."

"Great point, Johanna. I still have that Wei versus Drescher fight seared in my mind."

"So Wei is your pick, Turk?"

"I don't know. Being a soldier in the modern military era doesn't exactly train you to use something like a longsword. It really depends on how fast he's picked up the skill. But Cassidy has used weapons in probably at least a half dozen of his films, and even if it was prop fighting, some of that has to translate. But Wei is dangerous, we know that."

"Looking ahead, who do you think are the strongest options to take the entire tournament, and the billion-dollar first prize? Jayce, any thoughts?"

"It's hard not to say Drago Rusakov. The man was an absolute terror in *Prison Wars* and I think that experience makes him far and away the most formidable of any competitor here. Not to mention his sheer size and strength."

"True, but I wouldn't count out Matthew Michael Easton either. He doesn't seem like he'd really be built for this, but he's quick as lightning and showed in *Prison Wars* that if you give him a blade, he will find a vein."

"But what about the newcomers? Anyone jump out at you, Johanna?"

"Well, I know both Dan Hagelund and Asher Mendez personally, and they're each incredibly talented fighters. Not sure how they'll fare with weapons, but they've got a killer instinct all the same. I'm probably most curious to see how Soren Vanderhaven does, given her gymnastics background."

"Ah yes, and who could forget her whirlwind romance with Cassidy during *Heroes and Legends*? Reports say they're closer than ever heading into the tournament, and polling says they're the most popular of all sixteen combatants."

"Didn't Wei have a little thing with the dancer, Aria?"

"I know they had their breakfast club with Moses Morton and Ethan Callaghan, but I'm not sure anything ever came of that. She's way out of his league, in any case."

"Trying to get her number, Turk?"

"I'm just sayin'!"

"Well, Cassidy and Vanderhaven are on opposite sides of the bracket, so they'll be spared a potential match for a while yet, if it comes to that. Melanie, we haven't heard your pick yet."

"Well I mean, I'm not sure how he'll fight, but how can you *not* root for Ethan Callaghan? The man is a veteran, with a beautiful family and a wife who desperately needs not only the money for medical treatment, but for her husband to come home and be a father to his children. If that's not a reason to fight, and live, I don't know what is."

"And you, Turk?"

"I can see the appeal of Rusakov, Cassidy, and many of the others, but I'm telling you, I can't get Mark Wei out of my head. Something is seriously *wrong* with that dude, and in this situation, that might be exactly what's needed to win."

MARK WATCHED THE SAND swirl around the toes of his black metal boots. His sword was slung over his back and his helmet was in his hand. He supposed he should be looking at a flag during the national anthem, and lord knew there were enough of them streaming from a hundred poles planted around the top of Crayton's monument to American exceptionalism.

He didn't know the teenage pop singer belting out the rendition of the song, but it was well done and seemed to be moving Cassidy to tears. Twenty feet away, Mark had been sizing up his opponent's armor since he was introduced. It was indeed samurai inspired, with long, flat plates painted crimson. But instead of traditional pauldrons, he had hulking, snarling, golden lion heads on each of his shoulders. The design of his entire ensemble was much more ornate than Mark's matte black plating, and he definitely looked like he'd shown up to film *Shogun Rising 2*. But Mark knew the blade on his hip was anything but fake.

Brooke had tried to send him some last-minute motivation via S-lens. She'd done some digging and it turned out Cassidy was dangerously close to broke. Though he was the biggest action star of the last decade, in *this* decade he'd financed a number of awful pet projects that bombed at the box office and nearly wiped him out. Brooke's implication was that there was a good chance very little of his winnings would go to charity, if any, and would instead go toward his debts. He wasn't as squeaky clean as he looked, and that could explain the desperation of someone like him signing up for something like this.

Mark didn't really care. Whether he thought Cassidy was a shining paragon of heroism or a total fraud, he still needed to die. Even if he was the former, the mission required that, if given the chance, Mark would have to bury his blade into the man without hesitation.

The crowd wouldn't like that. He saw a sea of red and gold, and an endless parade of lion-themed gear. Though he was surprised to see a solid smattering of black in the audience with signs rooting for "Wolf Wei," as some called him. The audience hadn't completely forgotten his iconic bout with Drescher, which had earned him a lot of fans who wanted to see revenge for Carlo's unwarranted mauling. But he wouldn't have a quarter the support of Cassidy, and he had to just block all of that out.

But it was impossible. The view from the sand was like nothing he'd ever seen. He'd been to football games before, so his fight in front of sixty thousand people at Soldier Field, though overwhelming, had not been completely unprecedented.

This? This was something else entirely. 250,000 fans were shouting, chanting, cheering for the biggest "athletic" event in world history. It was a 360-degree tidal wave of human beings arching up toward the sky in the oval arena. Mark had no idea how many millions were watching on TV, but he was guessing that was breaking some records as well. And somewhere out there in the VIP boxes were Brooke, Carlo, Moses, Ethan, and Aria, watching to see if he would be the victor or the vanquished.

It was easy to forget that just a short while ago, Mark had been in a pit of despair and isolation. After Spearfish, he was left with no one, and nothing. But now? There were at least a handful who cared about him, and weirdly, millions of strangers cheering him on as well.

It consumed him. He couldn't help it. He forgot the mission. He was *living history* at this moment. Despite Crayton's insanity and the horror of what was to come, in that moment he was *proud* he was standing on that sand. The rush of it all could trick him into thinking it might possibly be the greatest moment of his life.

But for the mission, *or* for some twisted sense of glory, he had to win. He had to live. That was all that mattered now.

Crayton stepped forward to the edge of his box. It wasn't high up like the luxury penthouse suites; it was only thirty or so feet from ground level, the best seat in the house by a mile, and naturally, about where emperors and dignitaries used to sit when they attended arena bouts in ancient Rome.

The crowd went wild for the man, and after about five straight minutes of cheering, he had to start signaling for them to quiet down. He wore a light gray suit with a blood red shirt underneath. Mark was half surprised he didn't have a wreath of laurels placed on his golden head, but he supposed even Crayton drew the line somewhere.

"Gentlemen, if you'd take your positions," he said, motioning toward two faint circles in the sand about thirty paces apart. Mark and Cassidy walked over to them, their footprints evaporating with a fresh gust of wind. They turned to face him.

We who are about to die salute you, Mark thought. But despite all Crayton's delusions of grandeur, it really wasn't him they were dying for. It was the swarm of camera drones flying over their heads, capturing every angle of the carnage and broadcasting it to every inch of the country. The Crucible existed because *they* demanded it.

They're not ready for this, Mark thought, looking at the blur of faces in the crowd. *They think they are, but this will be like nothing they've ever seen.*

"We honor you, Chase and Mark, as two of the bravest men in this country. To risk life and limb for honor, for glory, for victory. Not only will everyone here remember you forever, but so will *history itself.*"

Mark's heart swelled involuntarily, and he swallowed a large lump in this throat.

Get ahold of yourself.

He couldn't get caught up in the moment, however larger-than-life it may be. He had one job. One mission.

"Please, address the crowd and your audience at home, for what may be the final time."

He gestured toward them. Cassidy didn't hesitate to start speaking, and a camera drone flew in to hover about three feet from his face.

"Above and beyond anything else, I want to thank my fans. Without you, I'd be nothing, and I'm so glad you've been on this journey with me. I want to thank you, Mr. Crayton, for giving me this chance, and also introducing me to the love of my life."

Soren. Gag.

"With all of your support," he said, "I know I will be victorious today. But I'd like Mark here to know I only have the utmost respect for him and his service, and it's an honor to face him on the sands today."

The crowd went wild as Cassidy ended his remarks, and Crayton turned to Mark. The camera drone drifted over to him. How many millions were behind this lens? Mark had a sudden urge to blurt out everything. The mission. Crayton's shady past. His government ties. He wanted to rant about the decline of America, that the country had crumbled into . . . this. Watching two men murder each other for money, their pending deaths celebrated. The Crucible was an abomination, and after today, everyone watching, cheering, would lose a piece of their soul.

He turned to face Cassidy.

"I'm sorry," he said softly, but the drone mic boomed it around the entire arena like he was shouting. The crowd took it as trash talk and started booing immediately, but Mark hadn't meant it like that. He didn't want to kill this man. No one deserved to die just for being a pompous asshole.

"Alright then!" Crayton said upon realizing Mark didn't have his own big last words speech planned. "Gentlemen, the countdown will begin shortly, and after that, your fight will commence. You cannot leave the ring, and the fight is not over until one of you has expired. The vital monitors embedded in your armor will be displayed onscreen at all times for reference."

On the giant, football-field sized screen above them, two pulsing lines showed each of their heart rates. Both were elevated, but Cassidy's was higher than Mark's.

It's not his fault, he's never stared into this abyss before.

Mark thought back to the *Hóngsè Fēng*, the massive ship looming ahead in the black water, full of probable death. But if he could survive it, his ticket to life, a future. A way home. He felt that way now. Maybe if he could live through all this, he could start over. Maybe.

Mark donned his helmet, which clicked into his neck plating seamlessly. He'd worn many combat helms before, but they always were alive with electronic readouts. This was just a blank sphere, a kind of fishbowl that dimmed the Vegas sun and muted the crowd a bit. No digital HUD allowed. It was oddly calming.

Mark cast another glance back to the crowd. This wasn't *Prison Wars*, which didn't have a live audience. This was a quarter of a million people about to witness an open-air execution.

They're not ready.

Suddenly, the countdown started. The arena became alive with bright LED lights that started on the north side balconies that separated the tiers of the building, and raced around the entire stadium in a circle to the south. When the lights hit the giant viewscreen, a number appeared.

5.

The lights reset, and coursed through the entire stadium again until . . .

4.

Crayton sat back down, shielded behind glass. He smiled . . .

3.

Mark's heart raced and matched Cassidy's lines on the monitor. Above them, the giant number . . .

2.

Mark watched the lights sweep across the balconies. He saw a thousands of camera flashes. A sky full of buzzing black drones . . .

1.

He tried to picture Riko. Instead he saw the crater, and the ashes. He was glad she wasn't alive to see this. He was glad Asami would never know what her father would turn into.

Zero. The crowd erupted.

Cassidy's blade hummed as he whipped it out of its sheath and sprinted toward Mark, not wasting a moment. Apparently he was hoping for a quick kill, to catch Mark off guard before he could find his bearings in the overwhelming surroundings.

But Mark's nerves were steel, forged in fire that Cassidy couldn't even begin to comprehend. He reached over his left shoulder and came back with Arthur's perfect blade. They were starting too far apart for Cassidy to catch him unaware. Mark easily brought the blade down and swatted aside the actor's aggressive swing. Sparks flew, and the crowd exploded with a fresh round of cheers.

By Cassidy's third swing, the crowd had already launched into a familiar chant.

"Cass-i-dy! Cass-i-dy!"

Mark shut it out as best he could. The helmet helped, but he had more pressing concerns than the unsupportive spectators.

Cassidy was incredibly fast, and had clearly spent the requisite amount of time mastering the katana, which was nearly the same length as Mark's bastard blade. The swords met over and over, sparks erupting with each clash, but none of them had managed to even land a glancing blow on either's armor yet.

Mark tried to control his breathing with each strike, knowing he'd need to conserve energy if the fight lasted longer than even a few minutes. The armor, though lighter than it could have been, was still oppressive without any electronic assists whatsoever embedded in the joints. Fortunately, the adrenaline surging through Mark's body was allowing him to move faster than he ever had in training.

Most of Cassidy's blows were overhand, and Mark found himself turning his own sword horizontal to deflect the hammering downward thrusts. He tried to find an opening to stab toward his midsection, but Cassidy had mastered a twisting deflection that cast Mark's blade off harmlessly to the side with each attempt.

Christ, Mark thought. *Why did he have to be good at this?*

Cassidy was no play actor. Not anymore. He had a real talent with his weapon, and fear was starting to infect Mark like a virus. Could he actually . . . die here? It had always been possible, but the threat never felt real.

Suddenly, Cassidy dove in with an unexpected straight lunge and bit into Mark's armor just below the armpit. Mark almost twisted out of the way, but not quite. At first he felt nothing, but then in a few moments liquid fire starting burning near his upper ribs. Blood dotted the sand. The katana was so sharp he'd barely felt it, but the aftereffects were excruciating. The crowd roared as soon as one of the drones spotted the wound.

FIRST BLOOD appeared on the giant screen above, and showed Mark putting his gloved hand to his side.

No more of that, he thought, and deflected Cassidy's next offensive lunge. Drawing blood had emboldened him further, and he would just. Not. Stop. Attacking. Mark blocked and parried but the strikes kept coming. Finally, as Cassidy went for a leaping overhead slice meant to split his head in half, Mark lunged forward and plowed into him with his shoulder. Armor met armor and Cassidy was thrown back, tumbling on the sand. Mark moved in for a downward thrust, but only managed to get his blade stuck in the ground as Cassidy rolled out of the way.

Mark gripped the handle of his sword to pull it out, but didn't have time as Cassidy was already on his feet and swinging the katana to try and slice through his neck. Mark ducked once, twice, and then finally wrenched the blade out of the earth.

Cassidy's next swing caused their swords to lock, and the blades ground against each other, their helmets mere inches apart. Cassidy wore a golden faceplate that mirrored his own handsome visage.

Mark's helmet was a blank sphere of nothingness, and he imagined Cassidy could see his own reflection in it.

The golden face lunged forward in an attempted headbutt, but Mark quickly retreated, freeing one hand from his sword and hooking it around the bottom of Cassidy's helmet. He dropped to the ground in a quick judo move, and Cassidy tumbled over his back. Mark rose, and realized he'd managed to rip off Cassidy's helmet entirely. He tossed it behind him, and looked into the actor's wild eyes. The drones zoomed in on Cassidy's face; a bruise was already starting to form on his cheekbone where the helmet must have caught it. He was panting, and Mark realized he was too.

"Is that it?" Cassidy said, raising his arms wide. He was far enough away where Mark couldn't lunge at him. The crowd ate up the taunt, and it seemed to imbue the actor with fresh energy. He sprinted at Mark again, and whipped the katana around almost too fast to see. Mark raised his sword just in time, deflecting the strike, but as soon as he did, another was on its way. But Cassidy's power had thrown Mark off balance. He couldn't bring the sword up in time so he . . .

Raised his left arm.

A direct slice might have taken his arm clean off, but the angle was such that the blade dug into the forearm plate and slid horizontally into his flesh. Mark's scream reverberated inside his helmet, and was broadcast to the entire arena through an embedded mic near his throat.

He twisted his arm violently and the blade dug deeper, but it became clear it was lodged in the plating so Cassidy couldn't extract it. The actor's smile from the damaging strike turned into a look of horror as he realized couldn't wrestle the katana away.

The sword was heavy in just his right hand, but Mark brought it around as quickly as he could manage. Cassidy jogged left, but the blade bit into a crack in the armor near his hip, and his face contorted in agony. The shock of the wound was enough that he finally did rip the sword out of Mark's arm, and both of them grasped their plating where blood was now flowing freely.

Mark tried a two-handed grip, but found he could barely close the fingers of his left hand. The entire appendage felt numb. But he forced them shut with the armored fingers of his other hand and swung downward toward Cassidy's collar. The actor forgot the pain long enough to raise his sword, but Mark bounced off the parry and spun around into an almost identical blow. The power of it shook Cassidy to the bone, and he nearly dropped his weapon.

Leaping forward, Mark lashed out with a straight kick that hit Cassidy right in the solar plexus. He followed up with a lunge that was only barely deflected by the katana, but it got him in close enough to smash an armored elbow directly into Cassidy's exposed face.

The blow stunned Cassidy, and he staggered back, clutching a newly broken nose. He raised his blade to deflect Mark's next swing, and managed to find his senses and counter with a riposte that sent Mark off balance as he dodged it. Cassidy darted forward with a one-armed straight thrust, and though Mark curved around it, Cassidy whirled around and Mark caught a flash of something silver in the air before the middle of his back flared with pain. The crowd gasped in horror before breaking out into cheers.

Cassidy had another weapon hidden in his armor, something smaller, and sharp, and now buried up to its handle in Mark's back. He had to look at himself in the monitor to see it, the handle in a gap in the plating between his shoulder blades. It looked like a Tanto, a Japanese knife that was often paired with longer katanas like the one Cassidy had. Mark gasped, but realized as the air filled his lungs that they hadn't been punctured. In one motion he pulled the blade from his back and raised his sword to deflect Cassidy's next strike. The bloody Tanto hit the ground silently. Through the pain, Mark remembered his own knife hidden in his shin plating, but his concentration was repeatedly broken by fresh blows from Cassidy, whose face was contorted into a mask of fury. The sparks from the swords danced in his eyes. Cassidy was a man possessed. The crowd hadn't stopped chanting his name since the fight started.

Mark was now losing a worrying amount of blood. He could feel it beneath his armor, seeping down his undersuit and saw it venting through the mesh soles of his boots, creating red footprints in the sand. Judging by how much blood he saw and how much his head was starting to swim, Mark knew this fight had a time limit, and it was just about up.

Deflecting Cassidy's next few strikes, Mark found a window. With his most powerful blows, Cassidy's swings sent him a little off balance because of his oversized lion pauldrons, something he obviously hadn't trained with.

Mark thought about Carlo and their fights with Drescher. He stopped deflecting. And started dodging.

Cassidy missing his swings completely caused him to stagger even further. Hitting only nothing but air began to frustrate him, and his swings became more and more aggressive, desperate. If he understood Mark's wounds, he would have realized he should be playing defense and let him expire on his own, but he was trying to be the hero. Trying to go for the money shot with a single strike to end it all in bloody glorious Hollywood fashion.

Cassidy had seen too many movies.

Finally, Mark seized the window he was searching for. After one particularly ambitious missed swing, Cassidy stumbled forward a few steps, carried by his over-heavy top half. Mark grabbed him by the edge of his left pauldron and wrenched him downward as he raised up his plated knee and smashed it into Cassidy's forehead.

The punishing blow righted Cassidy instantly, and his katana slipped from his fingers, his brain momentarily detached from the world around him.

Before Cassidy's eyes refocused, Mark's plunged the longsword straight through his abdomen, and out his lower back. The pain hadn't registered yet. It was all shock. They stood there for a moment, joined together by Mark's blade. Mark stared through his helmet into Cassidy's wide, terrified eyes.

"Is this . . ." Cassidy whispered, too low for the mics to hear. "I . . ."

Blood startled bubbling out of his mouth, choking out any other words. A hush had fallen over the crowd as soon as the blade went in.

Mark pulled back, taking the sword with him, which was red up to its hilt.

Cassidy collapsed to one knee, clutching his stomach, which was spilling blood and bile onto the sand. He lurched forward, and was now on his hands and knees, the ground quickly growing red all around him. He raised his head as the camera drones orbited above them. The handsome face was a mess of black, blue, and crimson.

It should have been over, but it wasn't. Not yet. Not while that heart rate monitor up above them still had peaks and valleys.

Mark looked over to Crayton, who had risen to his feet, along with the rest of the crowd. Mark asked an unspoken question, and Crayton nodded. Of course he had to. That was the point, wasn't it?

Cassidy started to shake in his ornate armor. His breaths were halted, his eyes starting to glaze.

It's a mercy, now, Mark told himself. *This is ugly. I knew it would be.*

Cassidy began to crawl toward his katana, a few feet away half-covered in sand. But he collapsed with each new motion before jerking himself back to his hands and knees.

Mark walked slowly over to him, bloody footprints trailing behind him. He raised the sword over his head and aimed at a slit in Cassidy's layered back plating.

The blade went clean through once more, but this time with better aim. Mark split Cassidy's heart, and the man fell one final time. Mark let go of the sword, which now pinned Cassidy's body to the ground, and dropped to his knees, his vision blackening. As the back of his head hit the sand, he heard tens of thousands of horrified screams echo around the stadium. Weeping. Sobbing. Wailing.

They weren't ready, Mark thought, before darkness took him.

28

*T*HE INK-BLACK WAVES SWELLED, pouring salt water down his throat. When they parted, Mark could still see the burning deck of the aircraft carrier, the *Hóngsè Fēng*, cooking the corpse of Admiral Huang.

Zhou's promotion was the key, it had turned out. Now a major, because of his peerless intelligence work with Mark, he had access to everything. Door codes. Personnel locations. Transport logs. Mark had siphoned off his login and fashioned his own ID chip with Zhou's credentials and his own face and DNA. Before he left the base, he took a tour of the armory, gearing up for the mission at hand. He took a truck to the port and snuck onto the carrier via a stealth-plated minisub in the dead of night, cleared to launch through Zhou's ID. Admiral Huang had fled to the edge of Chinese waters when the country started to catch fire, its most powerful leaders killing each other off. Or so it seemed.

Spearfish, the CIA's Mona Lisa, would cripple an entire superpower with only a handful of men. Huang, like the others, couldn't live. If there was a leadership vacuum, he could assume power and unite China, when China needed to stay broken. After the first team's success in the mountains, and the assassination of the rebellious Commander Wu by another embedded Spear shortly thereafter, it was Mark's turn. He couldn't fail. And he didn't.

How many had he killed? Six, no, seven soldiers on the way to the bridge, hiding their bodies after their lives were ended by whispered gunshots. He planted C4 below deck next to torpedoes as long as schoolbuses, then worked his way up the stairs near the rear of the ship and . . . ah, he'd forgotten one. The sailor. The young one. He slit his throat before he screamed.

The bridge was a bloodbath. Mark didn't know if his training would return to him, it had been so long since he'd seen action, but when he reached for it, there it was. He shot two soldiers in the backs of their heads before anyone even knew what was happening. Immediately after, he was forced to hook his arm around the neck of the nearest officer, and use him to absorb a hail of bullets as he snapped off shots from over the man's shoulder and the rest of the soldiers fell. He released the officer's bloodied corpse and found only Admiral Huang left standing, a short, paunchy man whose combat glory days had long passed him by. He was armed with a revolver, a big cowboy gun he could barely control, and his single booming blast went wide. Mark answered with a line of shots that ripped through him from his heart to his throat to his head. The admiral died three times over before he even hit the ground.

It was only once the room went quiet that Mark realized he'd also been hit. One bullet had passed clean through his arm, and another was still buried in the meat of his thigh somewhere, scraping against the bone. Both burned, especially the leg, but he had Zhou to thank for training him to manage far, far worse pain.

Using Zhou's clearance one last time, paired with the admiral's keychain, he overheated the massive engines so the ship stopped dead. He was three floors below deck by the time the alarms finally started blaring, and he killed four more to get to the escape sub.

The timing was off. Not by much, but enough. He couldn't remote detonate from the sub, so the bombs were on old fashioned timers. He wasn't far away enough. Shrapnel from the blasts raced through the water and tore through the rear of the mini-sub, which floated to the surface like a dead fish. Since then, he'd been swimming. For hours, it felt like. He had to make it to international waters, or there'd be no evac. They were right on the edge, so it was only a few more miles, wasn't it? It had to be.

Behind him, the fire burned, the ship slowly sinking into the Pacific. Whoever he'd shot now didn't matter. The *Hóngsè Fēng* was a flagship, one of the biggest in the Chinese Navy, with a crew of seven thousand. When the sub surfaced, Mark watched sailors engulfed in flame plunge from the deck of the ship, their cries echoing across the water. Who knew how many more had been incinerated, or were burning, or were drowning. Most of them, probably.

Mark knew the mission. Understood it from the start. Back in Zhou's chair, he swore he'd kill the entire country if it meant getting home to Riko and Asami. He would have flown a nuke over Beijing if they asked him.

But no, that wasn't the way. It had to be internal. Zhou would be blamed one way or the other. Would they execute him before or after they realized Mark had used his credentials? Either way, it was a reassuring thought. Mark was only sad he didn't get to pull the trigger himself, but Zhou living to face suspicion in the aftermath was part of the plan.

It can't be much farther now. A dozen intelligence satellites were scanning the waves for his heat signature. Gideon would find him. He had promised.

The waves were crushing. The salt ate at his bullet wounds. The night sky glowed hellishly and black smoke blotted out a line of stars. Mark's entire body felt strangely warm in the freezing ocean as he swam toward the vast nothingness ahead of him.

Not much farther now.

"THERE HE IS," SAID a familiar voice as Mark blinked his eyes open. Carlo was staring at him, but the rest of his surroundings were blurred. As they slowly came into focus, he realized he was in the medical wing back at Crayton's compound. The well-groomed Dr. Hasan crept into his vision.

"How are you feeling, Mark?" Hasan said.

Mark blinked again. Was he in pain? He didn't think so, but that seemed unlikely. He looked down and saw bandages wrapped around his chest and his forearm.

"I think . . . I'm alright," Mark said. "Though once the drexophine wears off, probably not."

Hasan shook his finger at him.

"Smart boy, very smart."

Drexophine was the only answer. His head was clear and he couldn't feel even a pinprick of pain.

"You made me burn through a fair portion of our reserve," Hasan said. "We'll have to switch you to regular meds so we don't run out for the other competitors. You wouldn't believe what it costs for a fluid ounce. But you know Mr. Crayton. Only the best for his athletes."

His athletes. Mark looked at Carlo, panicked.

"What day is it? How long was I . . ."

"Relax," Carlo said. "It's only been a day and a half. You missed a hell of a match last night though. I watched it from here."

"The tournament's still going on?" Mark asked.

"Of course!" Carlo said, giving him a strange look. "Six more fights to go in the first round."

What did Mark think, that Cassidy's death was going to cause some kind of national wave of nausea and Crayton was going to cancel the tournament out of a sense of newfound moral obligation? Of course it was still moving forward.

"Who fought today?" Mark asked, uncomfortable he'd missed even a single match.

"That billionaire asshole and the SEAL chick."

Rakesh Blackwood and Kells Bradford. The winner would face Ethan, if he got past Ja'Von Jordan.

"And?"

"Girl was armored up like a tank and the asshole only had one of those little needle swords they use in those musketeer movies."

"A rapier? So Kells won?"

Carlo shook his head.

"Dude is quick. He danced around for a while and ended up jamming that thing straight through her eye slit. Killed her dead on the spot. He didn't even get a scratch on that shiny silver armor of his."

Mark was taken aback. That was not what he was expecting. He really didn't know Kells at all, but her death saddened him all the same. He expected he would have been less broken up about Blackwood.

"Why didn't you go?" Mark said. "They gave you tickets for the whole tournament, right?"

Carlo shrugged.

"You stayed around when I was laid up. Figured I'd return the favor. That ambulance ride was *fucked* though. You had this foot-long flap of skin hangin' off your arm once they got the armor unclipped. Doc here stitched it up, but man, that was no joke."

Hasan returned with a new syringe.

"I know you already have quite the scar collection, but that's going to be a big one," he said. "But you'll get your mobility back in a week or so. The muscle damage was mostly superficial; you were lucky."

Lucky. *Christ.*

"Do I even want to know what they're saying about my fight?" Mark asked.

Carlo shifted uncomfortably.

"Well, let's just say the press doesn't love you. Everyone thinks you're scary as shit, though, so that's good!"

Mark glanced at the TV, which had been playing with no sound. It showed a live feed trained on Chase Cassidy's Beverly Hills mansion (that he'd just foreclosed on, Brooke said) where the front gate was covered in flowers and ribbons and signs.

A TRUE LEGEND, one read in block letters. NEVER FORGOTTEN, said another in looping cursive alongside a hand-drawn image of Cassidy's face. And then there was another written in red paint with a more ominous message, HE'LL PAY.

"You got flowers and shit like that too, but Crayton's people are keeping 'em in some room in one of the houses if you want to see the collection."

"*I* got flowers?" Mark said, incredulous.

"Man," Carlo said, smirking. "Seventy goddamn million people watched that fight. At least *some* of 'em were rooting for you. Hell, Charles Manson had fans, right?"

"Oh, thanks," Mark said.

Carlo laughed. He turned back to the TV where a blonde woman was speaking in mute, dabbing her eyes. Mark barely recognized her but . . .

Carlo turned on the volume with a gesture.

"Oh yeah, Soren Vanderhottie won't shut up about Cassidy. This is like her tenth interview since your fight, I swear."

"No one knew Chase like I did," she said, nearly sobbing. "People saw his face, heard his voice, but they didn't really *know* him. But I did, and I can tell you that he is . . . was, just as beautiful inside as out."

Mark rolled his eyes.

"Well, I did actually feel bad," he said, "but this is terrible acting."

"Fake or no," Carlo said, "public's eatin' that shit up. They were 'America's doomed sweethearts' or some shit. Fuckin' white people."

"And to Mark Wei," Soren continued, her ice-blue eyes staring daggers into the camera in a way that pierced Mark. "I only have this to say. Chase was a *hero*, and you? You're nothing. Just a murderer, a cold-blooded killer. If I meet you in the bracket, I'll have justice for Chase, I can promise you that. You better *hope* you die before then."

Despite the fact that Soren Vanderhaven was half his size and was probably jumping on a trampoline somewhere while he was being cut up in China, something about her chilled Mark to his core.

He waved off the TV. Soren could have easily met Chase *himself* in the bracket, and something told Mark that true love probably wouldn't have caused them to forfeit the tournament rather than butcher each other, given each's ambition. He was almost sad he wouldn't be able to see how that would have played out, but it would have required him to be dead. As it stood, Soren was still a ways off in the bracket. Her first fight was against Dan Hagelund.

"Well, *my* legs aren't broken, so I'm getting out of here," Mark said, and he flung off his covers to stand up. He was a little wobbly, but Carlo caught him by the arm.

"Yeah, yeah, asshole, I'll have these braces off soon enough. You're just lucky I owe you for saving my hundred bucks. Little bro is pumped you won too."

"You let him watch that?" Mark said, eyebrows raised.

"Pshh, whatever, Diego's seen the whole Max Rage trilogy, plenty of blood there. This is just another movie to him."

And that's the goddamn problem.

"Whole family's out here for the month," Carlo continued. "Crayton's passes get us flights, hotels, tickets, the whole deal. And I landed a few sponsors back home. Not a lot since I was just a city semifinalist, but enough to keep the lights on for a little while when we get back. But I am sick to goddamn death of these chalky protein bars they keep sending me, like I actually want to eat the shit I'm selling."

Mark felt a buzz in the air and Carlo checked his phone.

"Hey, uh, you mind if I take off? Shyla wants to meet up in the city before the fight. And you know, you're alive and stuff, so . . ."

Mark laughed.

"It's fine, you've been here for ages, seems like. I gotta get changed and talk to Brooke."

"Can't believe she went home," Carlo said. "Barely said two words during the fight. You would think—"

"Brooke's complicated," Mark cut in. "And she's got a job back in the city. No one's paying for her hotel. I don't blame her."

In truth Mark knew Brooke had been recalled by Gideon to discuss next steps. He was hoping it was something actionable before anyone else had to die.

"Who's up tonight anyway?" Mark asked.

"That mean D-town motherfucker Jordan and your boy Ethan. I hope he's got more than a pretty smile in his bag of tricks," Carlo said.

Ethan. Shit.

Mark hoped so too.

MARK'S ROOM IN THE main manor was exactly how he'd left it. Combatants were still mandated to stay on Crayton's compound between fights, and though the camera drones were gone, security seemed like it had increased threefold. Mark quickly found himself escorted by guards everywhere, and caught glimpses of mercs even walking around with Shin Tagami as he sauntered into the gardens. When he asked one of his escorts what was going on, he was told there had been an "incident" where a competitor had attacked a rival on the grounds ahead of the competition itself, presumably to get a leg up. Security was there to ensure that didn't happen again.

"What the hell?" Mark asked the young Glasshammer guard. "Who attacked who?"

"Sorry, sir, I can't disclose—"

"Was it Rusakov? Easton?"

Mark's mind to raced to Aria.

"As I said, I cannot comment on the matter," the guard said. "But there was no permanent harm done. The victim is recovering and the culprit is secured. But our mandate is to ensure such an event does not reoccur."

No more snooping around Crayton's mansion then, Mark realized as two guards stood at the exit to his room once he entered. He stripped out of his grungy clothes and put on pants, a shirt, and a sport coat. His TV told him that he was supposed to leave soon to head to the Colosseum for Ethan's fight.

As he finished with his final button, a dark shape loomed in his doorway, and Mark whipped around.

He broke into a smile.

Moses strode forward and wrapped him up in a crushing hug. Both his guards and Mark's guards flipped out and raised their rifles toward the pair of them, shouting at them to step back.

"Christ almighty, we're friends, you assholes!" Mark said. "Didn't you watch the goddamn show?"

"Sorry, sir, but we can't take any chances," Mark's guard said again. "We must remain in the room if you'd like to converse."

Mark rolled his eyes. Moses seemed unfazed by it all.

"I just went by medical after my run, but the doc told me you'd discharged yourself. Ran into Carlo on the way out too. How the hell are you feeling?"

"Fine," Mark said, raising his bandaged arm. "Drexophine is no joke."

"That fight, my god," Moses said, looking concerned. "I thought we were going to lose you. When you tried to block with your forearm. What were you thinking? I taught you better than that!"

"I know, I know," Mark said. "But once you're down there, it's different. Trust me, you have to improvise."

Moses stepped closer to him, and cast a wary eye at the guards, who stood still as stone near the front of the room.

"How . . . how was it?" Moses asked. "Are you okay? I mean really."

Mark looked into Moses's earnest, worried eyes. He saw

Cassidy's ruined face in his mind. Saw the sword sticking out of his back like a flagpole.

"You should forfeit, Moses," Mark said in a hushed tone, putting his hand on the man's hulking shoulder. "Your fight is in what, three days? Just go. Tear up the contract, give up the money. Go home and be with Nolan. Have a life."

"It was that bad?" Moses said, looking puzzled, and the tiniest bit afraid. "Actually killing him?"

"I've killed a lot of people, Moses," Mark sighed. "But none like that. I don't wish that on you. I know you think this is your destiny. That you were born in the wrong century and meant to do something like this. But trust me, *you don't have to*. You can just *leave*. You're not trying to save your dying wife or escape a tidal wave of debt. You can just *go*."

Moses looked confused.

"But . . . I can't. I've fought, I've trained. All this time. I'm strong. I know the weapons inside and out. My armor is . . . this is what I'm supposed to be doing!" he sputtered.

"It's a fantasy!" Mark said, raising his voice and gripping Moses by the shoulders. It caught the guard's attention, but they didn't make a move after Mark released him. "That's all it is."

"How can you say that?" Moses said, furrowing bushy eyebrows. "After all I've taught you this summer. I thought maybe some gratitude, support, advice. But now you're trying to play mind games? Trying to clear the field?"

"No!" Mark said. "Not at all. Moses, I just want you to *live*. Or I want you not to become a *murderer* by the end of the week."

The guards were muttering to themselves now. Mark realized he was probably taking this too far.

"If you don't think I'm good enough, fine, but there's no need for this," Moses said, anger flashing in his eyes. "I thought you were better than this."

He turned and stomped out of the room so forcefully the TV shook in its casing.

"Wait," Mark said. "What do you know about what happened here? Who got attacked? Have you seen Aria?"

Moses stopped, but didn't turn around.

"I don't know anything," he said. "And I haven't seen her since your fight."

Mark searched the compound as best he could before his guard escort shoved him in a limo to head into the desert for the evening's fight. He couldn't find Aria, but if she was hurt, apparently she was recovering, though not in medical. Mark knew it could have been any pair of combatants in an altercation; almost all of them were unstable. He thought of Manny's assault on the guards. He remembered Ja'Von Jordan and Rusakov's altercation during visitation weekend. Maybe they'd crippled each other. Wouldn't that be nice?

After trying Brooke for the fifth time, he gave up. Chances were she was probably deep underground somewhere with her phone in a Faraday cage. He popped in his S-lens and checked the messages there. He found what he was looking for.

GLAD YOU'RE ALIVE. NEXT STEPS. TALK SOON -B

Always a way with words, that one.

Mark didn't like the way he left things with Moses. The man seemed seriously hurt that Mark suggested he turn tail and flee the bracket. But couldn't he see it was for his own good? Probably not, given his borderline fanatical love for everything about Crayton's tournament, from the manor to the man himself. From the beginning, Moses had loved every aspect of the Crucible, and Mark told him to throw it all away. Still, Mark knew he wasn't wrong. Moses, Aria, and all the rest should get as far away from this thing as possible. Mark *had* killed before, but Cassidy's execution was . . . something else. Something not just unnecessary, but unholy. Something that would change him.

He hadn't stopped the Crucible. Not yet. Now it would change everyone.

29

THE CROWD WAS ALREADY weeping by the time Ethan Callaghan strode out onto the sand. His emotional introduction video from the city finals had been refilmed and updated with his wife's most recent prognosis, and featured the heart-breaking good-bye he'd shared as they parted for the last time at the end of visitation weekend. Ethan stared up at the giant screen and the enormous, looming faces of his three children. By that point there were tears in his eyes as well.

He was resplendent in his armor, which shined silver, red, and blue. A fearsome metal eagle stretched across the center of his kite shield, and his shortsword was polished to a mirror shine. His helmet in his hand, his blond hair whipped in the wind, and he looked like a cross between Captain America and a Crusades-era paladin.

"Now that's a heroic-looking motherfucker," Carlo said. Mark was sharing his booth with the Riveras, and was glad not to be alone. He'd hoped to find Moses or Aria at the Colosseum, but couldn't locate either once he'd arrived.

Ja'von Jordan's intro was . . . less heartwarming. It was mostly highlights of his brutal *Prison Wars* kills, and footage of him talking shit to the camera as his entourage spurred him on. His armor was black and royal blue, the colors of his old gang. Mark didn't recognize his weapon. It looked like some sort of oversized cleaver, and Mark saw a few other oddly shaped blades slung across his back.

It was a strange experience to watch all of it from the stands. The crowd was still massive, and from the low-tier box, they were only a story or two above ground level, so most of the fans were still towering above them. As Crayton gave another speech and the countdown started, Mark desperately wanted to be somewhere, anywhere else.

Ethan's wavy blond hair disappeared under his helmet. Jordan beat the scorpion on his breastplate and yelled some kind of war cry.

A second after zero hit, metal slammed into metal, and the crowd roared as one.

Ten minutes later, Jordan lay face up in the sand, hands wrapped around a slit throat. Ethan put a hand to his shoulder, which had been badly bitten by the monstrous cleaver, but he held his free arm aloft in victory, and crowd swelled to embrace him. Mark finally felt like he could breathe again. The kid had been brilliant, a born knight. Mark had sparred with him for ages, but he'd never seen Ethan fight quite like that before. But he understood. Everything changed when you were down there in the pit. You had to become something else, something better, or worse, than you'd ever been before.

TIME SPED UP. THE week started to fly by and Mark could barely process it all, bouncing between the compound and the stadium every few hours, it felt like. Brooke was still out of contact, and Aria was still missing, which had put a permanent pit in Mark's stomach. The sick feeling only left him during the fights, as there was simply no way to tear his attention away.

After Ethan's fight, it was Soren Vanderhaven who took on Dan Hagelund. Mark had no love for either, but a dark part of him wanted Vanderhaven to die.

Her outfit was every bit as preposterous as imagined. She'd fully embraced her "hornet" symbol, and the armor was all yellow and black. But to call it "armor" was something of a misnomer.

There was plating, yes, but on top it covered only her shoulders and part of her generous chest, leaving her collar, arms, and all eight of her abs fully exposed. On bottom, it appeared Arthur had figured out how to make something resembled armored undergarments, which left long, tan thighs exposed before they disappeared into spiked knee boots. She didn't wear a helmet at all, only an Amazonian circlet, and her curled blonde hair was billowing out of it. Her spear was much taller than she was, with a razor tip and ivy embroidery wrapped around all seven feet of the shaft.

It was a worrying amount of skin being exposed. When she was fighting in the city qualifiers? Sure, a pole-dancer's outfit could work. But this Red Sonja bikini armor? It was insane. Carlo and the rest of the audience was drooling over her, sure, and maybe the plan was that Hagelund was supposed to be too. But the risk was senseless.

Hagelund was a fortress by comparison. Not an inch of skin exposed from head to toe, an enormous tower shield on one arm and a chained mace dangling from the other. Like Cassidy, his pauldrons were also his designated animal, though his were rhinos, meaning a long spiked horn protruded from each of his shoulders. In the rust colored plating, he looked terrifying.

Mark braced himself for a swift resolution as soon as the chime sounded.

Instead, Soren destroyed him.

She was blindingly fast, and used the nearly nonexistent plating to her full advantage, flipping out of harm's way, cartwheeling over Hagelund's armor to plant her spear in his calf. Mark lost count of how many time she'd gored him through the cracks of his armor by the end. His flail had proven borderline useless, and was as unwieldy as Moses had said. He'd struck himself by accident a few times whirling it around, and Soren had countered with more jabs into his plating.

The crowd howled as Hagelund stumbled around, leaking blood from every gap in his armor. Soren waved and smiled and blew a kiss to the camera drone above her, right before she drove the spear under his armpit and straight through his heart. Mark was astonished at what the gymnast . . . the *gymnast*, had done in that ridiculous armor with a smile on her face.

I knew there was something not right about her, Mark thought as he looked at Carlo clapping wildly, his eyes glazed over as she bowed to each section of the stadium. The sand was littered with hundreds of bouquets of yellow roses.

Mark watched the next day's fight with particular interest. Though he wasn't friendly with either combatant, he felt some affinity for both of them, and would be sad to see blood spilled, however it went.

Shin Tagami had attacked Easton in the woods in defense of the maid. Manny had attacked Wyatt Axton outside the manor because well . . . he was crazy, but Mark appreciated the effort.

When Tagami took the sand, something Arthur had said a long while back clicked. The crowd gasped as he walked out with no armor, just a plain gray robe with a minimalist stitching of a white crane on the back. He was armed only with his long staff, though the wooden version had been replaced by a metal one. The crowd whispered about the man who would dare enter the arena wearing no armor, with less protection than even Soren Vanderhaven, surprisingly.

Mark thought he understood. It was probably how he was most comfortable. Wherever he'd learned his skills in decades past, he surely wasn't doing it with dozens of pounds of plating. And armor didn't need to block anything if you never got hit. Yet, it did seem a little like suicide in this context.

Manny's armor was patchwork, seemingly built by a madman. Misshapen plates locked together in odd formations, though knowing Arthur's design philosophies, it was probably more functional than it looked. On a random plate near his abdomen, Mark saw a scratched picture of a dog. The "hound" was meant to be Manny's symbol, though the representation on his armor looked like it had been doodled by a child or a caveman. The man was already swinging his dual berserker's axes at the air, and was practically foaming at the mouth.

Poor guy, Mark thought, remembering what Brooke had told him about the war-ravaged veteran. If the nerve damage was as extensive as she thought, at least he wouldn't be able to feel the pain of what was about to come next.

But regardless of what he thought about the two men, the fight was incredibly important because whoever lived would face Mark in the next round. This was his corner of the bracket, and he watched the entire fight on the edge of his seat.

The crowd didn't seem to know who to support. With his mangled face and mental illness, Manny had few fans in the audience. There were more rooting for Tagami, and he seemed to win a majority of supporters through his lack of armor and use of a non-bladed weapon, which seemed especially brave. But the man hadn't spoken a word on or off camera since even before he qualified, so he was as much of an enigma to the Crucible audience as he was to Mark.

After a low bow from Tagami and a violent twitching spasm from Manny, the bout was underway.

Tagami's fighting style was beautiful, in a way. While Manny lashed out like a wild animal in every direction, Tagami looped around him and away from the singing blades of the axes. Soon there were a few slices through his robes, but no blood. When he struck, his staff rattled Manny's armor and the man clutched his helmeted head with each fresh reverberation, but with just the staff, Mark didn't understand how Tagami would land a killing blow.

Eventually, Mark understood Tagami's strategy. He was going for the head, and only the head. Though the staff had no blade to open any arteries, it rang Manny's skull over and over like a bell. By the fifth blow, the helmet was dented, but the fifteenth, it was practically collapsing in on itself. Manny couldn't feel pain, but those violent vibrations and contusions clearly aggravated him all the same. He roared and finally ripped his helmet off, cutting his face as the bent metal dragged over it. Free of the oppressive, battered helmet, he lunged forward wildly and one swing finally nicked Tagami's side and the gray robes started absorbing crimson. But with Manny's head now exposed, Tagami had his opening.

Another wild lunge missed, and Tagami spun around backward, the staff a blur that cracked against the back of Manny's neck, just under his skull. Mark heard the bones crunch from the armor mics, and watched Manny's eyes widen as he sank to his knees, his body jerking like a broken toy. The axes dropped harmlessly to the sand.

He kneeled there, heaving, staring at Tagami. The old man planted his staff upright in the dirt and walked over to Manny. He too dropped to his knees and whispered something out of mic earshot to the crippled man. He bowed to his opponent, and Manny looked at him blank-faced. His eyes rolled back into his head and he toppled toward Tagami, who caught him in his armor, and lay his body down on gently on the sand.

Mark sighed. This was yet another man he didn't want to kill.

AND THEN, A MAN fought whom he didn't want to see die.

It was time for Moses to face Asher Mendez. Nolan had invited Mark and Ethan to watch in Moses's private booth, and the man looked distraught throughout the entire opening ceremony.

"It's what he wants," Nolan whispered over and over, as if trying to convince himself, but Mark was disappointed that Moses hadn't taken his advice and fled. He still hadn't spoken to Mark since their falling out, but Nolan assured him it was just nerves.

"He'll be okay after today," Nolan said.

No he won't, Mark thought. *Either way.*

Ethan stuck to the hard facts of it all. Moses's sizes and the reach of his maul gave him an advantage over Mendez, who had fully embraced his "tiger" persona with gaudy striped armor and double-bladed claw weapons that supposedly utilized some remnant of his boxing skills. Tactically, Mark agreed Moses may have a leg up, but it was hard to divorce that kind of logic from the fear of losing a friend. If Ethan felt the same way, he was hiding it well. He had spoken little of his own fight against Jordan, only to say he was glad it was over with. His next match had already been decided on day two, and he would face Rakesh Blackwood in the second round. Mark wished he could trade, and Ethan would have to be the one to execute the old man. Mark now had little faith he'd be able to stop the juggernaut of the Crucible in time to avoid more death. Brooke's absence was growing worrisome, matched only by Aria's, who had also been invited to the box but was still missing. Mark was now sure that she was the one who had been attacked and was lying injured somewhere. But Crayton's people always brushed Mark off when he tried to schedule a meeting with the man to ask him directly. The alternative was that she'd left the tournament entirely, and Mark secretly hoped that he'd see a breaking news story that Aria had been spotted back in New York, performing on stage. No such bulletin had appeared.

Moses had gone full barbarian with his ensemble. He was wearing half a bearskin (fake, Nolan assured Mark) that had very real-looking fur and claws over his metal gauntlets and the bear's head and upper jaw wrapped around his helmet. His outfit left some skin on his broad chest and muscled quads exposed, but if it was good enough for the ancient Gauls, it was good enough for him, Nolan said. Though he was one of the largest fighters, not becoming a literal tank on legs gave him a bit of extra mobility, which he'd need against the worryingly quick Mendez.

The fear was well-founded. After the chime sounded, Moses was cut three times over within the first two minutes. Nolan went pale white as Moses held his gauntlet to his wounds and he shifted his grip on the maul. Mendez had gored his abdomen, leg, and chest with quick claw strikes, but there was no way of knowing how deep the cuts were. Mark could only judge by his movement, and he was optimistic, as Moses was still reacting as quickly as he'd ever seen him during training, despite the injuries.

When the maul finally connected to Mendez's tiger stripes, the result was nearly apocalyptic. The boxer flew a half-dozen feet through the air before crashing to the ground. He didn't lose his grip on his razor claws, which were fully integrated into his armor, but it had clearly shaken him. Moses almost ended it right there with a crushing follow-up, but Mendez rolled out of the way just in time.

Moses pressed his luck too far. When he went in for another haymaker, Mendez was ready and slid under the swing, raking his claws against Moses's gauntlet as it passed by.

Mark heard Nolan cry out as two of Moses's fingers dropped to the sand, and crowd practically lost their minds.

Fortunately, Moses kept his grip on the maul, and all the injury did was enrage him. When Mendez leaped to press the advantage, Moses rushed to meet him. Mendez's right claws glanced harm-lessly off a chest plate and Moses slammed his head into Mendez's, knocking him straight to the sand, stunned. He tried to roll again, but Moses's maul caught his leg, and from the resulting, horrifying sound, it was clear every bone below the knee had instantly turned to gravel. Mendez's scream echoed through the entire stadium and everyone was on their feet.

Moses's chest heaved as Mendez tried, and failed, to limp to a standing position, his left leg little more than jelly inside the warped armor.

Don't, Mark thought. *Just walk away.*

Moses stood there, contemplating the fate of the beaten man. In any other fight he could have claimed victory, his opponent clearly unable to continue, but not here. Not in the Crucible.

Save yourself. Walk away.

Moses tightened his bloody grip, swung the maul up in a high, wide arc, and when it came crashing down, every organ inside Mendez's armored chest became little more than pulp.

Mark acted like he was supposed to. He high-fived Ethan. He hugged Nolan. He smiled, and tried to mask the urge to vomit.

Out in the sand, Moses didn't wave to the stands or roar in victory. He stared silently at the mangled corpse, and let 250,000 people celebrate for him.

Moses's injuries turned out to be more severe than anticipated, so Dr. Hasan stitched him up and pumped him full of drexophine. Mark let Nolan have a tearful reunion with his husband, and then went in alongside Ethan to try and talk to him. Their contingent of escort guards followed them. Ethan went on and on about the mechanics of the fight, and how much he'd kicked ass. Moses smiled and nodded and cast Mark sideways glances. As Ethan wrapped up, Mark simply nodded and said, "I just wanted to say congrats, man. Well fought."

He held out his hand and Moses shook it stiffly. Mark released his grip, but Moses kept his.

"Stay a minute?" he asked. Mark looked at Ethan who nodded and left the room.

"Sorry for being a dick," Mark said first. "I just . . ."

"I get it," Moses said, waving his bandaged left hand that was missing its last two fingers. Mark was a bit startled to see they were in a jar nearby. "I didn't before, but I do now."

"How are you doing with it?" Mark asked.

Moses paused and stared at the TV, which was showing the crowd milling out of the stadium as the Muses performed their daily post-show send-off. Mark saw blurry shapes in the background that looked like they were hauling Mendez's body away.

"It doesn't feel like a sport," Moses said. "Not really. I thought it would make it better because we all knew the risks and weren't doing this because we had to. We're not Caesar's slaves."

Aren't we, though?

"But it isn't like that," he continued. "It's uglier than I thought. And easier. Just one swing, and he was gone. I'm supposed to feel proud, aren't I?"

"It was a good fight," Mark offered.

"You know what I mean. You feel it too, or you wouldn't have told me what you did."

"So what now?" Mark said, itching the bandage on his arm.

"You know it's too late to walk away," Moses said. "Especially after today."

Mark sighed.

"You still can. You're alive. And you're not going to like what comes next if you stay."

"The girl?"

"The girl."

Moses held his palms to his eyes.

"I'm over the edge now. All I can do is keep falling."

Mark knew that feeling better than he'd like to admit.

A TV blared behind them, showing slow-motion tracking shots of the most brutal blows of the match.

The headline at the bottom read MORTON TO MEET VANDERHAVEN IN QUARTERFINALS.

30

MISSIONARIES? WHAT THE HELL do you mean, missionaries?"
Mark stared incredulously at Brooke's face through his
S-lens. She'd finally gotten back in touch after half a week in a crypto-
site under Chicago.

"Joseph and Heidi Olsson. The people in Crayton's photo. We
had to verify the find a dozen times over because the hit was just
from a single source. A random archived scan of a bulletin from the
Church of Righteous Light in Idaho, circa 1981. Read it."

Brooke flung the photo and excerpt up on the screen. In it were
the blond man and woman from Crayton's hidden photo, roughly the
same age, but posed somewhere else, in front of a small white church
that needed a few coats of fresh paint. He read the text under it.

> "Join us in praying for Joseph and Heidi as they take the
> light of the Lord to the darkness of China. Your offerings have
> funded their mission overseas so they may preach repentance
> to the heathens who would butcher children in the womb. The
> Church of Righteous Light goes where the Lord wills, and the
> Chinese people must understand the monstrous sins they com-
> mit daily. If they do not turn from their path, the Lord will
> smite them with fire and brimstone, and we cannot sit idly by
> as that happens. We are blessed that Joseph and Heidi have
> answered this call, and that little Joseph Jr. will be allowed

to witness the Lord work through his parents at such a young age. Please attend our farewell barbecue for the Olssons this Friday in the Narthex. Bring a dish if you can, and a smile if you can't.

"What in the holy fuck am I reading?" Mark said, eyes racing over the text for the third time.

"Facial recognition came up with this scan, and after ridiculously extensive analysis, we matched the photo," Brooke said. "We believe these are Cameron Crayton's parents, his true parents, who left the country in '81 to become missionaries in China. The Church of Righteous Light wasn't your average house of worship. Back then, the FBI had the congregation linked to various abortion clinic fires in the decade after *Roe v. Wade*. They were fanatics. An unpublicized raid landed a dozen members in jail and the chapel itself burned to the ground 'unintentionally,' the report says. That was in 1984."

"And the Olssons? China?"

"With China's one-child policy and all the abortions that led to, it was number one on their hit list. They'd been planning to go since the policy was enacted in '78, but it took them a while to save up to fund this mission. They could only send one family, and the Olssons were the most devoted of the most devoted."

"They never came back," Mark said.

Brooke shook her head.

"Their passports show the family going in, but not out. I can't imagine a bunch of white people screaming about the evils of abortion went over very well with the locals *or* the government. They were never reported missing because the church didn't want the FBI looking at them even closer. Even when they lost contact, they just told everyone the Olssons were still there, doing the Lord's work. In all likelihood they were dead or in prison."

"So Joseph Olsson Jr. is Cameron Crayton?" Mark said, rubbing his chin. "He survived?"

"That's the running theory, but it's unconfirmed. If those dots really are all connected, he was over there young, very young, and possibly an orphan."

This was huge. Mark's mind raced.

"What's it going to take to make this official?" he asked.

"We need Chinese intel. Either data showing the government scooped him up and turned him, or that he came back and had connections with the regime during his business years. Timeline makes it look like he was back in the States by seventeen. That's where things start to look genuine in his file, working odd jobs, then starting businesses, making investments and the like. But that's about a decade he's unaccounted for."

"Anything else? The box? The teeth? 'White Devil'?"

"Nothing on those. But there has to be a connection, however bizarre."

"We should take him and . . . extract the rest from him," Mark said, gritting his teeth.

"I ran that up the flagpole; Gideon shot it down. We'd tip our hand before we have proof and there's no way to know how China would respond. If they want him dead now, for whatever reason, taking him off the board could have . . . unexpected consequences."

Mark shook his head in disgust.

"People are dying every day we don't take him down and disrupt this entire freakshow."

Brooke nodded. He could see the pain in her eyes.

"I know, and I'm sorry. But he's too high profile to take into custody without a better case against him. This operation isn't even supposed to exist, and if it gets brought to light, everything we find had better well stick."

Brooke paused.

"I know people are dying, but compared to . . ."

"Don't even say Spearfish," Mark growled. "Yes, the body count is lower, but this is . . . something else. Something worse, in a way.

These are not soldiers. These are delusional people who think they have no other options."

Brooke shook her head.

"You shouldn't have gotten close with them, Mark. You're losing scale here."

"This isn't about Aria!" Mark snapped.

"I didn't say it was just about her. It's Ethan. It's Moses. You're so desperate to save them all you'll sink the mission and make all this for nothing."

Mark took a breath. He knew she was right. He didn't want to start whipping Brooke for Gideon's decisions either.

"You did good work on this," was all he said. "Just tell me what you need."

"We're reaching out to our remaining spies to see if we can get anything from China that way. But that's a needle in a haystack. We need you to keep an eye out for any more tails on Crayton that could be MSS. Someone keeping an eye on him, scouting him. And if they make another attempt to take him out, you need to secure him and also get to their agents before Crayton's people do."

"That's a hell of a longshot," Mark said. "And tell me again why we shouldn't just let them kill him?"

"If China wants Crayton dead, doesn't it stand to reason that we probably need him alive?"

Mark hated Brooke and her stupid fucking logic.

THE WALLS OF THE stadium were thundering from the bass of a thousand speakers. The Muses were off writhing on the sand somewhere, and Mark only caught glimpses of the pre-show on the monitors. The fight was less than half an hour away, and once he found out Aria was indeed in the building, he was going to be damned if he didn't see her before she went out there.

He had ditched his Glasshammer tail in a crowded men's

bathroom and was slinking in and out of the packed crowd on the way to the locker room. He had a hat down low over his eyes, and outside of a few people whispering, "*Is that . . .?*" no one had mobbed him yet. He pulled up the blueprints for the Colosseum that had been archived since he'd scanned them in Crayton's office on his S-lens and managed to find a service exit that would get him around what was assuredly a well-guarded front door. A few cracked locks later and he was creeping through the shower area into the dressing room, which could hold an entire football team but was only meant for a single fighter. Crayton had the entire area decked out in marble and imported oak, and it had training dummies, practice weapons, weights. This was even *more* extensive than the area where Mark had suited up before his fight. And was that . . . a bed?

"How the hell?" Aria said, eyes wide as Mark came around the corner. She was fixing the last few plates of armor to her suit, which covered her from neck to toe in shining silver with a few leaf green highlights that matched her eyes. On her breastplate were two mirrored, rearing stallions, and her dual swords were already slung across her back. A fringe of translucent fabric hung around her waist, with a few pieces streaming off her arms as well.

"I have half a platoon of guards stationed outside my room," Aria hissed. "You should *not* be here."

"That's why I came through the back," Mark said. "I needed to see you. I heard there was an attack. Did Easton . . ."

He looked over her for any sign of injury, but if there was anything to find, it was hidden by the armor.

"Mark, Mark," Aria said, putting an armored hand on his chest. "Calm down. I wasn't hurt."

Mark's brow wrinkled in confusion.

"What? Then where have you . . ."

"*I'm* the one who attacked Easton. Well, according to them. They've had me locked up in here for almost a week."

"What the hell?" Mark said. He looked around. The bed. The

training gear. The weights. And there was even more in the adjoining room. A treadmill, open lockers full of clothing, a dining cart with empty plates. The locker room had doubled as a prison cell and hotel room.

"Just tell me what happened," Mark said.

Aria leaned against the lockers and he sat on the bench in front her.

"I came to see you in the medical wing after the fight, but you were still out and Carlo was sleeping like a rock in the corner. I headed back to the manor and was going to try and get some sleep, but I heard a scream from down the hall as soon as my door shut. Easton's room. Of course, Easton's room.

"I yelled for security, but of course there was no one around when I actually needed them for a change. I heard more shrieks, and I kicked the door in.

"It was dark, but I could see them all the same. The lanky creep was standing there holding this poor girl's hair, which was no longer attached to her head. She was one of Crayton's maids, I think. Her face was sliced up and her scalp was stripped and bleeding raw. Easton didn't even look phased. Like I'd just walked in on them having tea. When she saw me, she tried to scream again. Before I could take a step, Easton jammed a knife in her windpipe.

"There were other knives. Ones from Crayton's armory. Ones from the dining hall. They were everywhere. There was practically nothing in that goddamn room but candles and knives. I grabbed the closest one and dove at him. He went for my neck and I went for his ribs. I got there first and stabbed him twice before security decided it was time to finally show up and pull me off him.

"They cleaned me up and took me to a little room, somewhere underground I'd never been. Crayton himself showed up, flanked by that goon, Axton. I asked him when the cops were coming, and you want to know what he said?"

"I can only imagine," said Mark.

"'Mr. Easton is a dangerous man,'" Aria said, doing her best Crayton voice. "'I'm afraid the law won't give him the justice he deserves quickly enough. Wouldn't *you* like to be that justice? To ensure he pays for what he's done? In just a few days, you can.'

"Axton was there to make it clear this wasn't a suggestion. The fight would continue as planned, and I'd be confined to make sure I didn't try to call the cops or finish what I started ahead of time. They told me they'd take care of the arrangements for the girl, but I've no idea what they did with her. I've been watching the fights and the news all week, and one word of this certainly didn't get to the damn press."

Mark thought of the girl in the garden. He wondered if it was the same one. He wondered if she had been the *only* one.

"He's fucking sick, Mark."

"Easton?"

"Yes, Easton, but *Crayton*. I always knew it. He'd rather have his pets keep playing than have something petty like a *cold-blooded murder* interfere with his game. God, I can still see her throat opening up. This isn't right. None of this is right. I should do something. But he and his henchman scared the shit out of me. I felt like they were about to tie me up and feed *me* to Easton next if I didn't comply."

Mark's head was spinning. It bothered him that the first thing he was thinking of was if he could somehow leverage this against Crayton, but it was Aria's word against his and Easton's, and no doubt any physical evidence had been destroyed, along with the body itself. The worst part was that deep down, none of this surprised him, given the picture of the man that had been forming over the past few months. But Aria was seeing Crayton's true face for the first time.

"How bad did you hurt Easton?" Mark asked. Aria shook her head.

"I don't know. Not bad enough if this fight is still on. And now I gave him a reason to be extra pissed at me."

"I'm sorry," Mark said. "I should have . . ."

"Mark, you should have done nothing. You were lying in a hospital bed sliced to bits."

"I know, I know," Mark said. "I just wish I'd been there."

"I am glad you came today," she said, her tone softening. "Nice to see a friendly face before . . . you know."

"I suppose I can't really give you the same speech I gave Moses."

"What'd you tell him?"

"To leave. To walk away."

"You of all people know it's too late for that now."

"It doesn't have to be. Not for you."

Aria moved closer to him and narrowed her eyes. Her long hair was in ringed curls and someone had clearly already been in to do her makeup for the camera. She was flawless. A Valkyrie.

"Would you leave with me?" she whispered. "If I told you I'd quit right now?"

The question hit Mark like a sledgehammer. With the mission at hand, he'd never even considered leaving himself. But . . . God. Would he? For her?

"I . . ." he began. And she saw the doubt in his eyes.

"I know you wouldn't," she said. "And neither would I. This is not a fairy tale, Mark. I am not your knight in shining armor to whisk you away from all this. And don't pretend you're mine either. You know better than that."

"I know."

"This is a road we both have to take, wherever it leads. You know why I'm here. You know why I have to see this through. And now I have to put down a true monster along the way. He needs to die."

"There are other paths to justice," Mark said. "Don't listen to Crayton's mindgames."

"What's *your* path, Mark? You don't think we're all trapped here now? That if we walked away our lives wouldn't be ruined in a thousand different ways, even if we didn't end up with our throats cut? I know Moses likes to go on about how we aren't gladiator slaves like in the old days. But we are. Slaves to greed. Slaves to pride. Slaves to the public. Slaves to our past. We all have to finish this, one way or the other."

Mark was silent. There was nothing else he could say. He was a slave to the mission, after all. *And a slave to the dead*, whispered a voice in his mind.

Aria kissed him then. Unexpectedly, as always. He kissed her back, his head reeling with the weight of the insanity around them.

"I think I could have loved the man you used to be," Aria said breathlessly as she pulled away. "The one I never got to meet, before the world broke him. And maybe you could have loved the girl I was, a long time ago."

It felt like good-bye.

The door burst open, and Mark found himself staring down the barrels of a half dozen Glasshammer SMGs. His guards and hers.

"Mr. Wei, you seem to have taken a wrong turn," one growled. "We need to escort you to your seat.

"Miss Rosetti, it's time."

EASTON WAS A NIGHTMARE.

His black armor was jagged and slick, like it had been dipped in oil. Strapped to his chest, ribs, and legs were long, sickly looking knives, at least a half dozen from what Mark could count.

But no one was looking at the knives or the armor. Rather, it was impossible to tear your eyes away from the monstrosity that was his helmet. It appeared to be a real pig's head that had been dismembered and stretched across a metal dome. Blood was still coagulating under the empty eye sockets and trickling from the holes in the ears and mouth. On Easton's back, it appeared the rest of the pig had found a home. He wore a long cloak of pink and black, the skin of the pig woven into dark fabric, which created a tattered stream of blood and flesh behind him. Mark wondered if Arthur had anything to do with this, or if Easton had just designed it all himself. It was something straight out of the mind of a psychopath.

Aria was a stark contrast. She now donned her helm, and a single plume of long brown hair erupted from the top. The silver helmet, presumably crafted from the same material as Mark's own armor, covered most of her face other than her lips and chin. The rest of the silver plating from her neck to her toes was mirror-polished and spotless. The wind tugged lightly at the translucent strips of fabric around her waist and on her arms. Mark's heart wouldn't stop thundering.

His box was crowded with Glasshammer guards, but also joining him were Ethan, his wife, Lily, Moses, Nolan, Carlo, and even Shyla, who had crept in right before the match was about to begin, still wearing her Muse outfit. The box was enormous, so it wasn't crowded, and Mark was glad he wouldn't have to watch this alone. Aria was talented, but the girl had a death wish, and Easton was clearly more than willing to grant it.

"Why so many knives?" Ethan wondered out loud. He'd turned into quite the analyst since his fight, rarely bothering to mention the emotional weight of the carnage itself. Moses, meanwhile, had become much more withdrawn since he'd killed Mendez, and sat quietly holding Nolan's hand with white knuckles. Shyla tried to make small talk with Lily, but was mostly met with silence and polite smiles. Ethan's wife looked constantly uncomfortable every time Mark had seen her, and she really only seemed to come alive when she was doing interviews for CMI streams. But anyone with a disease like that was allowed to act strangely, Mark supposed.

"I don't know," Mark said. "He's only got two hands. Just seems like extra weight."

Mark looked over the sheathed knives hung seemingly at random all over Easton's armor, and an involuntary shiver went down his spine.

"*Choose.*"

"She's got it," Carlo said, ever the optimist. "Not even worried about it. Dude's a freak, and she's got the crowd on her side."

It was true. Though Easton had amassed a number of fans through his *Prison Wars* performances, there were plenty who were disgusted by the fact that he was released to compete in the Crucible. On the way in, Mark had seen protestors holding signs with the faces of the dozens of dead girls Easton had scalped and slain over the past decade, and he'd slithered out of his death sentence with Crayton's help.

Aria, meanwhile, was generally well-liked by the public, especially since she was one of only two women left in the tournament. She wasn't quite the media darling that Soren Vanderhaven was, but as the match was about to begin, there were chants of "*Ar-i-a! Ar-i-a!*" reverberating throughout the stands all the same.

Crayton's speech was a blur of the usual buzzwords, "honor" and "courage" and "strength," with "beauty" thrown in there for good measure because of Aria's presence. The crowd ate it up, naturally, and soon lights ringed the entire stadium as the countdown began.

Mark watched the numbers tick down, and everyone in the box crept to the edge of their seats.

With one second left, Easton loosened his grip on the knife in his right hand, a twelve-inch straight blade. Mark watched in slow motion as the knife flipped around and he caught the tip of it between his fingers. Carlo saw it too.

"Oh shit he's going to—"

At zero, the lightshow exploded throughout the stands and the usual celebratory cacophony rang out. A millisecond later, the enormous knife was already sailing end over end directly at Aria's head.

She spun out of the way, arching her neck so the blade cut a few hairs from her plumed ponytail but missed the rest of her entirely.

The second knife didn't.

Despite the size of the weapons, Easton had learned how to

throw them with precision. The second blade was barbed and plunged directly into the side of Aria's shoulder as she spun, knocking her off balance, a teeth-clenched scream escaping from her lips. Mark and the rest of the stadium froze.

Easton didn't. He already had two fresh knives in his hands, pulled from their sheaths near his ribs, and was racing toward the wounded Aria.

Despite what had to be unimaginable pain shooting through her left arm, she still held both her swords, and she brought them up before Easton's curved knives could sink into her chest. She fended off strike after strike, her longer blades pushing Easton back, but he was able to quickly dive inside despite the reach disadvantage. A few times he just barely missed her stomach.

"Jesus *Christ*, they're fast," Carlo exclaimed.

He was right. The two were striking and parrying so quickly, it seemed like sparks were exploding from where their blades met nonstop. The knife was still sticking halfway out of Aria's shoulder, with no spare second for her to remove it, and Easton fought like he was enraged his initial trick shot hadn't killed her outright.

Aria finally found a window to fling a long-legged kick into the neck plating under Easton's pig mask, which sent him tumbling to the sand. She tried to lunge forward with a downward follow-up strike, but had to twist out of the way as, from flat on his back, Easton flung another knife toward her face. It sailed up into the air behind her. She nearly lost her balance dodging it, but wrenched herself around to keep her footing. Easton had already sprung back up and was on the attack with a fresh knife to replace the one he lost.

Deflecting his blows as best she could, Aria's left arm was starting to move noticeably slower, the shock of the impact slowly wearing off, replaced by pure, burning agony, no doubt. Easton dove in with both knives, but Aria crossed her swords in a bladed X and held him off. Mustering her strength, she shoved him back and he skidded on the sand a few feet away.

They paused now, circling each other like two predators convinced that the other one was prey. Blood was flowing from Aria's shoulder, where the knife was still embedded, and she kept shrugging to pump feeling back into the appendage.

Get that out, Mark thought. And it seemed she agreed.

She flipped one of her swords around and planted the pommel under the hilt of the knife. Using the flat of her other blade, she slammed it into the tip of the first sword, and drove it upward into the knife, which caused the serrated blade to pop out and drop to the sand. She winced, but rotated her arm around, and it seemed to be more mobile.

"Holy shit, what a badass!" Shyla said. The crowd was cheering relentlessly, and instant replay was already looping the knife removal on the big screen.

"She's a tough one," Moses said, a smile finally breaking across his face.

Easton stood opposite from her and broke into mock applause, clapping his metal hands together, still holding a knife in each. Aria was in no mood, and dove forward across the sand. He barely whipped his blades up in time to deflect the pair of slashes.

Aria was reinvigorated by the removal of the knife, and Mark saw her settle into her graceful fighting stance once more, gliding across the sand, weaving away from Easton's thrusts and diving in with slashes of her own. In the next few seconds, she'd caught him in the leg, the arm, and the ribs, a dance of slow destruction. They were shallow cuts, but his blood was mixing with the pig's blood all the same. Mark swore the armor mics were picking up *laughter* under his gory mask.

Once again, Aria charged in with a flurry of blinding strikes. A few clanged against his armor, and one of his counter-stabs bounced harmlessly off her breastplate. But Aria pressed forward, twirling past his blades, which sliced nothing but air. She lunged hard with a double-straight thrust with both swords that almost skewered Easton, but he leapt back, just out of range of the points.

Unfortunately for him, his heel caught his flesh-filled cape.

He stumbled and fell on his armored ass, dropping one knife in the process. Aria sunk down in order to leap on top of him and end the fight on the error.

But even dazed from the fall, Easton's remaining knife flashed forward, and planted itself straight through Aria's foot before it left the ground.

She cried out, stuck to the sandstone floor, and Easton scrambled upright, pulling out two more knives. He dove forward, but even with her foot trapped, Aria swung upward with one of her swords in desperation.

Easton was close enough where the blade swung clean through the front of his pig mask, cutting off the entire snout. The near miss stunned him for a second, and it was enough time for Aria to whip the other sword around and ram it straight through a crack in the armor plating on his left side, between two empty knife sheaths.

A ghastly shriek spewed out of the hole in the pig helm as Easton dropped a knife and sank to his knees. He brought the remaining blade overhead and tried to stab it down into Aria's abdomen, but she flung her second sword outward and cleanly sliced off his hand at the wrist. The blade and bloodied gauntlet went spinning into the sand as Easton continued screaming. Everyone in the box was yelling and clapping, drowned out only by the rest of the stadium doing the same.

Aria pulled the bloody sword out of Easton's ribs and stood all the way up, returning both blades to their sheaths on her back. She bent down and wrenched the knife out of her foot, taking a few gingerly steps backward. Leaning forward, she reached into the hole she'd created in the mask and pulled the entire contraption off Easton's head.

Underneath were the saucer-sized eyes of a lunatic, mouth contorted in an unhinged smile, teeth crimson. Aria's expression was
unreadable under her helm; only her lips were visible, tightly pressed
together. She towered above the crippled man, and raised Easton's
bloody knife.

She didn't stab him. Instead, she brought the blade to his forehead, where his wet hair met skin. She curled the blade around,
drawing a sharp line of red, and with her gauntleted hand, yanked
hard on his hair and started sawing under the flap with the knife.
She peeled back the skin to expose a round mess of gore and grizzle
where his scalp used to be. She tossed the matted, bloody trophy to
the ground.

"Oh my god," Moses exclaimed, hand over his mouth. Lily
looked like she might pass out. Ethan's eyes glinted with almost
gleeful malice.

This was her justice.

Aria pointed to a line of nearby fans in the stands who had
brought in the large signs with photos of Easton's slain girls. She
leaned down and said something out of earshot to the convulsing
man, and then drove the knife straight into his throat.

It was brutal. It was horrible. And Mark was on his feet cheering.

31

THEY LIVED. THEY ALL lived.

It was hard to believe that Mark, Moses, Ethan, and Aria had all made it through the first round. It gave Mark hope that with the recent break in Crayton's case, they could move on the man before the next phase started. But until then, they were content to all celebrate in Moses's box during what amounted to the closing ceremony of the first round, which the media was calling the "Clash of the Titans." The final fight was between *Prison Wars* god Drago Rusakov and NFL Hall of Famer Naman Wilkinson, the two most physically massive competitors of the tournament.

The four fighters in the box were nursing various wounds from their fights, each of them comparing recently sewn scars and boasting about how many milliliters of drexophine they'd been pumped up with. Aria's fresh wounds required the most meds, and she hopped around on an injured foot with a large bandage wrapped around her shoulder. Moses's scar by his ribs was pretty wicked, but everyone agreed that Mark's U-shaped forearm gash from Cassidy's katana was the ugliest wound. It was all horribly morbid, but they were flush with painkillers and ill-advised amounts of alcohol.

Mark cast a glance to a nearby TV rebroadcasting an interview with Miriam Easton, the dead killer's grandmother.

"Mrs. Easton. Did you watch the fight yesterday?"

"Oh yes!" she said, smiling with gray teeth. "It was a lovely play."

"Play?"

"I thought Aria and Matthew put on a wonderful performance. I think it's fantastic that so many people are taking an interest in the theater again!"

"Mrs. Easton, it isn't . . ."

"Matthew always wanted to be an actor. He has such a flair for showmanship! That silly mask was delightful. And those knives! I think he missed his calling to join the carnival."

"I don't think you . . ."

"It was a lovely time. I can't wait to see the third act."

Mark looked over at Aria, whose cheeks were red from drexophine and white wine.

"If only we could all live like her," she said. "Inventing our own reality."

"It's dementia," Mark said.

"It's bliss," Aria said. "A mind unbound. Shaping everything to your own narrative."

"And what's your narrative?"

"One where I don't have to fight the world's largest Russian next round."

The fight started, and Aria's expression quickly shifted from liquored-up peace to a look of looming dread. Wilkinson, in his shining silver and blue armor, mimicking the colors of his old NFL team, had a broadsword as wide as his waist. But like some of the other athletes who had fallen, he didn't have the skill to wield it.

Rusakov was something otherworldly in full black plate with an infernal-looking helmet with giant, twisting bull horns sprouting from it. His greataxe had to be eight feet long, something that no mortal man should have been able to wield. But Rusakov used it with brutal efficiency, making the final fight the shortest yet.

Wilkinson had deep gouges all through his armor by the time the first minute ended, all of them leaking blood. At ninety seconds, he was on his knees, missing his entire right arm, its twitching fingers still wrapped around the grip of his broadsword, which lay uselessly in the sand.

One final swing of the mammoth axe, and Naman Wilkinson ended the fight without a head. Fifteen feet away, his helmet danced and tumbled through the sand, and a dark, round shape rolled out of it, staining the earth. Rusakov raised his red axe high and screamed a primal roar that shook the very foundation of the Colosseum.

And then there were eight.

VEGAS HAD BEEN ON the verge of becoming a ghost town before Crayton's Crucible circus arrived. The city had been dying for decades, its former patrons either resting in nursing homes or six feet underground. Of course, the vices the city was famous for hadn't gone anywhere, but interest in showing up in person to play cards or see women strip had dwindled. You could get a lap dance from an S-lens and a few well-placed stim patches. You could lose your house playing poker, blackjack, or slots on anything with a screen. Vegas was redundant, and decaying.

"I got my start in Las Vegas," Cameron Crayton said in a recorded interview that had been playing non-stop in the city for months now. "I was a young kid with nothing. A torn $20 bill to my name. I prayed to the gods of luck and fate, and when I got off the bus, I walked straight into Caesar's and put it all on black. I won once. Twice. I won *eight* times in a row. I walked out of that casino with $5,000 in my pocket, enough to invest in my first business. I swore I'd never take another dollar for granted after that. I owe this city everything. I wasn't born here, but for the Crucible, I knew I needed to come home."

Mark suspected it had more to do with the massive tax breaks the state had offered to Crayton to build the Colosseum within city limits, but it had been a worthwhile bargain. With fans flooding the city to either attend Crucible matches if they were lucky enough to snag a ticket, or simply to see the stadium and watch the matches on the Strip, Vegas had come alive again.

The streets were packed as Mark took his seat on a small sound-stage outside a recently built casino, though "recent" in Vegas lingo lately meant that it was about a decade old. Across from him was a redhead swimming in makeup who was one of the co-hosts of SportsWire. Crayton's PR team had finally ordered him to plant his ass down in an interview chair now that he'd made the quarterfinals. All the combatants had to, apparently. Mark wore a trim blue suit, and he'd been swarmed by hair and makeup in the run-up to the interview. The lights were sweltering in the heat, but he fixed a grim smile and listened to the woman babble.

"Welcome back!" she said to the camera. "I'm Melanie Mitchell and this is a special late-night edition of SportsWire. We're camped out at the base of Emerald City Casino, where Cameron Crayton is celebrating the eight quarterfinalists who are continuing on in the Crucible. Joining me is one of the most fearsome competitors left, Mark Wei!"

"Thanks for having me, Melanie," Mark said.

"Mark, we've heard a lot about your military service, both for the US and for private corporations. Has that given you an advantage in the contest over those without military backgrounds, like the recently departed Chase Cassidy?"

"It's different for everyone," Mark said. "The training I've gone through in the Navy and with Glasshammer has been extensive. There are a few veterans here, but I'll go out on a limb and say I'm probably one of the most seasoned."

Careful.

"Seasoned. Were you *seasoned* fighting in northern Africa a few years ago during the controversial Glasshammer operations there?"

Mark kept smiling.

"Melanie, you know I can't discuss the specifics of my missions. And I think my former employer was unfairly maligned in that whole episode. But that's all I'll say on it."

"What does it feel like to kill a man like Chase Cassidy? A person so beloved by millions? A true hero?"

"A true hero?" Mark said, eyebrow raised. "I think by definition he was a fictional hero."

Melanie's eyes narrowed.

"His ten million in winnings were just donated to a children's hospital," she scolded.

A privately owned children's hospital where his business manager was on the board. That's what Brooke had told him, but he kept his mouth shut.

"Of course," Mark backtracked. "I didn't mean to imply . . . Chase Cassidy was a worthy opponent and certainly will be remembered as a legend."

Just tell them what they want to hear.

"Have you spoken to Soren Vanderhaven since the fight? Since you killed the man she loved?"

Oh god. Mark gritted his teeth as he forced himself not to roll his eyes on camera. The woman's clear agenda was starting to annoy him.

"I have not," he said slowly. "But I am sorry for her . . . loss."

"She has a match against your friend, Moses Morton, next week," Melanie said.

"That she does," Mark nodded.

"So you'd like to see her dead as well, then?"

Mark couldn't stop the eye roll this time.

"All I can say is that I will be rooting for my friend."

"And Shin Tagami," Melanie pressed. "The fanbase seems to think he's one of the bravest competitors in the tournament. He's nearly twice your age, and competes without armor. Do you think that's a fair fight?"

"From what I've seen, Mr. Tagami is more than capable of handling himself. I'm sure it will be a close match," Mark said, staring sternly into Melanie's malevolent green eyes.

"There have been reports that you and Aria Rosetti are something of an item," Melanie said, her lips parting into a smile.

"She's a friend," Mark said firmly.

"There are also reports that Matthew Michael Easton was attacked before his match with Aria. Attacked by another combatant on Cameron Crayton's estate."

"I don't know anything about that."

"Did Aria Rosetti enlist *you* to attack Mr. Easton in order to cripple him before the match? So that she could win?"

"What?" Mark exclaimed, caught off guard. "No! Look—" He tore off the skin-mic from his throat. "This has been great, but I've got a party to go to. Thanks so much."

"Mark!" Melanie called after him, reaching out with manicured fingers, but he pushed past two production assistants and headed up toward the towering doors of the Emerald.

"That was bad, man," Ethan said as Mark walked onto the cordoned-off casino floor, which was alive with light and sound.

"Oh god, that was *live*?" Mark said, burying his face in his hands. He looked up and saw TVs broadcasting a live feed of Melanie who had moved on to an interview with Rakesh Blackwood, who was being asked things like "Who made your suit?" and "Who are you here with?"

"Yeahhh, you're not exactly a media guy, huh?" Ethan said.

"It was that obvious?"

Ethan laughed.

"Yeah, me neither. I just speak from the heart and hope it comes out okay."

God, Ethan was charming even when he wasn't trying to be charming. That was a useful trick. For the first time, Mark wondered if Ethan might make a good agent. He was too bright to be just another Ranger grunt.

Mark felt a hand clasp his arm. He turned and saw that Cameron Crayton had snuck up on them.

"Boys!" he exclaimed. "So good to see you!"

"Mr. Crayton," Ethan said with a thin smile.

"Cameron," Mark said.

Crayton wagged his finger at him.

"See, Ethan, this is what I've been telling you. Not so formal! We're all friends now."

Friends don't let friends murder each other.

"Sorry, sir," Ethan said. "I mean, Cameron. Old habits."

"Of course," Crayton smiled.

Mark scanned the room to see if anyone was watching them, profiling specifically for Asians who might be MSS, though that didn't narrow it down. Unlike visitation weekend and the debaucherous End of the World party, there were far more guests all over the casino floor, fewer family and friends and more of Crayton's influencers and their entourages. Mark noticed one athletic looking Asian kid who was maybe about twenty-five and kept glancing their way as he chatted with a few guests. But given their profile, it wasn't unusual for people to steal glances at them or even stare outright. Still, Mark filed it away for later.

"A *hundred* million watched that Rusakov fight," Crayton said, raising his glass and inviting Mark and Ethan to toast with him. "That's a quarter of the country."

"No pressure then," Mark said.

"Just do what you do best," Crayton said. "Are we missing the lovely Lily tonight?" he asked Ethan.

"She wasn't feeling well, and wanted to stay with the kids," Ethan said.

"Give her my best," Crayton said. "Oh, before I forget. Your credits."

He handed them each a small stack of chips. Each one was $5,000. Fifty grand in total.

"Hell of a buy-in," Mark said.

"All for charity, of course," Crayton said. "Miss Rosetti has been tearing up the poker table since she got here. I'd stay away from that one."

With a nod, Crayton slid away, deeper into party, and was mobbed by a sea of admirers. Mark noticed the Asian kid from before watch him leave.

"Moses," Ethan said as the big man lumbered up. He shook his hand, but Moses winced.

"Ach," he said. "They finally got the fingers back on. Was worried they'd kept them on ice too long."

He flexed his fingers and Mark saw that the pinky and ring finger Mendez had sliced off had indeed been reattached and were wrapped in skin-colored pressure bandages.

"Side's actin' up too," he said, patting his ribs. "Quit a slice he gave me."

"Drexophine isn't helping?" Mark asked, curious. His own pain was still completely muted by the drug, which he had been pumped into him every day.

Moses shook his head.

"They said in some cases, you can develop a tolerance. Last few doses only seem to make it worse. But I'll be fine. Just stings a bit."

"Nolan make it out?" Mark asked.

"Yes, and he's currently losing most of my free money playing pai gow poker."

Mark looked over and saw Nolan playing with a few other tuxedo-wearing guests. At the end of the table, easily overlooked, was Shin Tagami in a plain silk shirt. Mark scanned the room and saw Soren Vanderhaven in a provocative midnight-blue dress commanding an entire craps table, blowing on her own dice and charming a bunch of rich-looking men who laughed uproariously at everything she said. She caught his eye from across the room, and he immediately averted his gaze.

His eyes kept circling the room, looking for anything out of the ordinary. Crayton was the sun, the party constantly in orbit around him, so it didn't help that half the eyes in the room were on him at all times. Mark lost track of the young man he'd been scoping out earlier.

Rakesh Blackwood walked through the doors in a blinding silver suit with three models in tow, and it looked like he'd cross their path on his way to try and steal some limelight from Crayton.

"Ugh, let's go find Aria," Ethan said, clearly not wanting to run into Blackwood, his opponent in the next round. They didn't move fast enough, and Blackwood lowered his shades and raised a drink toward their group as he passed.

"See you next week, soldier boy!"

"Cheers," Ethan said, all smiles, raising his glass, before turning back with a look of uncharacteristic contempt on his face.

They found Aria lording over a castle of chips in the private poker room, a half million dollars in faux-money laid out in stacks before her. Mark recognized at least one congressman at the table with her, and a Glasshammer board member as well, but a few hands later and more or less the entire field was cleared.

"Your turn," she said as she motioned to the newly empty chairs. Her hair was done up elaborately, and she had on gold eye makeup and a tight black dress.

"Uh, I don't know," Moses said cautiously. "I feel like I'm going to leave with you wearing the shirt off my back."

It was nice to see the big man slowing getting back to his old self again, though he was cringing with every breath, brushing his hand along his side.

"Oh come on," Aria said. "Sit, sit, and sit," she said, pointing to each of them. "And deal."

The dealer obliged.

Two hours later, the three of them were almost broke and Aria could barely even be seen behind her chips, but they were having a blast, with an unlimited parade of free drinks and the chance to all just hang out with the pending threat of death still almost a week away. They had the good fortune of not being matched against one another in the quarterfinals, but none of them dared to say what they were all thinking. If they all *won* next week, they would occupy all four slots in the semi-finals, and would have to face one another. If Moses and Mark both won, they'd face other. The same was true for Aria and Ethan. This had always been the risk making friends, but Mark had allowed himself to because he thought the Crucible itself would never even be allowed to *start*, much less finish. But Crayton had proven himself more slippery than anticipated.

I won't kill any of them, Mark said, looking around the table. Moses was laughing, having just been called on his ten-high bluff against Aria's pocket kings. *No fucking way.*

If it comes to that, Crayton will die first.

Could he really do that? Scrap the mission for them? Get sent to a blacksite to save the lives of three people he hadn't even known three months ago? That wasn't him. That wasn't the man who watched thousands of Chinese burn on the water. The man who was responsible in part for the deaths of hundreds of thousands more in the ensuing chaos.

They chose their fates, Mark reminded himself as she looked across at Aria checking out a fresh new pair of cards and smiling slyly. *They signed up to die.*

So did you, he reminded himself. It's why it bothered him. They had more in common with him than he wanted to admit. Half the Spearfish agents never made it back, Brooke's brother included. The CIA had assumed few of them would.

Mark placed a bet. Aria doubled it. He shifted his cards and called. Moses dropped out, Ethan stayed.

Nothing felt right about any of this. Crayton was wrong from the start, but the mission itself was starting to grate him. The stalling. The lack of support. This was too big to heave onto his and Brooke's shoulders alone.

Mark stayed, but Aria bet again. Ethan was out next, washing his hands of Aria's power plays. Mark eyed the board. Would his three jacks take it? Could she really have the flush? Her face was a playful mask of false intrigue, daring him to read her.

Behind her through the open doorway, Mark saw the guy from earlier passing by, alone.

"I'm out," he said. "Bully."

"Aw, come on. I was ready to take the rest of your tiny pile over there!" Aria said, scooping in the pot.

"Did you have it?" Mark asked, flipping his jacks as he stood up. She tossed her cards at the dealer, face down.

"Guess you'll never know."

Mark excused himself for an imaginary phone call and crept back onto the main floor. Almost immediately, he found himself trapped in a conversation with Vanessa Redgrave, Crayton's omnipresent VP of operations. He smiled and nodded and tuned her out as he watched the young man from a distance, who was now standing alone and blinking conspicuously as he watched Crayton play roulette with a crowd around him cheering at every win and gasping at every loss. "Blinking conspicuously" meant it looked like he had an S-lens, and was snapping photos discreetly. His lips were moving as well, just barely, indicating he had someone on the line. Mark eyed him and saw no protrusions in his slim-fitting suit that might indicate a gun, but that didn't mean much. He scanned around for other possible agents, but the kid was the only one that stood out. As he continued his search, he found Rakesh Blackwood and Soren Vanderhaven chatting at the bar, speaking in whispers and laughing, their eyes locked in his direction, assuredly having fun at his expense. He ignored them and panned back to the young man, but he was gone.

Mark quickly broke off his conversation with Vanessa, much to her dismay, and hurried toward where he last saw him. He looked toward the restrooms and caught a glimpse of the kid heading inside just as the door closed.

He tried to reach Brooke on the S-lens, but she didn't answer, so he swiped her a quick message on his phone.

POSSIBLE MSS CONTACT, INVESTIGATION.

As he reached the door, it swung open, and the massive frame of Drago Rusakov poured out. They exchanged a glance, Mark having to practically look straight up to make eye contact with the man, and in those black eyes Mark saw nothing but a void. Rusakov drifted by him like a glacier, and Mark slid inside the marbled bathroom.

There was only one other man there, white, middle-aged, and he zipped up and brushed by Mark without washing his hands in one of the gold-laden sinks. But in a far stall, Mark could see two shiny shoes. He turned back to the door and jammed the e-lock, ensuring no one else would join them.

Mark's mind raced as he tried to calculate his next move. He could remote wipe the guy's S-lens with his phone, but if he let him walk, he'd lose valuable intel. And he couldn't question him if he knocked him out and scraped the data manually. An all-out brawl with an MSS agent could spill back out into the casino and blow his cover. Or he could, you know, die, if the kid had a poisoned microblade up his wrist or a molar mine in his jaw.

The toilet flushed. Mark didn't have time to weigh any more options.

The lock of the stall clicked open, and Mark's foot plowed into the door a millisecond later. The hardwood cracked against the kid's forehead and staggered him, and in an instant, Mark was on top of the dazed would-be agent, a hand around his throat and the other searching him for weapons. But most importantly, Mark wrenched the stunned kid's face toward his and ran a siphon program in his S-lens, instantly transferring his lens data to him, eye-to-eye. Useful for sharing photos with friends, but also for complete data dumps, with a military-grade hacking program embedded in Mark's device.

Mark quickly scanned through the photos as the kid struggled. Crayton. Crayton. Crayton. Surveillance.

"Man, what the fuck!" the kid finally choked out as Mark's grip slipped a bit.

"Who are you?" Mark said, testing the cover. He wasn't fighting back. Not effectively anyway.

"Han," he sputtered. "Han Takeda!"

"Why are you here?" Mark asked forcefully.

"My buddy, Chris. Chris Westerland. His dad owns the casino. He's in Ibiza but he threw me his ticket for this. Knows I'm a huge Crucible fan! Just got off a call with him."

Mark checked the call log, which did indeed read "C-WEST," who had been online a few minutes earlier. He kept scanning the pictures in the S-lens as well. There were more shots of Crayton, but also of all the fighters at the party. Eventually he reached a few creepshots that had zoomed into Soren Vanderhaven's cleavage, and a suspicious-looking round, black shape that Mark recognized as Aria's ass in her slinky party dress. After that there were a few more of her from more traditional angles, laughing, smiling, playing cards.

His heart began to sink.

Wordlessly, he searched for the kid's name. Six forms of legit ID popped up immediately. Police record too. Arrests for two public intoxications, thrown out, three counts sexual assault, thrown out. Rich kid. Too dirty for a cover. Mark began to loosen his grip.

He's no one.

"Is this because you saw me checking out Aria? I'm sorry man, I watched *Heroes and Legends*, I know you two got . . . whatever it is you got. She's just so fuckin' hot! You know? Well, of course you do."

"Why Crayton?" Mark growled, his pulse racing, but the adrenaline was slowly starting to fade. "Why so many photos of him?"

"Did you just gank my whole S-lens roll? Damn, I gotta get that hack. I'd stop scrolling if I were you soon though."

Still sifting through the photos, Mark reached the end of the party shots and was greeted by a giant, erect penis next to a hand giving a thumbs up. He winced, and kept scrolling past several more like it, and then eventually found photos of Han at various clubs timestamped days and weeks earlier.

"Crayton's the man, dude. He put all this shit together! Other billionaires are sitting on their asses investing in fusion power and synthetic trees and shit, and he's bringing gladiator matches back from the dead. Fuckin' badass."

Mark finally released Han, his sportcoat wrinkled and his forehead bleeding, but otherwise unharmed. He sighed loudly.

"But for real though, sorry about the Aria pics," Han continued. "Guess subtlety ain't my strong suit."

Mark ran his hand through his disheveled hair. He'd heard of deep cover, but there was no way this was a front. He was jumping at shadows. Well, assaulting shadows in bathrooms, anyway.

"It's . . . fine, man," Mark said, slowly walking backward. "It's my bad. It's just been a hell of a month."

Han nodded and dabbed the blood on his head with toilet paper.

"Stressful shit, I get it. No worries. Just . . . you know, save the rage for that Tagami cranker."

Mark practically stumbled out of the bathroom when Brooke called him back.

"You made contact with MSS?" she said in a hopeful tone that made Mark extra reluctant to explain his fuck-up.

"Uh, about that . . ."

32

MARK STARTED TO SLIP into a dark place the next few days. The mission was at a standstill, and nothing he did seemed to move it forward an inch. Since Easton's death, the Glasshammer guards no longer forcibly accompanied competitors everywhere, so once again he had a window to dig. He'd mostly neglected his training, scouring every inch of Crayton's manor as best he could at night for more intel, and spent most of the days doing research through encrypted channels to support Brooke's work, but there were no new breakthroughs. His screw-up at the casino had potentially exposed him, and more importantly, it turned up nothing at all useful. The quarterfinals were mere days away, and despite all they'd learned about Crayton, there was still not enough to move on.

Aria invited him out for a late-night run, but he declined, instead lying on his bed with a fifth of whiskey and watching a replay of Drago Rusakov's SportsWire interview. Melanie Mitchell seemed afraid to even ask him anything, and just let him grunt and speak when he felt like it.

"These women," he said with a thick accent. "This cheerleader. This ballerina. They do not belong here."

Mitchell nodded slowly, her eyes wide.

"They will die. They will not die well. It will be ugly thing."

He rubbed his beard and his beady eyes glinted from the overhead lights.

"Ballerina will dance and dance. She will be pretty. Like flower. Crowd gives many kisses and cheers. Good TV, as you say."

Mark took another swig and kept watching.

"But this is not like the *Prison Wars*. Those men knew death when they were still living. This? These girls know nothing. They know smiling and curly hair and happy TV talking," he said, moving his hand like a puppet.

"They do not know death. I alone remain. The black man dead. The pig man dead. No more from the *Prison Wars*. Only me. And I know death. I am full of souls. Full to bursting."

Rusakov stared straight into the camera.

"This will be ugly thing."

Mark forgot about sleeping the rest of the night.

But it wasn't just that night, it was every night.

Mark was losing sleep at an alarming rate, throwing himself into an unhealthy, illogical cycle of training, drinking, and research. Even Brooke, doing all of it remotely with no imminent threat of death looming, was starting to wear out.

"I can't read through another interrogation brief," she finally said after an all-night S-lens session with Mark. "I'm serious. I'm going to claw my eyes out if I have to read 'prisoner unresponsive' as the answer to every goddamn question. Do they cut their tongues out over there or what?"

"Yeah, I know what you mean," Mark said, rubbing his eyes. His S-lens warped and reformed after being prodded by his finger. Brooke's exhausted face snapped back into focus. He saw her hand-waving through virtual docs on her end.

"Oh," she said, coming to a stop. "I forgot about this."

"What?" Mark asked, no longer even daring to hope for a breakthrough.

Brooke looked into the lens.

"How much do you want to know about Shin Tagami?"

"Huh?" Mark said. "What does he have to do with this?"

Brooke shifted.

"Erm, nothing. But I mean you're probably fighting him in a few days, and I know the public pretty much knows nothing about the guy other than he's old and quiet and badass enough to fight without protection or a blade."

"And you know something else about him?" Mark asked.

His curiosity was piqued. As much as he hated to say it, he was more engaged with prep for the tournament now than the mission, which seemed to be going nowhere. All he had to do was kill people there. Much simpler. Of course he didn't want to kill Tagami. The man had done nothing to him. But what the hell was Brooke talking about?

"During visitors' weekend, I may have snuck into his room to do some digging."

"Why the hell would you do that?"

"Gideon's suggestion. I mean, he's the only other Asian guy in the damn tournament, and this entire thing revolves around China. He, we, thought he could potentially be an MSS plant."

"I assume he's not, given that you're apparently pulling this out of your 'shit I forgot to tell Mark' file."

"He's not, but that doesn't mean there's nothing worth reading. At least for background. But if you'd rather just fight the mute old sage and leave him a mystery, I wouldn't blame you."

Mark thought about it for a few seconds, and took another sip of gin.

"Screw it," he said, waving his drink-filled hand. "I can't stomach any more briefings either. Just send it."

Brooke waved a document up onto the screen. It was a scan of a handwritten letter, written shakily.

"The man lives like a monk," Brooke said. "But I found this rolled up inside one of his bedposts."

"This is, what? Nepali?" Mark said squinting. "I've got a handle on five languages, but this isn't one of them."

"Me neither," Brooke said. "Here's the translation."
Another page appeared, in English.

Captain Hirota,

I remember my son's message like it was yesterday. He was so excited he had been placed in your unit. You were the great Iman Hirota, the hero of the Himalayas. Your victories against the Chinese invaders were legend in these parts. My son was proud to serve in your guard, and said all the other boys thought the same. For my part, I felt relief. There is no safety in war, but at least my Kamal would be looked after by one so brave and formidable.

But now? I spit. I spit on you, your memory. Your legend of lies. It must have been some other man who did those great things. It could not have been you. Iman Hirota was a hero. And you, whoever you are, are a coward.

My son is dead. And he is not the only one. There are grieving mothers all over my village who curse your name nightly. They say you sold them. You sold them to the Chinese for slaughter, and fled. Did they promise you position? Wealth? How much was my son worth? How much were all the sons of this valley worth? I want to know.

I do not know if you will ever see this letter. I send it to your last address, but they tell me your family is gone as well. A vacation, perhaps? Living a life of affluence with your blood money?

Know that an entire village curses your name, your soul. Carry that with you. Carry it like I hope you carry the faces of the dead. The face of my sweet Kamal.

You are old, growing older. Naraka will find you soon, and I know Yama shall not be kind to you. That is my solace. My only solace.

Your shame will stain your soul in this life, and throughout eternity.

The letter was unsigned.

"What the hell?" Mark asked. "Tell me you've got some context for this."

"I do, but you may want to leave it at that," Brooke said, shifting uncomfortably.

"What, because he was some kind of traitor in the border war? And sold out some kids? Now I'm supposed to make him pay, I guess. Bringing that karma around."

"Sure," Brooke said.

"What aren't you telling me?"

"Well, after I found that, I *definitely* needed the rest of the story to make sure he wasn't still a Chinese agent, if he'd been reportedly working with them. It took a while, but I tracked down a few sources who could retell this story. The whole story."

Mark sat and listened, pouring himself another drink.

"Before he was Shin Tagami, he was Iman Hirota. Japanese mother, Nepalese father. He grew up in Tokyo, but when the border war started, his father's village was on the front lines. He flew out and rose to captain in just a few, short guerrilla assaults on the mountain that soon became the stuff of local legend. It's hard to know how much of it is true, but one story had him taking out a twenty-man Chinese convoy singlehandedly. No record of that, but who knows.

"Eventually, he was given his own unit. A selection of the Gurkha Army's best and brightest. The toughest, smartest young soldiers. He caused even more havoc with them, to the point where China was almost forced entirely out of the mountain province.

"Rather than try and take on the guerrilla division directly, China sent an exfil team to Hirota's village. Soon after, they sent him a note attached to a video file.

"'Your unit for your family,' it said. The Chinese had taken his wife, two daughters, and three grandchildren."

"Ah," Mark said quietly.

"The sources are split about what happened next. Some say that he sold his unit. Told them to make camp and keep a lighter guard than normal so the Chinese could take them unaware. Others say he offered *himself* to save his family and his unit, but China found his camp anyway and took them all the same.

"Both stories end with his family being returned at a local Chinese base. And then as he embraced them, the soldiers opened fire.

"Hirota was thought dead for years, but bits of scavenged security footage showed a man killing at least a dozen Chinese in the base. But he couldn't kill them all, and fled to the mountains, reportedly to a monastery, and eventually to America where we granted him asylum and citizenship."

Mark flipped through the intel report of the incident, scarcely believing what he was reading.

"Jesus," he said, unsure of whether or not it had been a good idea to hear that story. Tagami was as much of a victim as Mark, losing his family to the Chinese, though whether he'd sold out his unit was unclear.

And what would you have done? Mark asked himself. *What did you do to see your family again?*

Was Tagami here punishing himself? Like Aria? *Like you*, said the voice in his head. Was Mark supposed to balance the scales for the grieving Nepali mothers? Or was Tagami supposed to do the same for Mark?

This tournament is not a tool of the gods, Mark thought. *Only of the devil. The blond, white, scheming, laughing devil.*

Don't lose focus.

Mark set down his drink.

IT FELT LIKE MARK was being constantly thrown into the future, each day scrambling out of his grasp as he was dragged toward the inevitable quarterfinal matches. His dreams were cruel and violent. In one, he stood outside a Chinese outpost as Riko and Asami were led out. He ran to meet them just as a dozen soldiers opened fire. Tagami's story had been warped into his own. Commanding the soldiers was a familiar white man with blond hair and blue eyes. He screamed in perfect Chinese and the soldiers closed in on the corpses of Mark's family. He was bleeding everywhere, and found himself staring into the barrel of a revolver. Behind it was a thin face flecked with scars. Zhou pulled the trigger.

Mark woke up, soaked with sweat. Aria didn't stir, tangled in the sheets of her bed. It was three in the morning, and they'd only been asleep for two hours, which is as much as Mark ever hoped to get lately. Aria usually didn't sleep much either. She frequently woke up, heart racing, saying the face of the maid Easton had killed was plaguing her dreams. Just because the man was dead, the scene wouldn't erase itself from her mind. The guilt wouldn't leave either. Mark knew that better than anyone. He quietly dressed and stole out of the room, heading for the expansive gym across the courtyard outside.

The facility was mostly dark. Way in the distance, Mark could hear the nearly silent whine of a treadmill, and saw a blonde ponytail bobbing in the distance that could only belong to Soren Vanderhaven. She wore shorts, a neon sports bra and headphones, and didn't even glance over when he entered. He likewise ignored her and he started up a lifting routine on the opposite end of the gym. It reminded him of the eerie, late-night workout sessions where he used to spar with Carlo. But his friend was holed up in a Vegas hotel somewhere with Shyla, and Mark was here, now training to avoid near-certain death in the Crucible.

Mark did a full body routine until he could barely lift his arms or walk. It was enough to convince him he might finally be able to catch another few hours of sleep, if he was lucky. He left Soren, who was apparently running a half-marathon at least on the treadmill, and headed to the men's locker room to shower and change.

The cavernous room was silent. Mark remembered a few weeks ago, when fighters and trainers were in there after a long day of work, the place was alive with piped-in music and chatter. Now it was stone silent, only the drip of a leaky showerhead echoing down the tile.

Mark took off his shirt and picked at his forearm bandage. He felt a tiny twinge of pain for the first time in a good long while. They must be scaling back his drexophine doses, he realized. It was probably for the best. Even if it wasn't a narcotic, a little pain reminded him he was alive during a time when he more or less always felt like the walking dead.

Footsteps on the marble floor. Gym shoes. Light gait. Mark's head snapped instinctively to the left, right before the owner of the sneakers rounded the corner.

Soren?

She was soaked with sweat from the run, and still wearing her headphones. She didn't even look at Mark and simply walked to a nearby locker across the room from his own. She stepped out of her shoes and put them inside. Finally, she pressed a finger to her right ear, and placed the deactivated set of headphones in the locker as well. Mark stared at her.

"Uh, I think you read a sign wrong," he said, now that she could hear him. She answered without looking at him.

"I'm exactly where I should be."

And then she peeled off her sports bra.

Mark's eyes widened, then jerked away out of chivalrous instinct, but not before he caught a glimpse of the most perfect man-made breasts money could buy.

"Uhm," was all he could say, his tongue and stomach both twisted in confused knots. But Soren didn't slow down. Next were her skin-tight shorts and underwear, and after she stuffed all her clothes in the locker, she walked straight ahead toward the showers on the other side of the mirrored sink wall wearing nothing at all.

"Coming?" she asked, still not bothering to turn his way. Soren disappeared behind the wall, and the sound of her bare feet on the floor was the only sound in the locker room.

Mark had no idea what the fuck was happening. He sat there, stunned, wishing that there was someone, anyone, around to see what was going on. Hell, he even wished the *Heroes and Legends* spy cameras were back. This was . . . what *was* this?

Mark heard the hiss of a distant shower and stood up. He was in a towel, and the only other thing he wore now were bandages. He knew something was off about Soren Vanderhaven, but he currently had no idea which way was up. This felt like some kind of surreal, sick drug trip.

He crept slowly toward the showers. Most men would have been gleefully sprinting toward the sight he'd just seen, but he inched forward like someone was about to spring out from the shadows with a knife. The dim lights of the locker room and the splashing of the water on the tile made everything feel foreboding.

Just walk away, he told himself. *She's fucking with you.*

Of course she was, he knew that. But morbid curiosity was getting the better of him with each step. Was she really doing this?

Mark turned the corner.

The showers were each individual stalls. Walls of stone with glass doors for privacy, to give off less of a "prison shower" communal vibe. But the stall with steam pouring out of it had the door wide open.

An invitation.

She's really doing this.

He still expected to wake up at any moment. The situation was dreamlike, something he would have fantasized about as a teenager. But the environment, the shadows, sounds, and sickening heat of the air was nightmarish. It was one of those alarming moments when Mark thought he might be losing his mind.

Mark reached the stall, and there she was.

Water from dual showerheads was pouring off her sculpted, tanned body in a thousand little waterfalls. She was clothed only in steam, and ran her hands through wet tendrils of hair, the blonde now a much darker shade when drenched. She didn't make any effort to cover herself after Mark's arrival, but instead for the first time locked eyes with him. She was impossibly beautiful, yet a wave of something cold and sharp and horrible spread through him when he looked at her. Mark half expected her gaze to turn him to stone.

"Took you long enough," she said, and sent two suds-covered hands racing through her hair. Shampoo dripped down her ample curves and disappeared into the drain.

"Soren," Mark said flatly. "What the fuck are you doing?"

"Oh come on, Mark," she said, her voice all sweet and light. "You know what the fuck I'm doing. And I will do it a hundred times better than Aria, if that's what you're wondering."

Mark laughed. He caught a faint flicker of anger in her ice-blue eyes.

"Is this what you do? Cassidy, Hagelund, Mendez I know about. I'm guessing Blackwood too?"

"I'm here for *you*, Mark," she said, her tone sharpening a bit. Her makeup was starting to run. Who wore makeup to the gym at three in the morning?

"Gross, don't tell me Easton or Rusakov?" Mark continued, wrinkling his nose.

"Don't forget Ethan," Soren said coldly, her sexy voice gone, replaced by something darker.

"Well now I know you're full of shit," Mark said. More mind-games. "And Moses too, right?" He laughed again.

Soren's expression twisted into disdain.

"I *know* you hate me," Mark said, leaning in closer. "I know you hate me in public, for all the cameras to see, and I know you hate me for real, because I see it in your eyes every time you look at me."

Soren leaned in closer as well, her lips nearly at his ear.

"Want to know my secret?" she whispered.

Mark's silence was a yes.

"I hate you *all*."

Honesty. Mark was taken aback. Soren pulled back and continued to shower in a more practical fashion. Though that didn't change the fact that she was totally naked a few feet away from him.

"Even Cassidy?" Mark asked, trying to maintain eye contact.

"*Especially* Chase Cassidy, Christ," Soren said, exasperated. "That sun-shiny asshole was going to steal my spotlight. *My* spotlight. So I fucked him until he loved me. And it made *America* love me even more."

"Who . . . *are* you?" Mark said, scratching the back of his head.

"No one understands this tournament," Soren growled. "Not really. Whoever wins will be a *god* among men. Or goddess, as the case will be. This tournament is historic. There's *never* been anything like it."

"You're doing this for *fame?*" Mark said.

"Fame is everything," Soren hissed. "Fame is power. Fame is control. Fame is immortality. I will be Cleopatra. I will be Helen of Troy."

"You will be dead," Mark said. "And no one will remember you in a few years, much less hundreds."

Soren's face was stone.

"I'll tell you what. You can take that towel off and get in this shower, and I might give your friend Moses a quick death a day from now."

He knew she was trying to get in his head, permanently. Trying to stay there if they met in the tournament, which they could in the next round. She had more weapons in her arsenal than just the spear.

"And if I don't?"

"He will die weeping. And so will you. And Ethan. And Aria. And whoever else crosses me before I become champion."

Mark stared at her. All of her.

Just do it.

No one will know.

You're as good as fucking dead anyway you stupid fucking—

Mark shook his head and laughed.

"You're insane, and Moses will crush you. Good-bye, Soren."

He left her standing there, goosebumps rippling across her flesh.

"You might want some shower shoes," he called out as he walked away. "You wouldn't believe what's growing on Rusakov's feet."

33

THE MORNING OF MOSES'S fight, Mark found him in the dining hall, eating an entire table full of breakfast. There was a literal vat of egg whites in front of him, and Mark couldn't even count how many pieces of turkey bacon Crayton's chef had whipped up for the big man.

"Mark," Moses said when he saw him. "Have a bite."

He gestured toward the seat opposite him, and Mark obliged.

"You sure you have any to spare?" Mark asked.

Moses let out an abrupt laugh that caused egg flecks to lodge themselves in his mustache, which he quickly wiped away with a napkin.

"Everyone always says they get so nervous before a fight, they can't eat. But I'm the opposite. The day of, I can't help but stuff myself. Hoping protein and carbs carry me to victory, I guess."

"This is an inhuman amount of food," Mark said, surveying the vast offerings on the table. Mark hadn't slept and had practically no appetite most days. The smell of the bacon was making him nauseous.

Moses glanced up at him, and bags under his eyes indicated he probably hadn't been sleeping much either.

"Just please tell me you're not here to try and talk me into quitting again," Moses said. "I can't get into this with you. I'm finally feeling good again."

"No, no," Mark said, leaning in. "The opposite, actually."

Moses arched an eyebrow.

"Look," Mark continued. "I know how Soren seems. She's all hugs and kisses for the cameras, America's Sweetheart and all that. But trust me, she's a sociopath."

"I—" Moses began, but Mark cut him off.

"I know you're dreading having to kill this girl. Don't tell me you aren't."

Moses was silent.

"But don't be. Do *not* hold back. Do *not* think you should go easy on her, or look for the most *humane* way to end it. She won't do that for you. She wants to tear you apart and smile for the crowd while bathed in your blood."

Moses's wide eyes showed that Mark was making an impact at least.

"Did something happen?" Moses asked. "Why are you—"

"Because I know you, and you're a good person. And I know her. Everything she says is a lie, and she's one of the most cutthroat competitors here. You can't underestimate her, or give her *any* special consideration because you want to play the gentleman."

Moses sighed.

"Alright. Treat her like a rival knight, not a princess. Got it."

"Whatever analogy floats your boat," Mark said. "Just give it *everything* you have."

"What's going to happen," Moses said, dropping his voice to just above a whisper. "If I win, and you win? What advice will you have when I'm standing opposite you?"

It can't come to that. It won't.

"I'd give you the same advice," Mark said. "Don't hold back. And I know you wouldn't want me to either. It'll be a glorious death for one of us."

Moses smiled and nodded. Mark knew that was exactly what he wanted to hear.

"A true honor."

WITH EACH NEW FIGHT, the crowd in the Colosseum seemed to grow a little louder, and a little more raucous. By this point, even the cheap seats were hundreds of dollars, with the competitors looking little more than ants from on high. Lower down, seat prices jumped into the thousands, and for the box where Mark was sitting with Aria, someone probably would have paid a hundred grand easily. Mark heard Crayton was increasing subscription rates as well for all Crucible televised content, but viewership was steadily growing anyway. There was little else anyone was talking about. The top two boxers in the world had just fought a bloody pay-per-view in Philadelphia, a rescheduled NBA title series had come and gone, and no one seemed to care. All eyes were on the Crucible.

The large box was oddly empty. Nolan, Carlo, and Ethan had all opted to watch the fight with their respective families, and that left Mark and Aria with a suite to themselves. An unopened bottle of champagne stood nearby, along with trays of appetizers that were quickly growing cold. Mark wasn't hungry. Didn't even want a drink. He was too nervous.

Aria had burst out laughing when Mark told her about what happened with Soren in locker room. He didn't see the need to keep it from her, as it had nothing to do with the mission, nor did he feel particularly guilty about it, considering he hadn't done anything. Something told him Aria probably would have laughed it off even if he had.

It sounded goofy from the outside, but it told Mark that Soren was cold, calculating, and dangerous, both mentally and physically. Moses was literally triple her size, but Soren was so desperate for the spotlight, she'd do anything possible to keep her star from fading.

"He will die weeping."

He remembered those icy blue eyes. That half-smile, half snarl. Men like Easton and Rusakov were the obvious sort of evil. But Soren? She was Lucifer, the beautiful angel of light. She reminded him a bit of Crayton, in that way.

Once again, the spotlight was on her, and Crayton gave her the usual chance to address the crowd before the countdown to the match. She said exactly what she was supposed to, thanking her family, friends, fans, and God, in that order. She smiled and waved and blew kisses to the love-drunk fans in the first few rows. The crowd *adored* her, and there wasn't an entertainment outlet on earth that didn't have her as their lead story half the time these days. That sort of power was unsettling.

Then it was Moses's turn. His armor was polished expertly, as Mark knew it would be. Most fighters had someone on staff do it for them, but Moses did it all himself, buffing the metal, treating the leather. Mark even saw him combing the faux-bearskin he wore over his upper half. He was the most finely groomed barbarian Mark had ever seen. He wasn't standing quite as tall as usual though. Mark caught him placing his hand on the same side that was giving him trouble days ago. It had been a week since his last fight, and he still didn't look recovered. It made Mark sweat even more.

Instead of giving the usual thanks to family and fans, Moses cleared his throat, and his armor mic picked up his big, booming baritone.

"Out of the night that covers me,
Black as the Pit from pole to pole,
I thank whatever gods may be
For my unconquerable soul.

In the fell clutch of circumstance
I have not winced nor cried aloud,
Under the bludgeonings of chance
My head is bloody, but unbowed.

Beyond this place of wrath and tears
Looms but the horror of the shade,

And yet the menace of the years
Finds, and shall find me, unafraid.

It matters not how strait the gate,
How charged with punishments the scroll,
I am the master of my fate:
I am the captain of my soul."

The crowd was silent, not knowing what to make of the poem. Aria was moved to uncharacteristic tears, and Mark felt a lump in his throat.

The blaring fanfare of the Crucible's orchestral theme played as the countdown ticked to zero. Mark watched Soren's face slowly morph from a carefree smile to a hard sneer in a matter of seconds. Moses, for his part, didn't look nervous either. His brow furrowed in concentration, and he bent low with his massive maul in a defensive position.

As soon as the timer hit zero, Soren sprang at him like a coiled snake, gripping the bottom of her spear with one hand and sending all seven feet of it racing right toward Moses's throat while still holding onto the end. Her horizontal leap was unearthly, and the length of her weapon brought the tip of her spear within a few inches of Moses almost as quickly as the knives Easton had flung at Aria in their match's opening moments.

But Moses wasn't like the other armored tanks that lumbered around in full-plate suits. He was surprisingly mobile, and spun out of the way of the spear, which glanced off his shoulder plating. He choked down on the grip of his maul, and whirling around, swung it like a gigantic bat toward Soren, who was now sailing through the air, unable to dodge what came next.

"Yes!" Mark shouted, leaping to his feet alongside Aria a millisecond after Moses's maul slammed into Soren's side. It threw her a solid dozen feet to the right. The crowd was stunned. She landed hard and rolled on the sand, her spear spiraling out of her grasp, her body too pulverized for her to even form a scream.

He had actually listened. No holding back.

She had to be done. Mark always suspected if Moses could land a single blow with that metal oak tree he called a maul, someone Soren's size would be dead on the spot. And yet, he watched in horror as the gymnast picked herself up off the ground.

"Are you *kidding*?" Mark said out loud. "She has to have half her ribs broken."

A large bruise was already forming on her side, and the minimal gold and black plating she wore had spiderweb cracks running through it, but she was standing. Breathing hard, she stared venomously at Moses, who looked as stunned as Mark felt.

Soren was the first to move again, none of her mobility gone, even after the potentially catastrophic blow. She dove and tumbled forward, picking up her spear from the sand, and coming back with it fast, swinging in a wide arc, which made Moses jump backward.

She began thrusting and lunging with the spear so quickly it was hard for Mark to even track it from his coveted close seat. The spearhead was just a blur, Moses having to back away from it, occasionally swatting the point with his maul or the back of his forearm plating, something Mark knew was a dangerous proposition.

But try as he might, the exposed parts of Moses's barrel torso were bloodied as a few light stabs managed to breach his defenses. He roared, seemingly to push past the pain, and pressed forward with a fresh assault. He slammed the maul left and right, forcing Soren to relent and roll out of the way as the metal cratered the earth where she'd stood only moments before. He was hoping to catch her with another haymaker, the maul built for single kill-shots, not rapid attacks. But Moses was making do, attacking more ferociously than Mark would have thought possible holding something of that size. He was expertly trained in a weapon most humans couldn't even hope to lift.

Soren tried to counter-spear him after he lunged toward her, but Moses twisted left and drove his bear-headed helmet straight into her. It bowled her over, but she had retained enough of her senses to keep her balance, rolling back and flipping up to a standing position while keeping ahold of her spear the whole time. Mark was searching her for hidden weapons like the ones he and Cassidy had, but there weren't many places to hide them, given her outfit.

Soren tried a move Mark had seen her use on Hagelund, sticking the butt of her spear behind Moses to try and trip him, but Moses had nearly a hundred pounds on her last opponent, and it was like trying to knock over a redwood. Moses went nowhere, an immovable object, and she wasn't quite the unstoppable force she needed to be. Moses took advantage of her failure and sent the handle of his maul into her face, which momentarily stunned her. He swung it around for what would have been a devastating blow, but she managed to duck under it just in time. Her nose was bleeding, possibly broken, and she did not look pleased about it.

Her next counter was more effective as Moses swung again. She jammed the spear upward and it caught Moses's bicep where there was just a leather support strap instead of metal plating. He winced as the spearhead dug into his flesh and blood poured out. Thankfully he was able to rip his arm away before she could twist the shaft and do any further damage.

The drone cams panned to various crowd shots which showed people cheering wildly at the fresh spray of blood. They were clearly hungry for more.

Soren obliged. She arced over a sweeping swing from Moses with a no-handed cartwheel, and thrust the spear behind her when she landed so it sliced through the wound on his abdomen he'd sustained in his fight with Mendez, reopening it. Moses howled, and Mark was thankful that he wasn't in the same room as Nolan, who was no doubt losing his mind, just then.

"He will die weeping."

Mark convulsed with an unwanted chill, and Aria put her hand on his shoulder.

Moses was starting to stagger now, his swings getting slower, his footwork slipping. He tried a lunging uppercut with the maul, but it missed Soren completely, and she responded by whipping the spear around so that it cracked against the metal of his helmet just under the bear's jawline. Thankfully, Mark couldn't see any more blood.

"He's still in it," Aria said, though Mark didn't know if she was trying to convince him or herself. All it would really take was one more solid blow, the kind he landed in the beginning. With the right strike, she could be dead before she hit the ground.

Moses kept swinging for her tanned collar and abdomen, but Soren was quick to dodge and deflect with her spear. Her exposed skin seemed like an easy target, but one that was impossible to hit.

Moses swung the maul hard right, and Soren went airborne yet again to dodge it, this time, launching herself off his shoulder pauldrons, and landing behind him before he could turn. Mark's heart caught in his throat as he saw her spear racing toward his exposed quadriceps, but he managed to fling his gauntlet back and sent the spear grazing off his calf instead, which drew a fresh line of red, but wasn't as crippling as it could have been.

Soren danced back, keeping him at bay with the spear like she was hunting an actual live bear. The bruise was darkening on her side now, but if she was in any pain, Mark couldn't see it on her face. Her look was feral and ferocious, blood streaming from her nose and smeared across her lips. Meanwhile, Moses looked like he was about to black out. The sand was stained with his blood from a half dozen major and minor wounds. The one on his side was flowing steadily, which worried Mark. He'd have to end this quickly. One decisive blow. That's all it would take.

Moses went in for the same maul sweep he'd just tried moments earlier, and once again, Soren left her feet, arcing over his back. Mark didn't understand why the man would try the exact same thing twice.

Because she'll do the exact same thing twice, Mark realized as Soren flew upward once more.

Moses stopped the swing short and twisted his right arm behind him. Just as an airborne Soren was bringing the spear around to try and plant it in the small of his back, he grabbed her by the leg with a meaty hand.

He slammed her down so forcefully, Mark swore he felt the box shake, though it was probably just his nervous system going haywire as he was on his feet yelling and screaming. The entire arena was a non-stop thunderclap.

Soren's eyes were unfocused as the drone zoomed in from above. She had no earthly idea where she was. Her spear was out of her grasp on the sand beside her, and Moses was already starting to bring the maul around for a crushing overhand swing.

"Yes!" Mark cheered, having never been so eager to see something so pretty smashed to a pulp.

As he pulled the maul up behind him and started to muster the last of his strength to slam it down, a screech rang out from the sand.

"*Wait!*" Soren screamed. Her face was bloody, tears were streaming out of her eyes. She was covered in dust and blood, her armor cracked, her bruise spreading endlessly.

"*Please!*" she begged.

"*No, no, no, no, no!*" Mark yelled so loudly his voice cracked. He pressed himself to the glass of the box, and slammed it with his hand over and over. "Moses, don't listen—"

Moses paused. Only for half a second. Only to consider the pitiful, broken, beautiful creature before him. Mark watched his heart break as he resumed the swing.

But a half-second's hesitation was all Soren had needed.

From the ground, she lunged left and grabbed the very end of her spear. As Moses's maul came down over his head, she twisted right, and in one fluid motion brought the spear around just before the maul smashed into vacant ground.

Mark watched as the razor tip opened up Moses's throat, showering Soren in a spray of blood. He dropped to his knees, choking, gasping, his armor mic picking up every horrible gurgle.

Mark screamed until his lungs burned and his ears were ringing so loudly he couldn't even hear the obscenities Aria was shouting next to him. The roar of the crowd was a volcanic eruption.

Moses's eyes rolled back in his head, and he fell to the red earth below. Soren's expression shifted from a cruel stare into a wide smile. She thrust her bloody spear into the sky, the wind tearing at her long blonde locks. The air was suddenly thick with a million yellow rose petals, flung by celebrating fans from every corner of the arena. She blew a kiss to the closest camera drone, an image beamed directly to the box's enormous TV to Aria's left.

Mark screamed a scream he couldn't even hear, and he flung a champagne bottle through the screen. Soren's beaming, blood-soaked face shattered into a thousand jagged edges.

34

THERE WASN'T TIME TO grieve. There wasn't time to do anything, really. Mark's fight with Shin Tagami, Iman Hirota,
whatever the hell his name was, was in nineteen hours.

He'd barely known Moses for a few months, and still the loss
was crippling, like it had blown a hole straight through him. He
ignored calls from Carlo, offering condolences, Gideon, demanding
mission updates, and Brooke, probably ringing him with some combination of the two.

He couldn't bring himself to go back to Crayton's compound.
Not yet. He told the autolimo to drive in circles around Vegas indef-
initely, and he just stared at the lights outside. Every so often, a
screen would show the highlights of the evening's fight. By the third
lap of the city, he'd seen Moses's throat slit a half dozen more times.

"I saw Nolan on the way out." Aria was sitting next to him,
resting her head on his shoulder. She was idly flicking through the
pages of a flexscreen. "His eyes were red and his voice was cracking,
but other than that, he seemed oddly . . . okay."

Mark raised his eyebrow.

"Because of the money?" That didn't seem like Nolan, from
what he'd learned about the man the last few weeks.

Aria shook her head.

"He said that Moses had never seemed more alive than he had

the past few months. That he'd never made friends like us. He said it was the first time Moses had been truly happy in years."

Mark didn't know Moses as well as Nolan, obviously, but he thought back to training. Moses did seem like he loved every second of it, albeit outside of the brief pit of regret he fell into following Mendez's death.

"That's a little bit insane," Mark said.

"This was sort of heaven for him," Aria said. "You have to remember that."

"I know," Mark sighed. "But this still sucks."

"We should go back," Aria said. "You need to sleep."

Mark kept staring out at the neon. The city was just coming to life as midnight approached. He thought about stopping the car and throwing himself down a well of drinks at the nearest casino. But he supposed he'd learned a lesson from when Carlo was injured. Tagami would kill him outright if he was even a fraction off his game. Especially with what Mark had planned for the following day.

It's a stupid idea, he thought, and he'd been wrestling with it for days. But it just seemed right to him, and after so much wrongness, he felt like he needed it. He'd figure out whether it was noble or idiotic the following day. He'd told no one about it. Not Crayton's people, not even Ethan or Aria. They'd all see tomorrow.

It's too much of a risk.

Mark pushed the thoughts from his mind, though part of him wondered if he *wanted* Tagami to kill him. To end this miserable tournament and mission that never seemed to stop going off the rails.

Mark heard Aria let out a tiny gasp.

"What is it?" he asked, and turned away from the window to look down at her flexscreen. He saw a familiar face he couldn't quite place. A young girl, pretty, Asian. Above her head was the word MISSING in block text.

"Oh god," Aria said. "It's her."

The maid. The one Easton had killed in front of her. The one he'd harassed in the park when Tagami put him in his place. The one Crayton had swept under the rug, and no one noticed but her family, it seemed.

"Her father posted it. It says she just didn't come home from work one day. He says CMI reported that she left, and nothing else. Her autocar is gone, too."

"Thorough," Mark said, wondering what Wyatt Axton had done with her body and vehicle. They were likely in a scrapyard somewhere, both crushed into a two-by-two cube.

"Christ," Aria said. "I should . . . I should have—"

"It's just your word against his, isn't it?" Mark said.

Aria paused hard for a minute.

"Yeah."

"Nothing will stick to him, and he'll probably put you in a soundproof room until your fight," Mark said. "You avenged her, it's all you can do."

"It's not," she said. "And Crayton needs to pay."

Mark wanted to tell her. Wanted to tell her everything, and explain how there was a very calculated plan of how Crayton *would* pay, and how hearsay about a murder/cover-up in his compound would probably only serve to derail that. The right thing for her to do probably *would* be to go to the cops or press, but Mark was worried that it would only complicate his own task even further. He was being selfish, letting her struggle with the guilt, but he told himself he didn't have a choice.

"He scares me," Aria whispered. "More than that goddamn giant Russian I'm supposed to fight in two days. I don't know why, but he does."

"Power comes in many forms," Mark said. "*Beware the evil behind smiling eyes.*"

He couldn't remember where he'd heard that before.

"Why do you just believe me?" Aria said, sitting up to look at him. "What have *you* seen?"

Mark stared blankly out the window.

"I've seen a man bring a country to its feet, cheering the televised deaths of men and women. Anyone who can do that is capable of anything."

"Who are you really, Mark?" Aria said as they reached the edge of town and the blooming lights started to fade.

"I'm someone who will make him pay."

It was raining by the time they finally pulled up to the compound and made their way through the entryway, surrounded by the underlit towering statues Moses had loved so much. When they pulled up to the rounded edge of the driveway in front of the main manor, another limo was already there. Mark saw a blonde woman get out and for a moment clenched his teeth.

Soren.

But it wasn't her. Their headlights lit her up, and Mark's eyebrows raised as he saw that it was none other than Brooke.

Aria saw her too, and punched in a command to the autolimo to have her take her to her own manor.

"Come by later," she said. "Or not, if you'd . . . rather stay here tonight."

"I told you—" Mark said, before Aria shushed him.

"I know, I know. I'm just saying, it could be your last night on earth, so spend it wherever you want." She smiled weakly.

Mark opened the door and the rain started blowing inside.

"I'll be there soon," he said.

MARK AND BROOKE DID retreat to his room, the only safe place to talk, both drenched even in the short window of time it took them to climb the stairs to the door.

"Why didn't you tell me you were coming?" Mark said as he toweled off his hair and threw Brooke a spare hoodie emblazoned with the Crucible logo. She changed quickly in the bathroom, and came out with her wet blonde curls spilling down her shoulders.

"Check your damn messages," she said. "Or answer your phone. One of the two. I'm here for your fight, obviously. Crayton's people reached out with airfare and a hotel offer like three times. It would raise flags if I kept turning them down."

"And I'm guessing you wanted to check on me to see if I was going to go off the deep end after Moses died," Mark said flatly.

"There . . . were concerns after the city qualifiers and Carlo, yes."

"Gideon's concerns?"

"Yes, and also mine. I watched that butcher Burton Drescher almost kill you because you were fighting drunk."

He could feel her sizing him up. She was standing close enough to smell the alcohol on his breath, but for once, there was none.

"Satisfied?" he said, holding his arms out.

She nodded, and then stood around awkwardly with her hands in her back pockets.

"Alright, well I'm sure you weren't in that limo alone, and there's a certain gorgeous gladiator waiting for you somewhere in this complex, so I'm going to head to the hotel. I just wanted to make sure you were alright."

Mark looked at Brooke with wet hair, no makeup, and in a lumpy hoodie, and the only thing that crossed his mind was how goddamn beautiful she was. He said nothing. He did nothing. She'd said her piece in this very room weeks ago about why nothing was going to happen. He understood, and respected her enough not to be an asshole.

"They can't keep dying," he said. "Or I'm going to lose my mind."

"You're trained better than that."

"I know that, in theory. But it's harder in practice."

"I know."

"Do you?"

"It's how I feel every day, knowing that you could be discovered at any moment and executed in a cellar somewhere, or that you could die at the hands of a crazed actor, a traitorous Tibetan commander, or now maybe a psychotic gymnast, and that's if things go *well*. I want to tell you to go AWOL. Or kill Crayton. Or both. I want this to be over."

"But it can't be."

"Not yet. And I think deep down we both know that. There's a larger picture here we're missing."

Mark knew that. He felt it. The mission was all wrong. Crayton made even less sense as time went on. China's involvement was murky and getting murkier. He understood why he couldn't go off book. Not to save anyone, not even himself.

"Wish me luck," he said. Brooke turned to leave, and surprised him by wrapping him up in a tight hug.

"Just survive."

THE RAIN RETURNED THE following afternoon. It turned the sky gray and the sand to mud. Two downpours in less than a day was unusual for Vegas, though in the last decade weather patterns had shifted in disconcerting ways almost everywhere. Still, the flood warnings hadn't kept the crowd away. That would have been too much to hope for, Mark thought.

Tagami's angle that Crayton's team had crafted for him was "mysterious old man." Not flashy, but great with older viewers and it got the job done in terms of building interest in his "character." His intro video was nothing but picturesque scenes of nature, spliced with past clips of his victories. The music was Tibetan throat singing, showing Crayton knew that much about him at least. But Mark figured only a few people alive actually knew the story Brooke told him.

Tagami's gray robe was almost black from the rain and mud. He stood silently, as he always did, and seemed oddly content, given the weather, his possible impending death, and hundreds of thousands of fans screaming all around him. He wiped away the rain from the top of his bald head, and stared at the sky. He didn't even acknowledge Mark when he entered the arena.

Do you really want to go through with this? said the doubting voice in Mark's mind. He tried to tell himself what he was planning would be better in the tactical sense, given the weather, but he knew he was planning on doing it anyway, rain or shine.

For honor? You're an idiot.

Maybe he was. But the old man deserved better. Mark could see in his eyes that he hadn't sold out his unit. This was the kind of man who tried to sacrifice himself to save everyone, but lost them all the same. Because he failed, shame was his only armor.

Crayton gave Mark his usual booming introduction, gesturing broadly at him from behind his glass booth, shielding him from the rain. Mark's metal feet sank into the mud as he trudged toward his mark opposite Tagami.

"So Mark, does Chicago's favorite son have anything to say on this lovely afternoon?" Crayton said, looking around at the rain. Laughter rippled through the crowd like a wave.

Mark paused.

"He deserves a fair fight."

The audience buzzed as Mark began stripping off his armor plating. Arthur had shown him how to do it quickly earlier that day, though he questioned the wisdom of him doing so. He was right, no doubt.

Mark planted the bastard sword in the mud, and dropped his helmet that he held at his side. It was easiest from the top down. First were the pauldrons, then his arm and forearm plates. The chestplate came off smoothly, and the wolf's head faceplanted in the mud. Then went his gauntlets, legs, and boots. In the end, the black plates were scattered in the muck around him, and he wore only his fiber undersuit. It was built to reduce friction from the armor, and offered no more protection than Tagami's robes. Possibly less, as you could stab at the billowing robe and hit nothing but air. The same certainly wasn't true of the skintight undersuit.

Mark wiggled his bare toes in the mud, as the suit stopped at his ankles and wrists.

The audience was murmuring in confusion, and even Crayton looked a bit concerned, which Mark was curious to see. Was it not bullshit? Was Mark really one of the man's favorites? That would be ironic, considering rarely a day went by where Mark didn't imagine killing him in a dozen different ways.

"Are you sure you want to do this, Mark?" Crayton said solemnly into the mic.

"If he can, so can I," was the only reply Mark could come up with. He was just trying to do the right thing. Hopefully the right thing wouldn't get him beaten to death in the next five minutes.

Tagami finally turned his attention toward Mark, sizing up both him and his gesture. Would he take it as an insult, or a sign of respect, as Mark meant it?

The old man went rigid, and then gave a low bow with his arms at his sides. Riko had taught Mark the nuances of polite bowing before he'd met her ultra-traditional parents in Aoyama-Itchome, the old money section of Tokyo. Mark returned Tagami's gesture with the most formal bow he could remember. If the man was pleased, he didn't show it. Still, something passed between them, and it wasn't animosity.

She'd be proud you remembered that, Mark thought. But Riko wouldn't be proud of anything he'd done the last few years.

If she lived, where would you be now?

Mark didn't know. It made him too sad to fantasize about what could have been, so he simply lost himself in memory. The photos, the videos. The life he once had. But it had been too long. When was the last time Mark had heard Riko's voice, even on a recording? He'd forgotten himself in this mission, this tournament.

You're coping. You want *to forget her. Forget them.*

No, no he didn't. He tried to picture Asami's face. Round and bright with joy. He saw nothing. He tried to hear Riko's voice. Hear her sing again in his mind. But there was only silence.

He should have died in China. Perhaps the man in front of him should have too.

One of them would find peace at last.

Mark hated that it couldn't be him.

Not yet.

When the countdown concluded, there wasn't booming thunder or flashing lightning. Nothing so dramatic as that. Just cold, gray rain that made it very difficult to see a gray staff whipping towards him at a few hundred miles an hour. Mark absorbed the first blow to his ribs, and felt far less pain than he imagined he would, the lingering drexophine in his system doing its job, perhaps. But the second, third, and fourth shots made him realize that shedding his armor had probably been a very, very bad idea after all.

Mark finally got his sword up, learning on the fly how to block the insanely fast blows from a man who looked far too old to possess such speed. Mark had only trained against a staff a few times, and when he had, it was Moses wielding it, who was a much larger target. Tagami was practically darting in and out of raindrops, and as the downpour intensified, Mark was losing him in the mist, despite the fact they were the only two people on the arena floor.

The mud limited both their speed somewhat, making for sloppy footwork. There was a hard layer of stone a few inches down, but the goo covering it was something neither had had to deal with yet. The crowd was just a dark blur punctuated by pinpricks of light from flexscreens and phones trying to take photos.

Mark swatted Tagami's staff aside as it whirled overhead, sending crashing blows toward his unarmored head that he was barely able to deflect. When that didn't work, Tagami launched himself into the air and whirled around with a one-armed backhand that connected with Mark's shoulder and set him sprawling into the mud, his undersuit now more brown than black. Mark scrambled back to his feet and barely dodged a follow-up slam that would have likely broken both his legs.

He was disoriented. Every side of the arena looked the same. He couldn't make out Crayton's box, nor the one where Carlo, Aria, Ethan, and Brooke were all huddled together to watch him. Of course it would be his luck to be fighting in the middle of a monsoon in the Nevada desert. Behind Tagami, he could already see water starting to pool where the drainage systems had been clogged.

Mark finally went on the attack with a pair of spinning strikes that Tagami dodged easily. Eventually, one close swing made the old man stop it cold with his staff, and Mark was secretly hoping the razor edge would slice clean through the metal staff, but he had no such luck, and the result was only a shower of sparks, which were quickly extinguished by the rain.

Readjusting his grip, Mark realized how much his forearms were aching. His armor normally absorbed a huge portion of the shock from these metal-on-metal clashes, but now his arms were taking the brunt of it, and they already felt like lead.

Tagami was relentless. The bottom of his robes was thick with clinging mud, but he kept striking furiously, fighting like a man possessed. It had taken Mark all of a couple minutes to understand that all the stories were true about Iman Hirota.

But he was just a man. Mark had to remind himself of that. He was a legend in the Himalayas, and was built up to be some kind of force of nature through his mysterious Crucible promos. He was skilled, especially for his age, and Mark didn't even want to know how many years he'd trained while in exile, but he was human. He could die. He would die.

The crowd got behind him, though. Mark heard the dull roar of a chant beginning to build over gusts of wind. "*Shin! Shin! Shin! Shin!*" Mark really couldn't catch a break. In an age when the country was largely distrustful of Asians in the wake of Cold War II, he was still the least favored out of the two in the tournament. They were all still sore about Chase Cassidy, Mark supposed. As usual, he just had to put it out of his mind.

Tagami lunged forward with a low, pointed strike meant to take out Mark's knee, but he side-stepped it, then brought his shin crashing down the staff, which caused Tagami to topple forward ungracefully into the muck while retaining his grip on the staff. But when Mark leapt forward with a double-handed downward strike at his skull, the man was forced to leave the pole in the mud and fling himself out of harm's way. The staff slowly sank into the brown earth, and now Mark stood between Tagami and his weapon.

A tiny part of Mark wanted to flick the staff out of the mud and hand it to Tagami as a show of sportsmanship, but his aching ribs reminded him he'd been far too chivalrous already. When he had an advantage, he had to press it. He dove forward at the unarmed man, blade first.

Tagami was even quicker without his staff. He *palmed* the blade aside with his left hand and gripped Mark's wrist with his right. A half-second later, Mark found himself cartwheeling through the air over Tagami's shoulder. By the time his ass hit the ground, the crowd was already going wild, and as Mark leapt back to his feet, he turned and saw Tagami had already fished his staff from its resting place and the rain was washing it clean.

They circled each other, and the rain was starting to lighten, just a bit. It was easier to see, and for a moment, Mark saw a new face in front of him. A narrow one littered with tiny scars. Mark blinked, and the wrinkled visage of Tagami returned.

This is no time for a psychotic break, he thought. A drone looped slowly overhead, projecting the pause in the fight up on the mammoth screen to their right. Underneath the image, Tagami's heartbeat was slow, almost inhumanly so. Mark's was racing, peaks and valleys spiking as he tried to catch his breath.

He's just a man, Mark thought. He lunged.

Tagami deflected the blade down and spun left, bringing his entire staff with him. Before Mark knew what was happening, something hard slammed into the back of his head, and his eyes exploded with stars as he fell face forward to the ground.

He turned so he hit the ground facing upward, blinking through the encroaching blackness as his skull was screaming in agony. His vision returned just as he saw Tagami moving in for the killing blow, a huge downward swing aimed straight at his forehead.

Mark went to clench his fist around the grip of his sword to bring it around, but realized he wasn't holding it. The staff flexed as it whipped toward him, and he had to squirm sideways so that it planted itself just next to his ear. Looking left, Mark realized he was lying in the middle of his own armor pieces, scattered on the ground after he'd stripped them off before the fight. His shoulder plates were behind him, and his boots were sinking into the mud to his right. It gave him an idea.

Tagami went to lift the staff back up for another swing, but Mark had enough sense to grab it. Tagami froze, unable to win the tug of war just long enough for Mark to knock his leg sideways with his bare foot, causing him to lose his balance. He wrenched the staff forward as Tagami pitched toward him.

They both rolled. Tagami to avoid falling directly on top of Mark, and Mark so that he could pull out the dagger hidden in his shinplate of his disembodied boot a few feet away. Once he had it in hand, he spun around and planted it through the corner of Tagami's robe, halting the man's escape as it pinned him to the ground. Mark flew at him with a hard cross punch the now immobile man couldn't dodge, and his fist cracked against his jaw.

Stunned, Tagami went to yank his robe free of the blade, but Mark beat him to it. In one motion, he kicked out Tagami's left leg and pulled the knife out of the ground with his right hand. The man hit the mud and twisted out of the way as Mark's knife dove toward his chest.

While the blade missed the man's sternum, he couldn't move fast enough to dodge it entirely. It plunged into the left half of his gut, and blood bloomed through the mudded robes. There was deep, horrible pain on his face, but still, he didn't cry out. Instead, he kicked Mark back and grasped his side, scrambling for his staff.

He found it and brought it around, but his strength on that side was gone. Mark caught the staff in his armpit, and wrenched Tagami toward him. Again, the knife plunged into the man's stomach and the entire crowd was now on its feet.

Mark knew he'd speared something vital that time. The energy simply evaporated from Tagami as Mark held him. They both sank to their knees, the blade still lodged in Tagami's abdomen.

Mark looked over the lined face in front him. He saw pain and regret. The same thing he saw in the mirror most days.

"Just one more," Mark whispered to Tagami in Japanese, hopefully out of mic earshot.

Tagami nodded stiffy. Mark's head was throbbing. Tiny scars kept appearing and fading on Tagami's face. He had to end this. The knife slid out easily.

"*Arigato,*" Shin Tagami said, his voice hoarse after untold years of silence.

Tears welled in Mark's eyes. He didn't even know why. This man was nothing to him. A stranger from halfway around the world.

He is you. What you will be. Alone.

The knife found his heart. Mark was doomed to live another day.

35

UNLIKE HIS LAST FIGHT, Mark was still conscious and able to walk out of the arena to a mix of boos and cheers. He was treated by on-site medics who constantly blinded him with tiny flashlights to check the status of his head, but he was supposed to be shipped back to Dr. Hasan in the estate's medical wing. He blinked and was losing seconds, sometimes minutes, but he was still standing, still walking. His head felt like it was full of cement. He was pretty sure at least three of his ribs were free-floating.

"No stretcher," he said, pushing it away as some EMTs showed up at the door. Ethan and Carlo were waiting outside and rushed to his side as soon as they saw him.

"We got him," Ethan told the EMTs, and both he and Carlo took one of Mark's arms over their shoulder as he forced himself to walk barefoot down the long, curving hall toward the back exit.

"Hell of a fight," Carlo said. "You about gave me a heart attack when you let him smack you upside the head like that."

He pulled lightly at the bandage wrapped around Mark's head. The question wasn't *if* he had a concussion, but how severe it was, and whether or not his skull had been fractured. But he could walk and talk, so that was a good sign, though he suspected he was slurring a bit from the painkillers they jabbed into him. The fogginess in his head told him it wasn't drexophine, which could probably only be administered by Hasan himself.

"Where's Riko?" Mark asked, slurring.

"Who?" Ethan said, eyebrow raised. "You mean Aria? She and Brooke are meeting us at the compound, don't worry."

Shit, shut the fuck up you idiot, Mark thought, momentarily panicked about the slip. But the meds mellowed him out again almost immediately.

"You've got a fight tomorrow," Mark said, looking at Ethan. "You should be with your family."

"Well I've got a brother in need at the moment," Ethan said, flashing that disarming smile of his. Mark felt his vision go black again for a second, but Carlo and Ethan steadied him. He started to ask where Moses was, but caught the question on the tip of his tongue.

To their left, Mark saw a young man in a suit keeping pace with him. He had shiny hair and a tiny camera drone floating above his shoulder. A reporter.

Shit.

"Mark, how are you feeling?" he asked, holding out a thumbnail mic. Carlo swatted it aside.

"Chill, man. He ain't in the mood for this bullshit."

Mark cast a sideways glance at the camera drone.

"I'm fine. Just need some rest."

The man was soon joined by two women, each with their own camerabots.

"Mark, why did you remove your armor before the match?" one asked. "Why taunt Mr. Tagami like that?"

"Taunt?" Mark said, surprised. "I was doing it out of—"

"We're almost there," Ethan said, motioning toward the double doors ahead of them. They picked up the pace and his escorts pushed them open.

Mark was blinded by a hundred flashes of light, and deafened by another fifty questions being shouted his way. They'd stumbled into an absolute *swarm* of press camped out in the parking garage. Behind them, Mark could see the flashing red lights of the ambulance.

"Mark!"

"Mark, over here!"

"Hey, Mark!"

Goddamnit.

All three of them shielded their eyes, and pressed forward. CMI security was there, pushing the reporters out to either side, slowly forming a path to the ambulance.

"Mark, why resort to using a hidden weapon? Isn't that a cheap trick?"

"What?" Mark said, stopping and whirling around, though he had no idea who in the mob had asked the question. He was able to speak more coherently now, at least. "Chase Cassidy stabbed me in the back with a 'hidden weapon' last week! Do you want to see the fucking scar?"

He started pawing at his undersuit, which was designed not to rip. Ethan tried to stop him, and he gave up in frustration.

"Have you heard Mr. Crayton's statement yet?" another reporter asked.

"What statement?"

All at once, the closest dozen reporters to him brought up a clip on their flexscreens, and they all began playing at once in some kind of nightmarish symphony.

"Shin Tagami was a private man," Crayton said, addressing the camera from inside his box, it looked like. "But in the wake of his passing, I would be remiss not to mention that we've learned he was an instrumental leader in the Tibetan resistance against Chinese incursion in the Border War of '21. It was an honor to see him eventually call America home, and compete in this tournament. He was a skilled fighter, but a gentle soul, and he will be missed."

Of course this would come out now.

"What do you have to say about killing a war hero?" a red-haired reporter yelled at him.

"I don't—"

"Come on," Carlo said, pulling him toward the ambulance. "You should not be talking right now, bro."

"He's right," Ethan said, forcing a smile. "Live TV's not your thing, remember?"

Suddenly, the reporters grew quiet. The camera flashes didn't stop, but the questions did. Mark felt the hairs on the back of his neck stand up.

Drago Rusakov waded through the crowd. No one else even came up to his shoulders. He wore a suit tailored to fit a silverback gorilla, and his black hair was pulled in a tight ponytail, while his beard was as wild and unruly as ever. He spoke with the gruffness of a diesel engine.

"Good fight."

He started clapping. He was the only one. Mark knew better than to thank him for the compliment.

"Good fight," he said again. "Kill old man with little knife. Much bravery."

Mark's eyes narrowed.

"And before that, kill Mr. Hollywood. Mr. Smiling Man. Very impressed."

Mark was in no mood for this. The press were furiously snapping photos of the confrontation, Ethan kept trying to pull him toward the ambulance.

"Come on, Mark, leave him."

"Now he fights cheerleader," Rusakov continued. "Blonde pom-poms. *Big* challenge I am sure."

"Big talk, big man," Carlo said. "But Mark would *destroy* you in the arena."

"Quiet, little crippled boy," Rusakov growled.

"What the hell do you want?" Mark asked, gritting his teeth. Rusakov switched to Russian. Mark suspected he was the only other one there who also spoke it.

"Ya budu naslazhdat'sya ubivat' vashu shlyukhu."

Mark's eye twitched.

"I will enjoy killing your whore."

Aria.

Mark shrugged off Carlo and Ethan and lunged at the towering man. He was aiming for his jaw, but ended up punching Rusakov just under the eye.

The man they called "The Undying" countered quickly and brutally. His head snapped back from the blow, but after Mark's follow through, he grabbed him by the back of the neck and simply *hurled* him.

Mark flew through the air in a flat spin, and slammed into the open door of the ambulance. He heard something pop in his arm, and when he hit the wet pavement, fresh pain blossomed from the point of impact.

He turned back toward the press, who were snapping a hundred photos a second and back to shouting. He saw Carlo try to land a leaping uppercut on Rusakov, but the man hit him with a palm the size of a dinner plate, which plowed him and his braced legs into a bunch of reporters who toppled and broke his fall. Ethan rushed to Mark and was saying something he couldn't understand. Rusakov started walking toward them, but he was swarmed by CMI security. He flung off two, three guards before six more packed in around him. He started to toss them aside too, so they broke out their tasers. They were electric blue and brighter than the camera flashes.

"Goddamnit!" came a familiar, bloodcurdling voice. Wyatt Axton burst through the press line, taser in hand. That had to mean Crayton was nearby. "Sit your ass down, Drago!"

With four other lit tasers already being pressed into his skin, Rusakov still managed to take a swing at Axton, who dodged and countered with a straight cross to his jaw. He jammed his long taser up into Rusakov's tattooed neck, and Mark lost sight of them as the press folded around them. He was hauled into the ambulance and the doors shut just before he blacked out.

Mark woke to a terrifying vision.

He was back in Crayton's compound, standing on the hill with the lone tree that overlooked the man-made lake in the center. Where he and Aria had shared many a memory the past few months.

But it was all wrong. The sky was rolling with red clouds and crackling lightning. The tree, the massive willow, was fully aflame, so bright it seared Mark's eyes.

All around the base, there were animals. Vicious, violent, tearing into one another with primal fury. Mark recognized a few. A massive brown bear was biting the haunches of a howling tiger. A rampaging bull was goring the legs of a towering elephant. Mark saw a chestnut stallion with its mane on fire. He heard the ghostly howl of a hound and the shriek of an eagle.

But it wasn't just familiar animals. There were more. So many more. Boars, leopards, panthers, polar bears, biting, slashing, tearing. Hawks and falcons ripped the feathers from each other's wings in mid-air. Hyenas and vultures were already descending on the corpses that littered the hill.

Is this what a coma is like? Or just brain damage? Mark thought as he slowly backed way down the hill from the horrifying scene. His movement was odd, and he looked down. His legs were narrow and covered with black fur, ending in clawed paws. He was suddenly aware that he tasted the rust of blood in his own mouth. In his jaws, rather.

He could smell not just smoke and fire, but fear and rage. He could hear not just howls and moans, but the scream a soul makes when it leaves a body. He backed up more quickly now, panicked, hoping none of them would see him. His paws made squelching sounds in the hillside grass, which was drowning in blood.

He retreated all the way down to the water, the animals now mere silhouettes, dancing in the fire of the tree.

Disturbed water splashed behind him. He didn't even have time to turn his head before the teeth sank into his flesh.

He was pulled down into the black water. Trying to scream, all he could emit were muffled yelps. Something was dragging him down, deeper and deeper. Red poured out of his flank and the pain was excruciating. Finally, he wrenched his head to the right, and found himself staring into the cold, dead eyes of a great white shark. Deeper and deeper they went, the pain never-ending, the drowning eternal.

"YOU SAID YOU WANTED me to let you know when he was waking up, so here he is. He's mumbling nonsense, but he's coming out of it."

Mark blinked. His vision was blurry, and he could see only shapes. He recognized the voice, but it seemed so far away.

"I just gave him the injection to speed things along. He'll be coherent in a minute."

Mark moved his mouth, but his tongue felt like styrofoam.

"Water," he finally said, and an unseen figure granted his wish. It was freezing, but glorious.

He felt something coursing through his veins, and it started to light up his nerves like a Christmas tree. A few more blinks and his vision went from blurred to crystal clear. He was in a locker room, not the med wing, though Dr. Hasan was standing over him all the same. And down by his feet he saw Cameron Crayton in a dark blue suit and white striped shirt. Leaning against the door was an always-armored Wyatt Axton, regarding him with his usual scowl.

Mark sat up, and was immediately dizzy. Hasan steadied him, and Crayton leapt up to do the same.

"Careful now, Mark," he said, smiling. "You've had quite an exciting day."

Day. Thank god. That meant he hadn't lapsed into a coma for days or weeks. Though his head certainly felt like that could have been a real possibility. He felt behind his skull and found a knot the size of a tangerine.

"Shin got you pretty good, didn't he?" Crayton said, feigning a wince. "But your scans are clear. Concussion, but no brain damage. Right, Doctor?"

"That's correct," Hasan said, "But I would advise against—"

Crayton cut him off with a look. Mark guessed the second half of that sentence was something Crayton didn't want to hear. Nothing would derail his tournament. Nothing.

"Now, Mark," Crayton said, "I just want you to understand there aren't any hard feelings, but this is for your own good, and the good of the Crucible."

"What is?" Mark said, the feeling starting to come back to his mouth.

"You had an . . . altercation with Mr. Rusakov after your fight. Do you remember that?"

"No," Mark lied.

"I think you do," Crayton said with a glint in his eye. "And I think you know we can't have competitors going after each other outside of the arena."

"But he—"

"Said something very nasty about a young lady friend of yours, yes, I know. But you hit him first. And you cracked his orbital socket before he fractured your arm."

Mark looked down at his arm for the first time, which was in a very thin fiber cast. It felt completely fine, the hallmark of drexophine.

"And it's also the second time you're rumored to have attacked a combatant who was about to face young Miss Rosetti," Crayton continued.

Mark couldn't hide the contempt on his face.

"I didn't—"

"I am not accusing you of that. What happened with Miss Rosetti and Mr. Easton was a private affair, and will remain that way. Your encounter with Mr. Rusakov, however, was very public."

Mark knew where this was going.

"As such, you'll have to remain here until your next fight with Miss Vanderhaven in the semi-finals. Know that Mr. Rusakov is under a similar restriction, as he's hardly blameless in all this."

Mark looked around. This wasn't the locker room Aria had been kept in, but it was similarly stocked with a bed, workout equipment, and Mark spotted a replica practice blade that was a stand-in for his bastard sword. He searched the room, but there were no screens. Panicked, he reached for his phone, which was gone. And he hadn't been wearing his S-lens when Rusakov attacked him.

Crayton knew what he was thinking.

"I'm sorry, but communication with the outside is restricted as well. We will keep you apprised of the match results, but you won't be able to watch them."

Ethan vs. Blackwood. Aria vs. Rusakov. Bullshit he couldn't watch them. Mark began scanning the room and was already working on five different ways he could possibly break out. Brooke had to be flipping out. God only knew where his phone was. She'd figure it out though. She'd come for him.

But what then? Mark knew he could break out. This was a locker room, not a Chinese blacksite. But he'd be tossed right back in and draw even more attention from Crayton's security. If Brooke or, God forbid, Carlo tried to get him out, they could be exposed as well. Better to play the good little prisoner, as much as it pained him.

"Not even a flexscreen?" Mark said through gritted teeth. "Just for the matches?"

"Something tells me you have the capacity to wreak a lot of havoc with a flexscreen, Mark," Crayton said with a sly smile. "As I said, you will be notified of the results. Play nice, and you may even land yourself a visitor or two."

"This is bullshit!" Mark barked. He stood up and paced. Axton pushed off the wall and was immediately tense. Mark wondered if he could snap Crayton's neck before Axton unloaded his pistol into his face. *Probably 50/50*, he decided.

"This is me protecting my investment," Crayton said, shrugging. "And my investment is you. If my combatants are going to brawl, it needs to be on the sand, not in parking garages with a fraction of the audience."

Crayton put his hand on Mark's shoulder.

"What would I do without you, Mark?" Crayton said. "We've come so far together, haven't we? You're a star. And you need to stay safe and sane if you're going to have a chance of winning this thing."

Crayton leaned in close to him.

"Don't you understand?" Crayton whispered. "I'm *rooting* for you. And I promise I don't say that to everyone."

The strangest thing was, Mark actually believed him.

36

MARK COULDN'T SEE THE fight, but he could hear it. No amount of soundproof paneling could keep the roar of the crowd out of the locker room. A quarter-million screaming fans were impossible to silence, and when they started cheering a few hours later, Mark knew the match was about to start. He heard dull, thumping bass and rhythmic clapping, which told him that the Muses were performing. He heard a long silence, followed by furious cheers, which told him someone had just sung the national anthem. More silence said that Crayton was giving Ethan and Rakesh Blackwood time to say their final words to their loved ones, the crowd, and the audience at home. Mark heard the muffled chant of a countdown. Five. Four. Three. Two. One.

It was impossible just to sit around and do nothing, so Mark grabbed a practice sword and attacked the training dummy with blind rage. Strike after strike hit the kevlar target, the dull blade leaving it undamaged. He mirrored moves Moses had taught him during training. He copied some Chase Cassidy had used against him. He tried to replicate ones that he had been forced to make up on the fly. He swung, and swung, and swung. Cheers from the crowd could mean anything. Cheers meant blood. But whose? It was infuriating not to know.

Mark had watched Blackwood's fight against Kells Bradford on replay, since he'd been unconscious when it originally happened.

Blackwood hadn't even been touched, and he had killed her with a single, pointed thrust penetrating a wall of armor. When she died, she didn't fall, but stood hunched in the metal suit until Blackwood kicked her over in an obscene victory celebration.

The Crucible audience had grown to hate him. He was rich and good looking and the media couldn't shut up about him. But to the common man? The guys watching fights at the dive bar with twenty of their buddies drinking cheap beer? To them he was the worst kind of rich prick. Mark knew that he wasn't exactly the most popular man in the tournament, but even he had amassed more fans than Blackwood. And almost no one was more beloved than Ethan, the war hero with the cute blond children and dying, beauty queen wife. You had to be some kind of sadist to root against that. Though you had to be some kind of sadist to watch the Crucible in the first place. Still, Mark hoped that the crowd being on Ethan's side might give him some kind of edge. Cheers and chants had power. They could mask fear and boost adrenaline. They could make you feel like a god.

Shit, he was starting to sound like Soren Vanderhaven.

As he listened to the roars and lulls of the crowd, he kept attacking the dummy furiously, hammering with blow after blow for two minutes, five minutes, ten minutes, until the blade started to bend. He tossed it aside and lashed out with punches and kicks. He watched his knuckles split open as the drexophine masked the pain. He knew he should stop but he kept hitting. He kept hitting until . . .

It was loud. It was so loud that it had to mean he fight was over. It was so loud the words were finally unmistakable. The crowd told him exactly what he wanted to hear.

"*E-than! E-than! E-than! E-than!*"

Mark dropped his fists and broke into a smile. The kid had done it again. He banged on a nearby locker with his palm, and shouted the chant along with the crowd.

When someone knocked on the door an hour or so later, Mark didn't know who to expect. Guards? Crayton? Ethan himself?

Instead, Mark found himself staring at Carlo, flanked by two Glasshammer mercs. He wore a crumpled sport coat and pants. He was holding a few grease-soaked paper bags.

"Mind if we bring our dinner date in here?" Carlo said. Shyla popped into view from outside the doorframe. She gave a little wave.

"Hiiiii Mark!"

Mark smiled.

"By all means."

Carlo relayed, in graphic detail, pretty much every blow of Ethan's fight. The long and short of it was that Ethan had used his shield expertly, allowing him to keep Blackwood's shorter rapier at bay while countering with his own slashes. Ethan had been stabbed about a half dozen times, Carlo said, but none were enough to take him off his feet. Worryingly, he was escorted off the sand in a stretcher, but Crayton was already broadcasting that he was perfectly fine, and it was just precautionary. Blackwood, who ended the fight with a crushed skull thanks to a timely shield slam from Ethan, was not as lucky.

"You see Brooke?" Mark pressed. There were cameras everywhere in here, so he had to be careful about what he was asking. He kept an eye on Shyla as well. She seemed like a perfectly nice girl, but he couldn't be sure she wasn't Crayton's creature. Once upon a time it had been *him* that Crayton was trying to attach her to, after all.

"Yeah, I ran into her," Carlo said, munching on a barbecue burger. "She said to tell you she knows where you are, and she hopes you're comfortable."

Mark wasn't precisely sure how to read that, but it sounded like she was telling him to stay put.

"What about Aria?"

Carlo shook his head.

"Haven't seen her."

Mark poked at his fries, lacking an appetite.

"I saw her!" Shyla suddenly chimed in. She blinked her wide, green eyes.

"You saw Aria? Where?" Mark asked, surprised.

"She was . . ." Shyla hesitated. "Erm."

Mark wanted to shake her.

"Where was she, Shyla?" he said calmly.

"After our performance, I saw her outside Mr. Crayton's box. She and Mr. Crayton were . . . arguing."

"Arguing?" Mark said, confused. "About what?"

Shyla shook her head. Her curled red hair danced across her shoulders.

"I don't know. I couldn't hear. Mr. Axton told me to keep moving, so I did. But they were both pretty upset."

Mark didn't know that he'd ever seen Crayton actually angry, so that was significant. Were they fighting about his imprisonment?

"I just heard them say one thing before I left," Shyla said. "Something about . . . a maid?"

Mark froze. After a long stretch of silence, Shyla spoke again.

"Maybe her room was messy?"

Mark's anxiety tripled after Carlo and Shyla left. Was Aria seriously confronting Crayton about Easton and the murdered maid again? What was she doing? What possible good could come from that? From her view, maybe now that Easton was dead, Crayton could tell the police what had happened to the missing girl, but that could come with potential blowback on him. He wasn't going to risk that, or more importantly, risk this getting into headlines when everyone was supposed to be focused on the tournament itself. Not to mention, Easton had supposedly been cleared of the exact kind of crime Aria had witnessed, thanks to his legal team. Maybe there *was* something to this that Mark could use. It had nothing to do with China, but it was potentially significant.

It's not the mission. He could already hear Gideon's voice in his head.

No way in hell was Crayton going to let him see Aria before her match. Her match with the most brutal competitor in the tournament.

He wouldn't dare, Mark thought. Not that he would put it past Crayton to kill Aria to hush this entire thing up if she was just some random witness, but in this context, she was too high profile, and it would destroy his precious bracket. No, Crayton expected he was marching her to her death in the arena tomorrow. Mark wasn't sure he was wrong.

Sleep didn't come. Mark wrestled with the enormity of everything, and didn't want to see any more mangled animals when he closed his eyes. He ran on the treadmill until his legs burned. He lifted weights until his arms screamed. By the end of it all, one thing was clear. He wasn't staying in this room another day.

It wasn't Mark's best plan, but it would have to do. It felt like China-lite, working within the situation at hand and concocting his own escape.

He managed to get himself into the digital temperature display of the room, which he used to jump over to the camera feed and set up an incredibly rudimentary stutter that Brooke would no doubt be ashamed of. But it could work for his purposes. It would show him lying in bed, motionless, over and over. Not ideal, but better than showing what was about to happen next.

Mark took a few swings at the now-battered practice dummy with the bent blade. He gripped it hard, too hard, squeezing every muscle in his forearm. He squeezed like he was trying to crush the grip into jelly, but naturally, his arm went first. His forearm, still healing after its encounter with Cassidy's katana, popped at least a dozen stiches, and blood immediately soaked through the bandage. Mark felt a sharp stab of pain, meaning the drexophine was fading, and blood was soon dotting the floor.

"Ah fuck!" he yelled, acting like the injury was an accident. He banged on the door with a bloody hand. "Need some help in here!"

The door opened and a helmeted Glasshammer guard answered. Mark held up his bloodied arm. The other still gripped the practice sword.

"Shit," the guard said through his helm. Mark backed into the room and the man followed him. "Hey, you got a kit?" he said to the other guard. "We're gonna need a medic in here. Call it in."

The other guard pressed his finger to his ear, but Mark was too quick. He lunged forward, grabbing the man by his neck plating and wrenched him into the room.

"What the f—" the other guard began, but Mark spun and planted a kick straight into his visor, which bowled him over. Still holding onto the other guard, Mark smashed the side of his helmet with the pommel of his sword, once, twice, until the man went limp. He flung a kick toward the door, which slammed it shut, and fell onto the first guard who was now trying to rise after Mark's kick.

"Wei—" was all the man said before Mark tore off his helmet and locked him in a chokehold. He slipped into unconsciousness, and both guards lay still. It had only been about twelve seconds.

Mark stripped all of their armor off and pieced together an un-bloody, un-smashed uniform from the two of them that he donned himself. He found the one guard's medkit, and after re-bandaging his cut, injected each of them with a tranquilizer compound he found, which would keep them out for a few hours. Regardless, he smashed their remaining comm unit, and used their own cuffs to bind them together. He gagged them with the torn-off sleeves of a CMI fleece he found in one of the lockers. Messy, but a believable escape for an alleged ex-SEAL. He'd be caught eventually, but it would be a little while yet.

Mark looked over his new black Glasshammer ensemble in the mirror. He was every bit the stormtrooper.

He needed to hurry.

The guards had all their data pumped directly into their visor displays. Mark sifted through a virtual map to quickly locate where Aria, one of the so-called "assets," was supposed to be before her fight. Naturally, it was another locker room halfway around the giant stadium. Mark walked briskly, cutting through the amassing crowds

-389-

like they weren't even there, returning curt nods to other guards when he passed by.

It was nice to walk in a crowd for a change without being recognized, something Mark hadn't felt in months. But his heart started racing as he approached a cluster of guards who were all in a circle talking outside the entrance leading to Aria's room.

"I'm supposed to re-dress one of Rosetti's wounds," Mark said, holding up the medkit he'd pulled from the guard.

"You're in the wrong place then," a guard said, breaking from the conversation. "She ain't here. Supposedly still at the Estate, but Roston just phoned in and said they can't find her there either."

"Bitch musta skipped town," said another helmeted guard. "Pussied out of the fight with Rusakov."

"I mean, can you blame her?" another guard said. "$50 million might not seem so nice once you realize you're gonna be too dead to use it."

Mark's mind raced. Aria was missing. Last time this happened, Crayton had her. Had her in that very locker room, in fact.

"Let me get in there," Mark pressed. "If she shows up late, there's gonna be a rush to get her patched."

The lead guard shrugged and waved him through.

Mark realized he was shaking as he walked down the hall to the locker room. He stopped at the door, afraid of what he might find if he went inside.

The electronic lock clicked its approval of his security clearance, and he pushed the door open.

It was empty. Or at least appeared to be. After setting down the medkit, Mark made a quick sweep of the room. She wasn't hanging from the rafters or lying in the shower with her wrists slit, an Axton-induced suicide, which he wouldn't put past Crayton. She simply wasn't there, as the guards had said.

Mark opened up the medkit and laid out some bandages in case someone was watching the monitors. He made another sweep, and started casually opening lockers and wardrobes. Nothing but CMI Crucible merchandise, the same as his own. The bed was gone, the workout equipment remained.

Mark thought about his next moves. Trying to head to the compound was a bridge too far. She could still show up here, even if she was running late.

I hope you ran, Mark thought. *I hope you got the hell out of here, and the next time I see you, you're on a stage dancing in Italy or France or Austria.*

Mark waited for what felt like hours, being the patient medic, waiting for his charge to arrive. But he was woken up by a sharp crackle of static in his headset.

"Wei is gone. Knocked out his detail. Was or is posing as a guard. Check exits. Check all the boxes. Check Rusakov and Rosetti's rooms."

That had actually taken longer than Mark expected. He calmly stood up and walked to the shower area, exiting the way he'd come when he snuck into the room when Aria was locked up there last time. They still hadn't bolted the paneling shut.

He shed the armor in the walls, but not before dumping the entire contents of the helmet comms unit to Brooke's encrypted remote storage to sift through later. He'd pulled a Crucible-branded tracksuit from his locker room before he'd left for this very occasion, and emerged wearing it along with a baseball cap and wraparound sunglasses. He left the wall in a utility room and found his way back to the main strip. Walking a quarter of the way around the stadium, away from Rusakov and Aria's locker rooms, he bumped into a slouchily dressed teen in section G21 and came away with a slim phone that he slipped into his pocket. He held it up to security as he entered the arena area itself, and as he expected, the scanner read the kid's ticket and he was waved through.

Mark entered the sun-drenched stands and a gust of hot Vegas air hit him. He was already pretty high up, but turned and trudged even higher toward a section in the nosebleeds. He'd never seen the crowd like this before, from among them. The boxes he sat in didn't do the experience justice. Here he was part of the endless ocean of humans. They were laughing, eating, drinking (quite heavily in the cheap seats), and waiting for the festivities to kick off. Mark looked across the bowl of the Colosseum and saw infinite faces stretched out around him. Lining the rim of the stadium were tiny figures Mark knew were snipers, watching over everything with eagle vision and rifles that could punch a hole through a concrete wall.

Mark found an empty seat and sat down. It would take them a while yet to find him, even if they had a derm tracker on him, like he suspected they might. Those were imprecise enough to only tell them he was still in the stadium.

Mark wanted to watch Crayton announce that Aria was gone. That she'd forfeited. That she'd fled. That she'd escaped his horrible game.

The sun started to set. Music blared, and tiny figures bounced out onto the sand. The enormous viewscreen zoomed in on Shyla and her Muse sisters. They began to dance, and Mark found himself tapping his foot along with the beat.

She ran, he told himself. *He didn't kill her. She ran.*

By the end of the national anthem, he'd almost convinced himself.

Rusakov entered like a massive stormcloud moving through the desert, clad in nightmare black, executioner's axe already in hand. There were more cheers than boos, reflecting his legend status from the *Prison Wars* era, but the man had the power to make your blood run cold just by looking at him. The spiral horns on his helmet were polished to a mirror shine. If Soren wanted to be Helen of Troy, this man was Attila the Hun, destroyer of worlds. His intro video now included a clip of his recent TV interview.

"Ballerina will dance and dance. She will be pretty. Like flower."

A quick cut to Aria's beautiful destruction of Easton.

"I know death. I am full of souls. Full to bursting."

A cut to Rusakov decapitating Naman Wilkinson.

"This will be ugly thing."

As the crowd settled down, Aria's video played next. It was a classical score set to a collage of her taped fights, juxtaposed next to recordings of her dancing on stage from before the Crucible. The editing was fantastic, and so was she, in both sets of clips. The video ended with a line from an interview Mark had never seen.

"Well, you only get one life," Aria said, smiling at the interviewer off camera. "And you haven't really lived until you try to do something impossible. I guess that's why I'm here."

The crowd cheered the sentiment, but when their approval died down, Aria still hadn't emerged from the tunnel. After a minute, a hundred thousand whispers were heard rippling through the audience.

Mark stared hard at Crayton's box.

Say it, you bastard. Call the match. Call it.

The camera zoomed in on Crayton himself, who sat stonefaced with his hand on his chin, blue eyes narrow. The shot panned to the blackness of the entry tunnel. Nothing. Back to Crayton. The tiniest hint of a smile.

No.

Aria strode out onto the sand, wind pulling at her long brown curls, her helmet in her hand, and her mirror swords on her back. She smiled and waved, the setting sun making her polished silver armor glow. The crowd loved her.

You love her, Mark finally admitted to himself. *And you should have taken her far, far away from this place.*

37

IT WAS HARD TO describe how Aria fought, because it was more of a *feeling* than anything else. Mark knew that the best fighters let go of themselves when in combat. You didn't think, you just *did*. The closest anyone ever came to putting it into words was Bruce Lee, with his famous "Empty your mind, be formless, be shapeless, be water, my friend" quote that had been on a poster in every dorm room in America for the last four decades. But it was true.

And Aria was water.

She flowed in and out of Rusakov with a delicacy that seemed improper for the situation, but it was entirely effective all the same. Rusakov didn't flow. Rusakov was not water. He was an iceberg, waiting for one solid smash to destroy whatever was in his path. But Aria wove all around him and his terrifying axe like it was some sort of elaborately choreographed routine where she was paired with a partner who had two left feet.

Her swords tested his armor, massive interlocking plates that Naman Wilkinson certainly hadn't been able to breach in his ill-fated, minute-long attempt. She finally found a gap, and drove her blade into the meat of his leg, before whirling away from the butt of his axe. Rusakov and the crowd both roared, but for very different reasons.

The foot that Easton had gored in her previous fight was still hurting her, Mark could see that in her micro-movements that favored the other leg. But she was still fast enough. Fast as she needed to be, it seemed.

Aria stabbed Rusakov once, twice. Five times. Careful slices that sometimes took minutes to set up. The fight was already one of the longest on record, and Mark expected she was trying to wear the big man out. How many times could a human swing an axe the size of a street light before getting fatigued? But that was assuming that Rusakov was human, not an infernal machine powered by hate and pain and death.

If he was hurting from Aria's stabs through the cracks of his armor, he didn't show it. Nor was he slowing down. Not a bit. In fact it was *Aria* that seemed to begin to tire first, her foot becoming more of an issue as time pressed on. Her balance wobbled, her form slipped. But still, even Aria fighting at less than full capacity was a sight to behold. No, she wasn't doing backflips like Soren Vanderhaven, but there was a grace in her movements that the gymnast lacked. It was like—

Ah shit.

Mark saw a group of guards talking about thirty rows down near the entryway. They weren't looking at him, but they were scanning in a complete circle around them. Despite his makeshift disguise, he might have triggered facial recognition on one of the thousands of security cameras in the arena. Mark shifted in his seat, but acted natural. And that meant cheering when Aria's blade sunk into Rusakov's arm, along with the rest of the crowd.

Before she could retract the sword, Rusakov brought the butt of the axe around and smacked it into her shoulder. Aria spun like a top, landing on her injured foot and hitting the sand, unable to keep her balance. She scrambled to pick up one of her dropped blades, but Rusakov stomped on her hand and sword with an iron boot, which caused her cry out. After trapping her, he thrust the axe down toward her back, but she managed to bring the other blade around and sink it into his knee. He didn't scream, but he staggered, and the axe bit into the ground to her right. He lifted his foot enough for her to pull her arm out, the armor now crumpled around her gauntlet. A fracture or break seemed likely, and as she gingerly tried to grip her reclaimed sword, she saw the blade was bent awkwardly from being crushed under his heel.

Mark had to watch all of this from the drone cams that were projecting the fight on the massive screen overhead. To try to follow them in the actual sand was impossible. They were just tiny shapes skittering around like insects from this height. The drones were looping lower and lower to get prime shots for the audience, and a zoom on Aria's helmeted face showed that she was grimacing from fresh pain, her teeth locked together in agony. Her heart rate on the monitor was spiking.

She tossed her bent sword away and charged in with her remaining good blade held in her remaining good arm.

It's just a broken hand, Mark told himself. An easy fix. She was fine. Rusakov may not have been showing signs of fatigue, but he was now making red prints in the sand and blood was trickling down his armor in a half dozen places.

He yelled something in Russian Mark couldn't make out and deflected Aria's flashing blade with the back of his gauntlet. He turned and immediately flung the axe up in a high, overhead arc, nearly sheering a rotor off one of the passing drones, which were circling dangerously low to get tighter tracking shots.

Aria deftly dodged the earth-shattering blow, which lodged the axe firmly in the rocky ground. Then, to the entire arena's amazement, she leapt over the head of the enormous axe and *sprinted up the grip* toward Rusakov's head.

Yes. Goddamnit, yes.

Her blade dove forward, but Rusakov shifted slightly so that it sank into his collar, not a gap in this throat plating. Aria flipped off his shoulders, missing his helmet's sharp bull horns. She took the red blade with her, and landed behind him.

It was like he hadn't even felt it.

The giant wrenched the axe out of the ground and whipped it around toward her. His fresh wound made his grip slip, so when it hit Aria, the flat of the axe smacked into her chest plating, flinging her against the stone wall that made up the edge of the arena, when it could have easily cut her in two.

Mark winced, but in his peripheral, saw the guards now pointing in his direction, and beginning to charge up the stairs, tasers out.

Shit shit shit.

He balled his hands into fists. His eyes kept darting between the screen and the men racing up the stairs.

Aria was reeling on the wall. Her armor had actually cracked the curved stone. But she was still standing.

The first man made it to within six steps of Mark.

"Mr. Wei, I need you to come—"

Mark lashed out with a front kick that sent the man flying into the other guards behind him.

Aria leapt forward with a desperate swing at Rusakov, but he dodged it, and landed a hard hook with his mallet fist that sent her hurling back into the wall.

The tumbling guard took two others with him, but that meant the other ones were done being polite. The next two came with tasers, crackling blue with the promise of pain and unconscious ignorance.

No.

As a drone veered in to get a better shot of Aria lodged up against the wall, Rusakov actually jumped. With such a massive wingspan, he *grabbed* the flying metal annoyance and hurled it at a still-recovering Aria. The three-foot drone plowed into her chest and the crowd just about lost their mind. The feed it was broadcasting cut to black until another drone looped in for a new shot. Aria was reeling, barely able to stand, her armor marred with deep scrapes and gouges.

Mark let the first taser inside, but turned his chest so it sailed right past him. His elbow met the guard's helmeted face, and he tumbled into a confused bunch of onlookers who were just starting to realize what was happening around them. The second taser bit into his abdomen and he clenched his jaw so hard he thought he heard something crack. He broke the man's wrist with a quick twist of his own, and shattered his visor with a headbutt, managing to keep his footing.

Rusakov lumbered toward Aria, who held up her sword, which now looked no more threatening than a knitting needle. Mustering her last bit of strength, Aria leapt at the hulking black monstrosity, and drove the blade into a slim gap near his ribs.

More guards arrived. The air was now thick with stinging pepper. He could barely see the screen anymore, and more tasers buzzed all around him.

Rusakov cross-checked Aria with the handle of the massive axe, sending her one more time toward the wall, stumbling over the downed drone as she went. As she hit the stone, his axe was only milliseconds behind her.

The last thing Mark saw before the voltage of the tasers shut his brain off was Aria two feet in the air, pinned to the wall with the axehead running straight from her right shoulder to her left hip. Her head hung limp. Her hair blew softly in the desert wind.

He tried to scream. Instead he gurgled through clenched teeth, and a gloved hand shoved his head into the concrete stairs.

Maybe that shot in the head from Shin Tagami gave you brain damage, and this is what insanity looks like.

Maybe Chase Cassidy put that katana through your throat instead of your arm, and these are the last spasms of your mind before oblivion.

Maybe Burton Drescher put you in a coma, too. Maybe this is a lucid dream.

Maybe it was you who blew up in that car, not Riko and Asami, karma for the thousands killed by the Red Death.

Maybe you died on the Hóngsè Fēng. Maybe this is purgatory, as you wait for the devil to make more room in hell.

Maybe you're still in China. Still in that hole. Maybe Zhou broke your mind, and this is your descent into madness.

Maybe not.

Maybe you're alive. And sane. And that's even worse.

It WAS A FULL day before CMI lifted Mark's security detail and let him go to the morgue. His head was still pounding, and he had a new collection of fresh bruises, but Crayton had no interest in escalating things further with him, it seemed. With the quarterfinals over, Mark was no longer under lock and key.

The morgue was freezing. It was a part of Crayton's great gleaming Colosseum that no one ever talked about, and most probably didn't know existed at all. It was half a dozen floors underground, far from the hot Vegas air. It kept the bodies of the fallen competitors on ice until the conclusion of the tournament.

At first, Mark didn't even realize they were doing this, but it was in the fine print of the paperwork he'd signed. Bodies were held until the conclusion of the Crucible, and no funeral services, sans coffin or otherwise, were to take place until then. Presumably it was about not killing the "mood," as since the tournament started, there would have been a dozen very public memorials broadcast all over the country with how many combatants had lost their lives. Their loved ones had to wait to mourn. Wait until the country was done cheering for the winner.

Mark walked past the labeled storage lockers of the bodies as he entered the room, the mortician agreeing to wait out in the hall. All were familiar.

C. Cassidy
M. M. Easton

S. Tagami

K. Bradford

A. Mendez

M. Varkas

N. Wilkinson

J. Jordan

D. Hagelund

R. Blackwood

M. Morton

And there on the table, covered by a sheet to the neck, was A. Rosetti.

She was pale. Just a shell. Just a shadow of her former self. How could something so perfect be sacrificed like this? Offered up on an altar, for what? A memorable Thursday night for a hundred million viewers at home?

Mark lifted the sheet. Even clean and loosely stitched, the wound was horrific, slashing diagonally across her body to the point where it was a miracle she hadn't been fully cut in half. Mark still didn't even *understand* her fight. She'd stabbed Drago Rusakov so many times, in so many seemingly vital places. How was she the one laying here? Granted they called the man "The Undying" for a reason, but *Christ.*

Mark checked his phone, which was lit up with news alerts.

Wei Involved in Yet Another Arena Brawl read one, as his fight in the stands with security had gone viral just like his altercation with Rusakov before that. He was exhausted trying to deal with the press. He was exhausted from everything.

He looked around the room. These corpses represented $160 million of the nearly billion-and-a-half prize pool. He never asked Aria what she was planning on doing with the money. She never asked him either. In the end, Mark thought she knew who he was. Who he really was. Or some version of that, anyway. And he always knew it was never about the money for her. She had a death wish, and now here it was, granted.

Mark wanted to believe in some kind of afterlife. That Aria and her sister were now dancing in harmony in the clouds somewhere. But it was hard to delude himself like that, standing there in the frigid room of the dead, looking at the body in front of him. The last time he was in a place like this, there was an unrecognizable scattering of ashes and black bone fragments on the table that was supposed to be a woman and her child. At least Aria still resembled her former self, even if her soul had fled.

Moses's death had hit him hard, but after Aria, now he was just numb. He didn't weep or wail over her body. He simply stared.

Rusakov was a monster and clearly needed to die, but Mark didn't really even blame him for any of this. It was like throwing someone into a lion's den and expecting them not to be eaten. But the person who bred the lion, starved the lion and sent the person in to die? *That's* who you would blame. And there was only one person who met that description.

"Tell me where we are," Mark growled, shifting the ice around in his empty glass. The bar was dingy and deserted, way off-Strip in Vegas, and he'd had to slip his Glasshammer shadows to get there. Brooke was drinking water and wore a leather jacket with her hair pulled back into a curly ponytail.

"Mark, I'm sorry about Aria. I know—"

Mark waved her off.

"Do you really think I want to go there right now? Do you really think I want to talk about any of this shit for one second longer than I have to at this point? I need to know the plan. I need to know when and how this ends."

Brooke shifted nervously in her seat. She stared past him to the muted TV on the wall. Like every TV in the city, it was tuned to CMI's Crucible coverage. They were already plugging Mark's upcoming fight with Soren in the first semi-final match. The subtitle: VANDERHAVEN: "I'LL GET JUSTICE FOR CHASE."

"Did you know some companies are actually letting employees go home early to watch fight pre-coverage?" Brooke said. "I heard there's even a petition to make the finals a federal holiday. Bet Crayton floated that himself."

"Stop changing the subject. There will only *be* a final if we keep fucking this up," Mark said coldly. "Tell me where we *are*."

Brooke sighed.

"The early investment case is the strongest. I have almost a dozen cases where start-ups Crayton invested in had their competition decimated by something that traces back to China.

"We can place Crayton in Beijing at a young age, but we have little actual proof that he's 'Joseph Olsson Jr.,' and we don't know what actually happened over there.

"We have Crayton's head of security on tape executing a woman we believe to be an MSS agent, but we have no way of tying her directly to that organization. We have found nothing on Crayton giving the order to possibly kill Justice Wright, and that feels like something that would never have been documented if it *did* happen."

"And?" Mark said.

"And I'm going to write all of it up for Gideon to send up the chain. He's flying out to Vegas as we speak, actually, and will want to meet up. But we still don't have what the Agency and Homeland are looking for."

"Chinese confirmation of Crayton's status as a plant. Or former plant, I guess, seeing as they're apparently trying to kill him," Mark said.

"That's what I'm guessing they'll say," Brooke said, taking a drink.

"This is bullshit. We can extract the rest out of him once we have him. This is not just something he's going to let slip in casual conversation or have written down in some stray email. We have *more* than enough to book him as is. If we dug into this Easton murder on his grounds, that could be rolled up in it, too."

"That's completely unconnected."

"It's accessory after the fucking fact."

"That's not the mission."

"If I hear that one more time I'm going to lose it."

"Sorry," Brooke said, and she looked like she meant it. "But I'm just trying to make sure everything you've gone through so far actually ends up being worth it. Otherwise . . ."

"I don't think Gideon, McAdams or any of them understand the position they've put me in here. My life is effectively *over* after this. If I don't die in the tournament or get outright murdered by Crayton's security, this thing has made me so goddamn high profile I'll never be able to show my face in public again, no matter how this shakes out."

"What are you saying?"

"I'm saying if they don't greenlight this, I'll kill him. I have nothing to lose, and I'm not going to sit around and watch poor Ethan Callaghan get sacrificed to Drago Rusakov next. I will kill Crayton, and Axton, and Rusakov, and maybe Vanderhaven just for good measure. And then I will disappear and you will spend the next thirty years trying to find me. I am *done* with this shit."

Mark's chest was heaving, and the look on Brooke's face said that she was considering launching into yet another 'talk Mark off a ledge speech' that he was in no mood to hear. Instead, she surprised him.

"I understand," she said. "I'll make sure they get the message."

"See that you do," Mark said. "Or I will burn this whole goddamn thing to the ground."

38

IT WAS A STRANGE feeling, that Crayton's desert estate now felt more like home than anything else. It was the only place Mark could exist free from the prying questions of the press. He'd take patrols of armed guards any day over vultures with camera drones and thumbnail mics. Security had been beefed up yet again, and though Mark always seemed to have eyes on him, it was as if Crayton was almost gearing up for war. Whatever the issue with Mark and Rusakov had been, it seemed far from Crayton's mind now. The winds were changing.

Outside of the guards and the staff, the population of fighters had now been reduced from sixteen to four, and as such they rarely ran into one another. Mark had seen precious little of Ethan, who had gone quiet after Aria's death, knowing that he was next on Rusakov's hitlist in the semi-final, and mostly spent time with his family. The hulking Russian lumbered around the compound, occasionally visited by other hulking Russians, but he seemed to have no further desire to push Mark's buttons. Mark's blood hadn't stopped boiling since Aria's death, but taking on Rusakov here in the middle of Crayton's private army would do nobody any favors.

Mark checked his phone and S-lens incessantly, waiting for any information from Brooke. If the higher-ups didn't greenlight Crayton for take-down, Mark was determined to put him down. And that wasn't a bluff. He might die trying, or have to spend the rest of his life on the run, but goddamn did he truly believe he'd be doing the world a favor.

Still, these days Crayton's compound made Admiral Huang's aircraft carrier look like day care. He was so high profile he turned every guard's head from a hundred yards or more. And besides, Crayton was almost never on the estate anymore. Like Soren, he spent most of his time in Vegas itself. Mark saw him frequently on TV meeting with the execs of Crucible sponsors ("Odor Destroyer, the official deodorant of the Crucible!") or giving interviews to hype up what was still to come. And Mark's fight was next.

"Mark is a dangerous fighter," Crayton said to the silver-haired man across from him. He only gave interviews to streams he owned, ensuring Crucible viewership remained his sole property, in the arena and out.

"I don't think anyone underestimates him at this point, much less Miss Vanderhaven. She of all people knows what he's capable of."

"Do you think that she can match him?" the interviewer pressed.

"Soren has surprised us all with her brilliance in the arena. I absolutely think the two are evenly matched, and she is out for revenge, after all."

"Did you get to spend much time with them during *Heroes and Legends* filming?"

"Chase and Soren? I did, and they really were wonderful together. The gossip streams aren't exaggerating. I did not plan for love to blossom among Crucible combatants, but you can't control the human heart."

What would you know about the human heart? Mark thought. Naturally, the interviewer didn't say a word about Mark and Aria.

"And what of young Ethan and Drago Rusakov? It's your old champion versus the young upstart. Is it even possible for anyone to take down Rusakov?"

"Sure, it's a bit of a David versus Goliath situation, as is clear to anyone, and yet we know how that turned out. Young Ethan has been a hero both on the battlefield and for his family these past few years with his wife's illness. While Drago is a force of nature, anything is possible when you step out onto the sands, as we've seen already."

"So can we get your official picks for the fights?"

"Hah, Tom, you know my friends taking bets in Vegas wouldn't much appreciate me anointing one fighter over another. Suffice to say, I am hoping for exciting, entertaining matches, and for the best competitors to emerge victorious."

Shortly after that last interview, Mark had an unexpected visitor at his door, a young Glasshammer guard. One who had been on his personal detail a few times.

"Mr. Crayton would like to apologize for the business between you and Mr. Rusakov, and for the ordeal that took place in the stands during Miss Rosetti's match."

Mark leaned against the doorframe.

"That it?"

The guard shook his head.

"No, sir. He'd like to issue this apology in person, which is why he will be escorting you personally to your Crucible match with Miss Vanderhaven on Friday. You'll take his private car to the Colosseum."

Mark shrugged, though something clicked in the back of his brain.

"Alright. He's the boss."

ON THURSDAY NIGHT, MARK kept blinking to refresh his S-lens inbox. There was nothing. Still no word from Brooke. He knew she'd already gotten the answer, but one of two things was happening. Either they were mapping out a plan to bring Crayton in, or she was pleading with them to reconsider, relaying Mark's threats.

The newscast was replaying reports that Ethan's wife, Lily, had slipped into a coma. He'd fled the compound to go to the hospital before Mark could even wish him well. He tried calling a few times, but with no luck.

With little else to do, Mark had kept up training during the week. But there would be no more fights. Either Crayton would come in and this would be over, or he would be dead, and Mark would either flee or die in the attempt.

Are those really the only two options you're leaving yourself?

Mark shrugged off the notion. He could tolerate another fight, especially if it meant killing Soren, but he was *not* going to let Ethan get slaughtered by Rusakov the way Aria had. And with Crayton riding with him to his fight tomorrow, he may never get another shot like this anyhow.

Finally, the indicator in the corner of Mark's eye lit up. It was Brooke, and she was actually calling. He answered, and didn't even need to hear her speak. It was written all over her face.

"They said no. They need a Chinese source. But Mark, if you try to do anything to Crayton, they will—"

Mark didn't say anything. He closed the call, and ignored Brooke's frantic attempts to redial him. Soon she switched to written messages that all started with "MARK PLEASE, DO NOT . . ." followed by all the ways the CIA would dismantle him if he went rogue. Mark wondered if they'd actually try to take him out, but ironically they'd made him too famous, and too well-guarded, thanks to planting him in Crayton's camp.

Mark closed down the S-lens and began planning the assassination of Cameron Crayton.

In the morning, Mark woke up for what he knew could be the last time. It wasn't the first time he'd had that feeling. Over the years there had been many days he thought might be his last. Most of those were in China, but he'd certainly felt it before his last two Crucible fights, even if he wouldn't admit it. But this one felt different.

There were two scenarios Mark thought likely. Either Crayton would be sitting in the car alone with him, with Axton up front behind glass. Or Axton would be right next to him. In the first situation, Mark felt like there was a slim chance he could escape with his life. In the second, it didn't seem likely he'd leave the car alive.

He thought about killing Crayton with his bare hands, cracking his throat like he'd done to Burton Drescher. It would be twice as easy on an older man like him. But if Axton was there, he needed *some* kind of weapon to stand a chance. Brooke wasn't exactly going to be sneaking him in a concealed gun or syringe, so he had to make do. Kitchen knives were too big. Combat knives were too hard to lift from guards in such a short time window. He had a hunch, and followed it into a particular room in the mansion. The old living quarters of Matthew Michael Easton.

Aria had described the room as all candles and knives. A few candles were still there, but the knives were gone. Mark's heart sank a bit, but given the crime that had been committed there, it seemed reasonable. Crayton would take no chances when it came to trace evidence. Surely the furniture had been replaced, and it even looked like the flooring had been replaced. But Mark remembered Easton's case back when it had been on the news. In his remote cabin they found endless secret chambers and stashes of new horrors. At one point, Easton only was being accused of a dozen murders, but eventually investigators knocked down a wall to find a secret trophy room that provided DNA evidence for twenty others. In short, the man knew how to hide things, and that's what Mark was counting on.

Mark searched every square inch of the room, top to bottom. He checked the furniture anyway, but found nothing. There were no loose floorboards to pry up, with everything having been replaced.

What wouldn't a clean-up crew replace? Mark thought as he scanned the room. His eyes landed on a small picture on the opposite wall. It was a long painting. A simple grayed-out landscape with Chinese characters on top.

You've got to be kidding me.

It was a Wang Meng. Rather *the* Wang Meng, *Zhichuan Resettlement.* Though the value of Chinese art had plummeted recently, it still had to be worth at least a few million. It wasn't something you'd just tear off the wall and trash when you were gutting a room. Mark saw no flecks of blood on it, and when he took it off the wall, found it a bit heavier than it should be.

Mark smiled.

Gently, Mark peeled the picture out of the frame. Inside, he found two tufts of black hair, and three small, clean knives.

"I knew you wouldn't let me down, you fucking lunatic," Mark said aloud. He took the thinnest knife and put the other two back. He thought about pocketing the hair as well as possible evidence, but whatever poor soul he'd taken it from seemed rather inconsequential in the current scheme of things. The tufts went back in the painting, and the painting went back on the wall.

Mark slid the knife up his shirt sleeve and was reassured it was small enough to shift properly during a potential pat-down. It wasn't perfect, but it would have to do. And hell, it would even be a little bit poetic, considering who it belonged to.

From one monster to another.

The long walk down to the waiting car felt like a march to his execution. But he forced a smile when Crayton saw him, clad in a snow white suit with crimson shirt underneath. Axton stood inches from him, as ever, and seemed to be wearing even *more* body armor than usual, and had an extra pistol strapped to his hip.

"Mark, thank you for allowing me to escort you to the match," Crayton said. "Arthur assures me your armor and sword are polished and waiting. We're expecting to break viewing records again. And that beautiful Vegas sunshine is back, so you won't be slogging through the mud like you were against Mr. Tagami."

Chipper as ever.

"Yeah, should be a good day," Mark said, smiling.

"*That's* the confidence I like to see," Crayton said with a wink. "Let's get moving. We shouldn't be late for our own show."

Crayton motioned for Mark to enter the car. Axton gave him a pat down, and Mark rolled the slim knife around his forearm to avoid detection. A satisfied but still scowling Axton held the door open. Mark ducked inside the autolimo and Crayton followed. Mark held his breath and felt his insides melt as Axton piled in after him. Two other guards sat in the seats up front.

Well, I guess this is it then.

There was a very, very short window for Mark to make his move. The stadium was only a few miles out into the desert, across an empty stretch of sand. If you didn't mind the heat, you could easily jog from Crayton's estate to the Colosseum. That didn't give him much time at all.

Mark was surprised to see a crowd a few hundred feet from the walls of the compound as they exited. Some were waving Crucible signs, but others were the doomsayers that Mark had seen protesting the event since Chicago. They held signs that said things like Killing Is Not a Sport and Thou Shalt Not Murder and were screaming fire and brimstone at the car as they passed.

"A certain segment of the religious demographic has still not warmed to our little contest here," Crayton said with a smirk. "We've had some threats, but we've increased security, so there's no cause for concern."

Indeed their autolimo was flanked by a *second* limo, a decoy car, and two boxy SUVs in the front and rear. Mark knew it wasn't religious zealots Crayton was afraid of, however. Mark was already thinking about how he might use one of the other cars as a getaway vehicle, depending on if he could clear them of mercs.

God I wish I had backup.

As they passed by the crowds, Crayton launched into his apology about his treatment in the wake of his encounter with Rusakov, and how sorry he was that Aria had met her end. Mark smiled and nodded, but his ears were ringing and he could hear very little of what Crayton was saying. Instead, he was sizing up Axton. The man hadn't stopped staring at him since he sat down.

It was too risky to go for Axton first. Crayton was opposite Mark and a seat over from Axton. Going across the cabin to Axton was a death wish. If he was only going to get one opportunity before Axton shot him point blank with one of the various firearms strapped to his body, he was going to have to make sure that knife landed in Crayton's heart first, no matter what happened next. Mark thought if he was fast enough, he could do them both and actually set foot outside the car again. But there was truly no predicting how things would go down once he made his move.

Something in the back of Mark's mind told him not to do it. He wanted answers to the maddening mystery of Crayton, and they would likely die with him if he did this. He knew everything would play better if they could just do this the right way, but with no support from the Agency, time was up. Crayton was better in jail than dead, perhaps, because of his intelligence value, but better dead than free.

This man was everything Mark despised. A rich charlatan corrupting the masses with a vile product, and a traitor to his country for good measure. He was evil in its purest form.

The world needs to see what he is. They never will if you kill him.

Mark almost told the voice in his head to shut up aloud, but restrained himself. Still, Axton narrowed his gaze, and those steel-gray eyes pierced deeper into him.

It doesn't matter if the world knows. I know.

You'll be dead. And you'll be remembered as the evil one.

If I'm dead, I guess I won't mind.

They were deep into the desert now, Vegas hazy to the west, the Colosseum coming into view to the north. This was it. Mark rotated his wrist, and dropped the knife into his palm. His heart was hammering. One straight thrust to Crayton's chest, then he'd try to turn and catch Axton in the neck.

I love you, Riko. I love you, Asami. I just might see you soon.

"Mark, are you alright?" Crayton asked. "You look quite—"

Mark heard a distant sound. A crack, muffled by the nearly soundproof cabin. He had half a millisecond to consider it before he heard another quick succession of sounds.

A high caliber slug shattering the bulletproof windshield.

The sound of a guard's head exploding up front.

The whooshing tear of leather as the bullet plowed through the seat, bringing brains and blood and bone with it.

The gasp of Wyatt Axton as the round slammed straight into his chest.

Mark and Crayton's eyes widened at the same time. The car lurched and swerved. An explosion.

The car flipped, and gravity lost all meaning.

39

MARK WOKE UP IN a fit of coughing. Something was burning. Smoke stung his eyes and filled his lungs. He could hear the whine of autocycle engines nearby. More than one. Gunfire. Automatic, semi-auto. Close. Right outside.

He blinked blood out of his eyes. It was spilling down his forehead from an unseen cut in his scalp somewhere. As his sight returned, he saw the limo was upside down, and its seatbelt-less passengers were strewn everywhere. Axton was in front of him, face down on shredded leather and broken glass. Crayton was to his right, laying on his back, face contorted in pain. He was still alive.

Mark had clearly hit his head, but searching himself for other injuries, he couldn't find any.

What the fuck is—

More gunfire. A cycle whipped by and someone screamed outside. A muffled yell.

"*Zhè chē!*"

Mandarin.

"*This car!*"

China. They've come at last.

Two more gunshots rang out and Mark heard a body drop to the asphalt close by. Two legs came into view through the crunched window frame. They wore cycle boots and leathers. Not Glasshammer leg armor.

Before Mark could even think of what to do next. The figure crouched and a gloved hand threw a round object through the window. It skipped across the roof, which was now the floor, with metallic clinks. It rolled right in between him and Crayton.

"Shit!" Mark cried out as he grabbed the grenade and flung it backward out the opposite window. A split second later, an explosion rang out and Mark winced as tiny slivers of shrapnel peppered his right leg.

There wasn't time to even process the pain. Mark immediately lunged forward from his position on his stomach and grabbed Axton's Desert Eagle from his hip. The figure outside started to bend down again, but Mark ripped a shot into his kneecap. With a shriek, the figure collapse and Mark now had a full view of the leather-clad assassin wearing a tinted helmet. He unloaded the rest of the clip into the visor without hesitating, and blood started pouring out from the bottom of the helmet once the man lay still. More bike engines and gunfire told Mark there were still more assailants lurking. He pulled another magazine from Axton's belt and reloaded the pistol.

Crayton looked terrified. His suit was stained with soot and blood.

"I didn't think—" he said before trailing off.

Mark grabbed Easton's knife, which had also landed nearby. He looked at Crayton, and realized the choice that lay before him.

In this moment, he could kill the man no questions asked. China would have simply hit their target.

Or, he could capture one of the assassins and get what the case desperately needed. The reason why this insanity was happening in the first place.

As if an answer to his prayer, Mark heard shots ring out and saw an autocycle go tumbling past the window, its driver flying over the handlebars. Mark poked his head out and saw the man holding a wounded arm. Ahead of them, one SUV was fully aflame, a skeleton of metal and fire. Around it were the bodies of dead Glasshammer guards, leaking blood onto the pavement. But behind them, the other SUV seemed to be intact and drivable. Mark's decision was made.

He crawled out of the car and looked around. The smoke was drifting over from the second limo, which was in far worse shape than theirs. He drew his head back into the cabin and saw a stunned-looking Crayton still trying to process what was happening.

"Stay there," Mark barked. Glasshammer security was pushing up past the intact SUV toward their position, driving another four helmeted assailants on bikes backward, as they zipped around the road and surrounding desert. But some were making wide arcs and coming around from behind. Two more guards fell with armor-piercing rounds shredding their kevlar like paper.

"But—" Crayton said.

"If you want to survive this, stay in the goddamn limo!" Mark yelled. Crayton seemed content to obey, pawing at Axton's submachine gun. The man hadn't moved, as tended to happen when you took a .50 cal slug to the chest.

Mark turned toward the injured assailant on the downed bike. Immediately, a line of bullets tore into the man, and he lay still.

"Motherfucker!" Mark said aloud, turning back to see that CMI security had put him down for good.

A bullet whizzed by his ear as an autocycle blew by him. Autocycle was wrong, actually, these were full-on manual motorcycles, he realized. Mark fired several shots at the bike as it passed and hit the rear wheel. The bike pitched left and dumped the man into the flaming carcass of the lead SUV, and Mark heard him screaming as his body caught flame and he became a fused mass of skin and leather.

Double fuck.

Mark saw three Glasshammer guards taken down by another biker, who looped around through the desert holding a machine pistol in his right hand. He shifted his aim to Mark, who dove over the top of the upturned limo as the bullets ripped into the undercarriage. The man brought his bike to a skidding halt next to the limo and leapt off it, continuing to fire as Mark spun over the other side. He started to bend down again, looking for his true target, Crayton, who Mark knew was just feet away. Mark fired at the top of the man's head, but the gun clicked, out of ammo.

Suddenly, Wyatt Axton exploded out of the window of the overturned limo, spearing the helmeted assassin with the force of a freight train. He and the man slammed into the pavement, and Mark could only see Axton on top of the man, ripping his helmet off and pummeling his head into the pavement with his bare hands. He stood up, unslung his submachine gun from his back, and turned toward Mark. He was covered in blood, and had a crater the size of a salad bowl in his chest armor, but the sniper round hadn't pierced the plating after all. An engine whining turned his attention away from Mark, and he put a half dozen rounds into another passing attacker who spiraled off his bike into the brush.

Mark realized the attack was starting to collapse, and he was running out of time to secure a survivor.

As Glasshammer mercs swarmed the limo to cover Crayton, Mark leapt back over the undercarriage and dipped down to pick up the dropped machine pistol from the assailant Axton had practically decapitated.

"What are you—" Axton said, but Mark was still sprinting. He scooped up a submachine gun from a dead CMI guard and slung it over his shoulder. He also grabbed two pairs of metal cuffs from the man's belt. He righted the downed bike from the first attacker he saw crash, which didn't appear to have suffered any major damage, despite the dead rider crumpled underneath it. Ahead, the last two cyclists were starting to retreat. Mark gunned the engine and took off after them, watching Axton sprint to the lone remaining SUV, which lurched to life as soon as he got inside.

Mark was doing eighty in about three seconds, trying to remember the last time he'd manually driven a motorcycle. College? Thankfully, it was literally like riding a bike.

One rider was way out in front, the other lingering a touch behind. He started firing blind shots back at Mark with a subcompact of some kind, but they dug into the asphalt wide right. Mark fired back, trying to only hit the bike itself, or the man's leg at worst, but controlling the bike and firing was tough, and he missed completely, despite emptying half the machine pistol.

Axton's SUV had a monster engine and was keeping pace with the bikes. He was leaning out of the window firing at the rear bike as well, though also not finding his mark.

Realizing the SUV was also in pursuit, the biker emptied a clip into the windshield, but the bulletproof glass held against the smaller-caliber rounds and they only served to obscure Axton's vision. He hung out of the window and kept firing.

Mark saw the lead bike toss something over his shoulder, which bounced high on the pavement and rocketed past him. The explosion of the grenade caused Axton to lurch right, but he kept his wheels on the road and Mark could hear him yelling even through the deafening wind swirling around him.

It was clear Axton was making this entire situation even more difficult. Catching one of these assassins was going to be hard enough, but downright impossible with Axton on his tail as well. Mark pushed the bike to its redline and pulled even with the second bike. The attacker turned his attention back toward Mark, but before he could fire, Mark fired the last machine pistol shot into his front tire. At 130 mph, the result was catastrophic.

The bike flipped up into the air, the rider with it, and smashed back into the ground, immediately getting sucked under Axton's SUV, trailing too close behind it. Mark heard a sickening groan of metal, a muffled explosion, and watched the SUV's front axle snap. The truck pitched hard left and dove off the road completely. It crashed into the base of a towering billboard, dragging a streak of wet gasoline and blood behind it, the bike and its rider now no more than pulp. As Mark accelerated away from the crash, he heard Axton trying to restart the engine to no avail.

Now, it was just Mark and the lead biker.

Who had now disappeared.

"Shit!" Mark yelled as he searched the landscape. He found him almost instantly on the empty terrain, as the bike had pulled off the main drag onto a dirt road leading out to the badlands, which blew up a line of dust in his wake. Mark cornered so hard he almost flew off the bike, but regained his balance and took off in pursuit.

Here the road twisted and turned, and Mark had no idea if the tires he was riding on were cleared for dirt, but they seemed to grip well enough, so he tried not to think about it. The man lobbed a few shots his way that went well over his head from that distance. Mark didn't want to return fire until he was closer, and now he only had a single mag in the submachine gun to work with. He tossed the machine pistol away, and adjusted the knife in his belt, which was starting to dig into his thigh uncomfortably.

As he was heading to the fight, Mark wasn't wearing his secure S-lens that connected him to Brooke. He only had his phone, but going over a hundred miles an hour on a bike on a bumpy dirt road while holding a gun, he didn't feel like grabbing it to make a call. He tried to shout voice commands at it as he drove, but the roar of the wind was too loud.

"I'm sorry, can you say that again, Mark?" chirped the peppy little voice in his pocket.

"Fucking fuck—"

More bullets whizzed by his head as the biker swerved again. They were now in some rundown old ghost town that Vegas had crushed into oblivion decades ago.

Mark was gaining on the man. Smoke was trickling from the chassis of the bike ahead. It was possible it had already taken a bullet.

Mark saw several holes in his own bike, but from its performance, it didn't appear as if the rounds had hit anything vital.

They were down to about 60 mph now, which felt like crawling in comparison. Mark kept his distance as he didn't feel like taking a round to the face, but he knew he'd have to make a move soon.

He tried to make precision shots at the bike to further cripple it, but the rider veered left to avoid them and one only clipped the taillight. He returned fire and Mark felt a bullet tear through the tail of his suit jacket but miss his flesh.

He only had six bullets left, according to the digital ammo readout. He fired one of them. Mercifully, it found its mark. The tiny trickle of smoke coming from the fleeing bike became a large plume, which enveloped the rider completely. He swerved and braked and had to leap from the bike, rolling expertly as he landed in the driveway of an ancient, decaying autobody shop.

As soon as the assailant righted himself, he lunged for the gun he'd dropped a few feet away, but Mark took aim and shot the weapon, which sparked and spiraled away from his grip. The rider flung himself backward, dodging Mark's next shot, but the final bullet in the chamber dove straight into his leg. Mark heard him cry out under the helmet, and he ran up and planted his foot right in the visor, making it spiderweb and knocking the man hard into the pavement. Mark grabbed him by the back of his shredded leather suit and quickly hauled him inside the door of the body shop, slamming it shut behind him.

The man was still conscious, his head rolling around on his shoulders. Mark quickly flung him in a nearby rusted office chair and handcuffed his wrists and ankles to one another with the bindings he'd swiped from CMI security.

He dialed Brooke, thankful his phone still had reception in the middle of the desert. His message was short and curt, that he needed immediate extraction at his GPS coordinates. That he'd landed a whale.

He turned back to the groaning black figure and pulled off his helmet.

There he found a shaved head and a bloodied face full of old, tiny scars.

Not again. Not now.

He blinked. The thin, scarred face remained. His lips parted to reveal a red smile.

"Hello, Mark," Zhou said. "It's been too long."

40

*T*HE COAST GUARD REPORTED *Major Zhou boarded a watercraft at approximately 9:08 a.m., twenty minutes after the explosion at your residence."*

"You look surprised to see me."

"The craft was able to outrun local enforcement, so a V7 Hellbird was scrambled from Hickam AFB. It engaged Major Zhou's craft five miles off the coast."

"They told you I was dead, didn't they?"

"The fuel line of Major Zhou's craft was struck in the firefight. The ship burned, and divers were dispatched to recover the remains. Those remains are in front of you, and have been verified through dental and DNA testing."

"Of course they did."

"I hope this brings some solace to you, Agent Wei, in what the Agency knows is an incredibly difficult time."

Mark felt like he was choking. This couldn't be real. The man in front of him had to be some kind of hallucination. Zhou was dead. Zhou was soggy ash and bone in a bag somewhere, with the rest of him at the bottom of the ocean.

And yet here he was, smiling, talking, breathing.

Mark punched him.

Zhou's head snapped back and his eyes unfocused. Mark shook out his hand, he felt real enough.

Finally, he gathered himself to say only one word.

"*How?*"

Zhou winced, his eye swelling almost immediately. He dropped the smile.

"There was indeed an explosion out on the Pacific that day. But it was the Hellbird, not my ship. I had anti-air ordnance for such an occasion."

Mark's next question was why. Why would the CIA tell him that Zhou was dead? Why the *fuck* would they do that when the man had just killed his family?

"They did not want you going off book for retaliation. Re-invading China to kill me, I suppose," Zhou said, reading his mind. His English was almost flawless. Mark had never heard him speak it before.

"You killed my wife. My *child!*" Mark shouted, lashing out with another strike that rocked Zhou's head back.

"You think *you* lost things?" Zhou said, his tone changing. His eyes narrowed and his voice dripped with contempt. "After the admiral's assassination I was accused of *treason*. My entire family was rounded up and interrogated for weeks. My grandfather died in captivity from a stroke. My mother caught yellow lung and died a few weeks later. Even after I was cleared and reinstated, my family has never spoken to me again. Fathers forbid their daughters from marrying me."

"So you went back for what, revenge?" Mark said coldly.

Zhou spit out a gooey stream of blood onto the cracked floor of the garage.

"I came back to cleanse my shame. The Ministry sent me to kill the American spy who infiltrated our ranks to spark a civil war. But none of the other factions believed the US was responsible for the killings and the chaos. Or they just refused to accept it. By the time I missed my window with you, the country was crumbling and I was recalled. One man no longer meant anything, and my skills were needed elsewhere."

Mark had to push past the shock that Zhou was alive. The CIA's exfil team was on its way, and even though they were deep in the badlands, it was possible Crayton's people could find them. He would have to process this later.

"Tell me why you're trying to kill Cameron Crayton, why you're trying take your own piece off the board."

Zhou's jaw snapped shut, suddenly no longer in the mood to talk.

"Fine," Mark said. "Fortunately, you trained me for just this occasion."

Mark whipped Easton's knife out of his belt, and before Zhou could even blink, he tore through the restrained man's motorcycle leathers. The material and the skin beneath it split open, drawing a line of blood. Zhou clenched his teeth, but he didn't cry out.

"No?" Mark said. He sliced upward this time, perfectly bisecting the first wound.

Zhou grimaced again, but this time choked out a laugh.

"You are wasting your time. Your treachery saw to that."

Mark saw pale skin underneath the torn leather and something caught his eye. He grabbed a corner of the cut fabric and pulled. A patch of Zhou's chest was exposed, revealing long-healed, thin scars. The same kind that covered Mark's own body.

"The Ministry was . . . thorough when trying to determine my innocence," Zhou said. "You do not have the time or energy to carve the information out of me. Though I remember you were good with the knife. All those dissidents, offering up anything and everything at the end of your blade. And that poor American soldier too. What was his name? Oh-something."

Lieutenant Marcus O'Connor. United States Army. Service Number 8355521. D.O.B. 6/22/2002.

He'd never forget it.

But Zhou was right, and Mark knew it. It could take months to extract anything out of him by force, though more likely he'd die first out of pure spite.

Mark jammed the knife into Zhou's leg, the one that *hadn't* been shot, and the man finally cried out, a mix of surprise and pain.

"What . . . did I just . . . say?" Zhou said, cringing as Mark slowly pulled the knife out.

"I know, I just really wanted to do that."

He wiped the knife on his pants and slid it back behind his belt.

"So you'll admit to killing my family, but not why you just launched an all-out assault on the most famous man in America?"

Zhou glared.

"The man is a snake. He will explain this attack away. Just watch."

"If you hate him so much and want him gone, then *help* me. You know why I'm here, why I'm in this goddamn tournament."

"More of the CIA's little games," Zhou said. "You are their pawn yet again. Imagine my face when I saw you on *television*, of all places."

"I'm trying to take down a dangerous man. The same man *you're* trying to eliminate."

Zhou considered that.

"And what will I get if I share my knowledge?"

The man was a cockroach, and knew what it took to survive. Mark was counting on that.

"Immunity. Relocation. Money, even."

Zhou laughed.

"And then the CIA will feed you my address so you can come kill me in my sleep. No, thank you."

Mark couldn't deny that's exactly what he would do.

"If you don't agree to detail your government's involvement with Cameron Crayton before my backup arrives, they will take in a corpse, rather than a prisoner. That much I promise you. You may be worried I'll kill you later, but I can *promise* I will kill you now if you don't start talking."

Most MSS agents would indeed die before giving up anything, as the captured woman in Crayton's compound had. But after spending years with the man, Mark knew Zhou was a pragmatist, not a fanatic. And China hadn't exactly treated him well, it seemed. Mark watched the gears turning inside his head.

"In writing. All of it. The whole deal. Then you'll get what you want."

"I need something now. To understand what it is you have."

Zhou was silent, stewing.

"Let me see your eyes," Zhou said. Mark cocked his head. "Your eyes!"

Mark leaned in closer to the restrained man.

"No S-lenses, then. Take out your phone."

Mark hesitated, then slowly fished the phone out of his pocket. He thought he heard the distant whir of muted hexocopter blades overhead.

"Put it there," Zhou tapped the ground with his heel, his legs still cuffed together.

Mark obliged, and Zhou promptly smashed the thin screen to bits under his boot.

"No recordings until my deal is signed. But I can tell you who you are hunting. Knowing your government, you will kill the man outright before you let the world know he was ours. Heart attack. Suicide. The usual."

Finally, they were getting somewhere. Mark's heart was pounding. Was this it? Would it finally be over thanks to *Zhou* of all people? This didn't feel real. Every second Mark had to restrain himself from slitting the man's throat. Asami and Riko flashed before his eyes every time he opened his mouth.

"Who is Cameron Crayton?" Mark asked, pulling up another chair and sitting across from Zhou, who was now mostly covered in his own blood.

"Keep in mind all of this is years before either of us were born," Zhou said. "Crayton's story is legend in the Ministry, and legends can be embellished. And yet, I doubt much of this was.

"Missionaries have infected China for centuries. Invading to preach the word of their foreign lord under the pretense of helping the poor and sick. But in 1985, two came with no such noble aims. These two Americans, these 'Olssons,' were zealots. They planted themselves in the slums, and started shouting loudly about how the Chinese were murdering their children in the womb. They held signs with bloody masses of tissue, supposed infants, the words written in poorly translated Chinese, telling the populace they were doomed to a hell none of them even believed in.

"It was a district so impoverished and crime-ridden, there wasn't even a local police presence at that point. But their screaming upset the local brothel owners, their gory signs turning the stomachs of those who would otherwise be buying sex or drugs. A Triad lieutenant was finally called in to deal with the Americans. He quite generously gave them a day to leave the country, yet when he returned the next morning, there they stood. Even their child, a young boy no older than six had his own small sign with a message of damnation and blasphemy.

"The Triads had a good laugh before they dragged the Olssons off and cut out their tongues. They chained them up and let them bleed out, taking bets on which would die first.

"The boy was a special case. He could be killed too, yes. But he could also be sold. Such pretty blond hair and blue eyes. The lieutenant fetched a high price for him after a bidding war from local flesh merchants. They thought he would do well with tourists and diplomats, a booming market thanks to the depravity of Western society. But on his first job, the boy stabbed a Ukrainian businessman in a leg with a corkscrew, and he bled out on the floor. Rather than kill him, his owner had another idea. He was sold again, this time to a different sort of master.

"It's hard to overstate the plague of street children that surged through Beijing back then. Discarded second children usually died, but those that didn't roamed the streets, stealing, begging, becoming nearly feral. Some of the local gangs got it in their heads that there was money to be made from the hunger and desperation of these children. So they built pens. And cages. They turned them loose on each other, and made a fortune from the gambling returns.

"The boy spent a year in dark basements and hidden back rooms, beating other children to death at the behest of his various masters. He was their prize dog, and was sold repeatedly for huge sums of money. He destroyed every other child put in his path, and eventually one of his owners started collecting the milk teeth from his fallen opponents, and strung them into a necklace he wore to every fight. Whispers of the 'White Devil' began to spread throughout Beijing's underground. The undefeated demon child.

"Eventually, a young Ministry officer named Zhu Meng found himself at one of the Devil's fights. They were putting him against much older children now, to see if he could still win. After the child shoved half a broken bottle into the lung of an eleven-year-old kung-fu prodigy, Zhu Meng started asking around. He heard his story, and learned that because of the Olssons' outcast status in the US, no one was looking for the boy. He purchased him outright for triple his previous price, believing if he took him off the streets now, there would be some semblance of his sanity left. And he had big plans for the young Devil.

"At the time, there was a new MSS pilot program called 'Project Embryo.' It was a training initiative that took children from birth and raised them to be elite soldiers, assassins, and infiltrators. The training was extensive, and brutal, and many of the children were dying in the process. But in the young White Devil, Zhu Meng saw a child already hardened to steel, and *white* as well. It was an unimaginable opportunity, and Meng was given full authority to oversee the boy's training personally.

"It was there, in Embryo, that 'Cameron Crayton' was truly born. He was a construct, his story written by a panel of officers, scientists, and Zhu Meng himself. It took a full year to put his mind back together from what he'd endured since he'd arrived in China. He gave no indication he remembered his parents, or America, so he was a blank slate. They reformed him to their will.

"No one was even allowed to speak Chinese in his presence. He was given all Western teachers in every subject. Trained with Western mercenaries for his combat drills. He was to be the ultimate plant in the US. Not some politician the MSS would blackmail, or a businessman looking to make a few tax-free billion on the side. Such endeavors were unreliable at best, and dangerous at worst. But this, someone they could shape from such a young age to do their bidding. This was always the ultimate goal of Embryo, and Cameron Crayton was their best hope for success to date.

"Crayton grew up exactly how they wanted. How they engineered him to be. He was intelligent, well-spoken, and charming, without a hint of his previous insanity cracking through the surface. He loved Meng, and his caretakers, and understood his mission once he reached his teens. It would take almost a lifetime, but in the end, it would be worth it.

"After Crayton was smuggled into the States at seventeen, he was funneled enough money to start making investments in companies. His background was forged, but the money was real, and China ensured the companies he was funding succeeded, in one way or another. His fortune grew until he was able to found CMI on his own at thirty.

"The ultimate goal was to have Crayton become one of the West's most influential media figures. A country like the US is a slave to its news media, and Crayton would be in a position to push whatever agenda the Ministry wanted. If his influence expanded enough, he could sway huge portions of the American public with his programming."

"I don't understand," Mark broke in, his head spinning from the weight of all this. "Why the hell are you trying to kill him? You raised him from birth to be your man, and now you want him dead? That makes no sense."

Zhou glared at him. One of his eyes was now completely swollen shut.

"Would you like to keep talking, or should I continue? You should be on your knees thanking me I am telling you this much."

"You should be thanking me you can still talk because your throat isn't slit," Mark shot back. But he stayed silent, and let Zhou continue.

"During Cold War II, when Crayton was supposed to be working his hardest, his interest in news media waned. He owned streams, sure, he put out stories the Ministry wanted here and there, but he was growing increasingly unresponsive.

"Once you ravaged our country with your cowardly Red Death, Crayton broke off contact completely. He extracted all his finances completely free of the Ministry's grasp, using his billions for his own sick pleasures. He invented this '*Prison Wars*,' an *entertainment* program, and reveled in the attention. He turned his back on the country that raised him as it bled to death across the ocean. Once this 'Crucible' was announced, it was clear he had become an unstable liability. Not only that, but he had shamed his father nation. He had stolen billions and negated the life's work of his surrogate father, Zhu Meng, who now ran the MSS, and countless others who had given him the best training and care throughout his life. He had dishonored China.

"The problem is that there is no true Manchurian candidate. Someone who walks around asleep until you whisper the right code-word to weaponize them. You have to build a pet monster and then pray they do not devour you when they are grown."

Mark nodded. "And that's where you come in. The monster hunter."

Zhou puffed out his chest.

"Even if China has fallen, its soul lives on in the Ministry of State Security. I was dispatched to US soil to ensure Crayton's debts were paid in blood, one way or another. It was to be my pleasure to end the life of a traitor of his magnitude. When I saw you enter the tournament, I knew the CIA had their own plans for Crayton, and they likely suspected our involvement. It made the mission all the more urgent."

"Well, sorry to fuck all that up," Mark shrugged. "But in the end we both want this asshole gone. And now you can help us with that."

"Only if that deal comes through," Zhou growled.

"So even the 'Soul of China' has a price, huh?" Mark asked.

"And what did they promise you, Mark?" Zhou sneered. "A way to put your desire to die to good use? How can you trust the Agency still? If they lied about my death, what else are they keeping from you?"

"You don't realize how easy it would be for me to snap your neck before extraction gets here," Mark said. "So I would stick to the facts on Crayton before you start talking about the past again."

Mark heard the hexocopter for certain now, though it was so quiet it sounded like the hum of an electric current.

"If you tell them," Mark pointed upward, "what you just told me, they'll give you whatever you want. And I might be so grateful this goddamn shitshow of a mission is over, I may not even kill you. But no promises."

Zhou remained silent, apparently realizing it was probably not in his best interest to goad Mark into murdering him.

Mark breathed out a heavy sigh of relief.

Christ, this is it. This is really it.

41

*T*HE HEXOCOPTER DESCENDED INTO the lot behind the auto shop and an entire tactical team poured out, spreading out and aiming their rifles with fixed precision. Mark held the bound Zhou by the collar. He'd unhooked him from the chair and dragged him outside for collection. After the team surrounded them, Mark saw two more figures get out of the chopper, Brooke and Gideon. His current and former handlers smiled wide as they saw him.

"You got one," Brooke said, beaming. "He say anything?"

"He has the full story," Mark said with a less sunny tone. "Give him immunity, relocation, and some cash, and it's ours. So is Crayton, with everything he's got to tell."

"That's great work, Mark," Gideon said, putting a reassuring hand on his shoulder. "This was certainly worth the trip to Vegas."

Mark grabbed Gideon by the front of his shirt and pushed him up against the side of the hexocopter. The tac team descended on him, pulling at his arms and neck, and Brooke was shouting at him to get off. Gideon stared at him.

"Do you know who this is?" Mark shouted as the team ripped him away from Gideon. He pointed to Zhou. "Do you have any idea? Look at his goddamn face and tell me you don't remember!"

Gideon looked at Zhou, his lean, scarred face unmistakable. As his handler, Mark knew he would never forget it.

"Ah," Gideon said, motioning for the soldiers to stand down. "I see."

"You see?" Mark said. "You *see?*"

"What is going on?" Brooke asked, looking panicked.

"He's the one," Mark said, spearing Zhou's chest with his finger. "Who tortured me, who killed my family. He's alive, and the CIA *knew it!*"

Gideon raised his hand.

"I wasn't involved, I swear," he said. "I only found out a year or so ago, and the argument about it almost cost me my job."

"But you didn't tell me then either," Mark said, still boiling with rage.

"Because I knew what you'd do. I knew what *I'd* do in your shoes. Sneak into China and start hunting some ghost who had probably already been killed in combat or was rotting in prison. And you would die in the process."

"The Agency lies, Mark," Zhou chimed in, the blood starting to dry into a red mask on his face. "That is all they do. They—"

"And *you*," Gideon said as he hit Zhou across the face with a closed fist, "can shut the fuck up." The blow knocked Zhou out cold, so shut up he did.

Mark threw up his hands.

"I don't know what to believe anymore," he said. "But there he is, all wrapped up in a bow. Our ticket to Crayton. I will deal with the rest of this shit once he's taken down."

"If he gives us what you say he will," Gideon said, "We can move immediately after the testimony is recorded and verified. I'll rush his deal through the DOJ."

"How long?" Mark said.

"Day or two, tops. You'll need to stay in cover until then," Gideon said, then leaned in to Mark. "*And if you want Zhou's relocation information afterward, I wouldn't object to letting that slip over a beer or two,*" he whispered.

Mark was too exhausted to be angry at this point, at Gideon or even at Zhou. For now, the man being alive meant Crayton was done; that was the important point. What happened after that was a different story.

"Just get it done," Mark said. "This needs to end."

"And it will end. This will shut McAdams up for good," Gideon said. "Exemplary work, Agent Wei."

"Talk soon," Brooke said as she touched his arm lightly. Gideon hauled Zhou into the chopper with the help of the team. "I'm proud of you," she said, then stepped into the cabin as the rotors started up again.

Mark stood there silent, long after the hexocopter was a speck in the sky. He saw smoke on the horizon from the burning cars on the road miles away, and he righted the electric bike to return to the scene of the crime, with a tale to tell about how he lost the attacker in the desert. Most of all, he was wondering how Crayton was going to spin all this in his last few days as a free man.

HOURS LATER, MARK SAT on the grass with his back against the tall willow tree planted on the hill in the middle of Crayton's compound. His right hand was numb from the ice cold beer he was drinking, a reward to himself for a job well done. He sipped it slowly, watching the pink sunset in the desert. Right about now, his fight would have been starting. Instead, he watched CMI security buzz around the estate like disturbed wasps. Glasshammer had sent a literal army to the grounds to ensure no further attacks were attempted.

By the time Mark had made it back to the scene of the motorcycle assault, Crayton had been whisked away. Mark was treated for smoke inhalation, a few bruises, and a bullet graze on his side he hadn't even noticed. Security staff grilled him about the chase, but he maintained he lost the other bike in the desert, and never saw his face. Fourteen CMI guards had been killed, along with two chauffeurs and a valet. Crayton himself escaped unscathed, but no one was offering up any further information about his whereabouts.

It felt like yesterday that Aria had been dancing in the moon-light just a few feet away from where he was sitting now. He looked down toward the lake and remembered running along it with Moses every day for weeks. All of that felt unreal now, like it was the last, flickering moments of an early morning dream. But they *had* been real. They had lived, and they had died. For nothing, it felt like.

All this would have been easier if everyone would have been as hateable as Rusakov or Easton. Those were the types of psycho kill-ers who were supposed to sign up for something like this. Not Aria. Not Moses. Not Ethan, who thankfully could still be saved. Mark could do that much, at least.

Mark blinked and a call notification popped into his S-lens. With the nearest guards a ways off, he answered it. Brooke's face sprang into view.

"Did you see that press conference?" she asked, eyebrow raised.

Mark shook his head.

"No, what press conference?"

"Crayton just gave it from an undisclosed location. I'm guessing a darkroom in the stadium. He's blaming the attack on Christian fundamentalists trying to shut the Crucible down. You know, all those crazies with the doomsday signs?"

Mark couldn't help but choke out a laugh.

"Yeah, I don't think I know any local churches with access to illegally modded ultrabikes and machine pistols with armor-piercing rounds."

Brooke shook her head in bewilderment.

"Whatever he says is gospel to the media, and law enforcement too, it seems. He has Vegas PD in his pocket, and his Glasshammer guys were the ones securing the scene, and all the evidence and bod-ies. Supposedly he's sparring with the FBI about all of it now. But that doesn't matter to us anymore."

"Zhou still cooperating?" Mark asked, his heart beating a little faster, praying the asshole hadn't changed his mind.

Brooke nodded.

"Will trade for an ironclad deal. That's being drafted, and will have to be sent up for approval. I think it will fly, no question, but the process is still going to take a little time. We won't get a sworn statement we can move on for at least thirty-six hours, and that's with an insane rush on it."

"Okay . . ." Mark said, unclear where Brooke was going with this.

"The problem is that Crayton wasn't just playing the blame game with his announcement. He was saying that the Crucible rolls on, and despite you 'being present' during the attack, you're in fine health, and your match has been rescheduled for tomorrow. If you flee now, he'll know something is up, and will go to ground. Break cover and we could lose him."

Mark took another swig of beer and watched the last curve of the sun dip behind the horizon.

"What are you saying, Brooke?"

"How do you feel about killing Soren Vanderhaven?"

MARK LET HIMSELF EMBRACE it. All of it. He absorbed the energy of the crowd, let it race through his nerves like lightning and through his bloodstream like endorphins. Love, hate, it didn't really matter. This time, he was going to enjoy this.

Zhou had remained cooperative, and his testimony was nearly a done deal. By morning, Crayton would be in custody, and this entire circus would be shut down. Mark didn't mind staying in cover for one more fight. His only condition had been that they moved before Ethan had to fight Rusakov, no matter what. This first semi-final was how the Crucible would end.

He wished he could kill them both. Vanderhaven *and* Rusakov, avenging Moses and Aria at the same time. But he'd have to settle for Soren, the girl who had slit Moses's throat because the man had shown a glimmer of mercy toward her. The girl who had giggled and blown kisses while painted in his friend's blood.

That wasn't the angle being sold, however.

Rather, the fight was all about Soren getting revenge for her lost love, Chase Cassidy, against Mark, the man who had butchered him. She'd been giving tearful interviews all week, and her millions of fans had bought into her story like she and Cassidy were the modern day Romeo and Juliet. Crayton loved his narratives. But so did the audience, which was why they worked so damn well.

The boos and jeers hit Mark like bricks as he walked through the sand toward his appointed spot in front of Crayton's box. Mark didn't care. He raised his arms outward and smiled, embracing the insanity of everything around him for perhaps the first time. His entrance video played, which was now made up of a few of his interviews cut with his brutal fights. A loud, nukecore dance track blasted through the speakers. The crowd was on its feet, to remain there the whole fight. Mark felt that pull again, like he was living history. And there was the self-proclaimed Helen of Troy standing in front of him.

Soren wore her trademark armor, which featured much more skin than metal, but it hadn't failed her yet. Creeping up her exposed abdomen were the remnants of the sickly bruise she'd sustained in her fight with Moses, though either it had mostly healed, or it was covered with make-up. She wore a ribbon around her bicep, crimson and gold, with tiny little lion's head tassels on the end, a tribute to her fallen "love."

Mark hadn't realized just how long her spear was. It really was massive, towering above both of them at least nine feet from tip to tail. It was incredibly thin, but that made it pliable and easy to wield for someone of her size, and it gave her pretty much Rusakov's level of reach when she needed it.

Now, though, she held the spear outright and pivoted around toward the crowd. Mark turned and saw a cluster of fans near the front holding a collection of signs. On one end, there was a headshot of Chase Cassidy looking especially handsome and heroic in one of his windswept headshots. On the other, there was an old, blown-up photo of a younger Shin Tagami in full military uniform, an almost saint-like portrait. In the middle, more enormous signs held by fans spelled something out in black paint.

H-E-R-O-K-I-L-L-E-R.

Soren brought the spear back around and pointed it toward Mark, a beautiful, horrible smile on her face.

Maybe this was a bad idea.

42

THE SPEAR WAS A different animal than Tagami's staff. It was incredibly long and flexible and whipped around in entirely unpredictable ways. As soon as the contestants said their last words (Soren dedicated the match to Chase, Mark buttered up Crayton by thanking him for the chance to fight) and the countdown hit zero, the spearhead was constantly inches from Mark's body. No matter how much he swatted it away with his blade, Soren kept the razor's edge dancing dangerously inside his reach. Cassidy was methodical and controlled compared to her. Tagami was fluid and measured. But Soren Vanderhaven was a Fourth of July fireworks show, a never-ending explosion of color, noise, and fury.

Soren thrust the spear directly toward his helm, and Mark barely wrenched his neck out of the way before countering with a slash of his own. The blade missed its mark by a mile, the woman simply too far outside his range. He barreled forward, trying to close the gap, but Soren twisted the spear and the back end of it cracked across his armored jaw, causing him to stagger. Instantly, the bladed end was back, and Mark winced as it dug into his shoulder. He slammed his sword hilt into the spearhead, freeing the tip from the wound, and drank in air, trying to keep his concentration. Was there drexophine in his system? It felt like the cut should have hurt more than it did.

Mark had no time to consider it as Soren charged forward with a lower thrust. This time, Mark leapt up and stomped on the spear, but the metal flexed without bending permanently. Soren actually dropped the spear, but came at Mark with a no-handed cartwheel kick that struck him hard across the chest, her metal boots plowing into his own plating. The unexpected acrobatics bowled him over, and Soren tumbled and reclaimed her spear when he fell. From the ground, he twisted backward, just in time to deflect a new strike with his sword, and quickly leapt to his feet once the spearhead had bounced away from him.

Mark tried to catch her thigh with a quick jab, but Soren blocked the move effortlessly, along with the next two. He turned to try and thread his blade into her midsection, but she used the center of the spear expertly, twirling away his blow like he was trying to stab through a whirring fan blade. He nearly lost his grip on his sword as Soren rapped the spear shaft across his hand, then immediately jumped backward and raked the spearhead across his wolfshead chest armor, which left a jagged scratch, but hadn't pierced the plating. Before Mark even realized he wasn't hurt, the back-end of the spear swung back toward him, cracking across the side of his helmet with surprising force. The crowd cheered wildly as Mark shuffled back, disoriented.

Soren dragged the tip of her spear across the sand in front of her, drawing a curved line she dared Mark to cross. The tiny, tan woman in front of him exuded power in a way that was almost impossible to quantify, and it chilled Mark to his core. The vast majority of the 250,000 screaming fans were on her side and she knew it. So were the tens of millions at home, and she was riding them all like a wave. She wasn't simply fighting not to die, she was fighting for the chance to conquer the world as champion. She wanted to be worshiped.

Mark remembered Dan Hagelund, limping around bleeding from a dozen spear wounds. He remember the gurgling sounds coming from Moses's throat as he died. She'd smiled. And laughed. And the audience loved her.

He thought of the locker room, and those little waterfalls

dancing down her flawless skin, which was exactly what she *wanted* him to think of in this moment, instead of focusing on ways not to get killed in the next few minutes. He thought of that hard, cold smile and that pretty face, masking something dark and insane and sickening underneath.

She was the last doorway before Crayton. All he had to do was get past her. And despite her aspirations, she wasn't a goddess. She was very much mortal, a lesson Mark desperately needed to teach her. He sprinted forward across the sand.

Soren seemed momentarily caught off guard by how fast Mark was in his armor, which was much lighter than it looked. She barely pirouetted out of the way of his straight thrust, and though she tried to jab him in the back, Mark flung his arm out behind him and his elbow knocked away the spear. He countered with a quick kick to Soren's leg, which destabilized her, and as she hit the ground he tried to pin her there with an overhead stab that she was barely able to dodge.

She came back to her feet and jabbed at Mark again and again with the spear. He was able to deflect almost all the shots, but one found a gap in his side, and the spearhead came back red. She tried to go back in for the same wound, but Mark grabbed the spear and wrenched her forward. He tried to land a headbutt, but was amazed when Soren did a complete front flip, and landed with her legs wrapped around his neck. She used her momentum to swing herself around and fling Mark head over heels. As he flipped, her legs lost their grip, taking his helmet with them. He landed on his already concussed head, now exposed to the elements. Soren tumbled out of the move with ease, and gave a little bow to the roaring crowd, who had yet to see anything quite like that in the tournament to date. She kicked his detached helmet away with her boot, and dove back in with the spear, but her showboating had allowed Mark a split second to recover. Without the helmet, his field of vision was better, and it felt like his lungs were breathing twice as much air.

Mark swatted the metal spear shaft away as sparks showered the sand, and tried to dive in toward her exposed stomach once again, sitting there like a tan bullseye. But again, she anticipated the move, dodging and countering with a dangerous thrust that glanced off his shoulder pauldron.

Soren lunged forward again, causing Mark to dance back a few paces, but she dug her spear into the ground and used it to vault herself up and over Mark's back in a dazzling athletic display. Fortunately, Mark had seen Soren flipping over combatants one way or another for a while now, and so as soon as she landed, he made sure he planted an iron boot into her midsection, still bruised from Moses's fight. The blow knocked the wind out of her and caused her to roll back, barely able to retain her grip on the spear.

After being put on his back foot the whole match, confidence was starting to flood back into Mark, while Soren seemed to be scrambling to adjust. He lunged forward with a pointed stab at her exposed breastbone, an angle that could drive the tip of his sword straight to her heart.

Soren didn't block, she dodged. Insanely quickly. So fast that Mark and his sword sailed right past her, uselessly cutting through the air. Mark watched her spin around, spear in hand, as he stumbled a few feet past where she'd been. He ground himself to a halt and reversed his momentum to try and fly back toward her with a recovery counter.

By the time he turned around, he saw Soren gripping the spear low, and whipping it in a diagonal upward arc toward him. He was a solid eight feet away from her, but the spear was long. So goddamn long.

He felt a line of something hot and bright enter his vision as the spear passed by his face. It was a strange sensation, and he watched, confused, as the eyes of the fans in the front few rows widened beyond belief, their hands clasped over their mouth in horror.

Mark felt something wet tricking down his face. His vision was blurry and warped, like the all the angles of the world had just gone a bit wrong. Time seemed to slow to a crawl. He watched the spear continue to sail back up into the air, this time with a thin arc of red goo with it.

Then the pain hit. All at once. Like he'd dipped his face in boiling oil.

That's when Mark understood his eye was gone.

He watched the joy spread across Soren's face as she started sprinting toward him. He raised his gauntleted hand to his ruined left eye, and on the monitor above, saw a shot of his bloody, terrified face from one of the drone cameras.

The pain was excruciating, but he clenched his teeth and forced that part of his brain to shut off. At least for the next few seconds. If he didn't, his eye would be the least of his concerns.

Mark's head swam. He knew he was about to lose consciousness. His fingers fumbled with his sword's grip as he desperately tried not to drop it in the sand and remain standing upright. Despite his best efforts, he stumbled backward and nearly fell.

Soren left her feet, her spear a silver blur in his vision. He pushed off his own back foot and ran out to meet her. He summoned all his remaining strength to also go airborne, trying to twist out of the path of the spear, while bringing his sword around toward her with a two-handed grip.

Mark hit the ground with his ears ringing, his face on fire and the rest of his body numb. The crowd was a massive, fuzzy ocean of gold and black shapes and white noise. Mark spat out coarse sand and slowly rolled over.

He found himself looking at the blank, blue-eyed visage of Soren Vanderhaven, with his blade lodged in the side of her skull. Blood matted her wavy blonde hair and stained the sand around her head. Her glass gaze was cast into oblivion.

Mark followed her into the darkness, in that moment not knowing or caring whether he'd emerge again.

MARK FOUND HIMSELF ADRIFT in a freezing ocean somewhere between unconsciousness and the real world. He was vaguely aware of being carried, but it felt like he was floating. He tried to blink, but half his face didn't seem to work, and it took all his strength to even flex his fingers and toes. Heavy sedatives, traditional painkillers. Who knew what else. He was cold, and could see what looked like a burning ship on the horizon, but it flickered in and out of existence. He had won, hadn't he? Yes, yes he had.

Eventually he came to rest in a dark room. Or at least it looked dark, with his vision impaired. He finally was able to lift his left arm, and found an enormous bandage plastered over half his face.

"No, no, no," a deep voice said, and gently placed his hand back down. Something sharp pricked a vein, and he sunk into the icey ocean again. In the distance, he could hear shouting and wailing. Hundreds of thousands of voices. Millions. He felt like he was sailing down the River Styx to hell.

Eventually, his mind snapped back into focus. This time, a familiar face hovered above him. Gideon.

"What's going on?" he said, his tongue cotton.

"We're extracting you and moving on Crayton," Gideon said. "You've been out for about six hours, and we just got the greenlight." He held up a flexscreen, which shone brightly in the darkness and made Mark's remaining pupil shrink. As his eyes came into focus, it was an official-looking rendition warrant for Crayton full of digital signatures.

"Zhou testified," Mark said, hardly believing things were possibly going right. Gideon nodded.

"Said he told you the same story. Hell of a tale, wasn't it? Combined with the rest of the case you and Brooke worked up, it's enough to move on. We're taking him in, and shutting this shit down."

"Where is Brooke?" Mark asked.

"Debrief. And that's where you'll be once they bounce you out of recovery. It . . . uh, looks worse than it is," Gideon said, gesturing at the left half of Mark's face.

Mark pawed at the bandage again but felt nothing more than a dull throbbing.

"Is it—" he began.

"You lost the eye," Gideon said matter-of-factly. "I think we all underestimated that girl. Sorry to put you in harm's way like that. But the good news is they'll give you one of those new cybernetics. Permanent S-lens, plus UV, infrared, optic zoom, all sorts of shit. Few weeks, you'll be good as new. Better, even."

Mark sat up and realized for the first time Gideon was flanked by a half dozen armored soldiers all wearing full helmets flickering with internal displays. They wore no patches.

"Strike team?" he asked.

Gideon nodded.

"Leading the charge myself. Crayton isn't dumb enough to put up a fight though, so I don't expect any problems."

Mark swung his legs over the side of the bed. The room was dark, but he could still tell they were in the Colosseum somewhere. Where exactly had Gideon hidden him away?

"I'm coming," he said. "Give me a kit."

Gideon shook his head.

"Not necessary, and not possible. Mark, you just had your goddamn eye sliced out of your skull a few hours ago. You're in no condition to suit up."

Mark pointed to a trio of empty drexophine vials on the table.

"You know what that is, right? That means I'm ready to do fucking anything. And I'll be damned if I'm going to miss seeing the look on that bastard's face when we bring him in at last."

Gideon looked nervous at the steel in Mark's voice. He held up a finger and backed into the darkness to chat with one of the helmeted soldiers out of earshot.

"Alright," Gideon said, returning to his bedside. "I know how much you've put into this thing."

He cocked his head and a soldier came forward and presented him with a short shotgun and a tactical helmet. Gideon handed him a tiny case.

"Your S-lens," he said, as Mark popped it into his right eye. "But as soon as this is done, you're on a hexocopter to a military hospital. And, uh, watch your damn depth perception," Gideon said with a smirk. But there was something in his eyes that looked sad. Mark thought he must look particularly gruesome. He'd worry about the eye, or lack thereof, later. This was a moment he'd been looking forward to for months now. Crayton was finished. CMI would be broken apart. The Crucible would crumble.

Mark wore the helmet with a few light pieces of tac armor over his bloodstained arena undersuit, and stalked down the halls of the ghostly quiet Colosseum. Confused-looking Glasshammer guards approached them left and right, but Gideon held up his warrant and pressed on with impunity. Mark gripped the shotgun tightly and wondered if he'd get a chance to shoot Wyatt Axton in the face at last. Mark wished Brooke was there so they could celebrate the moment together. For what had essentially been a two-man operation, what they'd achieved was nothing short of a miracle. He'd take her out for drinks afterward, he supposed, and he hoped his face wasn't as badly mangled as it appeared to be.

"Target is in his arena office," Gideon said, consulting a map on his flexscreen. "Up the stairs on the left. Short hallway. Prepare to breach."

Mark was positively shivering with excitement. He felt fresh blood tricking out from under his bandaged face, but he ignored it. He could push forward a little longer, just to see this end at last.

The team hustled up the stairs and stalked down a hallway that ended in a pair of double doors. Right away, two soldiers knelt and planted a micro-explosive in the center, large enough to blow the heavy duty e-lock clean through.

Something flickered in Mark's vision. A call pushed straight through his S-lens with no warning. The floating screen was fuzzy, like the signal was being masked by interference. He could only see bits of a face.

"Charges set," soldier said. "Echoscan says only one body inside. It's him."

The image in Mark's eye shifted to become nearly clear for a moment. Mark's heart stopped. Zhou.

"They're [static] going to kill me, Mark. They did not want to hear what I had to [static] say."

"What? What are you talking about?" Mark said.

Gideon frowned at him, confused about who he was talking to.

"The Agency lies, Mark. I [static] told you. You are a pawn, once again. They gave me to Glasshammer. I've hacked their comms."

"Counting down in ten, nine—" a soldier began.

"Execution seems imminent [static], but it no longer matters. Things are in motion that cannot be stopped. Find me when you want revenge for what they've done to you, if [static] either of us are still alive. I will have the last laugh either way."

The feed went black.

Mark's head was spinning. Zhou was saying . . . he was in Glasshammer custody? And they were going to kill him? That was impossible, and absurd.

"Gideon," Mark said, turning to try and explain what he'd just seen to him, "I—"

His thoughts were cut off by an explosion, and two soldiers kicked the office door open. The team poured in behind them, and Mark was forced to follow.

What the hell is—

Cameron Crayton sat peacefully at his sprawling desk, looking over a flexscreen, undisturbed by the smoke from the bomb, the wooden splinters dotting his carpet or the heavily armored tactical team in his office. Wyatt Axton was nowhere to be found. Something cold creeped down Mark's spine. He frantically tried to redial Zhou's blocked number from his S-lens.

Crayton rolled his eyes.

"Really, Gideon, was that necessary?"

Mark turned to his former handler.

"How does he know your—"

He saw a thin wet coat of tears in Gideon's brown eyes. And that was when he knew.

Mark turned and tried to fire his shotgun at Crayton, but the weapon clicked uselessly, and the man didn't even flinch. Instantly, Mark's body twisted and turned as three tasers were jammed into his back and sides by the soldiers. Something hard and metal cracked across the back of his skull. A million thoughts flooded through his mind in the last millisecond before unconsciousness, and absolutely none of them made sense.

43

MARK WAS BACK ON the hill. The walls of the compound had crumbled. Out in the desert, enormous dust tornadoes drifted lazily around, feeding into the rolling red clouds above them.

In front of Mark, the giant willow tree was dead, blackened, burned to a crisp. In the grass around it were slaughtered corpses, splayed open and rotting. Whatever creatures they once were, they were no longer recognizable. The ground was just heaps of bone and flesh and gore.

The only sound was the wind. Mark could smell a thousand odors, all of them horrible. He turned behind him, but the lake was bare. The mansions lay in ruins like the ringed wall. Ahead, the tree looked like a dark, black crack in the sky.

Above it in the clouds was a shape. Just a shadow, swimming endlessly. A shark, as large as a warship, drifting a thousand feet above the earth. A black shape full of menace and dread. Mark couldn't breathe. He was drowning in the open air. He was—

Awake.

The room was dimly lit, but as it came into focus, Mark realized where he was. Crayton's private box in the Colosseum. The windows were tinted to pitch black, and there wasn't anything visible outside. Mark could hear absolutely nothing, and the weight of the silence told him the room was at least temporarily soundproofed.

Mark rolled his head around. What had happened? Had he—? Had Gideon just—?

He was restrained. Metal cuffs clipped into a plush armchair and his feet were bound. He felt scratchy growth on his face, which had been clean-shaven moments earlier. Or had it been hours? Days? He saw a pale reflection in the glass ahead and saw that he no longer had a bandage on his ruined eye, but a large black patch instead.

A shadow glided across the black windows in front of him. The shark. The man. In the silence, his voice was cold and clear.

"Wyatt, turn the lights up. It's the owner's box, not a dungeon."

The lights brightened a bit and Mark's pupils shrank. It was indeed Cameron Crayton standing in front of him. He wore a black suit, his hands stuck in his pockets.

"Welcome back, Mark. I'm sorry for keeping you under for so long, but we are on a timetable, and I just couldn't have you causing any more problems. Sadly, our time together is drawing to a close."

"What the hell are you talking about?" Mark spat out. His mouth was dry. He looked down and saw that he was in his armor undersuit for some reason. A fresh one. Panic started to constrict his throat.

What the fuck is going on?

"I'm sure you have many questions," Crayton said, his voice silk. "And there are some answers you'll need to move forward. So I'm more than happy to oblige."

Mark choked out a laugh.

"So what, you blackmailed Gideon into giving me up? You fucking moron. He's just a cog. The Agency will send another team. Five teams, after what we've got on you now."

"Ah," Crayton said, raising his finger. "I suppose you're referring to Major Zhou. He was annoyingly helpful for a Ministry operative. Usually they're quite quiet, as I'm sure you know. I guess you hold a special place in his heart."

Crayton wagged his finger, and the black glass of the tinted outer window became a screen. In it, Zhou was in an empty room, sitting across from a table with a mic. He was rehashing a version of the same story he'd told Mark. His recorded testimony. Had Gideon seriously handed it over to Crayton? Mark would kill him.

"*. . . spent a year beating other children to death for his masters. He was their prize dog, and they kept selling him for huge amounts of money as his record grew. He destroyed every other child put in his path . . .*"

Suddenly, Mark remembered. Zhou had called him. Warned him what was about to happen. Said that it was *Glasshammer* that had him. What the hell was—

"You're still not understanding," Crayton said, flipping off the video. "No one is coming. Because the CIA doesn't know about any of this. They never did."

Mark couldn't process what he was saying. It made no sense at all.

"There was never a mission, Mark," Crayton said flatly.

Something sick and cold took root in Mark's stomach and began to spread through his entire body. He felt like he was falling, drowning, all at once.

"What are you—" he began.

"I've been developing the Crucible for ages now. *Prison Wars* was just a trial run, to prove to myself, and the world, that America was ready for something that was forever thought too 'brutal' for the airwaves. My assessment was correct.

"But it couldn't just be a bunch of random citizens flung into the ring. I needed to tell a *story*. I needed the Crucible to *matter*. Some characters were easy to come by. I'd cultivated a few in *Prison Wars* who were perfectly suitable monsters who only needed to be released from prison, a simple feat. The rest came out of the woodwork, and there were a few shining stars, Chase, Soren, and your Aria, of course. But I needed someone else. I needed *you*.

"I asked my old friend from Homeland Security, General McAdams, if he knew anyone in the CIA willing to part with an operative, current or former. They would be the most well-trained, the most ruthless. And they would have the most skeletons.

"He found an over-the-hill handler, Gideon Gellar. Fresh off a messy divorce, drowning deep in debt and alimony. He had run one of the men who had made China fall, a 'Spear,' as they say. His was the triple-agent. The one who survived years of torture, and ended his mission by taking out an aircraft carrier, sinking a country with it. It was quite a story, and one I'd heard many times from the MSS directly.

"But now, the man was shattered. He'd lost his family to the Chinese, and was on his way to drinking himself to death after pissing away millions in recompense. But he was also an idealist, and wouldn't sign up for something as crude as the Crucible, no matter how well-suited for it he might be.

"So I manufactured a mission.

"This entire affair was my creation, Mark. A way to get you to stick around long enough to get to this point. I fed you little pieces of my story, my true story, and you gobbled them up, thinking the CIA would pat you on the head when you reached the end. Didn't you learn anything from Spearfish? Apparently not. But we've now reached the point where if I wasn't arrested, you'd suspect something, or just try to kill me outright. And we couldn't have that, hence the charade coming to an end."

Mark's head was buzzing angrily. This couldn't be happening. It was too massive. The scale of the thing was impossible. Wasn't it? And what about—

"Brooke," Mark said breathlessly.

She couldn't have.

"The rookie handler was harmless, and didn't have a clue, same as you. She believed in the mission. But more interestingly, she believed in you. Everything you fed her went to a private team Gideon ran, and ended up coming straight back to me. The CIA and Homeland got nothing. Not a thing."

Crayton paced across the hardwood in front of the black glass. His hands were crossed behind his back, and his chest swelled with pride.

And that goddamn smug smile.

"Between you and Brooke," he continued, "you actually ended up plugging quite a few holes in my own little 'cover story.' A useful side effect of the mission, and more than Beijing ever did for me. I know now I need to clean up my early business ventures, destroy that infernal wooden keepsake box and execute a certain chatty Chinese agent. And this week you actually saved my *life*, standing between me and the MSS. How serendipitous!"

"You're insane," Mark spat. "Why would you do this? Why the hell would you go to all this trouble to rope *me* into your disgusting game?"

"When I heard about who you were and what you'd done in China, I knew I'd found you at last. We have similar stories, as you surely realize by now. We suffered greatly at the hands of the Chinese, and were turned against our own countries, but only temporarily. And in spite of it all, we accomplished great things. I saw much of myself in you."

"I'm not your goddamn gladiator hero," Mark growled.

"Oh, of course not!" Crayton said, looking surprised. "You're my villain. My perfect villain."

"What?" Mark said, taken aback.

"Can't you see now?" Crayton said. "Everything you've done to get to this point? Yes, you had a brief brush with heroism when you killed Burton Drescher, but after that? Slowly, you've become the most loathed man in America. And that's even before what's coming next."

Mark didn't understand. *He's literally out of his mind.*

"The bracket was not as random as it appeared to be," Crayton continued. "Pitting you against Chase Cassidy, a beloved national treasure, was no accident. You slaughtered him without quarter 'for the mission,' as you liked to tell yourself. Then the old man, the monk, the war hero. You taunted him, and killed him too. And after that, Cassidy's better half, Soren. The woman all of America was in love with. You butchered her as a hundred million watched. And Christ, you even have a damn eyepatch now!" Crayton laughed. "That certainly wasn't planned, but it's delightful."

"None of this makes sense," Mark said, shaking his head slowly, hoping that he was in a coma or dead and none of this was real. "You recruited me, you forced me through the bracket and now—" something dawned on him. If he'd been out for days . . . "Ethan. What happened to Ethan?"

Crayton smiled and gestured. The screen lit up with a replay of a fight. It was the other semifinal, Ethan versus Rusakov, and the two were locked in furious combat. Ethan was ducking and rolling under the massive axe, and Rusakov was struggling to keep pace, possibly still reeling from the wounds Aria had inflicted on him in the last round. Still, he fought with unholy fury, and Mark thought that Ethan was about to lose his head at any moment, which made him cringe in anticipation. But this was a tape. Whatever had happened had already happened, which was even more terrifying. The video froze.

"Don't worry, Mark. I made it out alive."

The voice came from behind him. Ethan's. Mark twisted and turned, but his restraints and the high back chair wouldn't let him see the rear of the room. Instead, Ethan walked slowly around the row of outward facing seats and stood next to Crayton, clad in his blue armor undersuit.

"Ethan, what are you doing here? Crayton—" Mark didn't even know how to begin.

"Cut in the right places, and any giant will fall. I hacked him down to his knees, and made him faceplant into his own axeblade," Ethan sneered. Something was off about him. Something was wrong. This wasn't the man he'd spent the summer with, training, laughing, and sparring. This wasn't his friend.

"Still catching up, Mark?" Crayton said, amused. "Well, if you think I went to a lot of trouble crafting the ideal *villain* for my little show here, imagine all the work it took to make myself a *hero*. Fortunately, my son has been as determined as me to see this through."

"*Son?*" Mark said, feeling dizzy. "Are you fucking—"

"Bright little chap when I first met him a decade ago. Tried to blackmail me for a million dollars. Somehow got ahold of my DNA, and proved I was his. His mother was a model I'd slept with back in '09 who ended up throwing herself off a penthouse balcony when she was sky-high on coke."

Mark looked back and forth between Crayton and Ethan, who stood next to the mogul with his arms folded. He'd never seen it before, but there it was. Not the same eyes, nose or mouth. That would have been obvious. But the line of their jaw. The shape of their ears. The cut of their cheekbones. The barest hint of a resemblance hidden in plain sight.

"I could have let him simply become another tabloid rumor, but I kept him around. Took him under my wing, in private, of course. And when the Crucible first became a spark in my brain, I started training him. He started with the sword and shield before he even got his driver's license. He understood what we could do together."

"But Lily, the kids—" Mark stammered. Gideon. Ethan. Where did it end? This was a waking nightmare.

"Actors," Ethan said with thinly veiled disgust. "Who signed a very unique contract they will never want to break. Don't get me started on those brats. But they were necessary for the story to work. The war hero with the dying wife. The only competitor that *everyone* has to root for."

Mark thought back to all the times Lily had seemed nervous,

bordering on terrified out of her mind. The kids so polite and rehearsed. Except little Kellan . . .

"I want to see my daddy!"

Mark's brain felt like it was melting.

"Haven't you seen Ethan's rise, Mark?" Crayton said. "It's the opposite of your own. He's killed one horrible, spoiled billionaire and two of my *Prison Wars* monstrosities, one of whom was famous for *not being able to die.* Ethan has been on the hero's path from moment one. It's a classic tale, through and through."

"And now you," Ethan said, pointing, "are the last dragon to slay."

"What is the *point*?" Mark yelled. His entire body was shaking with rage. "What the hell are you hoping to *achieve* through all of this?"

"Billions of dollars and public approval numbers that would make any sitting governor or senator in this country nervous," Crayton said with a twinkle in his cold blue eyes. "But those are just the obvious perks. In order to cement a lasting legacy for the Crucible, I told you, I needed that *story.*"

"You're crazy," Mark said. "China broke you. The Beijing pits. The fights. The White Devil. That's why—"

Crayton acted like he didn't even hear him.

"Don't you remember what I told you in this very box weeks ago?" Crayton asked. "How America has been *thirsting* for a war, something that Cold War II never gave them? Well, this is it. This is America versus China at last. A fight out in the open, not lurking in the shadows. This is what they've been waiting for all this time."

Mark laughed.

"That's it? That's your master plan? Make me out to be a stand-in for China, when *you're* the one working for them?"

"I used them like they tried to use me," Crayton said flatly, betraying a hint of annoyance. "I took their money and built an empire. I have done nothing to betray this country. I *love* this country. That was their mistake in sending me here. No matter what horrors you've experienced, or what they drill into you for a decade, once you get to America, you can't help but adore it."

"So I'm the Chinese villain because what, I'm Asian and I killed a movie star and a Barbie doll? Fucking pathetic," Mark said.

"Fortunately, all the greatest lies have truth twisted into them," Crayton said, his smile growing wide. He motioned to someone behind Mark. "Wyatt, I think it's time. Let's take a look out the windows, and kill the dampeners."

There was a dull rumbling that Mark thought was an earthquake, but suddenly understood. It was the crowd. The window lost its tint and Mark could see out into the stands. 250,000 fans were roaring with anticipation. For the grand finals of the Crucible. Across from them on the big screen were portraits of Ethan and Mark with a countdown timer. Only minutes left.

"I should head down," Ethan said. "Have to armor up and start working on some tears for the cameras." If Mark could, he would have ripped himself out of the chair and strangled Ethan right then and there.

"Why?" Mark said, turning back to Crayton. "Why tell me any of this?"

"If I wasn't incarcerated after Zhou's confession, you would have been spooked and either run for the hills with your perky little sidekick in tow, or you'd be out in the crowd somewhere, drawing a bead on me with a rifle."

He paused.

"But you had to know about Ethan too, because I want the cameras to see the hate in your eyes as you try and kill my son. Now that you know the truth about your 'friend,' you will fight like you're supposed to. Like the cornered savage trying to murder the wholesome American hero."

"I won't fight," Mark said. "I'll stand there and I'll die before I let you finish this abominable 'plan' of yours."

"Oh you *will* fight," Crayton said. He pulled up a new screen on the window. Mark suspected no one in the crowd could see in at the moment.

Mark's heart sank as he saw what was on the monitor. Carlo and his family were in Mark's box, along with a worried-looking Brooke who kept checking her phone. The Riveras were excited and chattering away, sipping soda and eating popcorn.

"If you don't fight, Mr. Axton will slip something into Carlo's next soda. A few days later, he will die after a massive stroke. Complications from his injury. And though you won't live to see it, Brooke will disappear from the face of this earth. I might send her to my Chinese adversaries as a peace offering so we can put all this messiness behind us. I imagine they'll have plenty of use for a pretty blonde CIA officer."

Mark strained against his restraints, which only dug into his wrists and ankles. His eye hurt, his old wounds hurt. The drexophine had been purged from his system, it seemed. Out on the sand, Ethan's heartwrenching intro video played once more, and a few minutes later he strode out into the arena, dressed in American crimson, sapphire, and silver, burnished brightly for his final bout. The crowd chanted his name endlessly, and he waved to them with tears in his eyes. With Lily in a "coma," only his fake children were in attendance, and the camera showed them being held by relatives, who were no doubt actually CMI caretakers.

Suddenly, more men entered Crayton's box. Armored Glasshammer guards bringing several large cases. Leading them was Wyatt Axton. Mark's handcuffs clicked off, but before he could lunge forward, Axton had his Desert Eagle aimed directly at his forehead.

"Don't." The gun clicked menacingly.

The other men opened the cases and started pulling out pieces of Mark's thin black armor, attaching it to his undersuit. When they were done with his torso, his leg restraints were lifted and they fastened the rest of his armor to his lower half. After, he stood next to Crayton and all the cuffs went back on. Only then did they slide his sword into the scabbard on his back, but his body was bound too tightly to reach it. He watched the video of Brooke and Carlo on the glass. He felt the end of Axton's gun brushing the hair on the back of his neck.

"And now, there's only one last thing to share," Crayton said, seeming almost downright giddy. "The true face of evil, revealed."

Mark expected his entrance video to play, but something else appeared on the screen instead. It was a grainy, older video, filmed in a dark room.

Suddenly, a face came into focus. His own. The video cut to black.

Mark Wei is a spy, the caption read.

The video returned. Mark saw himself gaunt and pale, wearing the officer's uniform he'd worn in China after he'd gotten out of the hole.

Mark Wei is a traitor.

This time, the camera panned out. It showed a man tied to a chair. Mark was leaning over him, tearing into his flesh with a curved knife.

No, no, no. no. There's no way.

Mark Wei is a murderer.

"*Where is the rest of your squad?*" the Mark in the video barked before cutting into the man again. He'd been at it for a while, judging by all the blood. Zhou stood behind him with a thin smile on his lips. "*What is your extraction protocol?*"

The man's voice wavered, but he said the same thing he always did.

"*Lieutenant Marcus O'Connor. United States Army. Service Number 8355521. D.O.B. 6/22/2002.*"

The crowd gasped at the footage. Their screams were deafening, an angry hive agitated to a frenzy. And who could blame them?

How the hell . . .

"I told you," Crayton said with that sick smile. "The best lies are twisted with truth. And this truth came courtesy of the MSS data archives a few years back. *This* was the video that convinced me you were my man. You are *everything* they hate," he said, gesturing outward to the riotous crowd. "And now this entire country is on their feet, screaming at their televisions, waiting for you to die. No, *demanding* it."

"I—I," Mark stammered. "I had to. It was for the mission. *I won that fucking war!*"

"While *I* understand you're a true patriot, the rest of the world will not. And the CIA, the *real* CIA will deny all of this until the end of days, as you well know. China too, for their part."

Mark couldn't escape the fact that he *had* done it. That he had tortured and killed this innocent soldier to keep his cover. His sins were eating him alive right before his eyes. He tried to steel himself, and turned toward Crayton. Axton's gun pressed deeper into his neck.

"You want me to fight, I'll fight. But I'll kill him. I don't care how long you've been grooming him to be your little gladiator psychopath. He will die."

Crayton gestured to one of the guards.

"Even if you could defeat him in your current state, which I doubt, I'm not planning on leaving anything to chance. This bracket has been difficult to shape, but it's worked so far."

Mark's eyes narrowed.

"What's worked?"

"Whoever needs to win is often flooded with an overabundance of my miracle drug in their system."

"Drexophine," Mark said. He understood instantly. He thought about Rusakov shrugging off Aria's blades like they were nothing. He thought of Soren taking a maul to the ribs and staying on her feet. Hell, even a few of his *own* injuries he'd been able to push past with relative ease.

"But there's another side to that coin," Crayton continued. "The lab boys call it *nuravine*."

Mark winced as a small needle was jabbed into his temple, right outside the borders of his eye patch.

"My bio-dev team tells me it can amplify the sensitivity of pain receptors up to fifty-fold. It can make a papercut feel like you've just cut off your finger. I can only imagine what it's going to do to your poor eye socket."

The burning hit Mark like he'd just stuck half his face onto a hot grill. The pain was excruciating, unbelievable. What had been a dull throbbing was now a crashing wave of needles jabbing into every square millimeter of flesh around the wound on his face. He felt it in his other injures, his cracked skull from the Tagami fight, his forearm slice from Cassidy. He swore he could even feel it in his old scars, the ones Zhou had carved onto him years ago. He almost lost his balance, and the guards had to steady him.

"Heavy dose," Crayton said. "But I told Ethan to make it look convincing. And you should too, for the sake of your friends."

Mark thought back to Moses wincing from his gut wound and talking about his drexophine 'allergy.' Aria fighting on a foot that wouldn't heal. Hell, he'd probably even done it to Rusakov, to help him lose against Ethan. This was how Crayton stacked the deck. He made one fighter oblivious to pain, and hobbled the other.

Crayton took Mark by his armored shoulders and looked into his watering, remaining eye.

"I just want to thank you for making all this possible. It's been *such* a journey, and I'm sad to see it end. We've done a great thing here, whether you see it or not."

"Fuck you," Mark said through clenched teeth, trying to detach himself from the pain. The guards hauled him toward the door, and

Crayton turned to the windows. They became totally transparent, and he looked sternly across the crowd toward the torture video, which was still playing on the screen.

"*Lieutenant . . . Marcus . . . O'Connor,*" the dying man choked out. "*United States . . . Army. Please . . .*"

In the video, the uniformed Mark looked to his right. Zhou nodded, and Mark drove the knife into the man's heart. The Colosseum crowd lost their minds.

44

MARK RETREATED INTO HIMSELF as far as he could, trying to mentally flee from the pain radiating through his body. It was a technique he'd learned in China. But this poison, this nuravine was diabolical. He was dragged in cuffs through back tunnels and down to the arena floor. The Glasshammer CMI guards finally unshackled him at the wide-mouth entrance to the sand, where Ethan and the audience waited outside. The Muses were lining the tunnel as they always did, and Mark saw them all staring at him with wide eyes. Shyla was there too, leaning stiffly against the wall right before the sand, and she looked at Mark like a total stranger. Worse, like a monster. He kept quiet, and strode out into the light.

Mark had been booed before, but this was something else entirely. After that video outing him as a spy and apparent traitor, the crowd was in a complete frenzy. Mark heard every possible curse word and insult and racial slur all wrapped up in one droning torrent of hate. Mark looked at those closest to the edge of the wall, those who had paid tens of thousands to be there, and saw the disgust and rage on their faces. Those higher up were starting to throw trash at him, but security was moving in to prevent that. Many in the crowd held signs of Soren Vanderhaven, giant posters showing the beaming blonde, before his blade had split her skull. Others held signs of Cassidy or Tagami. No one seemed to be mourning Jordan, Blackwood, or Rusakov, the vile men whom Ethan had slain.

Crayton had delivered them a villain, alright. *Christ,* Mark still couldn't believe everything the man had just said and done. How Gideon had sold him out from the beginning. How Ethan had lied to his face the entire time. Now this video. His worst moment, broadcast to the entire world. It was unthinkable, impossible, and yet here he was. This was happening. He was marching toward his execution, a rogue agent at best, a traitor at worst. But above all else, he was an idiot for ever getting involved with the Crucible in the first place. For trusting anyone.

Mark walked toward an object in the sand and saw that it was his sword, planted blade-first in the earth. Lord knew they weren't going to let him touch it near Crayton. He picked it up and found that even gripping it made his forearm burn with amplified pain, and his face was still throbbing intensely.

He wanted to just lay down and die. The pain was overwhelming, and this entire nightmarish journey had been for *nothing.* But he couldn't. Carlo and Brooke were still in harm's way, and Ethan, his handsome face full of pretend shock and betrayal as he regarded Mark, needed to die. So did Crayton, of course, but that was out of his hands now. Mark couldn't believe he'd *saved* Crayton on the road from the MSS assault. How stupid. How monumentally stupid.

The mogul stood sternly at his box window with his arms crossed, and when he spoke, his voice was projected all throughout the stadium.

"I'm heartbroken by what my research team has discovered about one of our fiercest competitors, Mark Wei. We were unaware of his dark past and un-American allegiances. But now that the truth has come to light, it's hard to understate just how horrible I feel about turning this man into an icon. Giving him a place in our beloved Crucible. In the wake of this information, I've come to believe Mark Wei has orchestrated several attempts on my life, one recent and public, and a few others before that, which I've kept private. Trying to assassinate someone like me is all the fallen Chinese states can hope to achieve in their weakened form. *And they have failed!*"

The crowd cheered wildly for a moment before returning to booing Mark.

"The proper thing to do would be to turn Mark over to the authorities. To end the Crucible now, and declare Ethan champion. But I ask you, my beloved audience, should we do that?"

An earthquake of "*No!*" shook the arena.

"I didn't think so. I think we should keep Mark Wei around just a *few* minutes longer to face justice here, on the sand. Provided you are willing to be our instrument, Mr. Callaghan. Victory is never guaranteed in the Crucible, after all, and you still risk your life here today if we press on."

"As a veteran, as a patriot, I would be honored!" Ethan shouted from the sands, and the crowd roared its approval.

"And you, Mark. Have you anything to say in your defense? Any *possible* justification for your horrific actions?"

Mark almost laughed. What was he supposed to do now? Tell the world Crayton was a Chinese plant, supported by nothing but a bunch of wild accusations that would come off as insane? Explain how he *was* a spy and *did* kill that soldier, but it was in service of dismantling China in a secret mission both Beijing and the CIA would deny ever existed? And if he did speak the truth, Mark knew Crayton might go after Carlo and Brooke before he even finished the statement.

So he stood there in silence, glowering at Crayton, who masked his glee with a caricature of anger and disappointment. The crowd continued to scream obscenities at him relentlessly. "Fucks" and "chinks" peppered him like rocks. He stood tall and took it, saying nothing, twitching involuntarily from unceasing pain. He looked toward his box and could see only the tiniest glimpse of Brooke and Carlo's faces in the glass, their expressions unreadable. At this point,

Brooke would understand what was happening. At least most of it. Lord only knew what she was saying to Carlo about all this.

"Very well," Crayton said, raising his arms. "Then it's time to begin. Ladies and gentlemen, prepare to witness history."

The crowd chanted "USA! USA!" as the countdown began. Ethan clanged his shield with his sword, and let a small smile escape his lips just as he flipped the visor of his helmet down.

Mark winced as he slid his own helmet down over his mangled, burning skin beneath his eyepatch, and took the sword from his back.

He could do this. He could at least derail Crayton's master plan. This glorious US victory over the evil Chinese rogue. All he had to do was kill Ethan, the psychopath who had been training for this moment for years. And he had to do it while he was racked with constant, infernal pain that he hadn't felt since Zhou's knives. His only saving grace was that whoever Ethan was, who he *really* was, had never been to hell and back like Mark. He could push through. He would win. He had to.

He had to.

Two.

One.

"You were my *friend*!" Ethan yelled into his armor mic as he leapt at Mark with his shortsword. "I *trusted* you!" Mark deflected the blows, wincing each time. Ethan's voice boomed all around the stadium, and he was saying what Mark himself wanted to say to the stranger before him. Could he have known about Ethan? *Should* he have known?

There wasn't time to dwell on any of it further. Mark was one wrong move away from death, and though he'd sparred with Ethan many times, the man was on another level now. It was indeed more than just natural talent with the sword and shield. It was *years* of training, when his competitors had only had months at best. Mark frantically scrambled to keep his sword up to block Ethan's strikes, not only fighting through the pain, but totally unused to having one eye. He made one feeble stab forward, but Ethan batted it away with his shield, and Mark felt painful tremors race through his arm from the impact. His face was burning, a hundred different points of pain blurring into one giant blob of misery.

Ethan feinted forward, and Mark rushed to block, but found Ethan ducking and spinning with a metal kick that caught him in the midsection, something he couldn't see coming thanks to the black blotch that would have normally been visible through his left eye. Mark doubled over, and Ethan brought the grip of his sword down on Mark's head, the pommel strike sending him to one knee. Mark leapt back, avoiding a slower, third strike with the blade, but only barely.

Mark quickly realized that his only saving grace was that Ethan was trying to put on a show for the crowd, and his father. He probably could have gored Mark three times already, but he was holding himself back. Showing off instead of going for the quick kill.

But it was hard to feel like that mattered. Mark was a shell of his former self, lurching forward with uncoordinated strikes that were either deflected, or countered into stiff shield slams that rattled his entire body. Finally, Ethan stabbed forward with a pointed strike that slid in between the folds of Mark's wolf chestplate, and pierced his skin. It was a relatively shallow cut, judging by the volume of red on the blade when it was retracted, but it felt like it had gored Mark through and through, the pain indescribable. The nuravine was making a mockery of his nervous system, telling his brain that a small slice was a horrifying mortal wound. The crowd cheered the sight of his blood, and immediately demanded more.

Ethan went in for another strike, but this time Mark was better prepared. He dodged left, and managed to spin and rip his bastard sword up the side of Ethan's outer arm plating near his tricep. He drew blood from a gap in the armor, but if Ethan even flinched, it wasn't noticeable. His blood was thick with drexophine, no doubt, and nothing short of a killing or crippling blow was going to stop him.

Mark desperately tried to lunge at Ethan's heart, but was deflected by the kite shield, which caused him to teeter off balance. Ethan followed up with a hard slash to his back that didn't pierce the armor but sent Mark tumbling forward into the sand as the crowd jeered and laughed. Ethan didn't pursue him, and Mark was able to slowly pick himself up, cringing with every movement.

Was this really how it ended? Betrayed and alone, publicly humiliated and executed in front of millions? But he wasn't alone. Not yet. Mark cast a glance to his box, where something caught his eye. Black shapes were moving, struggling. Suddenly a large body went crashing into the glass, which splintered, but didn't shatter. No one in the crowd noticed.

It's Brooke. She understands. She's fighting back. She can get Carlo and his family to safety.

Mark had to get through this. He had to help them, whatever was happening up there. With renewed determination, he pushed past the pain, fracturing his mind to escape it, like he'd done with Zhou in the hole. He sprinted toward the waiting Ethan and lunged with a two-handed thrust directly at his neckline.

He could see Ethan's eyes through the slits in his helmet. They widened. Mark was faster than Ethan imagined he could be. This was not how things were supposed to go.

But it didn't matter.

Ethan flung his shield upward, and Mark's sword bounced harmlessly off the metal eagle stretched across it. Off-balance, Ethan hit him with a gut-punch with his sword hand, then righted Mark with a knee to his helmeted head. Mark stumbled back, not seeing the blade coming around in a diagonal arc from the left until it was too late. He strained to bring his sword around with one hand but—

Ethan's blade crunched as it ripped through the visor of Mark's helmet. It lodged itself there, millimeters from his lone remaining eye, barely cutting into his cheek and his brow. Mark blinked, stunned for a half second that he wasn't dead, then, on instinct, drove his forearm into Ethan's, and the sword was ripped out of the helmet. Mark followed up with a flailing kick that drove Ethan away.

The entire fishbowl visor was splintered, and Mark could only see through the crack the sword had made across the blank-faced visor, as if he needed any more vision problems. The crowd was still cheering, and they only became louder as he ripped the entire helmet off and threw it into the sand. The fresh cuts on his face, however superficial, burned furiously. He could feel Ethan's sneer under his helmet. The man clanged on his shield with his sword, taunting Mark to attack.

Mark looked back up at his box. The cracked glass was still there, but there were no figures in the window. What had happened? Where were Brooke and Carlo? Mark would have traded anything for an S-lens at that moment.

Ethan was hitting his sword on his shield in a rhythm now. *Clang clang clang. Clang clang clang.* It had the desired effect, and now the crowd was joining in with another "USA! USA!" chant to match.

"I'll make this more fair," Ethan said as he slowly removed his own helmet. "And I want to look you in the eyes when I put you down."

More fair, as Mark was flooded with pain, set against a man who had been training for this moment for nearly a decade. Ethan's gesture was for the crowd and the cameras, nothing more, but it worked. The "USA!" chants immediately turned into *"Let's go E-than!"* complete with requisite clapping and foot-stomping.

Look at him.

His armor was spotless, shining bright in the Vegas sun. His blond hair blew in the hot breeze, and he'd barely broken a sweat. He was handsome, brave, determined, and white. The perfect hero. And Mark knew what he must look like, bloody, black-clad, and broken, scars raked over a missing eye. Face seething with hatred. The spy. The traitor. Crayton's game was working. This is precisely what he wanted. America would never forget this moment.

Mark looked around at the crowd, swelling as an amorphous mass of faces and voices. Guards lined the rim of the arena floor, preventing the insane from trying to make the two story leap down into the sand. Snipers stood watchful on the upper outer wall, mere specks from this distance. Mark turned back to Ethan. He couldn't lose focus.

By taking his helmet off, the kid had showed that he was getting cocky. Even if he had every reason to be, that could be exploited. Mark summoned a boost of adrenaline and lunged forward to try and slash Ethan's newly exposed face, but it was predictable, and parried instantly. Ethan unleashed a series of quick cuts, shield thrusts, and front kicks that propelled Mark backward across the sand, absorbing blows and struggling to keep his feet. The shield smashed into his armor, and it felt like he had rebroken one of his ribs. The blade then caught him in the side, and fresh blood flowed from another hyper-painful wound. Ethan attacked until Mark was nearly at the outer wall. He looked to his left, and saw the long crack in the stone where Rusakov had pinned Aria with his greataxe. The blood had been washed away, but the deep gash remained, the lone marker of her death.

Mark was simply exhausted. The pain was creeping back into sharp focus, and he was simply unable to get past it. Ethan was indestructible, impossible to strike effectively thanks to years of training, and immune to pain through drexophine. Mark never had a prayer, just like Crayton said. No amount of willpower would get him out of this game alive.

Unless.

Unless he broke the rules. Unless he broke *all* the rules.

Ethan slashed again, and Mark deflected with his sword and sent a sharp kick into the man's chest, which had him skidding across the sand along the wall. Blood was pooling rapidly at Mark's feet, and Ethan barely seemed winded.

"It's time," Ethan said, his armor mic now muted, his lips barely moving. "The big finish. Come at me, and I promise I'll make it quick. I promise I'll get him to let your friends live."

"You're a liar," Mark said, heaving. His armor mic didn't work at all, unsurprisingly. "You're as bad as him. Worse, even. Do you even understand what you're doing here? What you've created? You will *destroy* this country."

"Said the peasant to the Caesar," Ethan sneered. "We will make it strong. Stronger than it's ever been. The people want it, Mark. Don't you see? They want strength. They want justice. They want heroes and gods."

"They're wrong!" Mark yelled.

Mark leapt forward, not at Ethan, but toward the outer wall. With one hand on his blade, he put his foot in the crack made by Rusakov's axe and launched himself upward as Ethan looked on in amazement.

MARK SUMMONED ALL HIS remaining strength and brought his sword around in mid-air, jamming it straight into the stone wall eight feet above the crack. He held on to the handle and used his burning arms to haul himself up so he could stand precariously on the crossguard and blade.

Again, he jumped. Toward the edge, toward the rim. His armored feet dug chunks out of the wall as he scrambled toward the very top. Finally, when gravity would let him rise no more, he flung out his arm, and grabbed the lip with his right hand. He froze there, hanging.

"He's running!" someone in the crowd shouted, and the Glasshammer guards raced to the point of the wall where he was

dangling. Those without masks looked confused and yelled into their comms for instructions.

I'm not running.

One guard drew close and aimed his submachine gun at Mark's exposed head.

"Get down!" he barked. "Get off the wall!"

Mark used his free hand and slid the hidden knife out of its sheath in his shinplate. He wrenched himself upward, over the lip, and grabbed the barrel of the guard's gun with his hand, pointing it away from his head. In one swift motion, he brought his other hand around and sliced cleanly through the strap anchoring the weapon to the guard's body. All of Mark's weight pulled on the SMG, and it was enough to rip it out of the man's hands.

Time seemed to slow as Mark slid down the wall, adjusting his grip to get his finger on the trigger of the weapon. He crashed into his sword on the way down, knocking it loose from the wall, and Mark pushed off the stone to leap toward Ethan, taking aim with the weapon.

"Holy shi—" Ethan began before disappearing behind his shield.

Mark fired, and shots ricocheted off the metal, sparking as the rounds were deflected in a half dozen different directions. He was firing actual lead, not riot rubber, just what he was counting on.

Mark hit the ground with a crunch, pain shooting through his legs and spine, but the armor had absorbed enough of the fall. And now there was more adrenaline surging through his system than poison.

The crowd was melting down, screaming in terror as Mark left his sword in the sand and charged toward Ethan with the guard's weapon, firing more rounds from the clip. One missed the shield and hit Ethan in the side of the knee, and he stumbled backward, crying out.

"You cheating motherf—" he began, but Mark collided with him, ripping the shield sideways with a free hand. Ethan tried to bring his sword around with his left, but Mark turned the weapon and fired a shot into Ethan's wrist plating. It went through a gap just under his palm and no amount of drexophine would save him from feeling it. His scream rebounded around the entire arena. The shortsword tumbled uselessly to the ground, and Mark grabbed Ethan by the lip of his silver chest armor. He turned the SMG sideways, and jammed the barrel up under Ethan's exposed chin.

The confidence had fled from his blue eyes. Instead, Mark saw the familiar black void of fear.

"Wait, just—" Ethan started, tears tumbling out of the corners of his eyes.

Mark thought of Moses's warm smile. He thought of Aria dancing on the hill. They never had a chance. They weren't fighters, they were prisoners, always doomed to a death sentence. Crayton staged it, and the crowds cheered.

Fine.

Then I'll give them one more execution.

Mark pulled the trigger.

An entire country let out a collective scream.

The Crucible had its winner.

45

MARK DID TWO THINGS then. First, he let the bloody mess that used to be Ethan Callaghan drop from his arms. Second, without pausing, he took aim at Cameron Crayton, a hundred yards away, standing at the window of his box. Before the man could even flinch, Mark fired the entire remainder of the SMG clip, a dozen and a half rounds, at the glass. More screams rang out as white spatters erupted all over the window, and Crayton dove out of sight. But as the gun clicked empty, it was as Mark feared. The glass was bulletproof, and the small caliber of the weapon in his hand had no chance of piercing it. He tossed away the now-useless weapon, and dropped to his knees.

Again, not wasting a second, he started rifling through Ethan's armor, pulling off pieces of it left and right, like he was looting the corpse. And in a way, he was. He was looking for one thing in particular, and he found it tucked underneath the plating on Ethan's shield arm. Three small syringes with a familiar-looking liquid inside.

Mark grabbed at them like a desperate man dying of thirst and jammed all three vials of drexophine into his neck. The autoinjectors sent the drug racing into his system, and he felt the unimaginable pain slowly dulling all throughout his body, and even his boiling face. It went from hellfire to an ache in the course of twenty seconds, but to Mark it felt like diving into a pool on a hot day. No kind of relief had ever been sweeter.

The ground was littered with garbage, hurled by a frenzied crowd that was about to riot after Ethan's death. Strangely, many *were* actually cheering, motivated by the violence alone, perhaps. Mark slowly picked himself up and retrieved his discarded sword from the base of the wall. He grabbed Ethan's eagle-embossed shield too for good measure, and walked into the center of the arena.

As he expected, Glasshammer troops burst in through the main entrance, pouring out onto the sand. They spread out in a circle around him, all aiming rifles and submachine guns at him. Looking at the rim of the Colosseum, Mark saw every sniper drawing a bead on his head, just waiting for the command. Everywhere, camera drones buzzed, projecting the chaos to untold millions of viewers at home.

And then, there was Crayton. He walked out onto the sand, escorted by a full contingent of guards, and Wyatt Axton himself. Mark had never seen Crayton look like this, face twisted with barely constrained rage. He was livid, just like the frenzied crowd.

Mark felt the last few pieces of his sanity slipping away. He chuckled. He laughed. Loudly. And then he couldn't help himself. He doubled over, sticking his sword in the sand to prop himself up, laughing uncontrollably at the absurdity of it all. Crayton drew closer, and Mark found another dozen weapons aimed at his head.

Mark wiped tears from his eyes and slowly got his breathing back under control. He stood up, still smiling.

"So what?" Mark said to Crayton, standing twenty feet ahead of him. "What are you going to do? Disqualify me?"

More laughter. He couldn't help it.

Crayton stood silent, wheels turning in his head. Mark *winning* had to have been impossible. Unthinkable. But here he was, alive (barely) with Ethan's crumpled body a few feet away, missing most of his pretty face.

Crayton let out a long sigh, and slowly his face morphed into a vague approximation of a smile.

"Well, you *did* put on a hell of a show, Mark."

He wished he'd saved a bullet, had he known Crayton would come down himself. Mark gripped his sword a little tighter. There were two dozen guards between him and Crayton. Making a run at him was suicide.

When has that ever stopped you?

"What happens now?" Mark said, slowly shifting his feet, ready to launch forward into certain death.

"I—" Crayton began.

The ground shook, ever so slightly. It wasn't much, but enough for everyone to notice.

An earthquake?

Then Mark heard distant screams.

Mark and Crayton searched for the source, and saw something odd in one of the northeast sections of the Colosseum. Smoke was pouring out from one of the entryways that led to the concession stands. A few tiny shapes were emerging from the blackness, and the crowd around the area was pulling back, frightened.

"What is—" Mark began.

Another rumble. Mark saw a flicker of flame this time. An explosion, shooting out from another entryway a few sections over. More screams. Louder. More of the audience saw it.

"Is this—" he turned to Crayton, but the man's eyes were filled with confusion and fear.

"Secure that area and find out—" he began, pointing at the fresh plume of smoke.

But the explosion of the arena wall stopped him short.

The blast was powerful, tearing through the eastern wall on the sand, showering the Glasshammer guards, Mark, and Crayton with chunks of debris. Everyone lost their footing, and Mark's ears rang.

He blinked through the dust and smoke, and saw a guard next to him with a piece of shrapnel sticking straight out of his visor. Mark scrambled to regain his senses. He searched himself for wounds, but in his full plate armor, he seemed to be okay.

What the hell was going on?

Zhou's words came to him.

"Things are in motion that cannot be stopped."

It's a siege, Mark realized. This was China. This was the MSS. This was Zhou's final move. It had to be, somehow. If they couldn't kill the man, they would kill the temple he built, and as many of his worshippers as they could.

Holy fucking shit.

He could barely see Crayton, who was being helped to his feet by Axton. The floor shook with more unseen explosions.

He pointed directly at Mark.

"Take him!" he screamed through the panicked roar of the crowd, as Axton dragged him back through the entryway. The guards who were just getting to their feet turned to point their weapons toward Mark.

Mark the spy.

Mark the traitor.

And now, presumably, Mark the terrorist.

Mark lunged forward and regained his grip on his sword and Ethan's shield. He brought it up just in time to deflect the first spray of bullets from the closest guard.

Mark watched Crayton disappear into smoke. His mind immediately raced elsewhere.

Find Carlo and Brooke.

But no. Something had changed. Mark's blood was molten. His vision was crimson mist. Everything around him was fire and smoke and death. There was only one thought that consumed him fully, all the way down to his core. He wouldn't get away. Not this time. This was his reckoning.

Kill.

Crayton.

Mark felt himself lose control of his own body. The drexophine had erased the last echo of pain from his body, and he raced forward into the surviving wall of guards sealing Crayton's exit out of the arena floor. He tucked himself behind his shield and charged as they opened fire.

A hundred rounds hit the shield before Mark closed the gap, but once he did, it was carnage. The Glasshammer guards wore kevlar, armored up for a different era of war. Mark tore into them like thresher maw, his sword slashing, hacking off limbs, feeling bullets glance off his armor. At close range, they fumbled with their guns, but once their ammo was spent, they were dead before they could even reach for a new magazine.

Mark ripped through a half dozen soldiers like paper, making sure to keep Ethan's shield actively blocking shots from the mercs that were farther away. Fresh blasts kept rocking the stadium, causing everyone's footing to slip, and their shots to fly wildly off course.

Dancing from the pile of butchered guards to individual soldiers near the mouth of the entryway, Mark sliced off the arm of a man trying to get out his combat knife and drove his sword through the chest of another fumbling with a fresh clip for his rifle. Mark didn't care who these men were. This was war. His mistake had been not seeing it sooner.

Mark heard a sharp crack and was knocked off balance as a .50 caliber sniper round tore clean through Ethan's shield and into the wall next to his head. That was his cue to dart inside the mouth of the arena floor, which guards had tried to seal shut, but an explosion had detached the hinges on one of the doors, so Mark was able to slip through.

Inside was literal hell. Everything was ablaze, from vendor stalls to human beings, and stinging smoke occluded Mark's already impaired vision. Alarms were blaring, and the CMI staff assigned to the ground level were as panicked as the fans as they raced toward the exits. Mark had stopped counting the explosions by now.

This is why Zhou didn't care if he helped you, Mark realized. *This was always the endgame.*

"I will have the last laugh either way."

Mark pushed away thoughts of Zhou and followed a column of guards in newly equipped gas masks that had to be trailing Crayton. Mark shoved the back few rows aside with his shield, but once they figured out what was going on, he had to start slashing with his blade again. Fans screamed in terror as impaled, bloody guards crashed into vending machines and hot dog carts. Mark almost lost his head when a guard at the front reeled around touting an enormous, drum-mag LMG, but the shield took the initial few blasts and Mark followed with a quick stab through the man's throat. As he fell, Mark could see more guards and in the smoky distance, the scarred, silver head of Wyatt Axton.

Mark picked up the pace of his run and leapt over the burning corpse of an unfortunate fan.

And then the ground gave way.

The blast was in the basement level somewhere, but it caused the floor to collapse completely, and Mark found himself tumbling down in a freefall. He hit the stone hard, along with a few other unlucky bystanders. He blinked, regaining his senses from the fall, which was mostly broken by his armor. Looking around, he saw one woman impaled on a piece of rebar. Another man had his head crushed by a twelve-foot-tall support beam. Mark scrambled to his feet and pulled his sword out of the rubble. Ethan's shield had slid down the mound and was baking in a flaming pile of debris behind him. Mark decided it wasn't worth going back for, and ran toward the nearest doorway marked STAIRWELL.

Halfway up, he ran into another pair of guards. He didn't hesitate to headbutt the first one so hard his visor shattered, and he threw the other one tumbling down the stairs with a judo toss. The cracked-visor guard let lose a pair of shots with his pistol. One hit Mark's plating while the other ricocheted off a railing. Mark grabbed the man's gun with his free hand, twisted it around, disarming him, then emptied the clip into his face, saving one bullet for the guard recovering at the bottom of the stairs. As the dead guard slid down the wall in front of him, Mark yanked the riot shotgun off his back and held it with one hand with the sword in the other. Both were heavy, but Mark was long past pain and fatigue. Adrenaline had taken over completely.

Three blasts with the shotgun cleared an unknown number of additional guards out of the top of the stairwell, and Mark pushed past their corpses to get back to ground level. He sprinted in the direction where he'd last seen Crayton.

Someone wearing a CMI polo was screaming at someone wearing a CMI windbreaker in front of one of the Colosseum's dozens of bars. Mark could barely make out what he was saying over the din of the panicked crowd.

"The kegs! They're in the beer kegs! I saw one go off!"

He pointed to the top of a silver keg behind the bar. Mark heard an electronic chirp coming from the metal cylinder as he got closer.

"Get the hell away from that!" Mark screamed and the two men started running with everyone else. When Mark was rounding the corner, he heard the blast and felt the heat from the fireball, which dissipated only a few feet before it would have engulfed him.

Kegs? Jesus.

Zhou's team had probably hijacked a vendor truck and loaded it up with lead-lined, C4-filled replacements to be distributed throughout the entire stadium. That's what Mark would have done. None of it mattered now. All that mattered was the hunt.

Crayton was sending guards backwards to try and stop him. They should have all been fleeing for their lives, but they were all trying to be heroes, trying to bring down the infamous Mark Wei.

They were idiots. The remaining Glasshammer mercs were disorganized and terrified and in no shape to take him on. Mark pumped through the last four rounds of the shotgun into too-slow guards before tossing the empty weapon and reverting back to the sword. He ran into a trio of mercs who had managed to get their hands on riot shields, but he simply rolled over the top of them and carved up their backs with his blade. From one of the bodies, he scooped up another SMG and emptied the clip toward the reappeared, fleeing shape of Wyatt Axton, turning the corner into another hallway marked EXIT. A flood of stampeding fans followed him, and Mark had to push his way through, knocking them left and right with his armor.

Mark could see wide double doors at the end of the hall. Flashing red and blue lights had appeared outside. The smoke wasn't as intense as the hallway widened near the exit, and Mark could finally see Crayton himself just ahead of Axton. Mark pulled the trigger on the SMG, but it clicked empty.

Another blast. Close. Disastrously close.

This time, it was the ceiling that was raining down in chunks above them, pieces of the second and third levels hammered the ground like meteorites, crushing people left and right and blocking the exit. Mark kept his balance, and through the fresh plume of dust, saw Axton rushing to Crayton, the mogul's lower half trapped under concrete, and screaming something into his radio. All the other guards were dead, had fled, or were walled off by rubble and the mass of fleeing fans behind Mark.

Crayton was stuck under a hulking slab of stone, one or both his legs crushed, from the looks of it. He had nowhere to go. All that was standing between him and Mark now was Axton.

While his back was turned, Mark shoved recovering fans out of the way, grabbed his sword, and sprinted forward. But even over the screams, Axton heard his metal feet clanging on the cement, and turned toward him, his Desert Eagle in his extended hand. Fans had spread out and cleared the space in between them, watching in transfixed shock.

There was no more shield to protect Mark. Instead, he simply threw his armored arm over his exposed head, dipped down and shoulder-charged toward the gunfire.

He felt the bullets hit. A few glancing shots, but the direct hits were like sledgehammer blows to his armor, with a few breaking the metal and burying themselves in his body. But still, he made it, and slammed into Axton, throwing him into the rubble blocking the exit. He turned to Crayton, who was wide-eyed, and brought the blade up for a downward stab. But Axton didn't even need a half second to recover. He leapt up and speared Mark, sending him sprawling onto the cement. Mark lost his grip on his sword, so instead sent a steel fist in Axton's side. Axton countered from his mounted position by plowing a forearm into Mark's face, which dazed him and wrenched his head to the side.

He turned back toward Axton, and his lone eye was bleary and unfocused. He saw the man towering above him, his eyes blazing with rage, raising both his hands far above his head. In them, he held an eight-inch, black-bladed combat knife, the one always dangling off his chest, and as he reached the arc of his swing, he drove the blade down toward Mark's skull.

There was a sharp pop, and Axton's head snapped back. The knife fell from his grip, and skittered off the concrete next to Mark's head. Mark scrambled back as a figure walked right past him, firing more shots that riddled Axton's chest, neck, and face.

Her blonde hair was brown with dust and soot, but Mark knew the curled ponytail immediately. Brooke turned back to him, her face blackened, her nose and mouth covered by a torn cloth. She extended her arm, and hauled Mark up to his feet.

"You alright?"

Mark nodded, but looking down at his armor, and saw that there were more than just dents in it, there were bloody holes. He couldn't feel a thing.

"I'm good," he said anyway, as Brooke looked concerned. She held the Glasshammer-issue sidearm at her side, the barrel still smoking after emptying its contents into Wyatt Axton, who was now missing most of his head.

Now there was just Crayton. The devil trapped in a hell of his own creation.

Mark turned to Brooke.

"Gideon, he . . . it was all—"

"I know," she said, coughing through the cloth on her face. "I know what happened, what Crayton did. Or I have a rough idea, at least. But we have to get out of here. I got the Riveras out, but this whole place is coming down."

"Not yet," Mark said, turning back toward Crayton.

"No," Brooke said. "No, Mark, not—"

Mark wrenched himself free of her grip, took a few steps forward to pick up his dropped sword. He stumbled forward toward Crayton, pinned in the rubble. The man's eyes opened wide as he saw him approach.

Mark was weak, but he thrust the blade straight at Crayton's already bloody chest.

Crayton *caught* it. He clenched the stained silver blade with his bare hands. Red erupted from his palms and streamed down his forearms. The tip of the blade was just inches from his heart. Mark pushed, but his body felt wrong. He couldn't feel the pain, but his strength was failing. Axton's shots had broken something inside him. He could barely breathe, his breaths halted and hissing. *Is this what a bullet in the lung feels like?* Still, he pushed. The blades cut deeper into Crayton's hands as the man's eyes clenched in unspeakable agony. The sword's tip grazed his skin.

Crayton looked like he was trying to choke out words, but the pain was making it nearly impossible.

"*Mark, wait—*" was all he could get out.

"You wanted a killer," Mark said, heaving, trying to remain standing, despite weakness flooding his body. "You got one."

Mark threw all his armored weight into the blade, and it slipped through Crayton's mangled hands and sunk straight into his chest. No scream, just a surprised gasp, and then nothing. The malevolent light in his eyes flickered.

He deserved worse. He—

Mark didn't hear the next blast. Didn't process the light or the heat. Didn't see the east wall disintegrate. Didn't feel the jagged chunk of stone that slammed into his skull.

He only knew darkness.

Finally, relief.

46

AFTER MARK WAS PULLED out of the Pacific, it took him a while to fully process what was happening. There was a boat, then a helicopter, now a military cargo jet that had been turned into an aerial hospital wing.

They'd found him eventually, drifting miles from where the aircraft carrier had burned and sunk to the ocean floor. He'd been shot twice and was hypothermic, and he'd been wrapped in a heated blanket for hours as medics treated his injuries.

"Welcome home, son," Gideon told him when he was transferred into the plane, wrapping him up in a hug. It was the first physical contact he'd had with a human in years, at least one who wasn't beating him senseless or carving his skin open with knives.

Mark tried to launch into full debrief mode, but so long as he confirmed Admiral Huang was dead, Gideon said the rest could wait. The Agency brass was celebrating what he'd done, and he'd set up the other Spears to finish the mission. News reached him that a member of the first team of Spears had died in the mountain attack, so Mark was already ahead of the curve. The years-in-the-making plan was working. China was on a knife's edge, and soon it would be cut into pieces. But Mark didn't care about any of that now.

"Will they be there?" Mark asked Gideon, who smiled warmly.

"They'll be there," Gideon said. "They were put on a plane as soon as we knew you were coming home."

Dawn was breaking, and Japan came into view at last. Mark wasn't cold anymore. He wasn't in pain. This wasn't a dream. The mission, the nightmare, was over.

It felt like an eternity as the plane dipped lower and lower toward the runway of the island airbase. Mark jolted as the wheels hit, wondering if in one last cruel twist of fate, some horrifying accident could befall his return flight. But the plane coasted toward the hangar and stopped without incident. They wanted to put him on a stretcher, but he refused. He shed his medical gown and the blanket, and Gideon handed him a pair of dress blues. No name, no rank. That would be his legacy, but that was fine by Mark. That was the job.

When the ramp lowered on the rear of the cargo jet, there were no cheering crowds welcoming him home. There were no rows of soldiers to salute him as he exited. The president was not there to shake his hand and tell him job well done.

No one was there. No one but them, and they were the only ones who mattered.

Riko crumbled when she saw him, dropping to a knee and clasping her hand over mouth. Her hair had grown long again, down to her waist, curled at the ends. She wore a blue sundress stamped with white flowers, and was twice as gorgeous as Mark could even remember. He knew how he must look, gaunt and pale and barely able to stumble forward, but they were tears of joy in her eyes, not grief.

Someone else was there too. A little girl in a tiny yellow dress, hiding shyly behind her mother, unsure of what was going on. As Mark ran to embrace Riko, she slid behind her back completely, peeking out, her pigtails blowing gently in the island breeze.

After an extended embrace and dozen kisses, Riko and Mark separated, and Riko drew the toddler out from her hiding place.

"Mark," she said, her voice breaking. "This is Asami."

It had been so long. She was so big. Too big. He had missed so much. Three and a half years of her life past already. It seemed like both an instant and an eternity.

"Hello," Mark said softly, holding out his hand to Asami. She slunk further behind Riko, and started wailing.

"I-I'm sorry," Riko said, distraught. "I showed her pictures of you every day. We watched videos every night. She can't stop babbling about you. I don't—"

Mark didn't care, he was crying too now. Her cries, her scrunched little face. They were the most beautiful things he could possibly imagine.

"It's him, Asami!" Riko said, picking her up and setting her on her knee in front of Mark's face. "Don't you see? It's Daddy!"

Asami stopped crying and reached out toward Mark's face. When she touched his tear-stained skin, she looked a bit shocked, like she'd expected to touch the surface of a flexscreen.

"Asami, what do we say to Daddy every night before bed? You remember, I know you do!"

Asami looked at him with the wonder only a child could possess. Those eyes. His eyes.

"Love you, Dad-dy! See you soon!" she said, her voice a tiny little melody. She finally broke into a smile and threw her arms around his face. She planted a kiss on his forehead and he started shaking, he was sobbing so hard.

Nothing could ever compare to this.

Not anything.

Not ever.

HE WAS HOME. AND he would never leave them again.

EPILOGUE

INT. TRANSCRIPT: MAJOR XIN ZHOU
INTERROGATOR: AGENCY ASSET GIDEON GELLAR
8/22/35 – SESSION FOUR – 01:34 AM
GLASSHAMMER HOLDING SITE [REDACTED]

GELLAR: "Is that the full extent of your testimony, Major?"

ZHOU: "It is exactly what I told Mark. And it should be more than enough for you. Impressive how fast you put my deal together."

GELLAR: "It was a high priority."

ZHOU: "Strangely fast, in fact."

GELLAR: "We're done here. Guards?"

ZHOU: "You realize you are playing with fire with Mark, I hope. You are going to lose him for good soon, once he finds out."

GELLAR: *[pause]* "What exactly are you referring to?"

ZHOU: "While I am grateful you told him I was dead after

Oahu, you really sold him on his daughter as well? Where did you even get the remains to falsify that?"

GELLAR: "That incident is not the focus of our discussion here."

ZHOU: "What, you knew he would chase me back across the ocean to find her?"

GELLAR: "Are you saying you know the whereabouts of Asami Wei?"

ZHOU: "That isn't her name. Not anymore."

[inaudible scuffling]

GELLAR: *[loudly]* "Where is she?"

ZHOU: "They wanted her. The wife was expendable, but they wanted the daughter of the man who could do so much damage to us. Imagine what she could do if given the direction. The right training. The proper motivation."

GELLAR: "Where—"

ZHOU: "Project Embryo, of course. Fourth generation. She is a prodigy, and I have overseen her development personally. Only eight years old, but you should see her *fight*."

GELLAR: "Tell us where the site is."

ZHOU: "This is not part of the deal. And something tells me, if you did not tell Mark then, you will not tell him now. She is ours now."

SESSION TERMINATED – 01:38 AM

WARNING – CONTAINMENT INCIDENT CODE 43554: DETAINEE AT LARGE
CONSIDER ARMED AND DANGEROUS
11 KIA ON SITE, ASSET GELLAR KIA

PLEASE ADVISE

ABOUT THE AUTHOR

PAUL TASSI decided after years of consuming science fiction through a steady diet of books, movies, TV shows, and video games that he wanted to write his own stories in the genre. Now the author of the Earthborn Trilogy from Talos Press, Paul also writes for *Forbes*. He lives with his beautiful and supportive wife in Chicago.